Quantum Chaos

Douglas Phillips

For the physicists, astrophysicists, astronomers, and cosmologists
who create and verify the astonishing explanations of reality,
known in science as theory. You make my job easy.

CONTENTS

PROLOGUE

chaos

/'kā͜ˌäs/

noun

1. A state of disorder and confusion.
2. In Greek mythology, the primordial entity from which sprang the first deities Gaia, Tartarus, Erebus, and Nyx.
3. The formless condition that is assumed to have existed before the creation of the universe.

Human

/'hyü-mən/

adjective

1. Pertaining to or characteristic of the people of Earth: the Human brain.

noun

2. A person from Earth. A Human being.

   Etymological note: Since the discovery of extraterrestrial civilizations, non-capitalized usage (human) has been discarded in favor of a capitalization standard when referencing any intelligent species by name: Sandzvallon, Litian-nolo, Szitzojoot, Chitza, Human. For the general noun applicable to any intelligent species, see people or person.

"All Human beings, by nature, desire to know." – Aristotle

"Funny how there are always consequences." – Daniel Rice

1   EXPLORERS

SATISFIED WITH HIMSELF, his crew, the universe, and everything in it, Captain Zeeno tugged off his boots, leaned back in his padded seat, and extended furry legs across the only sliver of the control panel not crowded with dials, switches, and displays. In the cramped cockpit of a Chitza scout ship, there weren't many places to stretch.

Their final course had been loaded into navigation. Soothing green lights pulsed on a secondary panel overhead, confirming a faultless performance. A gentle vibration in the floor produced a hum in the air—outside, twin compression turbines were spinning like precision drills.

Zeeno slapped the throttle quadrant between two pilot seats where a large red handle angled forward. "She's purring like a Cheeble kitten. Time for some tunes, ya think?"

Zeeno's first officer, Aussik, sat in the right seat. Technically, Aussik 8. His brother, Aussik 7, had been copilot on the last mission.

Aussik's chin quills twitched. "You got it, Boss."

The copilot twisted a dial then jammed a curved claw into a recessed button. Audio speakers hidden among an array of complex electronic components resonated with smooth notes and a syncopated rhythm.

"Damn fine choice, my friend," Zeeno said. "Your family reeks of quality." Competent, loyal, and resourceful, Zeeno couldn't ask for a better copilot.

Aussik grinned with a display of razor sharp canine teeth that all Chitzas regularly flaunted, partly out of style, but mostly because ritualized displays of aggression reinforced an aura of bravado. Chitzas were well known for their bravado.

Zeeno smoothed his backbone quills and settled in for the remainder of their long journey. The ship's forward viewport provided a sweeping vista ahead—not that there was anything to see. Since morning coffee break, they'd traversed nothing but a black, empty void. A million light-years of it. Space so deep they'd left the stars behind. "Let's see those jockin' Toraks do what we do. Ha!"

Aussik's crown quills pulsed in time with the oh-so-groovy rhythm filling the cockpit. "Toraks are amateurs. Nobody beats a Chitza." Truer words were never spoken.

"Nobody beats a Chitza!" Zeeno yelled, loud enough for everyone else onboard to hear.

"Together we live and together we shall die!" came the spirited response from the deck below. Probably the ship's safety officer, Onner. It sounded like her, but distinguishing between squeaks was hard even for Chitzas.

Every scout ship required four crew members, located on two decks connected by a ladder and a whole lot of enthusiasm. Nobody beat Chitzas because no other space-faring species even knew what Chitzas could do. By any measure, this small but agile ship had journeyed a long way from home. Beyond the Milky Way and a whole lot more.

Zeeno couldn't have been prouder if he'd taken first place in the Triannual Chitza Danger Games. Which, in fact, he had.

"Humans too. Can't touch us," he bragged.

"Especially Humans," Aussik agreed. "I gotta say, though, she is kind of cute... at least, for a—."

"Don't say it," Zeeno warned, looking over his shoulder through the open cockpit entryway.

Humans, the newest species to join Sagittarius Novus, often suggested that Chitzas resembled a small rodent on their home planet—something called a hedgehog. Chitzas took no offense. Physical comparisons were how newcomers made sense of the menagerie of life found in the galaxy.

Not that there weren't comparisons for Humans, there were. But calling out their resemblance to a hairless dookah, a lumpy cave-dwelling scavenger back home, just wouldn't do. Not on Zeeno's ship. Humans would eventually see it for themselves. In fact, their passenger already had. Shown a dookah photo, she had laughed until she cried, an unusual combination of emotions. Which pretty much summed up Humans.

"Hey guys, crank it up!" cried the Human voice from below.

Aussik bumped up the bass.

"Nice!" came the muffled response, along with some rhythmic thumping against the ship's bulkhead.

Compact scout ships weren't exactly spacious even for Chitzas, and a Human stood three times taller. How a creature so large could even fit below deck was surprising, but she hadn't complained.

"She's fun, I'll give her that," Zeeno admitted. "Laughs a lot."

"Curvy," said Aussik.

"Curvy, too." Zeeno ruffled the fur across his chest. "Funny how their males don't look that way."

They'd provided a Human-sized seat squeezed behind the two lower-deck workstations where Onner and Beets maintained the machinery that kept this marvel of technology running. A *wedge*, as the scout ships were sometimes called, could go almost anywhere, its range only limited by how high they were willing to set Tau, the ratio of 3-D spatial compression. Compression turbines affixed at two corners of the ship's triangular shape would do the rest, sucking in the appropriate amount of vacuum energy extracted from empty space to create a surrounding 4-D bubble. Always magenta. Never the purple or pink hues of more fragile bubbles. These things had to be done right.

They could also decompress the space they'd just traversed simply by swiveling the turbine intake ports to align with a reverse vector, then scaling back on Tau. The technique provided the ability to *go deep*, subdividing an immense journey into manageable segments while leaving behind nothing more than a thin 4-D communications filament.

But even a segmented strategy wasn't enough to cross a billion light-years. For that, the Chitzas tucked several more tricks into their boot sleeves, but they weren't about to divulge those secrets to anyone. Especially not the Humans.

Onner had been assigned babysitting duty for this mission. Luckily the Human had behaved herself—except for that weird thing she'd been doing with her hair. For some reason, Human head fur grew ridiculously long, and she'd bugged Onner to help tie down the unruly mess during the few periods they'd run without the gravity generator turned on.

Zeeno kept one eye open to monitor gauges and lights as they progressed ever deeper into the unexplored void. Just when he thought this segment would be as routine as the last, Aussik raised his paw and pointed out the forward viewport. "What's that?"

Zeeno looked up. Where there had been nothing but darkness, light now appeared. Uneven, but attention grabbing. A spark here, a flash there. The first departure from empty in a while.

Zeeno eased back on the red handle, scaling Tau to a more leisurely pace. More sparks popped to their right. A series of streaks zipped past on their left. The view from any 4-D bubble limited visibility to an oblique 3-D plane, but there was little doubt the sparks of light spread across their path in every direction. Something big lay ahead.

Zeeno pulled the handle again. Turbines wound down. The ship slowed to a crawl. "It's got to be the boundary?" he half-stated, half-asked. They had no science officer onboard. Probably should have thought of that before they left home.

"Maybe ask our passenger?" Aussik chirped.

These hairless dookah lookalikes weren't stupid, and this one had already demonstrated knowledge of galaxies, nebulas, and such. Zeeno queried with a shout to the deck below.

"Hell if I know," came the response.

Zeeno shrugged. They'd come a long way. Their ship hovered in uncharted territory—by design—but that didn't make their current position any less threatening. They'd need to drop out of 4-D to do a proper reconnaissance of this sparkling wall of doom.

"Prepare for a sniff test," Zeeno commanded.

"Gotcha, Boss," Aussik said.

"Three-D coming up," their engineer, Beets, yelled from below.

Aussik grabbed a visor off a hook and slipped it over his eyes. He'd need every bit of the infrared spectrum to monitor this maneuver. He toggled several big switches above his head, and the ever-present whir of compression turbines dropped in pitch. Vibrations in the ship's structure reduced to a low rumble.

A magenta circle on Aussik's display corresponding to the four-dimensional bubble that surrounded them, shrank to nothing. The collapse of artificial space came with an unsettling twisting sensation and produced a dramatic change in the view outside.

What had been a squashed plane now expanded to a vertical wall. It roiled with multicolored mists. Glowing layers of blue, white, and pink shimmered in undulating waves that traversed its surface. Random pops, sparkles, and streaks of light shot out like an out-of-control fireworks display.

They hovered in front of an impassible cliff—if cliffs were electrified.

"Damn big," Zeeno said as he scratched the shorter quills protruding from his chin. Over years of exploration, he'd never seen anything like it. "You're recording this?" He tossed a look toward Aussik who nodded back.

Zeeno studied the enigma, but not for long.

"Uh, Boss... we're still moving," Aussik said with a hint of alarm in his squeak. He scanned the readouts flashing across his panel. "It's nothing I'm doing. I don't know, I've got a bad feeling about this. Something's pulling on us."

Sparks of light loomed closer. Nearby flashes now fully illuminated the cockpit. Zeeno had seen enough.

"Give me a compression vector backward along our last segment."

Aussik touched several buttons on his control panel and when the whirring spun up, Zeeno eased the big red handle backward.

"We're moving," Aussik called out. "But the wrong way."

The multicolored wall of churning mist and spontaneous sparkles loomed over them as if a giant electric tarp were being slowly pulled over their heads. Zeeno jammed the Tau lever to its limit. The whine turned into a roar as compression turbines spun up on either side of the wedge, but no magenta bubble appeared.

"Some kind of gravitational anomaly!" yelled Onner from below. "Whatever it is, it's getting stronger."

Zeeno furiously pushed more buttons. "Frack balls! Where the hell is our 4-D?" No one answered.

One side of the turbulent wall burst into a sheet of white light as brilliant as any sun. Zeeno flinched and covered his eyes with one arm. Pain came instantly.

"Ultra-gamma blast!" Onner screeched.

Cracks appeared in the ship's viewport, spreading like a sheet of ice struck by a hammer. The glass quickly hazed over, which did little to temper the intense explosion of incoming light.

"Emergency dimensional burst!" Zeeno yelled. "Get us out of here!" At this point, getting back to a higher plane of existence was their only hope.

"On it, Boss!" Aussik's paws flew across the controls at his workstation.

"Hull breach!" someone from below decks yelled.

"Oh hell," Zeeno said to himself, covering his mouth with a paw. The quills on the right side of his chin had curled up like burned tree needles. Sharp pain stung his face.

Zeeno took a deep breath. When things went south, they did so in a hurry. Alternatives were disappearing quickly.

"Abandon data." It was a decision no Chitza pilot ever wanted to make and might be the last command he would ever give.

"On it!" Aussik flipped a metal cover marked *Do Not Open* and jerked a handle beneath. A slim cartridge the size of an Elitrean tea saucer rose from its electronic slot. "Ejecting data pack." He jumped up from his workstation and ran to the ladder leading to the deck below.

Zeeno called over his shoulder, "Take Onner and Beets. The Human too if she fits."

Already three rungs down the ladder, Aussik paused. "You sure?"

"Just get it done." Zeeno pressed a button that would send an automated emergency communication packet down the micro filament they'd stretched across distances too large to comprehend. In all likelihood, he wouldn't be around long enough to see the response.

2   LITIAN-NOLOS

THE HOSPITAL ATTENDANT folded multiple knee joints spaced equally down two articulated legs until her broad, flat head lowered to window height. She peered through the glass, blinking large green eyes that protruded above iridescent skin sparkling in aquamarine and violet colors. The lanky Litian-nolo was profoundly puzzled by what she saw.

She waved her coworker over to the window, one of many positioned uniformly down a quiet hallway. "He hasn't moved since planet rise."

The Human male inside the barren and dimly lit room lay prone on a flat board hung between chains attached to the ceiling. He wore a narrow white cloth around his midsection but nothing else.

The second attendant blinked. "Are all Humans so sluggish?"

Being mostly bone and ligament, giant Litian-nolos were reasonably agile, but the attendants had been all the way to the hospital commissary and back three times since planet rise, and in that time the Human hadn't so much as raised one of his keratin-topped fingers.

The attendant curled the edges of his flexible head—matching the curvature of a Human tongue. "He's still alive, isn't he?"

"Not to worry. See his chest? It lifts as he breathes."

"Ahh, yes. And look there! Movement!"

The Human twisted his neck one way and then another. A slight popping sound echoed across the nearly empty room. He didn't seem to be injured by the bone snap. Perhaps even oddly satisfied.

"He is not asleep. I have seen time mentors do this, even our own. It is a state of relaxation."

"It's called Zen. He told me." The attendant sharply curled his head.

She stared at her colleague with a mix of mistrust and jealousy. He wasn't lying about his direct contact with the Human—their species was incapable of deception—but Litian-nolos regularly engaged in one-upmanship to gain social standing. Not another living being in the galaxy could raise a Litian-nolo's social standing as much as this Human could.

The man lying before them was not only the first of his species to stand upon their planet, but widely praised across the galaxy. Ask any member of Sagittarius Novus, and they would repeat his name: Daniel Rice, the scientist who had solved the riddle of the Star Beacon.

****

Daniel lifted from the long plank and gave the wood a gentle pat. "Thank you."

No ordinary board, the intricate hand-carved inscriptions along its edges were hundreds of years old and told an ancient story of life renewed. The wood came from the semi-conscious lei'i kai tree, proven by scientifically rigorous tests to be self-aware, a rarity among plants. Litian-nolo time mentors—advisors with finely tuned responsibilities over key future events—treated these surfboard-like resting platforms with great respect. Daniel wasn't about to break with their tradition.

The plank was as long as a church pew and twice as hard. Daniel had expected that his forty-five-year-old body would rebel against multiple hours of prone meditation. But strangely, each session brought a feeling of rejuvenation. Perhaps there was merit in the Litian-nolo claim that these wooden planks spoke to their occupant. Or perhaps—and more likely, given Occam's razor—it was simply the lighter gravity of this planet.

Daniel glanced up. Two Litian-nolo attendants stared through the room's only window. Daniel lifted a hand to wave. The attendants curled the edges of their iridescent cephalopod heads— a smile in Litian-nolo gestures. He'd say hello on his way out, a chance to practice their language, and honestly, the celebrity thing was a lot more fun here than on Earth.

He'd first met this species at Jheean but a visit to their home planet had given him a much better perspective of these people. Here, they wore no breathing device, which revealed a rather cute upside-down nose. When expanded, the breathing slits also served as a double mouth which seemed overkill for a species that ate so little. With no chin or neck, their head simply merged to a broader torso, always covered by the brightly colored slim dresses ubiquitous to this world.

Once, he'd seen a Litian-nolo without clothing. In a word, she was lanky. Multiple knobby joints allowed her to fold to Human height or extend to the ceiling. Curiously, the skin covering all those bumps was luxuriously smooth to the touch. On the whole, she was quite beautiful in a gangly kind of way. The details of that scientific but intimate encounter would remain forever private, shared only by those who had been in the room, Daniel, Nala, and Theesah-ma.

Theesah-ma hadn't stopped by for several days now, not since Nala had *gone dimensional*, as they liked to say here on Litia. No doubt Nala was having the time of her life participating in a 4-D survey—essentially popping in and out of four-dimensional space to scout for undiscovered intelligent life in other star systems. Her last subspace message had indicated their mission might continue for another week.

He and Nala had been guests on Litia for two months, enjoying local hospitality often accompanied by perks no government scientist could or should expect. The first Humans to visit in person, they'd been provided with a clifftop residence that overlooked a tranquil sea. They had sampled exotic foods and tipped glasses with important people. Through it all, Theesah-ma had been their gracious guide and good friend.

As much as Nala cared for both Daniel and Theesah-ma, she'd gotten antsy. Advanced science and new discoveries seemed to be everywhere in this progressive society. When the survey opportunity had come up, she'd jumped.

"You stay put," Nala had said. "Recover. You're doing so well. I'll be back before you know it."

They had come to Litia for recovery. Daniel's condition, explained by Zin as the *entanglement of conscious experience across multiple probability pathways*, was a long-winded way to say that his brain was still messed up from time traveling.

He had checked into a Time Mentor's Hospital, which turned out to be more of a retreat for the body, mind, and spirit. The daily regimen included consciousness cognition exercises, attention training, Zen-like sessions on the lei'i kai board, and a truly weird experience involving a dunk into a vat of Slinky-style worms.

He had to admit his mental issues were improving. He had learned to manage the nightmares that had previously plagued him. He zoned out less during the day and slept better at night.

The primary benefits, so-called, of being an entangled consciousness were the oh-so-weird *future memories*. Daniel had experienced only one since coming to Litia, a not-terribly significant case where he'd visualized Nala accidentally cutting her finger trying to open a stubborn cardboard box. A day later, the same event happened for real. The minor injury was easily resolved with a bandage and a kiss, but the advanced warning made him wonder.

Nothing else weird had come up, and if the Litian-nolo time mentors could be believed, none would. Ever the skeptic, Daniel refused to use the word *cured*, but Nala had celebrated anyway by hosting what she'd called a "spontaneous future party" among the time mentors, complete with taste testing for margarita recipes that wouldn't be invented until next year.

Now this spontaneous, live-for-today woman was gone. Goodbye hugs had reminded him of his vow at Jheean never to lose sight of her again. But illogical promises were hard to keep, and Nala wasn't the type to be nailed down just because Daniel felt a twinge of separation anxiety.

She'll be back by Starday for sure, he thought.

Litian-nolos added a leap day to each month in their calendar to account for sidereal time as the planet Litia—really a moon—completed one orbit around their companion gas giant, appropriately named Nolo. Starday realigned the calendar with the stars, making astronomers happy. For everyone else, it had become a planetwide holiday where city lights dimmed, and people came out at night for an enthusiastic—and somewhat uninhibited—outdoor celebration under the spread of the Milky Way. Sort of a nighttime sex, drugs, and rock 'n roll thing. Nala was a big fan. Daniel too. Earth could use a similar holiday.

Daniel exited the treatment room into an adjoining closet and changed into his usual button shirt and lightweight pants. The rest of the day would be time to catch up on news from home and the latest goings on at Jheean, where Earth's newest ambassador to Sagittarius Novus was doing a bang-up job lifting Human status from deficient neophytes to that of every other consortium member.

If he was lucky, there would be a new message from Nala waiting for him at the office. She'd been good at keeping him informed. Mostly. Except for yesterday, which had been a terse, "You won't believe where I just went!" Followed by a promise to relate all the juicy details later, since "Zeeno says I have to keep it short."

Whoever Zeeno is.

On his way out, Daniel thanked the hospital attendants for their help, then quickly realized he had used the Litian-nolo word *atakai* instead of *atako*. He hadn't *thanked* them, he'd *invited* them. To what? He'd deal with that little faux pas tomorrow.

Outside, a typical day on Litia was only subtly different than a crisp autumn day on Earth. Lighter gravity made walking a breeze. White clouds decorated a blue sky, but here their edges were often tinged a pale green. The color came from the reflected light of giant Nolo, its quarter crescent easily visible even in the full light of day.

Daniel followed a curving walking path to the city's public transportation system. Litian-nolos were definitely not car people. Instead, they used an efficient train of plug-in modules that detached at predefined destinations allowing the rest of the train to continue on without slowing. Modules could be configured to move people or products and some even sported a compact minibar serving drinks and food. For a busy city of more than ten million residents, the system worked well.

There were stares as he boarded the train module—there always were—but a few smiles, hand waves, and common courtesies went a long way to making ordinary Litian-nolos comfortable with the alien in their midst. Of course, Humans were only the most recent. Various species regularly visited this planet, which was open to anyone who could manage a nitrogen-oxygen atmosphere with a touch of hydrogen sulfide. Litia smelled approximately like the geyser basins at Yellowstone National Park.

Daniel exited the train to a dense sector of the city dominated by surprisingly thin office towers. By Human standards, the floor count wasn't large but given the Litian-nolo standing height of about six meters, even a fifty-story building reached nearly to the clouds.

He greeted the receptionist as he entered. Metelca-kah? Meshalca-kah? Something like that. Names weren't easy to remember, but he did try. Nala was better at it, but then Nala was nearly fluent in their language after only two months. Theesah-ma had been an excellent teacher.

He took a lift to the twelfth floor and walked a curving hallway to the temporary office they had provided for his use. Tall glass panels gave the feeling of a modern museum or symphony hall back home. The ceiling was high enough to accommodate a volleyball court.

Outside, the sprawling city nestled among rolling hills. A magnificent view on a clear day. Only the best for a visiting celebrity. Daniel sat at an ordinary desk on a swivel chair shipped from Earth. His rather archaic laptop stood open on the desk. He had no need for the more modern glowpads that everyone seemed to be using these days. Litian-nolos had even made coffee available, and it turned out to be a reasonably close approximation to brews back home.

He didn't find any messages from Nala, but something might come in later. Instead, he turned to the usual time wasters, and an hour of scrolling caught him up on the latest happenings both around Litia and back home on Earth. With space easily compressed by coherent neutrino beams, interstellar news traveled fast.

A chime sounded, the oversized office door opened, and a familiar form ambled in.

"Theesah-ma," Daniel said warmly. He stood, still only one-third her height. "An unexpected pleasure. How are you?"

The giant folded joints beneath her slim red dress until reaching Daniel's level. Eyes were often the best indicator of a Litian-nolo's expression, and Theesah-ma's were decidedly not cheerful.

Daniel placed a hand on her shoulder bump. "Something wrong?"

She blinked several times, remaining silent. It wasn't like her at all.

"Want to sit?" Daniel offered one of the larger chairs in the room.

"No, lovely Daniel," she finally said. "I cannot stay. There is much to do." Her whole body shook, then calmed. "News. Bad, I am afraid."

Daniel steeled himself. It couldn't be news from Earth; he would have already read it.

"Nala," she croaked, barely getting the name out. "A Chitza scout ship has been lost."

Daniel's pulse quickened. "Nala's ship? Lost?"

Theesah-ma took a moment to regain her composure, then spoke with the sure voice of a scientist. "Perhaps destroyed, we cannot be sure. The ship's last message reported intense gamma rays. Ultra-gamma, as it is known by Humans."

As the name implied, ultra-gamma formed the extreme end of the light spectrum with photon energies ranging from a trillion electron-volts to a billion times higher than that. Ordinary gamma radiation destroys DNA and leads to cancer. Ultra-gamma radiation kills—more than kills, it sterilizes.

"Are you sure?"

Theesah-ma nodded diagonally, as Litian-nolos did when they were confident of their facts. Daniel leaned against the desk, feeling suddenly weak. Theesah-ma had never once been wrong about any information she conveyed. No one was more trustworthy.

But he'd been in this situation before. Years ago, a similar report of Nala's death in a blast at Fermilab had turned out to be wrong. The blast itself was real enough, taking out a fifty-meter spherical scoop from the building and shredding a whole lab. But the debris had been blown into a fourth-dimension bubble, Nala with it. Somehow, she'd survived.

He probed. "A Chitza wedge generates 4-D space, right? It's really the only way to travel to other planets."

"Yes." Theesah-ma's eyes shifted, now more curious. "Would an extra dimension of space make a difference?"

Daniel pursed his lips. "I'm really not sure. This is ultra-gamma we're talking about. Deadly. Radiation can pass into higher dimensions, but I think it depends on the circumstances. Nala would know more."

But Nala's in trouble.

He hadn't seen it coming, yet something told him he should have. His unease had nothing to do with the Chitzas; they were widely recognized as skilled in dimensional technology, and their mission had been billed as routine. It wasn't even related to risk. He hadn't *seen* it coming. Unlike the cut on Nala's finger, there had been no advance warning, no visualization, no future memory of a ship destroyed. No inflection point in the multiverse of timelines.

I'm no time mentor, that's for sure.

Perhaps he had been cured. Perhaps he'd never been entangled. But there was one other possibility.

It didn't happen. Not, at least, as Theesah-ma describes.

The Chitza report was likely accurate, and ultra-gamma radiation would be a grave danger to any ship, but add four-dimensional space to the mix and things got weird fast. Directions

19

appeared that didn't exist a minute before. Corners turned toward nowhere. Light reflected and refracted in ways no three-dimensional prism could duplicate. Inside a 4-D bubble there were ways to stay safe. Even if the whole ship had been destroyed it didn't mean that all hands were lost.

Daniel closed his eyes, forcing the science in his head to solidify into an answer he could latch onto and believe. Instead, he found telltale signs of denial and nearly as much doubt that there was any answer at all.

Nala, what have you done?

3   DEEP SPACE

WITH A THREE-METER STRIDE, long-legged Litian-nolos could move rapidly when they wanted to. Daniel ran to keep up. Theesah-ma's assistant, Dihani-keh, an adolescent with two-thirds the physical stature of an adult, joined them. She offered condolences, which he accepted without drama. In this ultra-polite society, condolences were used for anything from a death in the family to a wilted flower arrangement.

Regardless, thoughts about Nala's chances for survival were hard to push away. Gamma ray bursts were deadly, but also very rare and short lived. Had the Chitza ship simply wandered into the wrong place at the wrong time? It didn't make sense, but the stress building in his body had nothing to do with logic.

They were on their way to a government facility that would provide more information about the accident. Dihani-keh assured him that the staff included specialists knowledgeable in Chitza technology as well as administrators who kept track of just about everything happening anywhere in the galaxy. They would have answers, she was sure.

If they didn't, he would find the answers himself. Being a galactic celebrity ensured friends in high places. He pushed emotions away, focusing as best he could on the facts. "Chitza messages come to us via compressed space, right?"

"Always," Theesah-ma replied. Her red dress flapped in the draft of each stride. "Their scout ships compress then decompress space in segments. But this method leaves a four-dimensional filament behind. A microscopic pathway for communication."

"And we can send messages to the ship through this filament?"

"Not us, but the Chitzas can." She seemed to anticipate his next question. "Yes, they have tried to regain communication. Please know that for Chitzas, trying is an exhaustive effort."

Daniel agreed with her assessment of Chitza tenacity, in part because he'd seen it himself. These quill-covered, rodent-sized beings were certainly no hedgehogs.

A quick ride on the modular train brought them to a domed building constructed from polished metal and glass—essentially, a giant mixing bowl turned upside down. At the entrance, a security guard checked and double-checked his visitor's badge before finally waving him through.

Ramps crisscrossed the cavernous interior leading to open decks and balconies where Litian-nolos and android helpers gathered around tables. Banks of electronic equipment provided half height walls, though the open-air design gave the whole place the feeling of a big city library.

Dihani-keh led them up a series of narrow ramps to a level perched well above the ground floor. A sign at the entryway was written in Litian-nolo script. Daniel recognized a few of their complex characters but not enough to read the sign.

Dihani-keh translated, "Galactic Operations."

Theesah-ma engaged in rapid-fire conversations with several staff members. Daniel watched silently, unable to make out more than a word or two, though Theesah-ma's status was perfectly clear. Whatever she asked, the staff answered.

Dihani-keh finally stepped in, speaking in hushed tones. Her English was nearly as good as Theesah-ma's. "They are specialists. They collect news from everywhere. The Chitza wedge issued distress... a signal... automated. Humans say... mayday?"

"Yes, I understand," Daniel replied. "But the Chitzas sent data too, right?"

"A report. Also automated. Ship's position, compression vector, Tau, and others. The Operations Commander says some numbers do not... understandable?"

"The numbers don't make sense to him?"

"Yes, that is it. The Chitzas were too far. The Commander says the numbers are not possible. In your light-year measures, ten exponent nine."

Daniel asked her to repeat, which she did.

"Ten to the ninth. The Chitzas were a billion light-years away?" he asked, and she nodded.

"Minimum."

Daniel shook his head in doubt. "A billion light-years is not just deep space, it's beyond the Milky Way, past Andromeda, past every galaxy in the Laniakea Supercluster. How could anyone even go that far?"

He had once asked if any species had yet reached the far side of the Milky Way, and the answer came back a very proud "yes". A commendable achievement, to be sure, but the galaxy measured a hundred *thousand* light-years across.

A billion?

Even if such a distance could be achieved, it made no sense for a mission searching for new civilizations. They would have passed dozens of suitable galaxies within the first twenty *million* light-years. Daniel agreed with the Litian-nolo commander. There was something fishy about the Chitza report.

"The radiation data is also in question," Dihani-keh translated. "Too large, the Commander says." She picked up a small electronic device and typed. "Humans use electron-volt for photon energy, yes? But most people do not know."

"Don't worry, I do," Daniel said. She might be unsure how to relay scientific information knowing that the average person had little familiarity with some scientific units. Electron-volts were one of those measures, rarely used outside of particle physics and astrophysics.

Dihani-keh looked up from her device. "Ten exponent twenty-one electron-volts."

Daniel stared, unsure if he'd heard her correctly. Litian-nolos were unqualified math wizards. Students here probably learned about exponents in second grade. Perhaps the unit translation had been garbled. "Ten raised to the power of twenty-one. Electron-volts?"

She checked her numbers once more. "Yes. Very large. Ultra-gamma, yet so extreme."

She wasn't kidding about extreme. Radiation at 10^{21} electron-volts would be the highest energy ever recorded. Even gamma ray hot spots produced in supernovae were 10^{15} electron-volts, at most. They were talking about radiation a million times more powerful.

Daniel whispered to himself. "Far beyond our galaxy... and hit by planet-destroying power..." He hesitated to finish, and perhaps there was no need. Even if accurate, there were other factors to consider beyond position and energy. Daniel focused on the main one, the only factor that might make a difference. "Were they in 4-D space at the time?"

Dihani-keh understood his question but didn't have the answer. She spoke briefly with Theesah-ma who brought the Operations Commander into the conversation. When they were finished, Theesah-ma explained.

"The answer is unclear. The report shows Tau set to zero. Which suggests the Chitzas had returned to ordinary three-dimensional space. A grave danger given the radiation. But another value conflicts. Their scout ships are equipped with a dimensional scanning device, like radar. They use it to search for extra dimensions. It is how they locate advanced civilizations. The scanner reported two small bubbles of extradimensional space nearby. We don't know why."

Puzzling information but a hint of good news. Four-dimensional space wasn't natural. Bubbles didn't randomly pop up, they were purposefully stretched into existence by someone who had the technology to do it. A blast of ultra-gamma radiation at 10^{21} electron-volts would vaporize every scrap of matter, but only if that matter floated in 3-D space. With a fourth dimension of space in play—however small— geometry would be turned on its head. Straight lines would lose their meaning. Radiation blasting out in "every direction" might neglect to turn the corner into a fourth dimension. The reported bubbles represented hope.

"This story isn't over," Daniel declared. "Far from it."

Daniel peppered the Operations Commander with questions about Chitza scout ship design, structural integrity, and reaction times to a major event like this. The Litian-nolo responded to each but admitted that some details could only be answered by the Chitzas themselves. He would need to contact his counterparts and establish a *technical union*—an interplanetary conference call of sorts, complete with political advisors who would likely slow any response.

Theesah-ma placed a suckered hand on Daniel's shoulder. "There is another way. While our commander contacts the Chitzas, we may find answers here on Litia. Come." She asked Dihani-keh to remain with the operations team, then led Daniel down the ramps and out of the building.

They hurried along a gently curving path forming the boundary of a circular field planted with a wheat-like grass, a reminder of the two-mile track on prairieland just outside Chicago where Nala's Fermilab teammates accelerated protons close to light speed. Somehow, the Chitzas packed the same technology into a flying wedge no bigger than a Cessna SportJet.

"It'll be fun to see how they do it," Nala had said on the day she'd left. She'd always had an affinity toward the diminutive hedgehog lookalikes. She called them adorably cute, clever, and resourceful—and they were. But they were also technologists with extraordinary abilities. Nala wasn't so taken by their cuteness to miss two important facts: One, that Chitzas were her direct colleagues. And two, that they shared the same personality trait. *They're daredevils. People who rarely say no.*

When the Chitzas had offered, she'd given them an enthusiastic yes. Daniel shouldn't have expected any other answer. In all likelihood, the Chitzas had delivered on their promise of adventure. They'd taken Nala on a thrill ride into deep space, perhaps deeper than anyone realized.

But they'd also discovered something unusual out there. Something unexpected and potentially deadly.

4   HORIZON

A BRISK WALK BROUGHT DANIEL and Theesah-ma to an enclave of tan stone buildings set within a grove of purple trees. They looked like giant stalks of rhubarb. Daniel instinctively noted the retinal based plant life of this alien world, then returned his mental focus to the issue at hand: a deep-space disaster that directly involved his wife.

Nala was missing. Not dead, *missing*. And not critically injured either, since any visual that included Nala floating among tangled wreckage would only slow him down, keep him unfocused and angry. A worried Daniel wasted his talents. A grieving Daniel lost his effectiveness and squandered potential solutions.

For now, he tucked Nala into a safe cubbyhole somewhere in his psyche and embraced this single kernel of optimism if only as a way to cope: Nala had found a way to stay alive. Somehow, he would find her.

A billion light-years away.

The absurd distance aligned with the correspondingly low chance of rescue. But with new sciences and bold technologies cropping up everywhere, Daniel felt far less encumbered by limits. Maybe those limits had never existed. Careful analysis, a critical eye, and attention to detail had always gone a long way to resolving the most difficult of problems. New friends in high places took care of the rest.

Friends didn't get much higher than Core, the cybernetic gatekeeper for the consortium of civilizations known as Sagittarius Novus. Daniel had first spoken with Core four years ago, and they'd maintained an odd relationship ever since.

Unfortunately, among planet-sized cyborgs, this one was decidedly non-interfering. If Daniel asked Core for help, he could guess the answer and was beginning to see Core's point. Solutions came from gaining new insight into a problem, as Core had pointed out more than once. Moreover, insight was not merely a beneficial side effect to exploration or study, it should be the principle ambition of any inquisitive species.

Core would never be the solution to a missing scout ship, but simpler paths were still available. If they worked together, Humans, Litian-nolos, and Chitzas had the ingenuity and technology to solve the problem. No need for an all-powerful entity to interfere.

Daniel smiled, recognizing the same reasoning religious people gave when asked why their god never showed up for duty. *Roll up your sleeves and get it done yourself.* Core would have said the same thing, though not quite in those words.

Even now, Litian-nolo Galactic Operations staff were reaching out to their Chitza counterparts. Good would come from it, but they weren't about to stop there. Theesah-ma had her own list of indispensable friends.

"Alosoni-eff is a professor of cosmology," she explained as they passed through the ground-level entrance to a stone pentagon with gothic spires that reached skyward at each of its five corners. "You and he see the world in the same way, lovely Daniel."

Daniel's world view had never come up in previous conversations, but it might not be the comparison she had in mind. Litian-nolos tended to speak in larger contexts than Humans. A shared world view might mean that you both liked milk in your coffee.

"Right now, anyone that can help us find that Chitza ship is my dearest friend," Daniel answered. "At least the professor will know about ultra-gamma radiation, right?"

"Yes, exactly." Theesah-ma's voice drifted down from above. She'd stretched back up to her full height. It felt like walking next to one of those oversized puppets the Brazilians made for Carnival.

They entered a curiously curving walkway that corkscrewed vertically up one of the building's five towers. Unlike a moving sidewalk back on Earth, the exterior frame of the spiral structure turned, lifting its occupants up the corkscrew to higher floors.

Theesah-ma exited at the third level. Daniel followed past a series of tall entryways with no doors. Open floor plans dominated Litian-nolo buildings, Daniel's own office door being an exception, added when they'd learned of the tendency for Humans to work in isolation.

Theesah-ma led him into an office with walls covered by maps, star charts, and deep space photographs. Thick oversized books with worn covers leaned against each other in a disorganized stack across a desk. The place carried the musty smell of aging paper.

A smaller Litian-nolo rose from a chair.

It stood the same height as Theesah-ma's young assistant Dihani-keh, but that's where the similarity ended. This Litian-nolo didn't have Dihani-keh's fresh face, far from it. Wrinkles abounded across its flat, tongue like head. Eyes drooped, and knobby joints wobbled as though the ligaments holding everything together weren't quite up to the task.

An elder, Daniel thought. He'd only seen a few and had never met one directly. In their young society, advanced age was the exception, not the rule, with each person's lifespan governed by a complex gene not fully understood.

Theesah-ma introduced her friend without flourish. "Alosoni-eff. Daniel Rice."

The old professor leaned to one side and spoke to what looked like a potted plant on the desk. A single yellow leaf atop the pot folded itself into a crouch, then leaped to the desk. The surprisingly mobile leaf stood about ten centimeters in height on a flexible stem that flattened into a tripod at its base. Darker veins spread from the stem to its serrated edges. It looked like a leaf plucked from a cherry tree in autumn.

The leaf's edges pulsed with a red glow as vibrations spread across its surface and words filled the air. "My apologies, Daniel Rice," Alosoni-eff said in Litian-nolo, with the leafy device instantly translating to English. "I have not the time to learn your language. And at my age, not the remaining intellect either. My assistant will help." He patted the standing leaf at its point, which flexed from his touch.

Daniel had encountered several translation devices since leaving Earth, but none quite so organic. He smiled, then offered the standard Litian-nolo greeting. "*Et-tah mishi doh*. No reason to apologize, Professor. I'm afraid these few words are the sum of my Litian-nolo."

"Not true," Theesah-ma admonished. She had taught him more of their language, though how much he could recall varied from day to day.

Daniel hooked a hand under Theesah-ma's arm. "She is being kind. While on Litia, I lean on Theesah-ma and on my wife who are both fine linguists compared to me. I wish my wife could be here. She is the reason we came to see you."

"I have heard the news," the professor said via the leaf's vibrations. "My condolences, dear Human. How may I help?"

Theesah-ma answered, "Share your experience, dear professor. How and where could a Chitza ship encounter ultra-gamma radiation? Better knowledge of the source could help us understand their chances for survival."

"I will try," the old Litian-nolo said. He ran a suckered hand along the serrations of the leaf, paused, then repeated the stroke in the opposite direction. There seemed intent in both the motion and location of his touch.

"One moment," the leaf said on its own.

A few seconds later, the leaf stretched to a narrow point. A rectangular window popped into the air just above it, displaying a three-dimensional graph. A curving magenta line appeared above the axes.

"This graph maps position reports received from the scout ship," the leaf said. "We are looking at the Chitza communications filament left behind." More than a translator, the leaf's comments hinted of intelligence built into what might be an organic robot.

Daniel studied the line drawn in air. It began from a green point at the bottom, meandered gently for much of its length, then made an abrupt turn toward the right, ending at a second point colored red.

With no labels, Daniel needed confirmation. "The Operations commander suggested they were a billion light-years away. Frankly, I have a hard time believing that. Could the position reports be wrong?"

Alosoni-eff stroked the edge of the leaf once more.

"The position reports are correct," the leaf responded. "But the Operations commander is wrong. Not one billion. Fifty-two billion."

Daniel paused. With a variety of players, including one that looked more like it had fallen from a nearby tree, they might not be on the same wavelength.

"Light-years, as Humans measure?"

"Light-years, yes," replied the leaf. "If you prefer, sixteen gigaparsecs, a direct-line measure from the red endpoint to our current position on Litia."

The answer was clear enough, and expressed in two different Human units, yet once again the numbers seemed impossible. In fact, they were trending in the wrong direction, farther away not closer.

Notwithstanding the variety of star charts decorating the professor's walls, their conversation had veered toward lunacy. "You're suggesting that the Chitza ship ended up not just beyond our galaxy but beyond *every* galaxy. Fifty-two billion light-years is beyond the cosmic horizon."

"Yes, the Chitza position reports come from beyond the horizon of the observable universe," the leaf agreed.

"Astonishing!" Alosoni-eff stroked the leaf once more. "But if my assistant computes such a distance, then it is so."

Daniel couldn't claim to be an expert in cosmology, but he had googled crazy ideas like "the edge of the universe" once or twice. Surprisingly, our universe does have an edge, though horizon is the better word. Sixteenth-century sailors talked of sailing off the edge of the world, but their captains knew the ocean continued beyond the horizon, they just didn't know how far. In the twenty-first century, the same could be said for the universe. Not a single cosmologist could say with any certainty how far space might extend, but every one of them could accurately point to the horizon. The cosmic horizon.

Like the ocean, the cosmic horizon represented not a cliff but a limit of visibility. Telescopes couldn't see stars or galaxies beyond it because there hadn't been enough time in the 13.8-billion-year history of the universe for their light to reach us. In fact, light from such remote places would never reach us—the rapid expansion of space guaranteed it. Twentieth century astronomer, Edwin Hubble, discovered that space itself stretched. The further away, the faster it stretched. Go far enough, and spatial expansion would outrace light itself. There would be no point in searching further.

"Okay," Daniel said, holding up a hand. "Chitzas are proud and for good reason. But how does anyone find a place that we can't even see… and in fact will *never* see?"

Alosoni-eff seemed to agree with the absurdity of the numbers being recited. "It is one of many dilemmas introduced by spatial compression. Until now, no one has needed to grapple with locations beyond the cosmic horizon." The giant Litian-nolo settled into his chair and placed both bony arms on his desk. "The Chitzas may have accomplished more than we knew."

"There are rumors," Theesah-ma said.

Alosoni-eff nodded slowly. "Rumors of additional dimensions."

Daniel put a hand to his mouth as the light came on. "Of course… a fifth dimension of space… hell, even a sixth."

String theory reared its incomprehensible head once more. According to the physicists who had provided the evidence, our universe was built on a foundation of three ordinary dimensions of space, and seven more curled up at quantum sizes.

"Compression superimposed upon compression," Theesah-ma said. "An exponential effect carried into higher dimensions. Litian-nolos have no such technology, but perhaps the Chitzas have accomplished it?"

Alosoni-eff added, "Expanding a four-dimensional bubble into five-dimensional space could indeed compress a gigaparsec of ordinary space, though I cannot say how theory becomes reality."

Daniel shook his head in wonder and newfound respect. *Bloody geniuses, those Chitzas.*

Conceptually the technology wouldn't be hard to grasp. A bicycle could do it. A car too. Simply shift into a higher gear and the same engine could double its efficiency. But had the Chitzas accomplished such a feat? They may not have been entirely honest when they'd offered a ride to Nala.

33

Or had they?

Damn it! How could I be so stupid? They told her!

The pieces quickly fell into place. The Chitzas had accomplished something no one else had. They'd hinted to Nala, knowing that her scientific voice would provide credibility to their claim. Worse, they'd offered her a seat on an expedition to test their latest advances, dangling a shiny bauble to tempt her.

We're going beyond the cosmic horizon, they probably bragged.

Nala would have jumped at the opportunity. A front row seat to an unreachable viewpoint, plus a chance to see for herself how they had pulled it off. Upon return, it wouldn't hurt to have a Human as their spokesperson—someone who would, no doubt, tell everyone else how clever her Chitza friends had been.

She'd left without mentioning any of this. They might have sworn her to secrecy, or she may have rationalized her silence as a way to prevent him from worrying. Daniel closed his eyes and clenched his fists in frustration.

5   ZERO-G

NALA ARCHES HER BACK, vaulting upside down, twisting, scrambling, arms flailing, scratching for something to hold onto. There is nothing but blinding white light and the shouts from her companions.

Aussik? He'd pushed her. Onner? It sounds like her.

There is air to breathe, she is thankful for that, but the chaotic tumbling in zero-g becomes more than her stomach can handle. She slams into something hard, sending a shot of pain through her shoulder but putting an abrupt end to the tumbling. Her stomach settles, though she still can't open her eyes to the shocking brightness that surrounds her. Eyelids aren't enough to fend off the invasive brilliance. Even hands cannot completely block it.

She kicks the air and strikes something small which flies away. Clanks of metal upon metal don't echo, they are muffled by a deadness all around. The shrieks drift farther away by the second. "Onner!" she calls out, thinking the Chitza may have called to her. She listens but hears no response.

The fierce light finally fades to the point where she can see. She peeks out from beneath wary eyelids. Debris floats everywhere, bits of metal, melted plastic, and torn cloth. It's not enough material to account for a whole ship but it gives a distinct impression of catastrophe. How many crewmembers survived the chaotic, last-minute leap into what Aussik called the *lifeboat* remains uncertain.

Aussik jumped after her. She saw him. She only heard Onner. Maybe Beets too. Captain Zeeno not at all. Now she can't find any of them, not in any direction.

There is no shape to this place. The brightness continues to diminish but no walls appear. It feels like a cloud. It might be a bubble, but it has no view outside—to space or the sparkling, cliff-like boundary. They should have never stopped.

She ducks as a larger chunk of debris flies past her head, but it's hard to do much more than twist in place. She's floating in zero-g with nothing to push off from. Even if she could move from this position, which direction would she go? It looks the same everywhere.

She scans her body for injuries. A red, three-inch scratch crosses her arm. It isn't deep. She's not sure if coagulated blood proves there's oxygen in the air, but she's not dead yet so there must be something to breathe. No broken bones. Strangely, her skin isn't burnt or peeling.

She's lucky. Others may not have been.

****

Nala drifts, accompanied only by the memory of how she'd gotten here. The horror story plays over and over in her mind. She's been here for eight, maybe ten hours. Nobody wears watches anymore and her mobile phone is back on the ship. Or melted.

Another hour passes. Maybe two. Her memory isn't lying, her friends were here, but now they are gone. Somewhere else, dead, or dying.

She closes her eyes as tears well up. She slams fists against her hips and screams. "Jesus, why them? It's not fucking fair!" Her heart thumps, easily heard in the soundless environment. She hangs her head and weeps for her brave and talented companions. She weeps for herself. She is far from home, at a remote place no one would ever think to look.

From here, and into whatever future might be left, she'll be alone. Alone with no water. No food. The breathable air that has been trapped inside this dimensional aberration won't last long either. Another blast of intense energy would be a cleaner way to end this.

She should never have taken the Chitzas' offer. She screwed up, big time.

Daniel's going to be so pissed at me.

6   ARRIVAL

"IT'S A PYRAMID SCHEME, of sorts," Daniel said. "String theory claims ten dimensions of space, seven of which are curled into quantum sizes. We've learned how to uncurl one quantum dimension, which in turn compresses ordinary space in a chosen direction. Uncurl another and you get exponential compression? It makes sense, I guess, but why stop there? Just keep uncurling all seven. Where would that take you?"

"Anywhere you wish to go," Professor Alosoni-eff said.

Daniel attempted to shake the cobwebs of neglected hyperdimensional physics from his head. Adding a brand-new direction that no one could point to had always been a bizarre reality of Nala's work in particle physics. But now there were *two* new directions? Maybe more? Daniel tried to imagine a graph where five axes spread out from a single origin creating five simultaneous and distinct right angles. He failed magnificently.

The bicycle gear analogy was easier on the brain. "Theoretically you could uncurl more dimensions to trigger—let's call it, a *supercompression* of 3-D space. So much compression, you manage to get beyond the cosmic horizon. So, what's out there?" Scientists rarely ventured into speculative areas beyond friendly banter at the local pub on a Saturday night. Maybe that was about to change.

Alosoni-eff settled into his oversized chair. "What is beyond the ocean's horizon? More ocean. Our universe is the same, isotropic. On a large scale, one patch of the universe looks the same as any other. This tells us with some certainty that a peek beyond the horizon would reveal more galaxies. More galaxy clusters. More gas, dust, nebulae. More planets and perhaps more civilizations. These remote places have enjoyed the same 13.8

billion years to evolve, just as we have. We cannot see them, but lack of visibility does not make them any less real. *Supercompress* space, as the Chitzas may be doing, and you could eventually reach such remote places."

"Except that you're trying to catch up to space that is expanding faster than the speed of light," Daniel added. He was back to the Hubble discovery that space itself continues to expand. Natural expansion might not be a big deal when jumping a few thousand light-years, but a billion was another story.

"Remember, the expansion rate is relative to our current position," Alosoni-eff said. "A person standing on a planet located at our cosmic horizon would say that it is we who are rushing away from them at the speed of light. They would see the Milky Way at their cosmic horizon with no knowledge of what might be beyond."

"So, it's all relative." Daniel spat out the words he had always despised. It was a meaningless phrase, casually tossed out by those with a passing acquaintance of physics. In this case, he wasn't even buying its premise.

"Saying that a measurement is relative makes sense for velocity, time, even length. But not for matter. The Big Bang produced a finite amount of matter and energy. It's a big number, but it's measurable, and anyone anywhere in the universe would agree on the result. A finite Big Bang implies a finite amount of expanding space. There's an absolute limit out there somewhere, right?"

Alosoni-eff shifted uncomfortably in his chair. "Some suggest a higher dimensional boundary much as an expanding sphere has both an inside and outside. Others suggest a torus shape where space eventually wraps back on itself. Both are finite cosmologies derived from a finite Big Bang. Unfortunately, since we cannot see or measure beyond the horizon, no one knows which might be correct."

"Except perhaps the Chitzas."

The professor gently nodded.

A low tone sounded, and Theesah-ma spoke to the electronic sphere floating at her shoulder. A small window popped up in the air next to it.

"How interesting," she said. "Another Chitza scout ship has arrived. It has landed here on Litia."

"Your Operations Commander contacted them?" Daniel asked.

"Apparently so. The Chitzas are asking for you."

"Me?"

"You."

Alosoni-eff rose from his chair and addressed Daniel. "There is only one reason for the Chitzas to send a ship. Will you go with them?"

The professor might be right. The Chitzas had lured his wife to join a groundbreaking but dangerous mission. They might be feeling guilty. Or responsible. If hitching a ride on a second scout ship helped find Nala, Daniel wouldn't hesitate. He glanced at Theesah-ma who nodded without comment.

"Take my assistant with you." Alosoni-eff ran a suckered hand down the leaf's edge. "Ets-tah is a fully qualified cosmologist and could provide insight you may need."

Daniel wasn't sure what to say. No doubt the leaf could be useful for a voyage driven by Chitza-sized ambitions. Chitzas were known for their brash nature and snap decisions, not their thoughtful science. But Daniel detected a close relationship between Alosoni-eff and his assistant.

"It's a generous offer, but what if this ship is heading into the same danger? I couldn't put that kind of risk on your valued assistant."

"I will go," the leaf said.

The professor bowed to his assistant. "Then it is decided. Ets-tah requires no nourishment, gravity, or even air. Quite a suitable companion for a long trip on a Chitza wedge."

Notwithstanding the leaf's resilience, Daniel had his own requirements to think about. He could get by without gravity, but a long voyage on any spacecraft would need to provide basic life support. Somehow, Nala had managed it.

Theesah-ma wrapped an arm around Daniel. "Come lovely Daniel, I will take you to the spaceport." She reached out. The leaf hopped from the professor's desk onto her hand.

The professor gave one last stroke to the tiny leaf. "You will come back to me, won't you dear fellow?"

The leaf vibrated not unlike a cat's purr.

"Thank you, professor," Daniel said. "I'll make sure…" He was about to say something reassuring, but safe passage couldn't be guaranteed for anyone, himself included. Instead, he lightly touched the professor's arm, as Litian-nolos did on parting.

****

Theesah-ma guided Daniel back to the station. This time, their train ride left the city behind and passed through several tunnels that pierced the surrounding hills. Eventually, they dropped below ground for good and their module detached at a busy station.

They traversed a long corridor decorated with designs of flying machines ranging from primitive to sleek. Several Litian-nolo portraits hung among the aircraft drawings, most likely the pioneers in their flight history. Finally, a lift brought them to the surface.

They stood inside a clear dome surrounded by a concrete apron where airships of various sizes and shapes were parked. The largest ship bound three huge tubes within a metal lattice that stretched to either side forming graceful wings. Each tube could have enclosed the largest Boeing fuselage ever produced, with room to spare. Giant Litian-nolos definitely needed their legroom.

Almost unnoticed beside the oversized aircraft, a small black wedge perched on three landing struts. Its pointy nose protruded from an isosceles triangle body with twin turbines hanging at the triangle's vertices. A single red light blinked atop a short pole near its aft end. The whole craft was about the size of a military jet. Though the wedge looked sleek enough to speed through any atmosphere, various antennae and several raised glass viewports belonged to a design better suited for frictionless space.

A lone Chitza stood on the boarding ramp leading into the ship. No taller than a fire hydrant but just as sturdy, the figure wore two belts that diagonally crisscrossed a chest thick with brown and black fur. Black boots reached halfway up stout legs. White-tipped quills ran down its backside—a male of their species.

"I guess that's my ride," Daniel said. He'd already decided that even if the Chitzas weren't offering, he'd insist on a seat, leveraging his standing in Sagittarius Novus if he had to. Nala was out there somewhere, and these intelligent hedgehogs most likely knew where she went.

"Do be careful," Theesah-ma said. "I worry about lovely Nala. But I could not bear to lose you both. Our Chitza friends are clever, but they are also—"

Daniel wrapped arms around the tall Litian-nolo as best he could. "Impulsive? I get it. And I'll watch for it. But I couldn't just wait here when Nala needs my help."

Theesah-ma nodded. "I would go too, if I could."

Daniel smiled. Even for a Human, climbing aboard the Chitza wedge would likely involve a lot of ducking and crouching. This was not a ship for giants.

Theesah-ma lifted the professor's leafy assistant from a perch it had found on one of her many arm crooks and held it out to Daniel.

"I'm not quite sure where to put it," Daniel said.

"No pockets please," the leaf said. "Anyplace else will do." The leaf flexed the base of its branching stem. Tiny claws at the tips of three branches could probably latch onto most any soft surface.

Daniel placed the leaf on his shoulder, and the stem clung to his shirt. "I'm sorry, what was your name again?"

"Ets-tah Lohabi Akaisal. In English, a type of sprig."

"It fits you."

"Please call me Sprig, if easier."

No question there. "Pleased to meet you, Sprig. Are you...?" He let the question die on his lips. There was no point in asking about the creature's anatomy. Organic, electronic, or something in between, it really didn't matter. They would soon be partners on a second Chitza mission—assuming the Chitzas would allow him onboard.

Daniel said his goodbyes to Theesah-ma, promising to return soon regardless of the fact that such an assurance was nothing more than hopeful thinking. They embraced once more, then Daniel proceeded through a doorway to the flight operations apron with Sprig clinging to his shoulder.

"Any words of advice, Sprig, on how we might approach these Chitzas?" Daniel asked. The leaf flexed with each of Daniel's steps.

"They will know who you are," Sprig answered. "And will assume I am your personal assistant."

"Are you?"

"Humans have a better word. Ally."

"I like your thinking, Sprig. We're going to get along just fine."

They continued across the flat concrete to the waiting black wedge. The Chitza guard stepped to the bottom of the ship's ramp.

"Daniel Rice," the Chitza said in a complex squeak that included guttural tones in lower registers. "You ready to go?"

"Does that mean we're flying together?" Daniel asked.

The Chitza tilted its head toward the open hatch. "We have a spot for you. But our destination is wickedly far out there."

"Anything specific I need for a trip to wickedly far space?"

"Guts."

Daniel suppressed a smile. "No food, water?"

"We have ChitzaPacks."

"Which are?"

"Provisions. Top quality. Humans love 'em."

Nala had left with nothing more than the clothes on her back, a bottle of water, and her mobile phone. Daniel carried even less. "I'm in. Where are we heading?"

The Chitza tugged on one of its belts. "We go where we need to go. This mission is a search for survivors, including your mate."

"Then let's get to it." Daniel bent down and held out a hand. "Nice to meet you, captain."

"Captain Zeeno's inside. Aussik is my name. Welcome aboard." The Chitza lifted a clawed paw, slapped it against Daniel's hand, and spoke with resolute enthusiasm. "We go in honor, together in life and together in death!"

Arrival

7 CHITZAS

DANIEL MADE HIS WAY down a dark, narrow passageway inside the Chitza scout ship, ducking under pipes and squeezing between components covered with blinking lights. It felt like a submarine both in terms of the complexity of equipment and the general lack of space for the crew. On the plus side, the scent of fresh bread baking in an oven permeated the air. Chitza provisions might very well live up to the hype.

A particularly low spar forced him to squat but once past, the corridor widened to form an open space about ten feet across. Storage lockers covered one side. Hand grips were bolted into the walls and ceiling, useful for zero-g. Once underway, they might be floating. On Litia, a gravity generator could be bought at any hardware store, but he had no idea whether Chitza ships used the technology.

His stocky Chitza guide, Aussik, climbed a three-step ladder through an open oval doorway. Daniel stopped at the doorway, having reached the limit of Human progress in such tight confines. He poked his head into a bright cockpit packed with aviation-style instrumentation plus a few cogs, cranks, and handles that a commercial jet would never feature. Two Chitza-sized pilot seats faced a wrap-around glass viewport looking out to the surrounding airfield.

"Got him, Boss," Aussik announced while climbing into the right seat.

The left seat swiveled, revealing a thinner Chitza with distinctive patches of grey in its facial fur. It wore hard plastic shoulder pads that connected to a vest of the same brown color as its fur—clothing that accessorized rather than trying to cover the body.

"*Gek eep, shteep dah?*" the captain asked.

Daniel shrugged at the foreign words.

The Chitza grinned, showing fine teeth. "Didn't think so. We'll use your language. Hell, we all went through immersion training last night, so we might as well take advantage of it." The Chitza rubbed the inside of one ear. "Painful, but *damn*, that shit works."

He beat a fist against his chest. "I'm Zeeno. You already met our copilot Aussik. The others are on the lower deck. Four of us, plus you." He stretched, examining Daniel more closely. "Is that thing your assistant?"

Daniel glanced to his right. Sprig hadn't moved or spoken a word. "My associate. Thanks for including us. Aussik says it's a search and rescue mission. I appreciate your concern for my wife."

Zeeno pointed a stiff claw. "No guarantees, my friend. We'll retrace their path. Recover the data recorder if we can. But it might not be pretty out there."

"I understand. I'm still thankful."

"Wife means mate, right? You're a pair?"

"Right."

The Chitza gritted his teeth. "We'll find her if we can."

"Thanks, Captain," Daniel said, not quite sure if he'd heard the captain's name correctly. Zeeno sounded a lot like the Chitza name Nala had mentioned in her last message, but you never knew what slight variations were meaningful to a different species. "I understand several Chitzas are missing too."

"Not just any Chitzas, brothers and sisters," Zeeno replied. Daniel was about to get clarification on the somewhat surprising new information, but Zeeno waved him off. "It's a long story. Ask your little leaf guy, I need to get us underway. Aussik, show him his seat."

"Right, Boss." Aussik squeezed past Daniel at the cockpit entrance, scurried to the right side bulkhead and dropped through a hole in the floor that until now, Daniel hadn't noticed.

He followed the copilot and peered down. The hole was less than two feet in diameter, easy for a Chitza but challenging for a Human. A rail on one side and wide metal steps seemed sturdy enough to support his weight. Daniel went feet first, twisting to get his shoulders through.

The lower deck wasn't any more spacious. In places, Daniel could stand upright but he had to duck under wires, valves, and pipes that crossed the ceiling. Two workstations were slotted into cubbies on either side of a narrow corridor. Complex control panels were covered with displays and dials. A third Chitza occupied one of the seats.

"Veronica," Aussik said. "Our safety officer."

Daniel reached down to her height and ended up doing an awkward fist bump with the Chitza. Gender distinctions were fairly obvious in this species. Females had red-tipped quills instead of white.

"Interesting name, Veronica. We Humans use it too."

"I know," Veronica squeak growled. "I used to go by Onner, but I liked the sound of Veronica better, so I borrowed the name. V, vvvv, vverrr. Cool sound. We don't use it in our words, but we should." She rubbed her fur-covered ear. "Human language hurts a little. Probably the immersion training. No matter, I'm getting used to it."

"You all speak it well," Daniel said. "Sorry it hurts."

Aussik and Veronica chanted in unison, "Pain heals a wounded soul!"

The Chitzas seemed to have a clever motto for everything, but the power of their existential messages might be forever lost on Humans. Daniel made a mental note to ask about this particular chant later, assuming his relationship with the crew moved into congenial territory. Veronica seemed nice enough.

Aussik led Daniel a few paces down the corridor and stopped at a Human-sized chair positioned next to a window. "Obviously yours." He slid back a panel in the floor revealing a second window that looked straight down to concrete. "Once we're underway, you'll have the best view on the ship."

Opposite the chair, a half-sized door interrupted the maze of pipes and wires crisscrossing the bulkhead. Aussik cracked the door open to reveal a narrow closet, dark. "Water, toilet, that kind of thing. Big enough for Humans."

"Ha!" Veronica laughed from her workstation which was only ten feet down the corridor.

"Give it a rest, V," Aussik yelled to his colleague then turned back to Daniel. "Yeah, maybe she's right. We don't normally get Humans on a scout ship. Hell, we built a giant dummy back at base just to measure stuff. Might still have a few things wrong."

Daniel surveyed the collection of equipment performing who-knows-what function covering every surface. "Don't worry, it feels cozy in here. Thanks for showing me around, Aussik."

A soft whir kicked in from somewhere further aft.

"Stations!" Zeeno called from the upper deck. Aussik scrambled back up the ladder to the cockpit, and Veronica flipped a few switches on her panel. The second workstation remained unoccupied. Captain Zeeno seemed to be missing his fourth crew member.

As whirring pitched higher, several clangs rang out from somewhere deeper in the ship. Was there a third deck? Given the window view straight down to the concrete tarmac, an additional deck couldn't be thicker than a Chitza's head, even with quills flattened.

"*Jeepsa crack fratz!*" a muffled voice yelled from below. "*Jockin' Humans!*"

Veronica looked up at Daniel and smiled, showing two rather sharp canines. "Sorry, she means well."

"No offense taken," Daniel said. He had no idea what might be going on below but staying polite would ensure their fourth crew member didn't bare her own sharp teeth in anger. He imagined a Chitza bite could easily take off a finger.

The whirring became a piercing whine, sending vibrations through the floor. Daniel found a seatbelt and buckled up. Just behind him, a floor cap the size of a sewer cleanout popped open. A Chitza head poked out, streaked with dirt. Drips of grey-green sludge hung from her chin.

Intense eyes beneath filthy fur locked onto him like a cheetah spotting a lame impala. Her head quills had been sheered down to stumps on one side and dyed pink on the other. A metal bolt skewered one ear, causing the normally upright appendage to sag. Luminescent paint covered the claws on each paw giving them a distracting shimmer.

Daniel smiled as best he could. "Hi, I'm Daniel Rice."

Eyes rolled to the top of her decorated skull. "*Fratz!*"

"Nice to meet you," Daniel said. "I'll try to stay out of your way."

He had no idea if her name was Fratz, or if he had just been the target of the most repugnant of Chitza swear words. Probably the latter by the foul look on the Chitza's dirty face.

The ship's fourth crew member climbed out of the drainage pipe then pulled off a red checkered cloth tied around her stout waist and started cleaning fur and quills.

"Stations!" came the call from above once more. The whine of spinning turbines outside had become too loud to ignore. "That means you, Beets."

51

Beets tossed the now-filthy rag into a bin then ambled up the corridor to the empty workstation. She punched a button with a balled-up fist. "*Fratz!*"

Context, Daniel thought, *is a wonderful thing*. Now that he'd separated Chitza swearing from names, this journey could begin in earnest. It was a good crew on the whole. He'd dealt with a few unapproachable coworkers in his career. One eccentric among four wasn't a bad ratio.

The captain of this mission would be the key to its success, and Zeeno was clearly in charge. Being sympathetic to Human participation helped, but the captain hadn't stated why Daniel had been invited. He knew about Nala, but that hardly seemed reason enough to have his crew take immersion language training or remodel his ship to accommodate another Human passenger. For now, Daniel tabled his questions. A long journey lay ahead. There would be time to get things sorted.

Daniel turned to the only other passenger, who still clung to his shoulder. "What do you think, Sprig? Are we in good hands?"

Sprig spoke softly, with the barest of vibrations flitting across its leaf. "Chitzas are excellent pilots. But they make poor confidants."

"How so?"

"Litian-nolos have a saying. When a Chitza tells you two things, it is only because they are withholding a third."

"Interesting. I hadn't heard that before."

"Now you have."

"What's the brother and sister thing Zeeno mentioned?"

The leaf adjusted its position on Daniel's shoulder, hopping closer to his ear. "Chitzas are born in litters of twelve. Every time, exactly twelve identical twins. Dodeca-twins you could say. But more than twins, clones. Identical appearance, identical personality. For their first year of life, all twelve even share a single consciousness, a fascinating pattern of brain development that has been widely studied."

"Huh."

"Littermates are given the same name too, though adults sometimes adjust their name, as Veronica did. More importantly, all twelve undertake the same profession. It is their way."

Daniel began to put the pieces together. "So, it works like that for every profession? Pilots included?"

"Yes. Pilots, copilots, safety officers, and mechanics. The Chitzas you have just met are siblings of those who were lost."

Daniel tapped his lower lip. "Important to understand, given the mission. Thanks for telling me."

"You are most welcome," Sprig said.

It explained the name Zeeno, used by both pilots of both missions. But it also revealed that the personal stakes in this mission weren't limited to Daniel. Every crew member had a reason to grieve if it failed. A littermate might not have exactly the same meaning as a Human sibling, but Zeeno had already distinguished between the value of a brother or sister versus any other Chitza citizen. Humans had no lock on compassion and might not even rank in the top ten when it came to empathy for others. Daniel would need to keep that in mind as their journey played out.

With a rumble, the scout ship lifted from the ground. Daniel peered through the floor window and watched the Litian-nolo spaceport shrinking beneath. They passed through several layers of clouds then banked to one side. The gas giant, Nolo, appeared through Daniel's side window. No longer filtered by Litia's atmosphere, its bold striped face looked a lot like a bluer version of Jupiter. A minute later, the last bit of atmospheric haziness disappeared, leaving only the stark darkness of space.

"Stand by for 4-D," Zeeno said from the top deck. His voice carried easily in the small ship. No need for an intercom or headsets.

Veronica kept her gaze fixed on a large display where colored bar graphs overlayed diagrams of the ship from several views. At the opposite workstation, Beets studied a stream of text—portions highlighted—that apparently were enough to keep her informed on system details. With no view into the cockpit, Daniel could only assume Zeeno and Aussik were busy manipulating controls that would soon put the vessel into unnatural space created from curled up quantum dimensions.

"Three, two, one," Aussik called out. A dull pop and a slight twisting sensation were the only indications of the magic that had surely happened outside.

Daniel peered out the window. Stars were still visible but now appeared strangely flat, like pinpricks on an immense sheet of black paper. A grin spread across his face. Soyuz astronauts who had been zapped into a fourth dimension of space several years ago had provided similar descriptions: a flat wall of stars.

Nothing like being there yourself.

Nolo's crescent still filled most of the sky, but it now appeared thinner, like a basketball that had lost its air. Its moon Litia, still visible through the floor window, shrank rapidly.

"Tau is within parameters," Veronica announced.

"Systems nominal," Beets said.

"Set Tau to minus nine, smooth transition," Zeeno said.

"You got it, Boss," Aussik said, then yelled what appeared to be a cue for everyone else. "Initiating…"

All four Chitzas shouted in unison, "Mash it, crash it, nothing stops us! Nobody beats a Chitza!"

On either side of the ship, the whine of spinning turbines ramped up to a roar. Colors on Veronica's display turned blood red. The wedge lurched, temporarily pressing Daniel into his seat.

"Minus three," Aussik called out. "Minus four."

Daniel had a vague understanding of what was going on. Nala had done much the same thing several years ago when she and Daniel had sent a cobbled-together probe thousands of light-years from Earth to a special place on an alien map. Now Daniel sat inside a similar probe. They had just ballooned a fourth dimension from its quantum size to a bubble big enough to surround the ship. As the bubble expanded, ordinary three-dimensional space along a chosen vector compressed. They weren't really flying through space, though it looked like it outside the window. Instead, one dimension of space collapsed, folding like an accordion toward them. They measured the collapse using Tau. A value of 10^{-9} would compress by a factor of one billion, reducing light-years of interstellar space to almost nothing.

"Minus seven," Aussik called out. Tau equal to 10^{-7}, already a compression factor of ten million.

"Systems looking sweet," Beets said.

"Safety check is damn fine extra sweet," Veronica said with a fist pump.

"Keep her going then," Zeeno said. "Take us up to minus twelve."

"Gotcha, Boss. Climbing to twelve."

Daniel no longer felt any pressure against his seat and wasn't sure why it had occurred at all. Compressing space wasn't the same as accelerating. More likely, the initial lurch had something to do with ramping up the spin on their turbines. Daniel was beginning to see why Nala had jumped at the chance to fly with the Chitzas. This small, claustrophobic ship was performing miracles of technology.

Out the window, stars began to slide by. As Aussik called out ever higher Tau numbers, their apparent velocity in this weird expansion-compression state of spatial dimensions skyrocketed. Soon a blur of stars streaked by like water droplets on an airplane window at takeoff.

Daniel checked in with his traveling partner. "You doing okay?"

"I've never traveled like this before," Sprig answered. The leaf bounced on its stem.

"But you're okay?"

"I think so."

"Not scared?"

"No. It feels… fun."

Daniel smiled. They'd been given a front row seat to spatial compression on an impressive scale. Indeed, nobody beat a Chitza.

Veronica noticed their quiet conversation and leaned back from her workstation. "Cool, huh?"

"Yeah, we're loving it," Daniel called back. "You really know your stuff."

"Guess where we are now." The Chitza ruffled her red-tipped quills. She looked quite delighted with herself.

"I have no idea," Daniel said. "A hundred light-years from Litia? A thousand?"

"Twenty thousand," Veronica said. Tiny quills just above her eyes twitched. "We're already leaving the galaxy!"

"Really?"

"No lyin', no cryin'. Check it out yourself." She waved him over to her workstation. Daniel unbuckled and gingerly walked down the short corridor. Except for a vibration in the floor, there was little feeling of motion.

"Look here." Veronica pointed to a display showing their current position among a field of stars. When she zoomed out, an arm of the Milky Way stretched across her screen. Their departure path, marked in yellow, crossed the arm and was just beginning to emerge from its top edge.

The floor window provided visual proof. The enormous spiral arm filled the view. Uncountable stars mixed with glowing gases of violet and green along with darker patches of dust. Still oddly flat, but the 4-D weirdness didn't subtract from their glorious perch above the Milky Way. More galactic arms stretched into view, each a magnificent spiral covering an impossibly vast region.

Like looking at the intricate threadwork of a European palace carpet from one inch above its surface.

"Definitely the best view I've ever had. Any chance I could get a peek of where we're heading?" Daniel pointed to the deck above, hoping for permission.

Beets grunted, but Veronica shrugged congenially. "Don't touch anything. But ask the Boss when you get up there if you can hang out."

"Will do. Thanks, Veronica. You too, Beets." Beets flashed teeth—more a snarl than a smile.

With Sprig riding on his shoulder, Daniel climbed the ladder, squeezed through the hole between decks, and surfaced behind the cockpit hatchway. He leaned his head and shoulders inside.

Zeeno held a yoke in one paw and stared at a panel that displayed a black wedge inside a magenta bubble. Lines to the left and right of the wedge seemed to indicate the boundaries of their trajectory through compressed space. Aussik had his own set of displays. One clearly showed a plan view of the Milky Way. The same yellow line marked their departure route, now poking well above the galaxy's edge.

"Mind if I watch?" Daniel asked.

Zeeno glanced over his shoulder. "No problem. This part of our cruise will be routine while we monitor systems. A good time to talk."

"About?"

"You, mostly."

Aussik called out, "Tau minus nine."

"What happens when you get to twelve?" Daniel asked. If the captain wanted to talk about Daniel's reason for being here, getting a few basic questions answered seemed fair.

Zeeno squeaked with gravelly elements in his voice. "My friend, getting to Tau minus nine is easy. We're currently squashing space a billion times over. Interstellar distances. Any adolescent Torak with a backyard particle accelerator could do it. But getting to a trillion, Tau minus twelve? That's intergalactic stuff. Way harder. Nobody gets that far without a Chitza compression turbine, and damn if we don't have two of them!"

He lifted one clawed finger in the air. "Now try a quadrillion, Tau minus *fifteen*. I dare you. Can't be done."

Daniel lifted his own finger. "Unless you've uncovered a few secrets about additional quantum dimensions?"

"Ha! I see the rumors were flying on Litia!"

Daniel grinned. "Only the best. Can you do it?"

Zeeno grinned with canines showing. "You'll find out soon enough."

Out the forward window, another galaxy came into view, still faint compared to the Milky Way behind them, but enormous. It already filled most of the viewport.

"Andromeda?" Daniel asked.

"Yup."

"Amazing."

"Big piece of real estate. But you have to get away from the glare of our own galaxy to really see it."

"Tau minus ten," Aussik called out. Andromeda grew larger and brighter, showing beautiful strands of red clouds intermixed among its innumerable stars.

"So, about you," Zeeno said.

"About me," Daniel replied. Time to talk. This mission wasn't just a joyride to the neighboring galaxy.

"We could use your help."

"You have it, but I don't know much about compression technology."

"Nah, we've got that covered. But you're good with alien *communication*, shall we say."

Daniel shrugged. "I've met a few species, but we're leaving them all behind."

"Not all. We've already discovered four compression-capable civilizations in Andromeda." He gestured to the giant galaxy filling the viewport like a tour guide who points out the sights. "Three more in Triangulum. A couple in Whirlpool. There's bound to be more too, but none of those places are where we're going."

"Fifty-two billion light-years, or so I heard," Daniel queried. "Is that distance even possible?"

"Not easily," Zeeno answered. "But you're not a passenger on an ordinary Szitzojoot tug. On my ship... aw hell, the numbers don't matter."

"Tau minus eleven," Aussik called out.

Andromeda drifted past the viewport like a mountain adjacent to a highway. They were already two million light-years from home. Dozens more smudges of light lay ahead, some with spiral shapes, some elliptical, some just amorphous blobs. Not a single one of them was a star. All galaxies.

"We're headed to a place we recently discovered. Beyond the horizon."

Daniel had no reason to believe the pilot was exaggerating. They'd already traversed a full *megaparsec* of space, several million light-years. A gigaparsec—even the estimated 14 gigaparsecs to the horizon of the observable universe—might be within reach. As Zeeno had suggested, distances were beginning to lose their meaning. Tau seemed more important now, and the captain had already declared that a compression factor of minus fifteen was a hard limit.

Daniel gazed into a vast emptiness sprinkled with galaxies. There would be many more swirls of stars ahead that his eyes couldn't yet resolve. Even a powerful telescope had its limits. "What's out there?"

"Yes, indeed," Sprig whispered from his shoulder. "What is out there?" The tiny leaf was clearly following the conversation but had intentionally remained in the background.

"Secrets." Zeeno's sly smile matched the wily squint of his eyes. "But Daniel, since you're our guest and my new friend, I'm going to let you in on one."

The captain swiveled his chair to face Daniel. "Four-dimensional space is out there. Heaps of it. And we're not talking about random bubbles scattered about. No sir, where we're headed there's a chunk of 4-D space bigger than a galaxy, and there's nothing natural about it."

8   RINGS

DANIEL'S CURIOSITY PIQUED with Zeeno's description of their destination. Not a black hole. Not a pulsar, supernova remnant, or x-ray source. Not even a bizarre planet populated by blobs of intelligent slime. According to Zeeno, they were heading toward a four-dimensional structure larger than a galaxy.

Daniel had seen one before, the four-dimensional torus surrounding the Star Beacon. Its donut-shaped ring had been designed to allow visitors to walk the circumference of a star in just a few minutes. Useful. Clever. Definitely not natural. But tiny compared to a galaxy.

To reach this newly discovered mega-structure, they would need to venture beyond the cosmic horizon. A place so distant no Milky Way telescope—regardless of size—could resolve. Daniel remarked to their captain about the astonishing distance ahead of them and the horizon they would have to cross.

"Don't get all tangled up about the horizon thing," Zeeno said. "Space is space. Watch this." He turned to his copilot. "How are we doing?"

"Minus eleven, plus a bit," Aussik said.

Zeeno swiveled back to his console. "Before we show our new friend how Chitzas really dance, let's give him a look around."

"You got it, Boss." Aussik flipped a switch and called to the others on the deck below. "Prepare for a full stop."

"Engineering, go," Beets called.

"Safety, go," Veronica called.

"Hold on to your ass," Aussik said. Daniel stood at the cockpit's entryway, but at least there was a sturdy rail bolted onto each side.

Aussik grabbed a large red handle in the center console and jerked it downward. The whine of twin turbines dropped to a whisper then suddenly roared back to life like a landing jet deploying its reverse thrust. The ship lurched violently. Daniel fell halfway into the tiny cockpit, barely holding on. Sprig's stem claws burrowed into Daniel's shirt. The blackness of intergalactic space visible through the forward window flashed bright magenta then back to black.

"Filament deployed," Aussik called out. "Bubble burst is nominal."

Whining turbines spun down. The ship quieted. Daniel righted himself, puzzled.

"Welcome back to 3-D space," Aussik said with the grin of a fox.

"Whoa," Daniel said. "Your stops are a bit more dramatic than I expected."

"Torque," Zeeno answered. "No big deal if you do it right. But hell... screw up a full stop, and you could blow out a whole fan blade assembly. Never have. Never will. Not this crew."

Aussik nodded in resolute agreement.

Daniel gazed out to a view that included one spiral galaxy off to the right and another more disorganized collection of stars to the left. Each galaxy remained rigidly in place. He imagined that an extended length of accordioned space had just relaxed back to its natural span. Relatively speaking, of course. Nobody beyond the confines of this ship would have noticed a thing.

Zeeno pointed to one of his displays. "We're now twenty-four million light-years from home, give or take a few hundred depending on where you call home. From out here, you'd need a good telescope just to spot the Milky Way."

Unadorned emptiness spread across the wide viewport. No stars, no nebulae, just a few minor galaxies that a handful of astronomers back home might identify with names like KDG 64 or Centaurus N. As they'd promised when he boarded, the Chitzas had brought him to truly deep space. It felt lonely.

"And off we go again," Zeeno called. "Take us back up to minus twelve, Aussik. Steep climb this time."

"You got it, Boss."

"Steep climb!" came an enthusiastic yell from below.

Aussik returned his big red handle to its original position and flipped more switches. Turbines spun up to a roar, a sharp pop echoed through the cabin followed by a strong twisting acceleration. Without the rail, Daniel would have been tossed to the rear bulkhead.

The floor vibrated. The ship rattled. Its copilot began callouts of Tau as he'd done before. This time, the callouts came faster. Steep climb was just what it sounded like. When they reached Tau minus ten, their motion against the backdrop of galaxies became apparent once more.

Zeeno explained, "Everything you've seen so far is standard practice. Segmented compression, 3-D waypoints, and a 4-D filament for communications back to base. Good enough for exploring nearby galaxies. But it gets better." Zeeno grinned and called out to the crew. "Get your boots on team, it's time to dance!"

Daniel felt like he should return to his seat. The cockpit held most of the action, but something told him they were about to kick it to a different level. No one said anything, though. "Am I good here?"

Zeeno turned around. "Sure. Maybe." He turned to Aussik. "Have you ever been standing up for five?"

"You kidding? Naw," Aussik replied with a wave of his paw, then called out. "Beets!"

There were a few clanks from below, followed by grumbles.

"Beets?" Aussik called out again.

"Yeah, yeah," came the response. "We're go for five but watch the turbine inlet temperature on number one. It's going bonkers on me."

Aussik seemed to have no objections to *bonkers*. "Veronica?"

"Safety is go for fivvve!" Veronica answered, lingering on the 'v'. Enthusiastic safety officers were apparently rubber stamps for Chitza scout ship maneuvers. Engineers, even grumpy ones, provided the plain stats.

Aussik reached once more to his big red handle, pushing it forward. "Initializing for five."

The ship lurched with a feeling of weightlessness that twisted toward one side like skiing off a cliff while spiraling sideways. Everything went black. For a moment, Daniel thought he'd just been ejected from the ship. When reality returned, his head was spinning. He braced in the cockpit entryway until his inner ear stabilized.

"Yow!" came a cry from below.

"Tau minus thirteen," Aussik said with the same steady voice he used for every other announcement.

A whole galaxy flew past the viewport faster than a freeway sign.

"Tau minus fourteen."

The forward view narrowed to a pipe filled with oncoming galaxies. Each splash of stars and gas emerged from a central pinprick, spread out along the inside perimeter, and flashed by either side, above, or below.

"Tau minus fifteen... and locked," Aussik said.

"Chitzas soar!" The crew shouted in unison. This species had plenty of enthusiasm for their accomplishments and rightly so. They'd just achieved what Zeeno had declared to be the upper limit of spatial compression.

"What do you think?" Zeeno shouted. Vibrations rattled through the ship, forcing everyone to speak up.

Daniel had to admit the thrill seeker in him was pumped. "Feels like a military jet about two feet off the water. Five-dimensional space! You should be proud."

Zeeno grinned. "Chitzas never falter, even when we do!"

Daniel would save the parsing of that fearless mantra for another time. A wispy touch from Sprig on his shoulder gently reminded him that Zeeno's brash statement might be part bravado and part confession.

Galaxies flew past, each pinwheel representing a vast collection of gas, dust, stars, and planets. Each bore billions of suns anchoring billions more planets, many providing yet another niche for atoms to bind together into the complex molecules of life. Yet at this grand scale, each galaxy was simply another tree at the side of the highway, zipping by too fast to distinguish one type from another. Millions more lay ahead in an expanse that could only be comprehended when its dimensions were traversed at such speed.

Chitzas might be reckless in their approach, but they had shown a talent for technology and a zest for discovery. Having already identified intelligent life in multiple galaxies, they had positioned themselves to explore the entirety of the universe.

Truly remarkable.

As galaxies flashed by, he was left with one overriding thought: life exists on an unimaginable scale. Many of the billion-planets-per-second that rocketed past the window would be inhospitable to anything more than bacteria or protozoa. But richer environments would certainly allow for complex organisms and specialized biological systems. A select few would evolve intelligent life capable of understanding nature itself.

Only twenty-four advanced lifeforms had been discovered so far in the Milky Way but if that number held for every galaxy, it assured billions of intelligences in a universe this big.

"Wow," Daniel said to no one in particular. "If there's a purpose to all of this space, it's got to be life."

He continued watching the never-ending torrent of galaxies until another thought occurred, something Sprig might be able to answer. "Have we reached the horizon yet? You know, from the perspective of back home?"

The intelligent leaf had been curled up against Daniel's shirt collar, but now it stood up straight. "The cosmic horizon lies fourteen gigaparsecs in every direction, a distance so vast that the view is not appreciably different regardless of where you are located in the Milky Way galaxy, or in Andromeda for that matter. I calculate that we have currently traveled eight percent of this distance."

Daniel had pretty much run out of wows. More galaxies than he could count had rushed by, yet their journey to the cosmic horizon had only begun. Much more lay ahead. And if that fact weren't enough to blow any Human's tiny mind, cosmologists could only guess how far the universe might extend beyond the horizon.

This could be a very long trip.

"Cup of coffee and an agberry pie?" Zeeno offered. "We'll be on this 5-D heading for a while."

Daniel had almost forgotten the pleasant aroma of baking he'd noticed when coming onboard. If the Chitzas had a kitchen somewhere on this tiny ship, that alone was worth investigating. He thanked his hosts and a few minutes later Veronica appeared at the cockpit entrance with four aluminum containers, each about the size and shape of one of those seven-ounce mini soft drink cans back on Earth. She passed them out to Daniel and the pilots, keeping one for herself.

The can felt warm but provided no clues how to extract its contents. Veronica came to the rescue. "You open it like this." She twisted the bottom third of her can, which split away from the top and rotated out on a vertical hinge. Inside the bottom cup was a crusty pastry about two inches in diameter. A meal for a Chitza, a bite-sized snack for a Human. It smelled delicious.

Veronica nibbled on her own pastry, then sipped at the can's top edge where a wisp of steam came out. Daniel tried his own, pleasantly surprised by the taste of coffee. The liquid must have passed through unseen micro holes along the can's top edge with the aluminum tempering its residual heat to perfection. The food-drink combo was as compact as any space food Humans had ever come up with, including a container that required nothing more than a small heating element embedded into one of the lower deck bulkheads.

Veronica folded down a hinged panel from the wall to form a jump seat. She sat, patting the remaining space for Daniel to join her. He was easily three times her size, but they made it work.

Daniel took another sip. "Veronica, I'm impressed. I knew Chitzas sent wedges on scouting expeditions. But this..." He waved a hand toward the complex cockpit then hoisted his equally satisfactory snack. "Reality is always more complicated, isn't it?"

"Chitzas don't worry about reality," she said. "We make our own."

"Damn straight," Zeeno agreed. He munched down his own pie. Apparently, ship systems were on automatic, though Aussik still kept one eye on the control panel.

Sprig scooted close to Daniel's ear. "For a complete perspective on Chitza reality, you might want to ask their safety officer about the Arcturus Prime Interdimensional Transition Catastrophe."

Daniel thought, then responded. "Thanks, Sprig. For now, I'm good. But I'll keep your advice in mind."

"Your leaf friend is right, you know," Veronica said without the slightest hint that she'd been offended, while proving Chitzas had exceptional hearing. "What we do involves a level of danger Humans might find hard to accept."

Daniel laughed. "Tolerance for danger depends on the Human. You haven't met my wife."

Veronica paused, then replied cheerily, "I'd like to."

Daniel eyed his furry companion. They still had gigaparsecs ahead with danger levels that might be off the charts, but if anyone could pull it off these four explorers could. "Let's make it happen, shall we?"

Veronica pointed at him. "That could be a good ChitzaCheer. Hey guys… Let's make it happen! Shall we?"

Zeeno shook his head. "Nah."

Aussik downed the last slug of his coffee, "Doesn't quite click."

A grunt sounded from Beets down on the lower deck.

Veronica shrugged. "Yeah, maybe not."

Daniel didn't mind that this tightknit crew didn't include him. It was enough that they all shared the same goal. He finished his miniature pie, then turned his attention back to Zeeno. "Before our little stop-and-go maneuver, you mentioned our destination. Unnatural 4-D space, you said."

"I did," Zeeno said. He pushed some buttons, and his main display zoomed out to a map where scattered white dots seemed to match the galaxies blowing past. A blue line with tick marks ran vertically across the display. A second yellow line wasn't quite as straight, gently meandering from the bottom to the top.

Zeeno pointed to a triangle at the bottom of the yellow line. "We're here. Yellow is our course. Anything magenta colored is extra-dimensional space detected by our sensors."

Daniel studied the chart. The tiniest of magenta dots occupied the center of the triangle noting their current position and clearly showing the 5-D bubble that surrounded them. The only other place with the same color was near the top, a magenta smudge at the end of the yellow line.

"That's where we're heading," Zeeno said, tapping the screen. "Chitza Command says I'm not supposed to show anyone who doesn't have a security clearance, but I'm making an exception in your case."

"This is where the previous mission got hit by ultra-gamma radiation?"

"Not yet. But it's related." Zeeno zoomed in on the magenta smudge. As he did, white dots grew into tiny spirals. The smudge grew too.

Daniel leaned through the cockpit entryway for a better view. As the view enlarged, features sharpened. The smudge resolved to a spiral galaxy much like the Milky Way but with banded magenta rings surrounding it. It could easily be a photo of an ordinary galaxy overlaid by a recolored version of Saturn's rings.

"The ring is real?" Daniel asked and received a head nod as confirmation. "Sprig, you're our cosmology expert. How does a galaxy get a ring around it?"

"It doesn't," Sprig answered. "If accurate, this image represents a phenomenon not observed in nature. In fact, I can think of no natural force that could produce a uniform ring on a galactic scale."

Zeeno said, "This is a real-time view. We've covered enough ground now that our long-range sensors are picking up blips that are normally beyond the horizon. The galaxy you're looking at lies in ordinary space, but the ring doesn't."

"And you think somebody built it? Like they built the Star Beacon torus?"

"Exactly, but this thing's a million times bigger. Two-hundred thousand light-years in diameter, and it's a perfect circle to a tolerance better than we can measure. Who builds something like that?"

"Chitzas don't know?"

"So far, we know two things. One, there's an inhabited planet orbiting a star at the ring's precise center. And I mean precise down to a whisker quill."

"Wow," Daniel said. "I wonder which came first, the planet or the ring? Either way, it's a significant relationship. What's the second thing?"

"The planet at the ring's center was the last recorded stop for the previous mission. They stayed for a couple of days, then headed out on a new vector."

"Wow again," Daniel said. He understood exactly why the Chitzas were retracing the previous mission's route, stops included. "They learned something there, didn't they?"

Zeeno nodded. "A scout ship pilot doesn't change his compression vector without a reason. Before we go searching for them, we need to find out why."

"So, we pay a visit?"

"That's where you come in. I'm going to level with you, Daniel." For the first time since they'd left Litia, Zeeno looked nervous. He set his coffee down and leaned forward. "You and I? We're not the second mission to this place, we're actually the third. Mission Two got hit by a gamma blast and is now lost somewhere in deep space, but at least they survived their stopover at this planet. I can't say that for Mission One. They reported in orbit and were never heard from again."

Two potential disasters? The level of danger had just taken a big leap. Worse, mission number three would be following the first two directly into the storm's epicenter.

"This place is no ordinary pitstop, and the natives who live there aren't exactly friendly, at least not to Chitzas. But we think Humans do better. It's why Mission Two offered a seat to your wife. And we think it's why they survived their stop here." Zeeno's eyes connected to Daniel's. "The people down there look like you."

Daniel froze, not sure he understood. "Humans?"

"Humanoid. Not an exact match, but close."

On one level, Zeeno's disclosure wasn't alarming since people were conditioned by countless science fiction movies to believe that aliens were simply Humans with pointy ears and blue blood. But on a scientific level, a humanoid shape with humanlike facial features would be exceedingly rare. On Earth, the closest equivalents were apes, and they only mimicked the Human form because they were DNA relatives. To discover a humanlike species produced through an entirely different evolution would be astonishing.

But it neatly explained Nala's participation. The Chitzas had already visited this place. They'd met the people who lived there and had decided that bringing a Human ambassador along might be just the ticket to avoid whatever disaster befell their first mission.

For that matter, it was entirely possible that Nala might still be on the planet at the center of the ring. The captain of Mission Two had learned something during their stop, then headed back into deep space. But if Nala had already fulfilled her role, she might have been left behind. In an odd way, it could be good news.

She's waiting for me there. It was a nice thought even if he had little reason to believe its truth.

9 PLANET

DANIEL BEGAN TO PIECE TOGETHER his role in this search and rescue mission. The Chitzas hadn't just permitted him onboard, they had *invited* him. And now he knew why: Zeeno said he would need Daniel's alien diplomatic skills. Apparently, the natives at their destination weren't especially friendly, but they looked like Humans.

Sprig had other ideas. "When Chitzas tell all, they don't. Candid is not in their nature."

Daniel absorbed the advice from a partner who hadn't led him astray yet but who definitely carried baggage from past contact with Chitzas. Maybe everyone on Litia did. Daniel found it hard not to like the adventurous rogues, but a fairer representation had to include their caginess.

If Zeeno was still hiding information, Daniel had little choice but to see how events would unfold. They were billions of light-years from home with Daniel entirely dependent on Chitza goodwill to turn a one-way journey into a round trip.

He sat in his lower deck seat, staring out the side window. Vast stretches of empty space transitioned into equally vast stretches where uncountable galaxies flitted past like cottonwood puffs on the wind. The past hour had viscerally demonstrated that the universe was ridiculously, impossibly, colossally large. He'd given up trying to comprehend it all. A single brain could not absorb it.

There had been more snacks, a bathroom break—with facilities that were bearable, if not comfortable—and even one semi-sociable chat with Beets, the ship's forever-irritated mechanic and engineer, whose interest in Humans seemed limited to hair dyes and facial piercings.

Sprig officially announced when they passed the cosmic horizon and, just as Professor Alosoni-eff had suggested, space at fourteen gigaparsecs from home didn't look any different than space just outside the Milky Way. Light emitted from this region 13.8 billion years ago had simply not had enough time in the history of the universe to travel the growing distance to telescopes back home.

An hour later—and a thousand more galaxies flitting past the window—Daniel nearly jumped out of his seat when Aussik screamed from above. "That's it!"

He hurried up the ladder to the cockpit. Near the center of the five-dimensional pipeline of upcoming space, a peculiar shape loomed from the darkness—a galaxy, but with a fuzzy halo surrounding it. Aussik pulled back on his red lever, noticeably decreasing the whine of the turbines along with the shudder that had been ever present throughout the ship.

"Let's drop down to 4-D and see what it really looks like," Zeeno said.

Aussik flipped several switches and pulled his red handle once more. Turbine pitch dropped further. The view outside magnified and sharpened, as if an optometrist had just flipped over another trial lens and asked, "which is better, one or two?"

What had been a hazy halo now resolved to an enormous flat ring extending well beyond the outermost arms of the spiral galaxy within its bounds. The ring had the same appearance of Saturn but without the gaps and on a scale that dwarfed any planet. It felt out of place among the collection of galaxies they'd been passing for hours. As incongruous as a ballerina wearing a truck tire.

"Whoa!" Veronica called out from the deck below. "I guess we've arrived."

"Big sucker," Zeeno said.

"Never seen anything like it," Aussik agreed.

"It certainly gets your attention," Daniel said. "I wonder if that's the point?"

"Like a signpost?" Zeeno asked.

"Sure. 'Come here', it says. You pass a million galaxies that all start looking the same. But not this one. It stands out."

"Compute a vector to its center," Zeeno commanded.

"Got it, Boss," Aussik answered.

They sank deeper into the unusual shape. A cloud of glowing dust embedded with newborn stars filled the viewport but quickly blew past as they blasted out its backside. The surrounding ring flattened further and grew in size. Only its far side now fell within the edges of their viewport.

"Slowing," Aussik said. "Target ahead."

A glowing galactic arm resolved into thousands of individual stars interspersed by red and green nebulae and darker dust. Individual stars now streaked past as the ship zeroed in on one unmoving point in the center of the viewport.

"Target is a yellow dwarf," Sprig announced.

"Same as Earth's star," Daniel said.

"Slowing," Aussik said. "Prepare for full stop."

Having already experienced one full stop and not ready to recommend it to inexperienced interdimensional travelers, Daniel decided to return to his seat on the lower deck. Besides, the lower deck had a view straight down, handy if they were going to land on this planet.

Daniel barely had time to buckle up before Aussik announced, "Three, two, one..."

Twin turbines quieted then roared into their reverse thrust mode. The ship lurched and Daniel grabbed a nearby handle which kept him in his seat but opened a bulkhead cabinet spilling a case of mini-can provisions across the floor in a loud clatter. Bright magenta flashed outside the window then disappeared. Beneath the ship, a planet appeared, blue and white.

"Filament deployed," Aussik called out. "Bubble burst is nominal. All stop."

A slight dizziness lingered, the only evidence of a dramatic restructuring of space. Daniel peered down through the floor window to a brightly lit planet of blue oceans, green-brown land, and white clouds. They were now something like sixteen gigaparsecs from home, but in orbit around a planet that could easily be mistaken for Earth.

Sprig, helpful as always, rattled off numbers somehow collected by its surprisingly perceptive epidermis, easily converted to Human measures by whatever computer might be lodged inside its thin body. "Gravity is 9.8 meters per second squared. Global average atmospheric pressure, 1027 millibars. Nitrogen, 71 percent, oxygen 26 percent, water vapor varies from trace to three percent."

"It practically *is* Earth," Daniel said. He glanced up to Veronica who was gathering the drink cans he'd inadvertently spilled. "If I didn't know I was so far away, I'd argue that's home."

"I'm glad you're going down instead of me!" Veronica quipped.

Daniel helped her gather the remaining cans and return them to the cupboard. "What, we're not landing?"

"Nooo. Boss's orders, and a good thing too. This place is too dangerous for my taste, but you'll do fine. Maybe your wife is down there somewhere?"

If plucky Chitzas were too nervous to step onto this planet, it didn't bode well for Daniel's diplomatic task. But it didn't change his resolve. "I had the same thought. She might be down there. So, if the ship stays in orbit, how do I get to the surface?"

Veronica laughed like a dog wheezes when it gets a bit of chew toy caught in its throat. "You thought we came this far with no way to get you down there? Ha!" She pulled a kit bag from one of the storage bins and withdrew a large syringe filled with purple liquid. "Don't worry, you won't even feel it."

Beets swiveled to watch, most likely fascinated to find out if their Human volunteer would survive the ordeal Veronica had in mind. Daniel became less enthusiastic by the minute.

He held up a hand. "Before I'm needlessly skewered, it's only fair that I know what I'm getting myself into. Who are the people down there? What did they do to your first mission? Sorry, I'm going to need some answers."

"No problem." Veronica put away the syringe, then yelled. "Boss?"

Zeeno dropped down the ladder full of energy now that the piloting part of their mission had completed. "Ready to go?"

All eyes were on Daniel.

He pinched his index finger and thumb together. "Not quite. I need a full briefing. I don't even know what you need."

Zeeno shrugged. "It's simple. Hop in the drop tank, pop down there, meet the locals, and find out what they know. When you're ready, we'll pull you back up."

It wasn't exactly a full briefing. Oversimplifying fit Zeeno's style, but at least he wasn't being tight lipped.

"And the injection Veronica has in mind?" With Nala's life and so much else on the line, Daniel could deal with alien first contact and whatever dangers might come with it. But he'd never been comfortable with needles. Veronica showed the syringe to Zeeno.

"Aw, that's just for your comfort," Zeeno said. "Keeps you calm while you're in the drop tank."

Daniel waved him off. "Let's dispense with the doggy downer. Tell me about the tank."

Zeeno waved a paw through the air. "No big deal. Chitzas do it all the time."

"You're a little smaller than me. No offense."

"And you're bigger, no offense. Don't worry, you'll fit, we took the seats out." Zeeno slumped to the floor with his back against the wall. He sighed in a big way. "Look... this part of the plan works better if Chitzas are not involved. Trust me, you're the right guy for the job. Hell, your wife did it, right?"

Daniel imagined Nala climbing into a *drop tank* for a fiery reentry down to an alien planet. Actually, it wasn't hard. Just last year, she had jumped into a mile long vertical tube high above the Jheean citadel on the planet Bektash... without a parachute.

"We have the landing coordinates. We even have a contact name: Osperus. Just ask around, I'm sure you'll figure it out."

"But make sure you bring back the map," Veronica added helpfully.

"The... map?"

If he'd been text messaging, he would have added a dozen question marks at the end. His guides had had fifty billion light-years to explain themselves. He wasn't going another fifty feet until they told him everything.

Daniel crossed his arms, leaned against the bulkhead, and glared with growing irritation over what had become routine Chitza concealment. "Spill it, Zeeno. All of it."

Zeeno held up both paws. "Okay, okay. It's nothing we haven't already mentioned. The last mission learned something when they stopped here. And yeah... we kind of know what it was. Not exactly, mind you! We don't have a copy because the dataset was too large to send across our 4-D filament. But it was a map of some kind. We think! We don't know."

"And this map will lead us somewhere?"

"Uh... yeah. To a boundary of some kind. Might be a wall or a cliff. But whatever it is, the last mission went there so we need to go there too."

"Where we'll encounter a gamma radiation blast?"

"Hey, it's a rescue mission. Danger is part of the deal."

Daniel paused in thought. Zeeno was right about their mission. It almost didn't matter where the previous ship had ended up, their goal wouldn't change.

While Daniel thought, Zeeno continued. "Look, that 4-D ring isn't natural. There's something special about a planet that's in the exact center. We could be on to something big. You want to know too, don't you?"

The captain looked as hopeful as a car salesman who really didn't care which model and options the customer picked as long as he drove something off the lot today. Appealing to Daniel's curiosity in addition to his rather obvious desire to get his wife back was exactly the pitch Daniel couldn't—and wouldn't—refuse.

"Okay. I'll go."

Zeeno hopped up. "Good plan."

"But Zeeno—no more secrets. Give it to me straight so I know what I'm dealing with. We'll make a better team."

"And spoil all the fun?" Zeeno held up his paws. "Yeah, yeah, all right. We'll make you an honorary member of the crew!

Surface Reconnaissance Commando, there you go. We'll give you a uniform with bars on your shoulders when you get back. Just uh... make sure you bring back that map."

Daniel had to chuckle. Chitzas had their quirks, but in the end, they were earnest players with enough enthusiasm to complete almost any task. This mission seemed crazy at times, but in an odd way Zeeno and his crew had shown every reason to believe they'd be successful. Now it was time for Daniel to contribute.

"If the map is down there, I'll get it. I understand why we need it."

"To find the previous crew."

"Exactly, but there's one thing I don't understand... why did *they* want it?"

"Great question." Zeeno waved Daniel down to his level. Daniel squatted. "Okay Commando... since we're now sharing every little thing, I'm going to let you in on a bit of Chitza lore."

Veronica gathered closer. Sprig perked up on Daniel's shoulder. Even Beets swiveled in her seat, looking on with interest while their captain continued with his latest reveal.

Zeeno's voice lowered to a whisper. "Chitzas are not just thrill seekers. I know... shocking. You see us as Danger Game medalists or maybe those guys who strap rockets on their back... you know the type. But we're not those guys. It's not even pride that drives us, though that's part of it. Litian-nolos don't have it. I don't think Humans have it either. We call it *akona*."

Veronica and Beets both nodded their heads.

"It's close to your word, *zest*, but more personal. It comes from a place that's hard to describe and can't be ignored. We do it because we have to. For a Chitza to disregard their akona? Unthinkable."

Daniel made eye to eye contact with Zeeno, then Veronica and Beets. These were passionate explorers, humble in their place among the stars, but full of pride in their ability to tease out whatever secrets the universe held. He admired them. And now they were asking for his help. He wouldn't refuse.

For whatever reason, the people on the planet below reacted better to Human visitors. Sort of an alien form of white privilege. Daniel's qualifications had nothing to do with science, his attention to detail, or even his ability to see the big picture when others couldn't. Daniel was Human. And that, apparently, was good enough.

10   ALONE

ANOTHER PULSE SHAKES THE PLACE where Nala floats, sending a shock wave through its air with an audible thump that sounds and feels like a powerful ocean swell pounding a rock cliff somewhere below her feet. It is the fourth such pulse since abandoning the ship and separation from everyone else.

Below. It has no meaning. She is suspended without gravity. There is no up or down. She's been here for at least twenty-four hours, an elapsed time measured only by the thirst building in her throat and the grumbles in her stomach. The brilliant light is gone now. White has dimmed to grey. The temperature has dropped too.

Scattered debris floats all around and provides a sense of distance. This cloud, this bubble, this *whatever-it-is* measures a hundred meters in width, maybe more. She spies what look like provisions floating among the debris. The collection of cans and packages aren't far away, but she can't figure out how to move herself in that direction. There's nothing to hold onto, nothing to push off of. She tries blowing air as a method of propulsion but that only makes her dizzy.

She does a few zero-g somersaults, stretches, and knee bends in an attempt to stay warm. So far, the air is holding out—one positive thing about her imprisonment.

"Onner!" she yells again. She's sure she heard Onner's voice when they bailed out, but not since. The others seemed to have drifted away. If this is 4-D space, perhaps the lingering energy from the gamma blast has split it into multiple pieces, carrying her friends away as new bubbles pinch off. It's a distinct possibility, but she can't be sure.

As expected, there's no response to her shout. But movement catches her eye. She twists around just in time to snatch a flat disc drifting by. It's the data disc that Aussik pulled before they abandoned ship. He slipped the disc under his body strap, but it must have come out in all the chaos. Does it mean Aussik is dead?

"Please don't be dead," she tells herself. She yells once more, "Aussik!" Her voice disappears without an echo.

Minutes pass. "Do something," she tells herself, then has an idea. She takes off one shoe and twists until the floating provisions are directly behind her. She winds up and throws the shoe, which disappears into the grey cloud. She twists around but can't tell if her position relative to the food has changed.

Not satisfied, she removes the other shoe and tries again. There's still not much progress toward the goal.

"F equals M-A," she says, reciting Newton's equation of motion. "Equal and opposite force, so my acceleration is proportional to the shoe's acceleration, but... the woman-to-shoe mass ratio is like a hundred to one."

She twists backward to look again. If she's moving toward the drink cans and food packets, it's hard to tell. She could continue throwing more clothes but the chill in the air makes naked unappealing. She'll give whatever slight drift she's initiated more time to reveal itself.

Has the ship been destroyed? If it has, a lonely death awaits. But Zeeno is resourceful. Once the abandon ship business started, she never saw their captain. He must have stayed at the controls looking for ways to return to higher dimensional space. If he made it, and with the gamma blast calming, it might only be a few more hours before he collects the crew. They won't forget her.

Stay alive. Wait it out. Nobody beats a Chitza... or a determined Human.

11 FREEFALL

VIBRATIONS SHOOK DANIEL to his teeth. Stronger jolts slammed his body against the barrel of a cigar-shaped tube the Chitzas called a *drop tank*. Outside, orange flames speckled with white-hot embers streaked past one of three tiny windows as Daniel plummeted through a thick atmosphere on his way to a soft landing on the planet below—or a very deep hole in the ground.

Tall enough to stand upright, the tank's diameter slightly wider than Human shoulders ensured its hapless occupant would be tossed around like the clapper inside a bell. Not by design, though. The landing craft was intended for three Chitzas strapped into reclining seats enjoying a view of their descent through conveniently placed windows. Zeeno had simply ripped the seats out to make room for a Human. The idea had seemed better from orbit.

Did you suffer through this too, Nala? She'd probably been laughing the whole way down.

The raging fire outside thinned to a stream of sparks. Jolts reduced to a rumble down a washboard road. A panel above his head provided a readout of his descent, but with symbols written in the native Chitza language. He had nothing to do but wait for the promised safe landing.

At first, Sprig had balked when Zeeno suggested the leaf might not be "sturdy enough to survive the plunge" but in the end, Daniel's ally decided to join him rather than remain behind with Chitzas, who would have nothing better to do than make up games like "Hide the Leaf". Sprig's words. Daniel had no idea where that fear came from.

"Besides," Sprig had told him, "previous Chitza missions to this planet recorded a language primer sufficient for simple conversations. You will need me as translator."

Sprig had been studying up on this remote alien planet, and Daniel welcomed its help. So far, the leaf had shown no signs of distress. Maybe the worst of their plunge was over.

A rapid beep preceded the distinct sound of a jar lid unscrewing somewhere above. Seconds later, blades unfolded outside the window and quickly spun up to helicopter speeds. Daniel's feet pushed into the floor. Clouds flew past the window. The craft's descent steepened and slowed further. Reentry had been pre-programmed to land near a village spied from orbit by Chitza sensors. Once down, the rest would be up to him.

With blades now thumping against thick air, the drop tank eased into its final descent. Tree branches appeared through the window and the craft settled to a gentle landing.

Daniel took a deep breath. "Show time."

He pressed the hatch release button—not the recall button, which would signal the craft to launch back to orbit—unless he had mixed up the unreadable labels. Thankfully, a hip-high door opened with a slight hiss. He squatted to peer out. The drop tank had landed in a small clearing in a forest. Leaves rustled in a light breeze that brought fresh air through the hatch.

With Sprig on his shoulder, he stepped out to hard ground covered by ankle-deep grass. Green trees surrounding the landing site could easily belong to any of the deciduous species common to eastern United States, Canada, or England.

Sherwood Forest near Nottingham came to mind. He and Nala had role played Robin Hood and Maid Marian there while on one of their more entertaining trips to Europe. As it turned out, the fair Maid Marian had shown a predilection for casually discarding every stitch of her clothing once they were sufficiently far from civilization. Nala had always known exactly how to grab his attention.

Is she here? He had no answer one way or another. Gutfeel was never his strong suit. Unless another future memory popped up, he had no connection to Nala in this timeline or any other. No Star Trek communicator, not even a working mobile phone. He'd need to go old school: inquire about her, assuming he could find someone to ask.

Daniel slung a ChitzaPack over one shoulder. "Water and food for three days," Veronica had told him when she'd handed the child-sized backpack to him. "You'll love it."

The only other item in the pack was something Veronica called a ChitzaShell, personal armor that instantly expanded like a car airbag. She had shown him how it worked. Like all things Chitza, the body shield turned out to be only big enough to cover Daniel's chest, but it deployed with a single touch, kept his hands free by way of ties to the ChitzaPack, and might protect him from bullets, laser blasts, and other mayhem as good as a police vest. With luck and diplomacy, it wouldn't be needed.

He surveyed the alien yet familiar surroundings, listening. Chirps matched small, brown critters that dashed between trees, disappearing as quickly as they appeared. The occasional deeper squawk hinted of a larger species. Birds, bats, or another kind of glider, he couldn't be sure, but a tree ecosystem with potential ground predators would virtually guarantee animals capable of flight.

"I don't suppose you can detect magnetic force lines?" Daniel asked Sprig. Based on Veronica's reconnaissance from space, due east would be the right direction to the village, but now that he was down on the ground, directions weren't obvious. With all the hustle before he'd climbed into the drop tank, he'd forgotten to learn the basics of planetary geography, like planetary rotation and sun angles.

"Easy," Sprig said from his shoulder, then pointed the tip of its leaf. "East."

Nice to have a competent associate.

Daniel memorized the landing site, then set off in the pointed direction. The village would be large enough that he wasn't likely to miss it even if their heading was off by a few degrees. The path was easy enough with undergrowth limited to grass and scattered shrubs.

A hundred meters in, movement in a nearby tree caught his attention. A furry animal the size of a cat with stripes down its back clung to the tree bark then skittered nervously to the far side of the trunk as he approached.

He walked on, looking up with interest as several more of the clawed tree dwellers leaped between branches. He became so absorbed in the familiar-yet-different wildlife, he nearly missed a dirt road that crossed his path. The road wasn't wide, but it curved eastward.

"Roads tend to end up at villages," Daniel noted.

Now on a well-defined path, Sherwood Forest felt more familiar by the minute, though he reminded himself that home was many billions of light-years away. Moreover, there could be nothing ordinary about a planet occupying the exact center of a galaxy-sized four-dimensional ring. Profound meaning hid here, and Daniel intended to uncover it.

As he walked, he sorted through what he would say upon arrival in the village. Unless someone had seen the drop tank, the locals weren't expecting him. But if reports were accurate, they had already encountered both Humans and Chitzas. They shouldn't be shocked to see another visitor. For this mission, "Take me to your leader," seemed the operative phrase.

A repetitive creaking sound came from behind. Daniel turned around. A wooden wagon pulled by a large four-legged animal appeared from around a bend. Two humanoid figures sat atop an old-fashioned buckboard. Behind the drivers, metal mesh cubes were stacked three high. Several of the cages were occupied by the same striped animal Daniel had noticed clinging to the tree.

Daniel stood his ground as the wagon approached.

Dressed in ragged clothes, the drivers looked Human enough. Two arms, two legs, torso, and head. Their facial features blended Human and... anime? Locks of dark hair hung over large, widely spaced eyes. Horn-shaped ears poked out from beneath the hair on either side. Where a nose might have been, a single vertical slit opened and closed rhythmically.

Daniel called out cheerfully, "Good morning!" He tipped his head to new acquaintances, and the wagon pulled to a stop. Sprig remained silent.

The humanoids sat still, staring. One finally spoke in deep guttural sounds with staccato consonants interrupting stretched vowels. Still no translation from Sprig but the leaf might be sampling and matching the sounds to whatever database it had built.

"Sorry, I'm not familiar with your language."

The largest of the two humanoids spoke again, and Sprig finally perked up. "An exclamation of some kind," Sprig said, "Then... road to Borah, forest creature."

"I'm not a forest creature," Daniel answered. He pointed straight up. "I come from the stars." Sprig vibrated, and surprisingly similar guttural sounds projected from its surface.

The humanoids exchanged a glance with each other. They didn't seem frightened by Daniel or the translation, but their attire and transportation seemed medieval at best. For these people, a visitor proclaiming himself from the stars might be regarded as a god—or an enemy to be burned at the stake. Chitzas had warned the locals weren't friendly.

The driver spoke again. Sprig followed in English, apparently getting the hang of the alien language. "Be gone... our bounty is not yours." The second humanoid withdrew a crossbow from behind his seat complete with a metal-tipped arrow already positioned in a grooved channel.

Daniel held up both hands. "Friends, I come in peace. Your bounty belongs to you." Sprig translated, presumably faithfully, though Daniel had no way to verify. Being on the alien side of first contact had its own set of disadvantages, but he felt sure he could deploy the protective ChitzaShell faster than the arrow could transit the distance. No need to panic.

Daniel moved closer, heading toward the animal hitched to their wagon. The humanoid followed with his crossbow.

"Hey there, big guy," Daniel said as he stroked the animal along its neck. It resembled a four-legged ostrich but without the feathers. It snorted at Daniel's touch but didn't bolt.

The humanoid slowly lowered his crossbow.

"See?" Daniel said as Sprig translated. "I'm a friend to animals and people. I only need your help. Can you take me to..." This is where the *leader* part came in, but Daniel also had a name that might work better. "... Osperus?"

The crossbow-wielding humanoid set his weapon down and grinned, showing a fused ridge of teeth. He held out a hand that ended in slender fingers and grunted. "We go," Sprig translated.

Daniel took that as an offer of a ride, grabbed the outstretched hand and climbed aboard.

"Starman meet Afeesh Tm," came another translation of guttural groans.

Daniel found a spot on the flatbed cart just behind the driver. He leaned against the stacked cages where several striped animals squeaked nervously. "Not to Afeesh Tm. Can you take me to Osperus?"

The driver snapped the reins and the featherless ostrich returned to a slow clop down the road. Oversized wooden wheels on either side creaked as the cart moved.

Crossbow-guy grinned again. "You are Starman. We are Afeesh Tm. Understand?"

Daniel nodded. "Got it." These people were called Afeesh Tm. Whether fur trappers could take him to Osperus was another question, but they were heading in the right direction. For the time being, he would be the Starman in search of Osperus. "How far?"

The driver pointed to the wagon wheel and rotated his finger in time with its motion. "Two hundred."

Two hundred wheel rotations. That seemed about right, assuming Sprig had accurately translated the alien number. The trapper had done well too, quickly identifying a unit of measure they could all agree upon. The means of transportation and their weapons might be primitive, but Daniel held hope that his mission to retrieve information and a map might yet be successful. These were people with intelligence, only marginally different than any space-faring species of Sagittarius Novus.

The road wound through more trees, then crossed a wooden bridge over a creek. On the other side, dirt turned to cobblestone pavement with adobe style houses along one side. The wagon continued past several houses, then stopped at the largest, three stories tall with windows on each floor. A tall metal box stood in front of the house with alien writing on it.

"Wait," the driver said to Daniel. His companion hopped down and began unloading the cages while the driver pressed buttons on the front of the metal box. A square door slid up, and they shoved each cage through its opening. Mechanical whirring came from inside, accompanied by animal squeaks and dull thumps. The cages popped out the other side of the chamber—empty.

Daniel had a bad feeling, but interfering in their work wasn't an option. More sounds of gurgling and whirring were followed by what could easily have been a hair dryer at full power. A slot opened and striped fur pelts rolled out from a conveyor. The driver withdrew each pelt and stacked them on his cart, six in all.

It was the most efficient killing machine Daniel had ever witnessed. The gruesome process made him queasy even though there hadn't been a single drop of blood. None outside the box, anyway.

"I hope they didn't suffer," Daniel said with a sigh. "No need to translate, Sprig."

The trapper spoke. "Geetback pelts fetch a hundred each, and the meat makes a great... some kind of food product, I believe," Sprig translated.

There was nothing more unappetizing than learning exactly how food arrived at the table. But Humans were no different when it came to efficient killing machines. Even in the mid twenty-first century, cattle were systematically slaughtered by the thousands every day.

No wonder the Chitzas didn't want to come. The size and shape of the woodland creatures who had been turned into pelts were no different than a Chitza.

Intelligence is the key. Daniel had always thought that the moral treatment of any lifeform should match its intelligence. On Earth where plentiful food could be harvested from plants, there was simply no ethical reason to consume a mammal, whether a cow, pig, dog, or dolphin. Each of these intelligent species deserved security from slaughter, even if the responsibility for managing their numbers still lay with Humans. But drop down to a bird or fish, and a fair argument for harvesting could be made. Drop further to an insect or nematode—if that's what someone really wanted to eat—and they wouldn't get any argument at all, at least not from Daniel.

The two indisputably intelligent Afeesh Tm trappers climbed back into their wagon and started once more down the road.

Rickety village houses grew more numerous as they went. Crossroads featured larger buildings constructed from metal girders. Some showed design features like arches and decorated columns. One in particular had a gracefully curving roofline that couldn't have been constructed without substantial engineering talents. It seemed an odd mix of pre-classical wooden structures with twentieth-century iron and steel. Perhaps these were people who never demolished anything, including wooden-wheeled wagons used by trappers.

The driver pointed his draught animal toward the largest and most elegant of the buildings. With a domed roof, stately columns, and a wrought iron fence around its parklike perimeter, the palatial building certainly looked like a figure of authority might live or work there.

"Here, we part," the driver said. He pointed to a high double door at the end of a curving walkway. "Osperus."

The communication had been better than expected, along with the helpfulness of the locals. Maybe the Chitzas were wrong about the dangers, but then Daniel bore no resemblance to a woodland creature. "Thank you for the ride."

He hopped down and approached the door with the poise of a visiting dignitary and Sprig as his entourage. The heavy door swung on hinges. He closed it behind him. A dim interior reached overhead to cathedral heights. Ornate carvings of leaves, trees, and other plants decorated stone walls. High overhead, a ring of windows on the inside of the dome brought sunlight into the grand room.

He wandered around, feeling like a tourist in a European cathedral. Beneath the center of the dome, shuffling sounds echoed. Dark figures passed behind columns. Daniel pivoted toward the metal scrape of a bolt being drawn across the door behind him.

"Hello?"

Four humanoid figures stepped out from the shadows. Slender in build, each wore a black one-piece jumpsuit with pant legs that tucked into high boots. A mask covered the lower portion of their faces. They carried weapons, and by the looks of a red beam flickering down the length of each barrel, these were significantly more advanced than a trapper's crossbow.

The guards shouldered their rifles, pointing at Daniel.

"Be careful," Sprig suggested not unhelpfully.

Daniel raised both hands. "I'm here to see Osperus." Sprig translated.

One soldier grunted, waving its weapon to the left.

"I think it wants you to go through that doorway," Sprig said.

"Happy to oblige," Daniel said as cheerfully as he could manage.

They passed through the doorway which led into a stone hall with a ceiling far overhead. The guards followed close behind, their weapons always pointed at him.

Nice welcoming committee, he thought. *Nala did this?*

Further down the hallway a heavy wooden door blocked the path. Light shone through the gap at the bottom. "In here?" Daniel pushed the door open.

The dark hallway opened up to a cavernous room, well-lit with colored stain glass windows down one side that looked outside to a patio decorated with trees and fountains. Heavy wooden benches stood around the room's circumference, with arched wooden supports on the ceiling that looked to be cut from the same trees. At one end stood an enormous desk with a gold table lamp on one side and a high-back chair behind it that looked almost like a throne.

Charmingly medieval, the Robin Hood and Maid Marian theme continued. He almost expected Nala to come waltzing down the spiral stone staircase in one corner wearing the sheer satin dress of the King's ward.

Or perhaps it will be Prince John, the villain of the story?

The guards kept their modern weapons drawn but made no more motions. Daniel stood in the center of the room and waited. Finally, a door near the spiral staircase creaked open, and a figure dressed in robes walked out. He stopped at the side of the desk.

The Afeesh Tm man had the same nose-less face as the trappers. He wore a hood fashioned from elegant cloth, wine-red. A trimmed beard at his chin was wiry and gray. He spoke with the same guttural sound, and Sprig dutifully translated. "You are Human."

"I am," Daniel replied. "I hope I haven't intruded."

The Afeesh Tm man nodded slowly. "Visitors are welcome here... with some restrictions. Our sensors detect a weapon in your possession."

Daniel started to object, then realized how the misunderstanding could have occurred. "I apologize. It's not actually a weapon. It's used only for defense." He slowly slipped the pack off one shoulder and withdrew the highly compressed ChitzaShell, no bigger than a coat button. "You see?"

One of the guards stepped forward and reached out, palm up. Daniel delivered the device. From here, words would be his only defense.

The robed Afeesh Tm elder walked around to the front of the desk, studied Daniel's face, then spoke with the sure voice of someone in charge. "I see it in your eyes, Human. You seek the map."

12   AFEESH TM

WITH A CASUAL FLICK of his wrist, the robed man waved the guards from the stone chamber, leaving Daniel standing alone like a minion summoned before the supreme leader. A mosaic of tiles formed intricate patterns across the stone floor. Roughhewn timbers supported a soaring ceiling at least twenty feet overhead. For all of its medieval castle feel, lighting in the room was surprisingly bright, a glow with no discernable source.

The bearded Afeesh Tm man remained standing beside his desk, examining the nondescript ChitzaShell his guards had confiscated from Daniel. He placed the button in a cabinet, then spoke in a deep, raspy voice. Sprig, who seemed to be getting better at the local language, quickly translated. "I am Osperus."

Daniel introduced himself. Finding Osperus had been as easy as Zeeno had suggested. So far, so good. Grab the map, and he'd be on his way.

Osperus stepped forward. "You follow the Human woman?"

It was an interesting start to their conversation. "She is my wife. She's missing."

"I am sorry to hear," Osperus said. "Her negotiations for the map were as unique as her beauty. I wished her well, as I do for all who stop by our planet."

"So, she's gone now?"

"She left, yes. We are not space travelers, but we know when visitors arrive… and when they depart."

The man had a direct style that would be useful since Daniel had little interest in remaining here any longer than needed. But if Nala had left, it meant he'd need his own copy of the map, and

Osperus hinted that a negotiated agreement would be required to get it.

First things first. Daniel would need to understand the game. "Your map is so valuable that you use armed guards to secure it?"

"Not *our* map. Afeesh Tm are custodians of a gift provided to us lifetimes ago—along with rules that we must follow. Rules that include security."

"I see. A map of great importance then… but wouldn't its true value depend on where it leads?" Daniel didn't know a single thing about the mysterious map, but he also didn't want to give the impression of a rube from a backwater galaxy. For a planet at the exact center of a galactic-sized 4-D ring, this place didn't seem particularly advanced. But variations among the population were stark—fur trappers drove primitive wagons through the forest, yet castle guards carried sophisticated weapons. Perhaps those weapons represented payments made from past negotiations?

"The map reveals many secrets, but only to those with the right technology. Do you have such technology?"

There could be only one answer to the old man's rather ambiguous question. Daniel nodded. "I believe we do. Inbound to your galaxy, we noticed a large ring not visible from ordinary space but quite remarkable when viewed from a higher dimension. I suspect that the map is related to the ring. Am I right?"

A sly smile from Osperus confirmed that Daniel's answer had been correct. Could it be that simple? One question and one answer? Mythical gatekeepers were supposed to ask three maddingly vague questions, and Daniel's answer didn't even rhyme.

Instead, this gatekeeper spoke plainly. "Afeesh Tm are simple people. We do not compress space as you and others do. Many visitors come here. All speak of the galactic ring. All depart and never return, including the first visitors who placed the ring in its current position long ago."

As Daniel suspected, the galactic ring and the map were two connected steps in an information quest, just as a highway sign guides tourists to a point of interest. But these people were only the distribution agents, not the source of whatever directions the map provided. The reveal raised still more questions.

"You give this map to visitors?"

"Give? Please understand, the map comes with rules that we must follow and a price that you must pay."

Nothing ominous about this deal with the devil!

Daniel consulted directly with Sprig to be sure any mistranslations wouldn't get in the way. The price for the map might not be his soul, but it wasn't likely to be a pot of gold either. Sprig didn't have any better suggestions, so for now, Daniel decided that straightforward would be his best approach to their negotiation.

"I'm still interested." Daniel pointed to a guest chair near the desk and lifted his brow to the old man who nodded his permission to sit.

The Afeesh Tm elder circled to the other side of the expansive desk and sat on its throne. "Do you understand your destination?"

Daniel answered as truthfully as he could, "I'm a passenger on a Chitza scout ship that is in orbit around your planet. My Chitza friends know more than I do about our destination. As for me, I only want my wife back."

Osperus nodded. "Daniel, the wife seeker. I see. Having met your wife, I can agree. She is quite worthy of your quest, even one that crosses the universe. But since you inquire about the map, my duty compels me to explain its dangers. Do you know of the Chaos Field?"

Daniel glanced to Sprig who had been doing a fantastic job of translating but couldn't offer any information about this particular location. Daniel shook his head. "It's a place on your map?"

Osperus smiled. "Indeed, the Chaos Field is the entire purpose of the map. It is place like no other. Deadly to those who dare to venture into its expanse without guidance. But navigable—once you have the map."

And there it was, the value proposition. Like any good pitchman, Osperus had identified a problem the customer didn't know he had, then offered a solution tailormade.

Daniel treasured his skeptical nature precisely for times like these. "Explain to me please, why my wife, or I—or anyone for that matter—would want to cross this deadly expanse?"

"To reach wonderous destinations that can be found on the other side," Osperus answered. "Or so I'm told by those who return. You see, Afeesh Tm have no direct interest in where the map leads. We don't have the technology to follow its guidance. Our visitors often speak of additional dimensions, compressed space, and bubbles. You may as well be speaking of gods."

"It's not that the science is—"

Osperus held up a hand. "None of your science matters. Afeesh Tm are keepers of a map given to us long ago. That it has great value to others is to our benefit. We simply trade its secrets for our own stability and prosperity."

Osperus paused, looking up to catch Daniel's eye. "You come to me because you wish to find your wife. I am a transactional man. Your interests become my interests too. Even if I knew your science, I could not describe to you where she went. The Chaos Field is complex. But by following the map, you will precisely trace her route. This much I am certain."

It was a bit like talking to a hang glider salesman who had never leaped off a cliff himself, knew nothing about aerodynamics, and had misplaced the manufacturer's training manual—but was ready to sell you one.

Zeeno couldn't proceed without the map, so that left Daniel with only one task: negotiate its price. Free would be a good starting point. After all, Nala had apparently pulled it off and she hadn't brought sacks of silver coins with her. Perhaps her beauty, as Osperus had curiously noted, had been enough.

Doubtful. This guy's a polished salesman, not a philanthropist.

Daniel began as cordially as he could. "Humans and Chitzas would be most grateful to receive such profound guidance." He raised his eyebrows in anticipation.

"And as the Afeesh Tm's representative, I will be happy to provide such guidance. In return, I will need the Chitza ship in orbit around our planet."

Bold. Very direct, and completely out of the question. "I'm afraid we'll need our ship to locate our missing friends. And when that mission is complete, there's the small matter of returning home."

"Not *your* ship, another Chitza ship which has remained in orbit around our planet for some time. Currently unoccupied, we are quite sure. Bring this ship to me, and the map is yours."

Daniel immediately recognized the ask but had to think about the implications. First, Osperus had just confirmed Zeeno's disclosure—that the first Chitza mission to this planet failed spectacularly. Its crewmembers were never heard from again.

But second, Osperus seemed to be contradicting his own words. "You said you're not space travelers. That you have no interest in the map's destinations or the science of extra dimensions. Why do you want a Chitza scout ship?"

Osperus dismissed Daniel's question with the wave of a hand. "The ship is not for me, you understand, but it has trading value. We have no way to retrieve it from orbit. You do. Bring it to me, and I will repurpose a useless derelict to provide modest gains for our people."

It wasn't a bad pitch, but there was still something distasteful about recovering an empty ship whose crew had mysteriously disappeared on the same planet administered by the guy requisitioning the dead crew's belongings.

"What happened to the Chitza crew?" Osperus had been direct. Daniel figured he could do the same.

"Attacked by Kyan Ta, I fear. Mongrels who inhabit our forests and will do anything to disrupt our peaceful society. They want the map for themselves, and it is my duty to prevent such a tragedy. Dealing with a businessman like me is easy. You would not relish a negotiation with the Kyan Ta—each wears a sharp blade at their hip."

There were clear dangers to obtain this map and still more dangers once acquired. The Chitzas had been justified in their concern about this planet. They had already lost one crew here, with another missing in deep space based on what they discovered here. He would need to be careful.

Osperus' suggestion that the map would lead him to Nala might be right, even if it was also a sales pitch. But their negotiations weren't complete. The Chitza ship that Osperus wanted wasn't Daniel's to surrender.

"I'll need to speak to my Chitza friends. It won't take long."

Osperus waved to the door. "Please do. While you are away, I will summon one of our mapmakers in anticipation of an agreement. This task too will not take long."

Daniel started toward the door, then paused. "I'll need the defensive device your guards confiscated." He didn't doubt for a second the story of dangers that Osperus had related.

Osperus called in one of his armed guards, then retrieved the ChitzaShell from the cabinet and placed it back in Daniel's hand. "Townspeople are merchants no different than me. But when in the forest, do not trust anyone you meet. I do not wish for you to end up like your Chitza friends."

****

Coming to the planet's surface without a communications link to the ship had been a mistake. Surely Beets could have rigged something up. Sprig even had an idea for adjusting one of its internal components to allow for radio reception, but any link would have required advanced coordination. At this point, Daniel would need to return to the drop tank and press the auto-return button to speak with Zeeno.

It's only a small delay, he assured himself as he started down the road out of town. *Twenty minutes to the drop tank, tops.* For the return trip, he would ask Veronica to reprogram the drop tank to land somewhere in the town. He could be back within an hour.

Daniel lifted his eyes to a setting sun and a darkening sky. Minutes later, the road led into the forest. Trees thickened. The remaining twilight dimmed quickly. Dark came soon after, though Daniel had memorized the turns in the road and still had a good idea where they had crossed it earlier in the day. Sprig double checked the bearing to the drop tank using its internal compass.

They reached the turnoff without encountering any person or beast. Beyond the dangers of knife-wielding attackers, natural predators would be harder to see as night fell.

"One moment," Sprig said as Daniel stepped off the dirt road to begin the final cross-country portion of their hike. The leaf shivered from tip to stem instantly producing a red glow radiating from its surface. Not exactly high-beam headlights, but the soft light managed to illuminate a twenty-foot circle sufficiently to avoid tripping over downed branches and rocks.

"Does your battery ever wear out?" Daniel asked his hiking partner, then shook his head. "Never mind. You do you. Just let me know if you need anything in the way of resupply."

As he walked, Sprig twisted on Daniel's shoulder to light up overhanging branches. Critters that had flitted from tree to tree were nowhere to be seen.

A rustle of leaves drew Daniel's eyes left. Bushes obscured the immediate area with nothing but darkness beyond. "Did you catch that, Sprig?"

"No, your neck is in the way. But I detect movement ahead. Beware."

Daniel paused and scanned ahead as best he could in the limited light. He picked up a rock. It might be enough to send an animal running. A fur trapper seemed unlikely, given the late hour, but Daniel acknowledged that his understanding of how people lived and worked on this planet was woefully limited.

Kyan Ta *mongrels* were a third possibility. Primitive warriors, as described by Osperus, who sought the map for their own profit. Had they discovered the drop tank? His landing hadn't exactly been a stealth operation.

Daniel took cover behind a bush and asked Sprig to douse its red glow, a liability if there were people ahead. The leaf had proven to be packed with internal devices capable of a broad range of remote sensing. Daniel imagined a built-in motion sensor that could detect a fly at a hundred paces. "Tell me what you see, Sprig."

"No further motion. My infra-red is also negative, though I would fail to detect a body colder than the freezing temperature of water." That probably ruled out the Afeesh Tm and every forest critter.

"Can you make out the drop tank?"

"Yes. In the clearing just ahead."

"Is it still upright?"

"Yes."

"And there's no one nearby?" They could make a dash for it.

"Correct."

"Okay, keep watching. Let's give it a minute just to be sure."

A soft padding sound came from behind. Daniel swiveled around to see a horizontal rope flying toward him. In one fluid motion, he pressed the tab on his backpack strap to deploy the ChitzaShell. The protective shield exploded around his upper torso just as the bolo-like lasso caught him in the throat, spinning weighted ends around his body and binding both arms to his sides. Sprig was thrown to the ground.

A man jumped from the darkness and pointed a long pole tipped by a stone spearhead with edges as sharp as broken glass.

"*Dho!*" the man yelled, hovering the spearhead beneath Daniel's chin.

Two more joined the first, each carrying the same primitive but effective weapon. Daniel lifted his bound hands in surrender. The Chitza's shield might have been useful to defend against lasers, but not a rope or a spear.

The three bearded warriors wore the same tattered skins as the trappers he'd met earlier but their fierce expressions bore no resemblance to merchants of animal pelts. One reached into the detritus covering the forest floor and pulled out Sprig, who quivered from the alien touch. The man held Sprig close to his eyes, turning the leaf over. He sniffed along Sprig's serrated edge.

Daniel struggled to reach out from beneath the rope binding. "Be careful. It's not just a leaf. My partner is a living being."

An Afeesh Tm woman joined the warrior ranks. She carried a crossbow and circled Daniel, never letting her aim drift even a millimeter from the target between his eyes. She reached into a pocket on her stitched skin jacket then smeared a sticky wax across his mouth, silencing him as effectively as a strip of duct tape.

The first spear-holder waved toward the trees, and the rest pushed him stumbling into the dark forest.

Sprig's voice came from somewhere behind, jittery and muffled. "The Kyan Ta tribe, I believe."

13 KYAN TA

ONE MAN LED AND TWO MORE prodded Daniel with the back end of their spears as they made their way through the dark forest. A second woman emerged from the trees to join the group at its right flank. She tapped a loose arrow against her crossbow in a cadence that matched the group's walking pace. No one spoke.

Daniel glanced behind and grunted through the layer of goo they'd spread across his mouth, "Sprig?", which turned out more like "Purrrg?"

"I am here," Sprig answered, muffled. Daniel couldn't tell which of the men carried the leaf but at least Sprig hadn't been left behind.

They walked for thirty minutes across flat forested ground with no trails and only an occasional car-sized boulder to detour around. Daniel tripped a few times on an unseen stick or depression in the rocky soil but had little choice but to soldier on through the darkness. Finally, a destination loomed ahead, a campfire.

Two more Afeesh Tm sat on rocks by the fire. As the group approached, both of them stood and ran to the leader. Skinny and half his height, they looked like children.

"*Dya da shtoo, ata ko,*" one child said. The words sounded vaguely like those that Osperus spoke. It gave Daniel hope that Sprig would continue to be useful for communication with these people.

The leader of their group unwound the rope that bound Daniel's arms, then removed his pack, which instantly compacted the ChitzaShell spread across his chest to button size. He tossed the pack to one side and pointed his spear to an unoccupied rock by the fire. "*Apo da, de tindee anakay.*" He pushed Daniel toward it.

Daniel sat, and immediately began to peel the sticky wax from his mouth. No one stopped him. With one more rip and an eye-watering wince, the glue came off. His eyes searched for Sprig without success.

Daniel motioned to his shoulder where Sprig had stood. "I need my associate."

Standing by the fire, the leader waved his spear toward one of his comrades. "*Ga peek.*" The other man pulled Sprig from a pocket on his fur jacket and handed the leaf back to Daniel.

Sprig quickly hopped up Daniel's arm to its preferred position on his right shoulder.

"You okay?" Daniel asked.

"I am, except for the smelly pocket. I detect no wounds on you either."

"Nothing a few kisses from my wife couldn't fix." He touched his tender upper lip.

Their abductors gathered around the fire. One woman put her crossbow down and placed an arm around the smaller child. The other kept her crossbow slung on a strap over her shoulder. Daniel didn't like his chances of running for it. These people seemed to see better in the dark than he did, and the crossbow's range no doubt eclipsed the distance he could run in the time it would take them to react.

All six adults and two children were dressed in skins stitched together with laces. Like Humans, the women had no facial hair and were smaller, but otherwise they looked the same as the Afeesh Tm men. The children in the group told a different story. This was more than just a band of warriors, but he didn't yet have enough information to piece together a strategy for how to deal with them.

"Time for some questions," Daniel whispered to Sprig. "Do you think you can translate?"

"So far, their words appear to be a dialect of the same Afeesh Tm language. I will do my best to adjust."

Daniel gave a thumbs up. "Damn fine extra sweet, as our Chitza friends might say." He spoke to his captors, keeping it simple in case the translation didn't work out right away. "I don't have the map."

The leader turned. Sprig translated his words, "We know."

"Then why did you take me?"

The leader laughed, speaking to the man on his left. "Another Starman comes begging. Osperus can't keep track of his inventory!" They moved further away and mumbled quietly to each other.

Sprig whispered, "They're talking about food for the trip. He may be ignoring your question. Sorry, I can't hear it all."

"You're doing great, Sprig. I was worried I was going to lose you back there." He stroked the edge of the leaf as he'd seen the professor do back on distant Litia.

Sprig stretched to his touch, then said, "In such a large forest, my survival depends upon you. But you are in danger too. While I am small and without weapons or physical strength, I will endeavor to keep you informed as best I can."

"Yeah, it's a tough situation, but we'll work it out together."

Small or not, Sprig's considerable talents to collect information gave them a fair chance to form a plan for their release. Since their captors knew he didn't have the map, they must have taken him for some other reason, possibly no more complicated than ransom. They'd need to learn what these people valued.

But there was another, more immediate option. Escape.

"How long is night here?" A dark forest put him at a disadvantage. Sprig's glow could help, but morning twilight would be better.

"Approximately eight hours, given the planet data I collected when we first arrived."

"Perfect. How about getting us back to the drop tank? You're pretty good with directions, right?"

"We meandered somewhat in our walk, but a bearing of 192 degrees and a steady pace for thirty-five minutes should return us to the clearing."

"You're way better than our migrating geese. How are you so exact?"

"Electro-magneto cells along the lateral leaf veins. Useful for magnetic headings and ferrous geology."

Daniel would have enjoyed an in-depth discussion of Sprig's internal structure, but he had more immediate issues to deal with. "Their campfire is well supplied with wood, they've put some effort into arranging rocks to sit on, and I see evidence of supplies." Daniel motioned to several packs piled together. "Their intent is to spend the night here. If they sleep, we might have a chance to slip away before dawn."

"Unless they tie you down." One of the kids was practicing throwing the bolo that had easily bound Daniel's arms. Its braided ends secured two baseball-sized rocks, providing the momentum required to tangle a foe with a single throw.

"Yeah, there's that." The rope didn't worry him. The crossbows did.

"Let's push our intelligence gathering a bit more."

Daniel stood up.

The woman with the crossbow slung over her shoulder swiveled expertly. With a single fluid motion, she flipped the weapon into her hands and pointed it at him.

He raised his hands. "I'm thirsty. Can I have my pack?" One of the men tossed over the ChitzaPack they'd taken from him. Daniel retrieved a cannister of water from inside and drank his fill.

"Are we spending the night here?"

The leader of the group came over and sat on a rock. Up close, his nose-less face looked the same as the other Afeesh Tm people but with oily smears across his forehead and cheeks. He smelled of fish. "You ask many questions," he said through Sprig's translation.

"And you dragged me away against my will," Daniel answered. "In my world that's a crime."

"It won't be long, a few days. We need you."

"Why?"

"We were unable to capture the Human woman. But you'll do."

In this planet's history only one Human woman had walked its surface: Nala. Daniel decided to hold his cards close this time and not disclose any relationship.

"You still haven't said why you need me."

"We will arrive at the cliff city tomorrow. Tennah will speak to you."

More information. They were intermediaries or possibly mercenaries, assigned to a task by someone named Tennah. It suggested an organization with structure, a more favorable situation than a band of outlaws who might do anything on a whim.

"What happened to the Human woman?" Daniel asked.

"She left before we could take her. In a Starman tube, like yours."

Confirmation that Nala had safely left the planet. "She had the map, you know."

"She *stole* the map." The rest laughed at their leader's words.

"Osperus had a fit," one woman added, unable to stop laughing.

Daniel kept the useful conversation going. "It seems you know everything about Osperus."

"Revolutionaries must understand their target."

"And when you overthrow Osperus, you'll take the map by force?"

Their leader laughed again. "Starman, you have waded into waters over your head. Osperus is not your friend, not your partner, and not your supplier. You would be wise to stay as far from him as you can. By capturing you, we're doing you a favor! At least you won't end up as a pelt!" He tugged on the stitched furs forming his jacket.

Daniel gritted his teeth. "That's disgusting. Those pelts you wear were once intelligent people."

The man shook his head. "Starman, you misunderstand. Yes, Kyan Ta wear skins harvested from the forest. But we do not kill visitors from the stars! Nor do we place a bounty on customers who are not willing to pay a steep price. No! If you're looking for crimes, point your finger at Osperus, and then be thankful there are revolutionaries like the Kyan Ta who will one day remove him."

They denied responsibility for murdering the first Chitza crew, turning the table to Osperus. Daniel would be willing to reevaluate the relationship, but he remained skeptical of this band's motives. "So, you'll overthrow a dictator who just happens to have a valuable map? Convenient for you."

"What value is a map that brings nothing but conflict and misery? I can assure you when we remove Osperus, we will free ourselves of the map's burden too."

The leader slapped Daniel on his back which made Sprig jump. "Sleep, Starman." He stood and pointed to the woman still gripping her crossbow. "But know that she won't."

The Kyan Ta leader returned to his group of revolutionaries, leaving Daniel to think about what he'd just learned. Osperus, they said, should not be trusted. But were they any better? He wasn't anxious to step into their local conflict. The natural world could be investigated through scientific methods. Probe it, and nature faithfully returned one answer. But people were different. People lied, especially when in conflict.

He continued to turn these thoughts over in his mind for much of the night, mixed with short periods of listless sleep and a pre-dawn breakfast of Chitza provisions. During periods of wakefulness, he watched the woman with the crossbow. She remained alert, patrolling their campsite and feeding the fire. Sprig, who never slept, confirmed that there had been no opportunity for escape.

When dawn arrived, the group roused, put out the fire, and gathered their belongings. They permitted him another snack and a chance to water the bushes, then they set off. This time he kept up with their leader with no prodding from behind. He wasn't ready to accept their revolutionary story, but it wouldn't be long before he would meet their leader and resolve the purpose of this kidnapping one way or another.

The forest continued with no sign of trappers, wagons, or even roads. The Kyan Ta seemed to make their own path between scrub undergrowth. The landscape became hilly. Deciduous trees gave way to pines as they climbed higher. Over the course of several miles, they never once encountered another village, house, or farm, a significant difference between this planet and Earth.

The pines grew taller, and the ground leveled. Ahead, blue sky between the trees hinted of an abrupt end to the forest. They arrived at the top of a rocky cliff with a glorious view across a deep canyon. Its horizontal stripes of red and white rocks reminded Daniel of any of the scenic places of southern Utah and northern Arizona.

"We have traveled a total of twenty-one kilometers from the drop tank," Sprig said. "I now estimate a bearing of 179 degrees."

"Good to know," Daniel said. "I doubt an escape will work, but if we can convince them to let us go, we can find our way back."

They continued along the rim of the canyon to an indentation in the rocks which dropped steeply over the cliff's edge. The Kyan Ta led in a scrambling descent where handholds and footholds had been carved into the rocks. The cliff became vertical with a sheer drop of at least a hundred meters to the next bench where bushes and a few trees grew, then a considerably larger drop below that. Overall, the canyon looked to be five or six hundred meters deep.

Each step dislodged loose scree which bounced down the slope like tiny missiles to anyone who might be below. A rope or guide wire would be a useful addition to their primitive trail, but a difficult entrance may have been part of this cliff city's design.

Finally, they reached a rock landing where a wooden ladder spanned a ten-meter sheer drop. The ladder seemed to be yet another element in their security, easy to climb down but also easy to remove from below. At the ladder's foot, a narrow ledge continued to the right. The ledge widened, undercutting the wall to create an overhang that grew larger as they walked.

Ahead, a natural amphitheater as big as a sports stadium spread beneath a hard rock ceiling. Across its flat floor, hundreds of small stone houses crowded into the cavernous space, in some cases stacking on top of each other until they reached its ceiling.

Dozens of people dressed in the same stitched skins were everywhere, on balconies, in doorways, climbing ladders.

"Wow, Mesa Verde," Daniel said. He had visited dozens of the Ancestral Puebloan villages carved into canyon walls in Colorado, Arizona, and New Mexico, with Mesa Verde National Park being the crowning achievement of those ancient people. Each of the spectacular villages had been designed to be secure from attacks that could come from above or below. The Kyan Ta village appeared to be no different.

These people have something to fear.

Revolutionaries rarely stayed under the radar of the government they wished to overthrow, yet this village showed no signs of recent battle. Their cliffside location might be more than defensive, it might also be a secret. They hadn't blindfolded him, and Sprig had recorded the exact compass bearing to this place. Once a captive learned the secret, could he ever be released?

Daniel peered over the cliff's edge. It would be a simple way to dispose of an uncooperative opponent.

A shove from behind pushed him perilously close to the edge. Daniel stumbled but regained his balance. His captors yelled something then prodded him with their spears toward a ground floor doorway. He stepped into a darkened room with a rock floor and wooden benches along the back wall. Two of the warriors took up guard positions at the doorway.

Daniel removed his pack and sat, leaning back against cool stone. He still didn't know why these people wanted him. He'd give their leader a chance to explain, but if they intended to keep him here indefinitely, he'd have to come up with a more aggressive strategy.

Nala needs me.

14 LOST

NALA MUNCHES ON A BALL of compressed granola pulled from a ChitzaPack she managed to snag while drifting across her debris-filled prison. She closes the pack, saving the rest for later.

Several cans of water were just out of reach, the distance to them now increasing. She has no way to turn around.

She remembers reading somewhere—probably a survival website—that even when you have no access to water, it's still wise to eat. Desert birds never drink a drop, the website said, they get all the water they need by eating seeds. It sounds right, but you never know about the internet.

Other than the granola pack and Aussik's data disc that she tucked into her pants, she doesn't bump into anything else that's useful. Even a collision with a heavier chunk of metal could strategically alter her drift trajectory if she hits it just right. But it doesn't happen.

In a shirt pocket, she finds two aspirin tablets and lint. Inside her jacket, a pair of sunglasses. She slips the sunglasses on, deciding the fashion accessory will make her look cooler when her stone-cold body is finally recovered ten thousand years from now.

If these are her final moments of life, she decides she'll split each hour into three components. The first ten minutes will be dedicated to thinking about Daniel. Then forty minutes to sort out the science of her surroundings—because, why not? Finally, she'll spend the last ten minutes kicking herself for being such a goddamn fucking idiot by joining a mission to the end of the goddamn fucking universe.

It seems a fair distribution of time.

She finishes an I-love-Daniel segment, using most of the ten minutes to obsess about the wave in his mid-length brown hair that gives him a sexy flourish especially when the wind blows.

Now she turns to science.

Nala motions with her hands as she speaks. "Okay, so a 4-D bubble views 3-D space as a flat geometric plane. It can hover above that plane or even touch it like a soap bubble on glass, right?"

"Right," she agrees with herself.

"But if it's *not* touching the 3-D plane, then the distance between the two implies a fifth dimension."

"Correct-a-mundo."

"So, anyone located in that fifth dimension of space would see both the 3-D plane *and* the 4-D bubble simultaneously."

"True, but they wouldn't perceive them in the same geometric sense."

"Why not?"

"Well, as you go up in dimensions, you always have to abstract the next level down by reducing one of its dimensions. A hypersphere becomes a sphere. A sphere becomes a circle. A circle becomes a point. It's just simple geometry."

"Nah, I'm not buying that. No matter what dimension you're in, you still have 3-D eyes. Nobody can actually see 4 or 5-D geometry in the way it really exists. Saying that a hypersphere is perceived as a sphere is purely a mechanism to explain the weirdness of extradimensional space to the Average Joe."

"But are we talking about a three-dimensional Average Joe? Or a hyper being who lives in a 4-D world with a 4-D body? Cuz… a roll in the hay with HyperJoe could be interesting if you know what I mean."

Nala shakes her head and sighs. "Damn girl, you're hopeless. Park that crazy shit for the next session on Daniel. This is science. Stick to the topic or go home!"

She stops talking and instead surveys her surroundings. Nothing stirs. Nothing could. She is alone.

"Can I go home now?" she whispers to herself.

Science is over. She picks up the next scheduled topic, kicking herself, and there are plenty of reasons to be ruthless.

15 CLIFF HOUSE

LEFT ALONE IN A ONE-ROOMED HOUSE with a stone floor, adobe walls, and timbers supporting the ceiling, Daniel shuffled along the room's only bench to get a view through a small window cut into one wall.

Outside people went about their daily lives in a remarkable cliff dwelling built high above the canyon floor. Unlike Osperus' marble edifice anchoring the center of the Afeesh Tm town, there were no signs of higher technology or wealth in this place. These people acquired what they needed from the land: animal skins for clothing, handmade ropes, log ladders, stone tools, and clay pottery.

"It feels like we've stepped into pre-Columbian America," Daniel said to Sprig. He hoped his meeting would fare better than the notorious first contacts between Europeans and native tribes in the Americas.

The guards at the doorway parted and a woman walked in. She stopped in the center of the small room and eyed Daniel with interest.

He stood up. She stepped closer, continuing her study of him head to foot without comment. The scent of wood smoke wafted from her stitched clothing.

She approached within inches, appearing unconcerned about the close contact with their prisoner. Her eyes were large like all Afeesh Tm, her nose the merest suggestion of a bump. The corners of her mouth twisted upward, giving the impression of a smile almost ready to break. Strawberry colored streaks decorated blonde hair worn in a long braid.

The braiding exposed a curving metal plate affixed to the side of her head just behind one ear. Tiny lights along the edge of the plate's comma shape glowed in multiple colors.

Bio-integration. It was the first sign of technology in this tribe and a bold reminder that she was not Human.

"Eeg nek abusant la cabeen da?" She had the same guttural voice but with a pitch complementing her smaller figure.

Sprig translated her words. "You look like me, why is that?"

Daniel shook his head, "I wish I could tell you. I'm just as surprised. Two species with this much physical similarity must be rare." Sprig translated back.

She reached out to touch the leaf. Her jointed finger ended in a rounded point with no nail. Sprig recoiled at her touch but remained secured to Daniel's shoulder.

"Ag spectah da neetz ka," she said.

Sprig responded, "She wants to take your language from me."

"Would that hurt you?" Daniel asked.

The leaf briefly conversed with the woman, then explained. "She says no. She says she needs your language to avoid misunderstandings, but I'm not sure how this *taking* would work." Sprig nervously danced along Daniel's shoulder.

Daniel felt sure Sprig had assimilated both English and the Afeesh Tm language well enough to avoid misunderstandings. There'd been none so far. Dynamics of negotiation were at play, and a position of strength benefited Daniel. "Tell her no. Tell her you are my valued partner."

Sprig did. The woman suppressed a smile.

Then she plucked Sprig from Daniel's shoulder and turned away. He lunged, but one of the guards jammed the sharp end of his spear an inch from Daniel's chest. He raised both hands.

The woman lifted Sprig to the side of her head. Lights flickered across the panel embedded above her ear and Sprig's leafy surface vibrated in time with the flashes. It was all over in seconds.

She turned back to Daniel, held out Sprig, and spoke in perfect English, "How interesting. I love that your partner vibrates its words." The guttural sounds remained in her voice, producing an accent that sounded vaguely eastern European.

Daniel carefully returned Sprig to a secure place on his shoulder, whispering, "Are you okay?"

Sprig tucked itself close to Daniel's collar. "I'm fine. Somewhat sullied perhaps."

"That's a good word, sullied," Daniel said. "Your language skills are now in her?"

"They are," the woman answered. "Your fascinating little friend is unharmed and is welcome to join our conversation. But now I am able to speak directly. Much better, don't you think? We have so much to learn about each other."

He could have demanded an apology. But aside from her snatch of Sprig, her tone came from a different place than Osperus or any of the other Afeesh Tm. She seemed curious. Almost scientific. She also represented his best chance for release.

With direct communication established, he would first need to gain her trust. He had no desire to become involved in their internal conflict and wouldn't disclose their location to Osperus— but it could be hard to convince her of that. For now, he would be cordial. "I'm Daniel. A Human, as we call ourselves. A Starman, as some of your own people have called me."

"Daniel," she echoed, quite closely to the correct pronunciation of his name. "I am Tennah, Sibyl of the Kyan Ta, Protector of Afeesh Tm. I thank you for joining us. Please forgive me for intruding upon your partner's mind and for any mistreatment by our scouts."

"We managed," Daniel replied. "In my culture, there's a difference between an invitation and abduction. If you brought me here, I need to know why."

She circled around to his side, studying him like a sample of something exotic yet familiar. "The Human woman slipped away before I could speak with her. We have questions. But now I have the opportunity to speak with you." Tennah ran her hand down Daniel's shoulder, stroking his shirt and pausing at his bicep. "So similar, even in the muscles beneath the skin."

Daniel didn't flinch. "I'm following the Human woman. I need to know where she went." Until he learned what they wanted, continuing to withhold his true relationship with Nala would provide detachment. He'd take whatever advantage he could.

"Most likely she went to one of two places, the same as any other visitor to this planet. Either back to her home, or onward to the Chaos Field."

"I'm sure she didn't go home."

Tennah nodded thoughtfully. "Then... the Chaos Field. Not a wise choice, but as I said, I was unable to speak with her. Will you now follow her?"

"As soon as you release me, yes. I understand the journey might get dangerous, but we'll manage."

Tennah laughed, turning away from Daniel. "You echo what Osperus told you."

"Only that the Chaos Field could be navigated with the map."

"And our cliff can be climbed with nothing more than bare hands and feet. But when you find the steps we have carved into the rock, your chances of success improve."

"I take your point. Do you have something better than what Osperus offers?"

"Perhaps. But much depends on you."

Now Daniel laughed. "Osperus wants to trade for an abandoned ship in orbit around your planet. Honestly, I don't have time or desire for a second negotiation."

"Then I will tell you what you need to know but Osperus failed to mention." She stepped close once more. "The map leads to a place that is not only dangerous, it is incomprehensible. It is reality without rules, a place not of this universe. I know because I have been there. In fact, I am the only person standing on this planet who has."

Daniel's attention perked up at the unexpected—and unlikely—information. "Afeesh Tm are not space faring people. I don't see anything here that contradicts what Osperus told me."

"You have much to learn." Tennah pulled his arm. "Come with me."

She guided him out the doorway, bypassing the guards. Outside, the Kyan Ta community bustled with people engaged in a variety of work from weaving to food preparation. Children mixed with adults, the younger ones playing, the older children helping with tasks.

Tennah led to the center of the village where the natural rock overhang soared at least a hundred meters overhead. They'd channeled a water seep on one side into an aqueduct that trickled into an enclosed pool. People gathered around, filling clay pots with water.

Tennah swept a hand across the mishmash of stacked houses, ladders, and structures that supported a population likely numbering in the hundreds. "My people, the Kyan Ta tribe of Afeesh Tm."

Daniel absorbed the alien version of an American southwest cliff dwelling. The village was impressive in scope and organization, if technologically primitive.

Tennah continued, "You are correct, we are not star wanderers by nature. We follow a simple life. We leave flying to the birds." She swiveled, lifting one finger. "But with one exception. Generations ago, the first visitors arrived. Powerful, they were deemed gods by our ancestors. They came with a single purpose, to select a few among us to become Sibyls—a kind of seer, a keeper of knowledge. Sibyls are always women, never men. They are set upon their path when the girl becomes of age, a tradition that continues to this day. Sibyls, you see, are the space travelers among us."

"But how? I can see that your people are industrious, but there's nothing here that could possibly take you to space. Unless..." Daniel pointed to the electronic attachment at the side of her head.

The turned-up corners of her mouth finally formed the smile that had been waiting there. She turned her head to give Daniel a better view of the brain implant. "We call it the Arc of Progression. Magic in its own way but not space technology."

She brushed back her hair in a prideful way. The silver panel gleamed in the sunlight. "Trust me, visitor Daniel, I have seen every type of spacecraft. Most recently the metal cylinder with rotating blades that brought you here. I've also seen a pyramid with legs on each corner. Another shaped like a fish. My favorite was an immense globe that alighted as softly as fog touches the treetops. Some visitors bring their marvelous crafts to the surface, others remain high above. I have been inside many of them, some with interiors grander than I could have imagined possible.

"No. Afeesh Tm have no such machines and I doubt we could build one even if you taught us the techniques. But visitors come here, one after another. On occasion, I have been invited to join their travels. I have been above our atmosphere fourteen times. Beyond our star six times. I have even walked the surface of another planet."

Daniel was enjoying Tennah's almost childlike description of the wonders she'd seen. No primitive, she lived at a crossroads for travelers lured here by the galactic ring that beckoned anyone with the right technology to stop by and satisfy their curiosity.

"As a Sibyl, my path was set long ago. It is both an opportunity and a curse. I have been to many places that I would gladly visit again. And one that I would not."

Daniel had a feeling he knew where. "The Chaos Field?"

She nodded. "The map Osperus offers could kill you. It is not crafted from sure steps. There are no directions, no distances, no signposts, only probabilities and uncertain outcomes. Yes, you might survive passage across the Chaos Field. Others have. But the odds are against you."

Even dressed in animal skins, Daniel had to admit that Tennah's credibility beat Osperus'. A brain enhancement that could absorb an alien language in seconds tipped the scales in her favor. But her advice began to feel worrisome, it certainly amped up the anxiety he'd been trying to keep in check.

The distances involved in this mission had always been imposing. A relentlessly ticking clock made every delay or detour a new concern. And now, as she had bluntly explained, the final leg of their journey would enter incomprehensibly dangerous territory. So be it, but the mounting warnings didn't bode well for Nala's chances.

Yet there was still something she wasn't telling him. "If you've been to this dangerous place, somehow you survived."

Tennah turned and walked straight to the edge of the cliff. A plunge of several hundred meters ended in trees and rubble on the canyon floor. Daniel wondered how many children might have fallen off. Maybe none, if these kids mastered their environment at an early age.

She stared out across the canyon. "Much like this cliff, there is an edge that separates us from the Chaos Field. I have been there just as I am here now. I peered into its abyss and saw its true nature, then convinced the pilot to turn his ship around. To this day I cannot tell you exactly how we managed to withdraw from the brink, but we did. Upon return, I vowed to put an end to the madness of a map that leads people to their destruction. Yet... over the years, I have come to see both plusses and minuses. Your arrival is a plus."

"Me? What did I do?"

"Nothing yet, but you might. Our struggle is deepening. We need your help."

Daniel rarely let a plea for help pass, and this woman had already been more enlightening than Osperus. Whatever secrets she held about the final leg of their journey might be worth Daniel's time as long as it could be done quickly.

"Tennah, I'm on a critical mission and I've already lost a day coming here. If you have something to offer, I'll do my best to help you. But I can't stay long." For the first time since his capture, Daniel felt the leverage swinging his way.

"I will not keep you. You are free to go anytime. But hear my story. It will save you much grief and needless deviations from a straight path."

Daniel nodded. "Fair enough, I'm listening."

Tennah lowered her head. "The map you seek is not drawn on parchment or skin. It is nothing you can hold up to the light and study its markings. It exists as countless sparks of energy, by themselves useless. The map requires a courier with abilities to analyze a given navigation system and configure a probability vector capable of guidance through chaos. Transferring the map to a machine is a complex task that involves both electronic and biological counterparts."

She touched the curving metal plate embedded into the side of her head. "The map you seek is here. The map is me."

16 SIBYL

TENNAH, SIBYL OF THE KYAN TA, protector of Afeesh Tm, guided Daniel up a sturdy wooden ladder lashed together with thick handmade twine. He had learned that a Sibyl was a map courier, trained to configure and install a *probability vector* into the navigation system of a visitor's spacecraft. If the complex task was done well, the vector would guide the ship across treacherous space. If handled poorly or not at all, the unlucky traveler might never be heard from again.

Sibyls were sometimes invited to join these travelers. They rarely accepted, according to Tennah, in part because their services were no longer needed. The probability vector—an everchanging path based on local conditions—would provide the required guidance into and through the Chaos Field. But no matter how well she had done her job, each Sibyl also understood that this path would involve unavoidable risk.

At the top of the ladder, several children gathered to see the Starman visitor. They touched his clothes as Daniel passed, gazing up with awe and the spark of youthful playfulness. Tennah caressed each child's head but continued across the first-level roof toward the only round building among the irregular Lego stack of adobe structures.

They passed through a wide doorway into an airy room decorated with colorful scenes of outdoor life on its curving wall: animals hiding in a forest, a cascade of small waterfalls along a creek, people napping in the tall grass of a meadow.

Sprig clung tightly to his shirt collar. "Everything okay?" Daniel asked.

"Absorbing," Sprig replied. "This tribe seems peaceful. Not the mongrels that Osperus described."

"They got a bad rap. Probably by design. Despots do that."

"On the other hand, they describe themselves as revolutionaries."

"True. There's probably no such thing as a peaceful revolution."

They exited through a smaller doorway to a semicircular balcony that overlooked the village. Flowers grew from pots at either end of a curving rail. Oval portraits of women hung at regular intervals along the rail, painted in full color by a master of the art. Each painting combined bold strokes with detailed realism in a striking rendition of the Afeesh Tm. Several of the portraits were of blonde haired women, but one included streaks of red— clearly a painting of Tennah.

She stood in the center of the semicircle, facing Daniel. "Seven paintings. Seven Sibyls. Some are young and still learning their craft. Some are older with experience. All are gifted with knowledge passed down over many generations via the Arc of Progression." She touched the small plate at the side of her head.

"The Arc is a computer?" Daniel asked.

"A vast store of mathematical procedures and data accessed and manipulated by direct contact with the brain. Is this the same as your computer?"

"Sort of. But we don't integrate computers into our bodies... at least, not yet." Daniel examined the paintings. The metal plate appeared in each portrait, often blended in with the woman's hair like an item of jewelry the artist considered secondary to her natural beauty. "These devices were provided by a visitor?"

She nodded. "We are a small sisterhood. Always seven but passed down from one person to the next over many generations. Once the Arc's neuronal transceivers burrow beneath the girl's scalp, she begins a training period to become proficient in its use. Today, six Sibyl's are under Osperus' control. They go where he tells them, they do his bidding and collect riches for the elite few. Osperus and his friends prosper. Our people do not."

She smiled with a devious twist. "And then there is me. Formerly obedient, I now follow a different path. The day I returned from the Chaos Field I redirected my efforts to lead our people toward a simpler life, a life not dependent on space travelers. Osperus would kill me if he could. He has done it before when a Sibyl disobeyed, but I'm too agile for him. The Arc—once a curse—has become my power."

Daniel smiled back. The device had already shown its value as a language adapter, but it had also elevated Tennah to a position of leadership, even if limited to one rebellious tribe. "I understand your struggle. It's not fair to burden any society with a job they didn't ask for. I can only imagine how Humans would react. And it must be hard to be the sole rebel among the seven Sibyls."

"The others are with me in spirit, but indoctrination is difficult to break. The bravest among them is Jazameh." Tennah stepped to a portrait of a young woman with dark hair and a Mona Lisa grin. "Sadly, she went missing just two days ago. It is possible that Osperus discovered our connection and killed her, but it is more likely that Jazameh's disappearance is related to the Human woman you follow. Her sudden departure and Jazameh's disappearance cannot be coincidental. As I said, we have questions."

Tennah reached beneath her skin jacket and withdrew a slender black blade long enough to do some serious damage and sharp enough to make it easy. With Daniel backed against the balcony rail, she flicked the tip of the obsidian knife an inch below his chin. Her steely eyes conveyed a realistic sense that she was fully capable of using the weapon.

Her words were ice. "If you value your life, hold very still."

Daniel swallowed hard, remaining silent. He tried not to flinch. Sprig froze too.

The knife hovered. "Why do you follow the Human woman? Is she a criminal? Or do all Humans simply take what they need without justice? Many in our tribe say Jazameh was stolen."

A quick upward jab would be fatal. He hadn't expected accusations, but under the circumstances he couldn't blame her. He had no idea how Nala had retrieved a copy of the map—now recognized as a person, not a scrolled piece of paper.

Daniel needed to diffuse the hostility that had come from nowhere, and he could think of no better way than to speak from the heart. "Tennah... we Humans have our share of scoundrels, but the woman I'm following is fair-minded and caring. She would never steal. I know this because she is my wife."

Tennah lowered the knife, if only a millimeter. "Your wife?"

"She's missing, caught in a gamma radiation blast somewhere in deep space, maybe inside the Chaos Field, I don't know. But I've come a long way to find her."

Keeping his head still, Daniel glanced down at the slender knife held by a strong sure hand. "I understand your sense of justice, and I agree with it. If my wife left with Jazameh, I assure you they went together in collaboration."

"And became lost in a gamma blast?"

"Yes."

Tennah huffed, then sheathed the knife. "Sorry. My blade is mostly for the benefit of our audience. Being a tribal leader comes with certain expectations."

Daniel glanced beyond the balcony railing. Villagers below stood frozen in place with their eyes locked on the Shakespearean drama unfolding on the elevated stage. These people hadn't been ignoring him, they'd been waiting to see what Tennah was going to do with him.

He took a deep breath. At least they were back on speaking terms with no weapons in sight. "My wife, Nala, was asked to be a representative to your planet for the same reason as me—we look like you. The Chitza pilots of our ships decided a Human would do a better job of obtaining the map. They had failed before, in fact, your guards told me Osperus may have killed the members of their first mission."

"I wouldn't be surprised."

"Of course, Osperus says you killed them."

Tennah tapped a finger on her sheathed knife. "In this case, no. We did not." She lowered her head in deep thought. "Osperus gets more desperate by the day. When your wife walked out of their talks, he became furious... throwing things, hurting people." She paused, glanced up as if an ancient spirit might be floating by, then continued. "If your wife did not take Jazameh, then the opposite may be closer to the truth—that Jazameh made direct contact with her, bypassing Osperus."

Tennah's eyes fixed on Daniel's. "If Jazameh acted on her own... if she left this planet with your wife... then the fire of revolution has already been lit."

She clenched her jaw. "Come. There is no time to waste."

Tennah dragged Daniel from the balcony back inside. He had a thousand questions, but she pointed to a decorative design on the floor and told him to stay put. She hurried away, privately conferring with several others in recessed coves around the circumference of the circular foyer.

She returned, highly animated with a quickness to her words that hadn't been there before. "I know where your wife went."

"Where?"

"To the boundary—the cliff I described. There is a fissure at one place where radiation leaks through. I don't know why, but

Jazameh believes it is a weak spot and the best place to enter the Chaos Field."

"Sounds promising. Can you take us there?"

"No, I am needed here. But your ship's navigation system will guide you there once I have installed the map. I will configure a waypoint at this precise location."

Daniel nodded. "I can work with that. What's the price? You said you needed my help."

Tennah's voice was sure. "You spoke of an abandoned ship in orbit. And of a Chitza crew killed while on the surface of our planet. They are one and the same?"

"Yes."

"I have been aboard many ships, and with the Arc of Progression, I can acquire complete knowledge of its systems within minutes. The abandoned Chitza ship will be no different. I will fly it myself and operate its blasters. With such a weapon, we can overpower Osperus."

Daniel hated to let her down. "Yeah, about that."

She waved a hand in front of his face. "A temporary loan, only. Once Osperus is gone, we will gladly return this ship. And no need for you to wait. I can configure your navigation system now, and you will be on your way. Kyan Ta can fight our own war."

As she'd said, she'd seen a lot of spaceships and most of them probably came with some level of weaponry. "I'm sorry, but a Chitza scout ship is designed for deep space exploration. It has no weapons."

She squinted, not comprehending. "No weapons?"

"Not a single blaster, atomic harpoon, or photon torpedo. In my pack is a small defensive shield. Nothing more."

"You're lying."

"I'm not."

She studied his face, then sighed. "You're not."

Daniel sighed too. He'd rather obtain the map directly from the source and avoid a middleman who was at best a con artist and at worst a ruthless dictator. "If you want the ship, I can probably get it for you, but unless you're going to create 4-D bubbles…"

Daniel paused, finishing the thought only in his mind. "Wait a minute." He remained motionless still working out the details. "I have a better idea. You don't need guns or blasters. Why fight a full-scale war? Your goal is to be rid of Osperus and his goons, right?"

She nodded quietly.

Daniel placed his hand on her shoulder. "Come with me, back to my ship. We'll talk to my Chitza friends. If my plan works out, you'll get exactly what you need, you have my promise."

Tennah gazed at him without words, then reached beneath her jacket and withdrew her obsidian knife. At first, Daniel thought she intended to slice their palms and consummate an agreement with a bloody handshake. Instead, she twirled the blade and offered its handle to him.

Sprig scurried up to Daniel's collar and whispered, "I believe it is a sign of trust. Take it."

Daniel accepted the knife, sliding it under his belt, pirate-like. "Shall we go?"

Tennah smiled, the kind of sly smile that hinted she likely had another weapon hidden somewhere.

****

They climbed handholds up the cliff to the juniper and pine forest at its rim. Now familiar, and with no armed guards accompanying them, the route back seemed far less threatening. Tennah carried her own pack of supplies. Daniel still had water and food in his ChitzaPack. Sprig rode comfortably on his shoulder.

As they walked, Tennah never once asked about Daniel's plan. For the leader of the Kyan Ta tribe, trust was trust. Instead, she spoke of Afeesh Tm history.

At one time in their past there were no tribes. Prosperity came by way of the map, with its distribution among seven Sibyls being the insurance that no single person could own it. Advanced civilizations came one after the other, drawn in by a four-dimensional signpost that could be easily detected even from a billion light-years away. Curious about where the map led, greedy for riches, or just plain adventurous, visitors traded for the map. Their payments ranged from technology to farming techniques. It helped to raise the local standard of living from nomadic hunters to a civil society with highly organized towns carved from the forest.

And then came Osperus. He seized power and confined the trading proceeds to himself and an elite group of allies. Security forces replaced egalitarian government. An iron fist replaced meritocracy. The seven Sibyls—keys to the whole enterprise—fell under his control.

Their population became intractably divided, with Osperus supporters fed lies, and detractors jailed or murdered. But like most authoritarians, Osperus never found a way to dominate absolutely. Multiple underground resistance groups thrived, notably the Kyan Ta, the only revolutionaries with a Sibyl as their leader.

She seemed surer of her theory as they walked. "Jazameh must have exchanged the map for protection."

"Highly possible," Daniel agreed. Nala would have considered it her duty to help a sister in need, and if Nala's Captain Zeeno was essentially the same person as Daniel's Captain Zeeno, his arm would have been easily twisted.

"Jazameh could be in hiding, possibly off-world. There is a second planet in our system that is said to be habitable. Perhaps she configured their probability vector in return for transit."

"Why do you call it a *probability* vector?"

Tennah had used the word to describe the map several times, but until now there'd been no time to ask her about its meaning. With the drop tank still miles away Daniel needed to get his head around what this woman would do to the Chitza's navigation system. Zeeno would insist on it.

"In ordinary space, a vector has two endpoints, each that can be described using three orthogonal axes and measured from an origin."

Daniel was surprised to hear mathematic terminology from a person who otherwise lived such a simple life. The panel screwed into the side of her head should have been the clue that this woman was anything but primitive.

"While my people have no means to compress space as you do, I understand the foundation of this science—the world of the very small. Probability cannot be ignored when quantum positions are measured."

"You're right about that."

The strangeness of the situation wasn't lost on him: hiking in a medieval world, speaking English with a Human look-alike whose brain had been enhanced with an alien extension. And now, their discussion centered on quantum physics. He'd never be surprised again.

139

"Waypoints are the basis of any navigation system," Tennah continued. "Two waypoints give you a vector to cross ordinary space. Reverse that vector, and you return to your starting point.

Simple enough. They were doing exactly that as they walked, returning to the drop tank where this episode began.

She continued her explanation. "But a path through the Chaos Field is fundamentally different. Quantum fluctuations require a probability vector, computed in real time, and never duplicated. Reaching your destination becomes a chance not a certainty, and the path leading *in* bears no relationship to the path leading back *out*."

Daniel began to see why this Chaos Field was nothing but trouble. Fortunately, Tennah seemed to think the Chitza ship and Nala could be found at the boundary. A wall, or a cliff of some sort, if such a thing could exist in deep space.

"Cross the boundary and the probability vector becomes your only guide. Successful navigation relies in part on chance."

"I get it. Like a ship navigating a rocky shoreline."

"With rocks that appear and disappear! Sibyls don't know how many visitors have transited successfully or what they find on the other side. The few reports we have come from a time before I was born. They speak of worlds beyond imagination, but the descriptions always reminded me of stories designed to enchant children."

Daniel shrugged. "When you put it that way, it's hard to imagine why someone would do it, but curiosity has always been a powerful motivator. What's beyond the horizon? I admit, I wanted to know. Now that I'm here, I have mixed feelings. If your map takes us to the edge of normal space, well… that's fascinating stuff, but only when observed from a safe distance." He laughed. "Unfortunately, my pilots are natural born risk takers."

"I could configure a key. Would that be helpful?"

"You mean, a way to unlock the map?"

"It would give you personal control."

She touched something on the panel above her ear. "Say the word *engage*." Daniel did. "And now, *disengage*." Daniel repeated, gaining a fair idea what she was up to.

"Voice control?"

"Most navigation systems can support such a feature. I will check yours."

"It's not that I don't trust the Chitzas…"

"I certainly do not," Sprig interrupted. "I value my e-consciousness. I expect to complete this mission and return home, better informed, enlightened, if possible, but whole."

"I'm with you there," Daniel said. He had little concern about an individual crewmember doing something crazy; Zeeno clearly had complete control over the ship. But the captain himself had been less than open and might still be withholding some aspect of the mission that could increase their risk.

Just hand over the map to Zeeno? Or maintain control? Tennah's offer seemed sensible, but not if it came with an element of deceit. His partnership with the captain would survive or fail based on trust. He had already demanded honesty from Zeeno, he could expect nothing less from himself.

"Thanks, Tennah. When we get to the ship, if the voice control option is available, let me know. But don't hide it. I want to see how our captain reacts."

Tennah smiled and walked on.

Junipers gave way to the deciduous trees of what Daniel had named Sherwood Forest. An hour later, they reached the clearing where the Chitza drop tank still stood. It had been a twenty-four-hour detour, but Daniel had learned much in the process and now had a map courier at his side. Mission accomplished, as long as Tennah completed what she'd promised.

Only one small issue remained. Daniel opened the hatch to the drop tank and peered inside. "It's a tight fit."

Tennah stood nearly as tall as Daniel. Packing two inside the cigar tube would require some finesse and an agreement that full body contact would be part of the deal.

Tennah stuck her head inside. "Perhaps we should remove our weapons, so no one is sliced."

She reached behind and pulled the anticipated second knife from a hidden scabbard. Daniel handed the knife she'd given him back. "I certainly don't need it, and if you're starting a revolution…" She took the knife without objections.

Daniel climbed in first and pressed against the metal wall, now cold and slightly damp from being parked overnight. Tennah followed, sliding a soft body against his. Her braided hair pushed against his nose. She smelled faintly of salt mixed with the ever-present smoke of her cliffside village.

"Sorry for the close quarters," Daniel said. He squeezed an arm over her shoulder to reach the hatch button. When it closed, the tight confines suddenly felt claustrophobic. Daniel pressed the only other button, the one that would automatically recall the drop tank to the Chitza ship.

At first, nothing happened. Then a green light flickered on, and helicopter blades outside began to turn.

For their return to orbit, their movements would be limited, with faces just inches apart and body contact no different than two people crammed into one sleeping bag. Tennah didn't seem to mind. As she had explained, she'd done this kind of thing before.

The rotor wound up, increasing in pitch. "Is your ship larger?" she asked. Maybe she did mind.

"If you'd asked me that when I stepped onboard two days ago, I would have said no. But compared to this tube, it's downright roomy."

Sprig climbed up Daniel's collar. Via a shank of hair, the leaf hoisted itself to the top of Daniel's head. It said it wanted a better view of a small control panel but getting away from the high volume of Human - Afeesh Tm exhales was more likely.

Seconds later the rotors came up to full speed. Branches outside swayed from the turbulent air. They lifted off the ground and rose above the trees.

The noise of thumping rotors forced Tennah to speak up. "Your wife has darker skin. Are all your women that way?" At such close proximity, it was only natural that physical features would be the topic of conversation. Her own skin color was closer to Daniel's—pale.

"Skin color isn't a male-female thing. We have several races within our species. You don't?"

"No. But some forest creatures do. Variations in color within the same animal."

The forest spread out below them. Daniel could make out the village where he'd found Osperus.

"Do you mate with only one woman?" Idle conversation continued. Daniel didn't mind. How many times would he share a flight with someone who looks vaguely Human but isn't?

"Depends on what you mean by mating. We tend to sample our options until we find the right person. Then we settle in."

"And your wife is the right person?"

It was probably the most profound question he'd heard from anyone in years. The obvious answer was yes, but that hardly answered her intent for asking.

Daniel lifted his eyes up. "How far have we come from home, Sprig?"

"Fifteen gigaparsecs," the leaf said from an indentation atop Daniel's hair.

He returned his attention to the not-so-exotic alien woman one inch away from his face. "There's your answer. I've traveled farther than the distance crossed by light from the very first star formed at the beginning of the universe. Why have I come so far? To find her... to pull her to safety... to bring her home with me. What does that tell you?"

"That you want her back very much."

Daniel's throat tightened. "It's simple. I'll go where I need to go to find her. And if I don't find her... there won't be much reason to go home at all."

Tennah placed a hand over Daniel's heart. "Uncanny how much alike we are."

"Yes," he said, covering her hand with his own. "Uncanny."

17 VECTOR

DANIEL AND TENNAH REMAINED WEDGED inside the drop tank for another five minutes while its automatic maneuvering systems brought them to the scout ship's orbit. The black wedge appeared outside the windows. The tank slowed, and with a gentle bump docked to the flat base of the ship.

The hatch hissed open, and Veronica stuck her head inside. "Gotcha back! And you've brought a visitor, I see."

"Glad to be back," Daniel said.

He squeezed out first, then helped Tennah. The Afeesh Tm woman glanced around the lower deck of the ship. Beets looked up from her workstation, grumbled, then returned to whatever she'd been doing.

Daniel waved a hand. "This is Tennah, Sibyl of the Kyan Ta, Protector of Afeesh Tm."

Tennah seemed impressed that he had remembered the whole title. "We'll need to get the revolution underway before that last part matters."

He still hoped to avoid getting caught up in her revolution. He had accepted his role as an arms dealer, but he'd need to clear a few more hurdles before his plan could be put in place.

Veronica introduced herself. Tennah seemed perfectly comfortable with the large differences in size, shape, and skin coverings between the species. "Welcome aboard," Veronica said. "Uh... why exactly are you here?"

Daniel pointed. "She's the map."

"Really?" Veronica walked around Tennah like a sculpture available for purchase. When she came around to the side where the fishhook panel covered her head, Veronica tapped her own head. "It's in there?"

"To be downloaded and configured to your systems," Tennah said.

"Great, let's get to it!" Zeeno clambered down the ladder from the upper deck. He did his own quick inspection of Tennah, keeping his distance.

Sprig hopped down Daniel's sleeve and leaped across to a shelf beneath a ventilation duct. Air blew across the leaf's surface, fluttering its edges with a gentle massage. It seemed purposeful.

While Sprig recharged, Daniel pulled Zeeno aside. "A word with you please, Captain, before we get to the map." He tugged the Chitza back to the ladder, far enough not to be heard.

"The map doesn't come for free," Daniel whispered.

Zeeno shrugged. "I figured as much, what does she want?"

"She's fighting a battle with Osperus. She wants weapons, but I told her we have none. That's true, isn't it?"

Zeeno hemmed. "Close enough."

Daniel ignored the equivocation. Zeeno probably had a dozen secrets still under wraps. "Regardless, I have a better plan for her, but I'm afraid it comes with bad news."

"How bad?"

"Well, first there's the revolution. We need to steer clear of that, and now that she's onboard, I think we can. She's what they call a Sibyl, a map courier of sorts. She says she knows where the gamma blast originated, and when she configures the map she can insert a waypoint there."

"Damn fine. Exactly where we need to go."

"But that brings up the second thing. We're heading to a boundary of some kind. It's at the edge of a place they call the Chaos Field."

"Good."

"Actually, it's bad, and not in a fun bad way."

Zeeno hesitated. Daniel cut him off before he could start into the joys of badness. "The Chaos Field is… chaotic. Survival is a coin toss. The Sibyls create what they call a probability vector for navigation. If we're lucky, we'll find our friends at the boundary, but if we have to cross, it gets dicey from there."

"High risk is what we do," Zeeno said.

"There's more bad news."

Zeeno braced himself against the ladder, and Daniel continued as gently as he could. "I confirmed that the first Chitza mission never left this planet. It appears all crewmembers were murdered."

"By Osperus?"

"I think so, yes."

Zeeno nodded bravely. "They knew the risks."

"They were trailblazers," Daniel offered, doing his best not to dwell since Chitzas never did.

"So, if we help this lady, we avenge their deaths, right?"

"We do. And here's how. The Mission One scout ship is apparently still in orbit. Tennah wants to borrow it in exchange for the map. It seems like a reasonable trade, but it's Chitza property. Not mine to give."

"Done. Give her the ship. Setup the map. We get on with our rescue mission."

"She'll need help learning its systems. I'm confident she'll pick it up quickly—that panel on her head gives her some pretty impressive abilities."

"Done. We'll find the ship, and Aussik can show her the ropes."

Now came the hardest part. "About those ropes. Can you reconfigure the compression turbines to expand 4-D space at an external target location? You know, instead of creating a bubble surrounding the ship, create it somewhere else?"

Zeeno shrugged. "Not standard practice but no problem. Beets could get it set up faster than you're explaining it."

Daniel pumped a fist. "That's it then. You're a fine captain with a great crew."

"That's it?"

"That's it."

"You said you had bad news. This is good news. Why are you Humans so damn timid about things?"

Daniel smiled, shaking his head. "I don't know. Just in our nature, I guess."

Zeeno made a straight line for Tennah. "You got your ship. Deal?"

Puzzled, Tennah finally asked the question Daniel had expected all along. "If this ship has no weapons, how can I stop Osperus?"

Daniel hoped his answer would make sense to her. She had already proven that she knew something about quantum physics. His proposal might be out on the edge of crazy, but he'd seen it in action twice. Once when the Chinese had been caught zapping space junk in orbit around Earth. And another, at Fermilab, when Nala had accidentally imploded a spherical scoop from the center of her laboratory.

"With compression turbines at your disposal, it won't be hard. You'll simply send him into the void."

"Ha!" yelled Zeeno. "Send him into the void. By Zog, Daniel, you'll make a Chitza crewmember yet!"

The captain yelled through the hole in the ceiling. "Aussik! There's another scout ship in orbit. Find it. Lay in a course."

"Gotcha, Boss," came Aussik's reply from the top deck.

"Beets," Zeeno pointed to his engineer. "When we get there, you're going to help this lady configure the compression turbines to External Targeting Mode. Show her how to set a target."

Eyebrow quills undulated in a slow-motion wave as Beets rolled her eyes. "Whatever."

Zeeno glanced at each of the players in the room. "Everybody happy? Good, let's get that map pulled out of her head." He snapped his claws in a distinctive click. Daniel had never seen such efficiency. He felt somewhat guilty after spending nearly twenty-four hours on the planet simply locating Tennah.

Beets climbed onto her workstation desk and scanned the side of Tennah's head with an electronic wand. "*Fratz!* Whatever she's got in there, it's jockin' big. Four hundred zettabytes."

Zeeno leaped. "What?! Who makes a compression vector that's four hundred zettabytes?"

"Probability vector," Tennah corrected. "You might be surprised by the difference. Every random variation of spacetime, vacuum energy, and quantum fluctuation must be considered and accounted for."

"Not your average line drawn on a map," Daniel suggested, though he really had no better idea than Zeeno as to what Tennah would need to do to reconfigure the navigation.

Tennah leaned past Beets' shoulder and studied the screens on her workstation. She touched a few buttons like she'd already been trained in their use. Maybe she'd just seen so many alien spacecraft systems that she could piece together how they worked.

Finally, she said, "I could make it fit within three hundred zettabytes. But no smaller."

Beets sat down and shook her head. "Damn. We'll have to dump all the audios, books, and vids to fit it in. Plus, the recipes."

Zeeno deflated. "The recipes too? Oh, hell." Zeeno paced, then stopped. "Fine. Just do it."

"You got it, Boss." Beets typed on a small keyboard, held one claw over the final key and pressed, wincing as she did. Zeeno stared at the floor. Veronica bit her lip, sighing.

With a wiped-clean data store, Beets finished the job by plugging a thin wire into a port on Tennah's head and routing the other end into the panel above her workstation. Lights flashed. A progress meter crawled even though Daniel imagined terabytes were flying through the hard wire connector every second.

Having lost their in-flight entertainment, the mood among the Chitzas remained glum. Eventually, Beets reported, "Almost done."

Tennah seemed no worse for the somewhat intrusive download. She stood patiently with eyes closed until the last byte had been extracted, then unplugged the wire herself. "May I borrow your seat?" she asked Beets.

Beets grudgingly gave it up, and Tennah squatted onto the Chitza-sized seat like an adult on a child's chair. She studied the screens and within seconds was touching, punching, and dialing.

After a few minutes, she pointed to one particularly complex diagram on the screen and explained to Beets. "Computed waypoints will display automatically. Never skip ahead in the sequence, but if you see this red failure indicator, reset to the last known waypoint, then restart the sequence. That will work one hundred percent of the time in normal space, and about twenty percent when inside the Chaos Field."

"Not liking those odds," Beets grumbled. "Hey Boss, are we really going into this Chaos Field?" She'd been listening to their conversation. In a ship this small it wasn't surprising.

"If we have to, sure," Zeeno said casually.

Tennah stood. "You'll need voice confirmation."

Zeeno put paws on hips. "What does that mean?" Tennah nodded toward Daniel. Zeeno glanced quickly between Tennah and Daniel. "His voice?"

"It's only an option," Daniel said, unsure if Tennah had already configured it.

"What?!" Zeeno's paws shot up in the air. "You two are taking over my ship?" Beets backed away. Veronica stared at the floor, eyes wide and lips zipped.

Zeeno scrambled onto the desktop at Beets' workstation, and directly a steely, unblinking stare at Daniel. "Have you been planning this all along?"

Daniel shook his head. He'd asked Tennah to find out if a voice override could be done. He'd also asked her not to hide it. Now it was time to get things straight. "This is no mutiny, Zeeno. You're still the captain. My job was to get the map. I did. Now I'm adding some advice. A map that hints of mysteries beyond our universe could be a significant temptation, especially for high seas adventurers like yourselves."

Zeeno shrugged.

Daniel maintained their eye lock. "The mission is search and rescue. Tennah has given us a tool to deal with dangers we might encounter, but there's every reason to believe we won't need anything more than her first waypoint... the location at the boundary where she knows radiation leaks through. We go there. We get out. Nothing more. Agreed?"

"You worry too much," Zeeno said.

"I worry just enough," Daniel answered. "Focus on search and rescue. Do that, and I won't need a voice override."

Zeeno reached out. "I'm in."

Daniel shook hand to paw. "Then I am too."

Zeeno hopped down from the workstation table. "Oh... don't worry. Just because we have the map, doesn't mean we're going to jettison you. You're way too famous."

The thought of being abandoned now that Zeeno had everything he needed had crossed Daniel's mind. But if avoiding bad press back home was Zeeno's only reasoning, their relationship still had some gaps.

Tennah noted that the voice override had been disabled and returned control to Beets. The Chitza plopped down into her seat and stared in awe, mixed with annoyance. "Damn, that's something."

Hundreds of orange pentagons overlayed a complex wiring diagram at key intersections. When Beets touched a pentagon, another diagram popped up with still more pentagons. Subsystems within subsystems.

Zeeno glanced over Beets' shoulder. "Let's see what it does. Fire up the compression vector—*probability* vector—whatever the hell it is."

Beets pressed a button and studied the changes on the screen. "Looks normal."

Tennah explained, "Waypoints are fixed coordinates while we're still in ordinary space. They only become quantum probabilities inside the Chaos Field. Your probability vector is configured. You're ready to go."

****

An hour later, and with Aussik at the controls, one Chitza scout ship slipped gently into place beneath a second. The two identical black wedges aligned, then docked. Daniel hadn't noticed an indentation in the ceiling of the top deck, but once Zeeno pulled a few handles, a hatch opened with a hiss.

He peered into a new passageway overhead. Another black metal hatch remained closed only a few feet away.

"Ping 'em," Zeeno told Aussik. "Just to be sure."

The ghost ship gave no answer to Aussik's hail. With a few more button clicks, and a password entered at his control panel, the hatch swung open.

"Going zero," Aussik called out, and gravity disappeared as though it had been nothing but an aberration all along.

Zeeno floated through the hatchway first and Daniel followed. They entered the lower deck of the ghost ship approximately where his Human-sized seat had been affixed in their own ship.

Lights inside were dim, the air stale. Nothing moved.

Zeeno pushed off, sailing across the lower deck. Two workstations stood empty. Putting this ghost ship into use against the tyrant responsible for killing its Chitza crew seemed like reasonable justice. At the very least, it eased Daniel's aversion to becoming an arms dealer for a war he had no business joining.

On the upper deck, a few lights blinked across the cockpit control panel, but the crew had left nothing behind to collect for loved ones back home—if there were any. Aussik floated up and flipped a switch. Gravity slowly returned and they each found their footing once more.

"Pull the data," Zeeno said.

Aussik flipped a metal cover and twisted a handle beneath, releasing a cartridge not much different than one of those old 3.5-inch floppy disks. He handed it to Zeeno.

"Show her how it works but make it quick." Zeeno departed with the data pack while Aussik waved Tennah over, who had just come up the ladder.

The training didn't take long, once Tennah managed to wedge herself into the small Chitza cockpit. She looked out of place, but she seemed to absorb everything Aussik taught her. There were only a few questions about how to use a joystick to maneuver in ordinary space, but once completed, Tennah said with conviction, "I've got it. Thank you for the lesson."

She pried herself out of the tiny seat and Daniel waved her to the ladder. "That's only half of it. Let's check with Beets on the rest."

On the lower deck, Beets had the engineering workstation powered up, its screens covered with diagrams and data. Tennah was already familiar with the workstation, if not the adjustments Beets had made.

"See this?" Beets pointed to a crosshair on a map. "It's now set to External Targeting Mode, and it's registered to the surface of your planet. Drag the crosshairs to your target—anywhere on the planet—set the spherical cut diameter, then tell any friends in the area to run like hell. When you power up the compression turbines, that chunk of 3-D is going away."

"Where?" asked Tennah.

"Don't ask," said Beets. "People, buildings, rocks, trees. Poof. Far away."

Daniel nodded. "I've seen it myself. It's like scooping a handful of sand and tossing it in the air. It's just gone. Technically, it's pushed into another dimension, but 4-D is nothing you can see or even point to."

"It's permanent?" Tennah asked.

Beets shrugged. "Well, if you have a ChitzaKit you can set a timer. The timer goes off, and *whomp*—rocks, trees, and people pop back to 3-D. Still alive, too, if you do it right."

"That could be useful." Tennah tapped her upper lip just like Humans did when they were planning something devious.

Beets shook her head. "Except that we don't have a ChitzaKit. This is a rescue mission, not first contact." Beets held up a paw, then rummaged through a drawer next to the workstation. "Almost forgot, I'm not on my ship. What do you know... here's one."

She groaned while lifting an oval metal plate from the drawer, then slammed it onto the desktop. About an inch thick, the polished disk had a curving line down its middle, which made it look like a 6 and a 9 fused together.

Daniel had seen one before. Years ago, discovered inside an empty Soyuz capsule. "Wow, a yin-yang!"

"ChitzaKit," Beets corrected.

Daniel's head spun with memories of the Soyuz incident—some that now made a lot more sense. "So, it wasn't Core after all, at least not directly. Chitzas brought our missing astronauts home!"

Beets shrugged. "Eh, we do that sometimes when rank beginners get into trouble." She ignored Daniel's open-mouth astonishment, instead pointing Tennah to a slot on the wall. "Drop the plate into the injection tube before you turn on the compression turbines. Once it's inserted into the bubble, the ChitzaKit will know what to do. You'll have about ten hours before it whomps back to 3-D."

Daniel imagined that anything Tennah sliced out of the planet's surface could be dropped somewhere else, possibly even onto the second planet in their solar system. It might be a good way to exile a dictator if that was the justice Tennah had in mind. He also realized that the same thing had happened to the Soyuz crew. They'd been offset only slightly into 4-D space, but the yin-yang's countdown had safely brought them back to three-dimensional space. Chitza technology, as it turned out.

Beets left, leaving Daniel alone with Tennah in her newly acquired scout ship. "What do you think?"

"Yesterday I was worried," Tennah said. "But today... I think we will win."

"Be careful. You have a lot of advanced technology at your fingertips. Don't let it go to your head."

Tennah turned to face him. "I am no tyrant. My goal is simple. Remove Osperus from power and let our people return to a modest but equitable life. We cannot avoid your technology, but we can use it wisely, then return it to its owners."

Daniel provided his last, best advice as an arms dealer to the Kyan Ta. "Go win your battle. Create a better society. But when you're done, if the Chitzas haven't returned to claim their ship, bury it."

Five hundred years from now, if the Afeesh Tm developed an ongoing interest in science, then advances in technology would come with matching knowledge. Until then, technology without science could get them into trouble. It was hard to say how the Afeesh Tm would fare in their struggle, but he'd made his deal and had learned in the process.

"Best wishes, revolutionary," Daniel told his new friend.

Tennah's eyes held a faraway look. The Kyan Ta leader put one hand over the stone blade at her hip and acknowledged with a quiet nod.

Daniel dropped back down through the hatch between ships, closing Tennah's side and then their own as he went. He poked his head into the cockpit where Zeeno and Aussik studied data scrawled across a display. "We're ready to go, Captain."

"You bet we are. Check this out." Zeeno pointed to the display. "That's the cartridge data from Mission One. It matches what we thought. They arrived here, took the drop tank to the surface, and never came back. But then, Aussik got an idea to compare the data from Mission Two to the navigation vector your smart lady just installed." He nodded to Aussik. "Show him."

Aussik touched two side-by-side lines on the display, one blue, one yellow. "Blue is the final navigation vector from Mission Two, pulled from their message. Yellow is the vector Tennah just installed, including the waypoint she says is at the boundary." A white circle stood at the top of the yellow line. Drawn next to the circle was a dagger icon with animated glints along its sharp edges. It looked surprisingly like the blade of the Kyan Ta.

Thank you Tennah. Even a scout ship novice like himself could watch over Aussik's shoulder and monitor their progress toward the dagger waypoint, clearly their final destination.

"I see two independently derived vectors, and both are well aligned," Daniel said. Zeeno seemed pleased. Perhaps open cooperation had finally created a fully functioning team.

"The new waypoint clinches it," Zeeno said. "As long as it sits on the boundary, that's as far as we need to go. A scout ship pilot doesn't abandon data then keep flying. They'll be there."

Zeeno yelled to his crew to take their stations for departure. Feeling more confident than ever, Daniel hurried to the lower deck to take his own seat.

He plucked Sprig from the nearby shelf where the leaf had been recharging and placed it back on his shoulder. He patted his leafy friend. "You know, Sprig, we've come a long way, but I get the sense that our journey is just beginning."

"The universe is larger than I had anticipated," Sprig said, which was quite the comment coming from a cosmologist.

"Larger and stranger," Daniel agreed. A boundary of some kind lay ahead. Gamma radiation too. But with the destination now pinpointed, they would soon reach a damaged Chitza scout ship and rescue its survivors.

Daniel watched out the window as their ship eased away from its twin. Inside, Tennah would be plotting her coup; he wished her luck, she'd need it.

Turbines spun up. A low rumble echoed through the floor.

Zeeno yelled once more. "Good job everyone. Final leg. Success is within our reach."

"Discover or die trying!" all four Chitzas yelled in unison.

18 DARKNESS

SOME PEOPLE AVOID risk at every turn. Others calculate the odds then proceed with caution. The most audacious among us simply close their eyes and jump. And then there are Chitzas.

Having obtained the needed map from Afeesh Tm who might have otherwise turned them into fur pelts, the mood of the crew turned jubilant, and their ship transformed into a party zone. Ever the source of inspiration, Captain Zeeno located the last remaining digital music that hadn't been erased to make room for the newly acquired *probability vector* and piped its exotic sounds throughout the ship for all to enjoy.

Grooving to a strong drumbeat, Aussik jammed the big red handle all the way forward, bringing them to Tau minus fifteen and another dizzying shift into 5-D space. New galaxies raced by, looking a lot like the uncountable galaxies they'd already passed.

On the lower deck, Veronica was out of her seat, dancing down the aisle. She twitched to each side, kicked her legs, and ruffled her quills like a mating peacock to the syncopated rhythm of the spirited music. Even Beets, who remained seated at her workstation, rapped on her desk each time a cadence of drums restarted another chorus.

"Wooooooo dawg!" Veronica squealed as she danced past Daniel, her arms churning and hips swaying. "It's Chiiiiitza time!" With paws in the air, she brushed erect quills against his leg, then proved the provocative move had been intentional when she did it again going the other direction. Daniel tapped his toe and bounced his head to the undeniably catchy drumbeat.

When the music crescendoed to an intense drum finale, Veronica screamed at her highest ear-splitting pitch. "Lovvve this place!"

"Damn straight!" Zeeno yelled down. "Chitzas do it better!"

It was hard to imagine a tighter crew or a better captain, no matter what Sprig might think of this vivacious species. The intelligent leaf had remained stoic throughout their impromptu celebration, latching firmly onto Daniel's shirt, and ducking behind his collar each time Veronica danced by.

"Is it over?" the leaf said once the ruckus had died down.

"I hope not," Daniel said. He felt their enthusiasm, even if only as a spectator. "If every team had this much motivation..." His logical mind would have normally finished with something about productivity going through the roof, but if Nala had taught him anything it was to enjoy the moment. Too much analysis killed the best of moods.

Veronica tapped Daniel's shoulder, and Sprig cowered. "Next time, I'm swinging with you, little guy." The leaf was less than half her height, but they might still make a sharp dance couple.

Enthusiastic hedgehog twirls oversized cherry leaf around the dance floor. Daniel wouldn't mind having a video of that to take home.

"Status," Zeeno called out.

"Tau locked at fifteen," Aussik answered.

"Turbines... good enough," yelled Beets.

Dancing Veronica jumped back into her seat. "All systems green and mean. And this tired girl needs a ChitzaPop. Anyone else?"

"Blue," Aussik responded.

"Orange," yelled Zeeno.

"Ehhh, I'll go with black," Beets said.

"Pick a color," Veronica told Daniel.

"Um… green."

"You got it."

He half expected a frozen treat but when Veronica finished rummaging around inside a cabinet, she returned with a collection of five colored peas in one paw. Daniel picked up the green one. Veronica tossed a blue pea in her mouth and bit down. A distinctive pop sounded from beneath her thick facial fur.

"Mmm." Veronica swallowed. "Try yours."

Daniel crunched down. A sweet and possibly alcoholic liquid poured from the ruptured ball. What would have been a full mouthful for a Chitza was a tiny shot glass for him, but he enjoyed the surprisingly thirst-quenching drink. "Good. Kind of like a bourbon and 7 Up on the rocks."

"Greens produce a nice mellow. Try the blue one next time, it'll jazz you up," Veronica said, heading off to distribute the rest. She looked back over her shoulder and smirked. "Oh, and don't forget the pink ChitzaPop, but save that one for when your wife is here." Veronica grinned like a fox at Daniel as she climbed the ladder.

A few minutes later she returned empty handed and with a more sober look in her eyes. "Hey, little leaf guy? Captain needs you up in the cockpit."

Daniel stood. "I'll take you up."

A call for Sprig? Zeeno must have seen something ahead that required a cosmologist. Daniel climbed up the ladder and poked his head into the small cockpit. Both Zeeno and Aussik studied their control panels.

"What's up?"

Zeeno pointed out the forward viewport. "That."

He pointed to nothing but darkness. No stars. No galaxies, not even in the weirdly distorted view of 3-D objects rushing out of a 5-D tunnel. Their latest view outside felt unnatural, like someone had drawn a black shade over the glass. With nothing to see, the view forward provided no sense of movement, yet Aussik had reported Tau minus fifteen only minutes ago.

"Do you mind?" Sprig asked. "I'd like to get a better view."

Daniel set the leaf onto Zeeno's control panel, and Sprig hopped up to the viewport's glass. He scurried along its bottom edge from one side to the other, then back again.

The complete absence of light in any direction baffled Daniel. Something fundamental must have changed but with all the partying on the lower deck, he hadn't been paying attention to the last few megaparsecs. "How long has it been this way?"

"For a while now," Zeeno answered. "We've passed through pockets of empty space on this trip, but nothing like this."

No more stars, galaxies, or even hazy blobs. They'd left all structure behind. If the universe had distant corners, this one was beginning to feel extraordinarily remote.

Sprig finished its impromptu survey and turned around. "I detect no light in any part of the spectrum. In fact, few quantum particles of any type. We have entered a void."

"Gotta say, it matches the vector," said Aussik. His display showed their path as a yellow line crossing a black background. The only other mark was a white circle with Tennah's dagger icon next to it.

Sprig continued, "A void of this scale does not conform to cosmological theory, which assumes a uniform distribution of matter, a direct result of the inflation that occurred in the first moment of existence."

"Translation?" Zeeno asked Daniel.

"Sprig is relating standard Big Bang theory. At its birth, the universe expanded from a sub-microscopic dot to a volume about the size of a solar system, all in less than a millisecond. Then inflation abruptly ended, transforming a stupendous amount of energy into a stupendous amount of matter. That's where every particle, atom, star, and galaxy came from—the sudden end of inflation and the beginning of our expanding universe."

"So, what's this?" Zeeno pointed to the blackness outside.

"Not accounted for in theory," Sprig answered. "We have reached the edge of knowledge."

"Or the edge of the universe?" Zeeno asked.

Sprig didn't answer. Daniel had no answer either except for a fundamental concept he believed to be true: regardless of the size of the universe—even an infinite size—the matter contained within it *must be finite*. The Big Bang ensured such a limit. A finite amount of energy at birth could not create an infinite amount of matter. All those galaxies and stars had to end somewhere, even if space itself didn't.

Zeeno absorbed the science but insisted they continue as planned. Daniel had no argument. No matter how dark, there were people to be rescued out there somewhere. They continued on, with no indicator of their motion other than a Tau compression factor displayed on Aussik's control panel.

Sprig hopped back to Daniel's arm. Without making a sound, the tip of its leaf jerked toward the ladder. If the leaf had eyes, they would have been subversively twitching in that direction too. Daniel got the hint. "Back in a minute, guys."

He descended the ladder and headed for the aft bulkhead where he had to crouch to keep from bumping his head on a myriad of ductwork covering the ceiling.

Once they were out of earshot on the lower deck, Sprig hopped off Daniel's arm onto a horizontal pipe bolted to the wall at eye level. "I have a theory." The leaf began pacing back and forth on its stretchable three-footed stem.

Daniel waited in silence until Sprig paused in its pacing.

"The previous mission measured a blast of ultra-gamma radiation at 10^{21} electron-volts. If correct, this number represents the most intense radiation ever recorded. The only event in history capable of producing such a value was the Big Bang itself and then only at its birth. Therefore, the previous mission may have discovered evidence of a *new* Big Bang."

Daniel understood right away. "That's the Penrose theory, right? A new bang springing from an existing universe."

"Not quite. Your Penrose theorized that new bangs would arise from the vacuum energy of empty space. He suggested a linked chain where a new universe is triggered when an expanding old universe finally reaches heat death."

"And since our universe is still very much alive…"

"This theory is ruled out. But there are other cosmological models that suggest finite space confined to a bubble universe."

"Which implies a boundary and something outside the bubble." Daniel was aware of the cosmology models even if he hadn't kept up with recent developments. Now that humanity had joined Sagittarius Novus there were far more experts in every scientific field.

"Tennah spoke of a boundary," Sprig said. "Cosmologically speaking, boundaries are tricky. But any bubble model requires something outside. A containment structure of some kind."

"The Chaos Field, you think?"

"Possibly."

The history of the word 'chaos' matched Sprig's concept. Ancient Greek philosophers had used the same word for the confused state of existence prior to the creation of the universe. A place before and outside of the universe.

"Horizons I can deal with, but a physical boundary? How does space end? And what could possibly be on the other side?"

Sprig paused in its pacing. "There are two possibilities, and both have been examined by cosmologists. Shall I describe them?"

"Please do."

"One is the eternal inflation model based on your description to Captain Zeeno."

"Exponential expansion. Two, four, eight, sixteen, et cetera. Very small to very big just like that." Daniel snapped his fingers.

"Yes. Inflation is well accepted as the correct theory governing the first millisecond of existence. But the *eternal* inflation model proposes that—outside our universe—exponential inflation never ended. It continues even now."

Daniel rubbed his temples. "Ouch. I've read about that. Space doubling in size every second, and somehow continuing to do that over billions of years. It's really hard to get your head around something that big."

"I do not get headaches," Sprig noted, "but I understand them."

Daniel stopped rubbing his temples. "As they say, the universe is not only stranger than we imagine, it is stranger than we *can* imagine."

"It gets worse," Sprig said.

"Of course, it does."

"There is the second possibility for what may lie outside of our universe… I don't wish to harm your brain. Are you ready?"

Daniel shrugged.

Sprig continued. "The second possibility is that *outside* is a vacuum energy landscape of the quantum wave function that fluctuates in eleven-dimensional string space."

Daniel rolled his eyes. He had definitely *not* read about that one.

"I warned you," Sprig said, pointing the tip of its leaf at Daniel.

"Okay, I'll bite. What is a vacuum energy landscape?"

"A combination of things. First, it is a quantum field, which is simply the mathematical probability of finding a quantum particle at a location in three-dimensional space. In this case, the quantum particle would represent not just our whole universe but every possible universe. The probability of a particular universe coming into existence is then computed by the quantum wave function, an equation introduced in your history by Erwin Schrödinger."

"I get it, I think." Sprig had just described any quantum field and its relationship to a quantum particle, though he'd taken the concept to the grandest possible scale. Strangely, a quantum field also matched Tennah's description of the Chaos Field. Sprig, a certified cosmologist, and Tennah, the leader of a decidedly non-scientific tribe who carried stone weapons seemed to be converging upon the same answer.

"The second part of this theory is the landscape itself. Not space, and not even three-dimensional. Some cosmologists say this landscape could be eleven-dimensional as proposed by string theory. Ten dimensions of space and one of time. Overlay the quantum field onto the landscape of ten-dimensional string space, then introduce the vacuum energy of empty space and a nonzero probability of quantum fluctuation, and you have it."

Daniel did his best to piece it together. "Um... a probability... that vacuum energy exists at a given location within this landscape?"

"Quite close. Picture the landscape as hills and valleys. Something like this." The leaf stretched its point and a colorful projection appeared above the tip, a three-dimensional view across a wave pattern spreading out in two directions like a frothy ocean surface.

"The highest probability for a quantum wave to become a quantum particle always occurs in valleys which represent stable potential energy. In this case, the valleys are places that could power a new bang."

"So, somewhere in this landscape is a valley of potential energy that aligns with a high probability of its existence."

"Well done. A probability landscape that fluctuates chaotically will eventually create a unique quantum particle called an inflaton. The inflaton then explodes exponentially into a new physical universe. Many valleys produce many bangs and many universes from the landscape. In fact, string theorists estimate the number of distinct vacua—the ever-changing hills and valleys within the landscape—to be in excess of 10^{600}. That is, one followed by six hundred zeros, a spectacularly large number. It is the number of potential universes that could be created."

"Colossal numbers," Daniel said. "I guess we shouldn't expect anything less from reality. So, which of these models do you think we're dealing with?"

"I have no idea."

"But you said you had a theory."

"I just told you. The ultra-gamma radiation may have come from a new Big Bang which was generated by either one of these theories of cosmology."

Daniel absorbed the heavy thinking as best he could. Sprig had been helpful in outlining options, connecting scientific theory to Tennah's words and to the evidence of ultra-gamma radiation. Cosmology sometimes ventured into unverifiable topics, but while this was primarily a rescue mission, they might also be in a position to answer one of the biggest questions of existence— where did our universe come from?

"Thanks, Sprig. If you're concerned about including the Chitzas, I wouldn't be. They're pragmatic explorers who could use a dose of pure science now and then, and Zeeno has already shown that he values your input. If Nala was here, I think she'd agree. Quantum physics can get weird fast. I suggest we advise the Chitzas, not hide from them."

Daniel twisted as Aussik tapped him on the back of one leg. Their copilot rarely left his controls and, with head quills standing on end, seemed disturbed about something. "It's not black anymore. Come on." Aussik waved a paw.

With Sprig riding, Daniel followed Aussik back to the cockpit. The view out the forward window hadn't changed from its featureless black.

"Did you see—"Daniel started.

"Just wait," said Aussik. Zeeno stared out the window too, scanning from side to side. Their vision might be better than Daniel's. He leaned forward for a better view.

"There!" Zeeno pointed, but whatever fleeting thing he'd spotted, Daniel had missed it. They continued to watch in silence.

Out of the corner of his eye, a light passed. No more than a pinprick and gone in a flash. A second later, another streak briefly sparked then vanished to black like a meteor in a dark night sky.

"You see them now?" Aussik said, and Daniel nodded.

"Any ideas?" Zeeno asked. A longer stripe nearer to the viewport's center was the brightest yet and slightly blue in color.

Several more popped up randomly like the first drops of rain on a moving car's windshield. Then from the darkness, a dim horizontal line formed. It glowed with a steady white light unlike the flashes that continued to sprinkle above and below.

"Whatever it is, we seem to be getting closer," Daniel said. "Ideas, Sprig?"

"Not enough data. Analyzing," the leaf said.

Aussik slowed their forward progress in multiple steps. The glowing line brightened considerably, and the scattered flashes grew in frequency and in brightness, becoming a full-fledged fireworks display, left, center, and right. The streaks coming toward them seemed to arise from the horizontal line. Some started blue and changed to green before disappearing. Others were red from start to finish. Still more, the same white color of the horizontal line.

"Getting crazy," Aussik said.

Sprig hopped onto the control panel for a better look. "No detectable gamma radiation. So far, it is visible, infrared, and ultraviolet only."

An intense spray of streaks now filled the view, silently displaying a rainbow of colors. The horizontal line brightened too, now glowing in fainter blues and greens that varied along its length, like a Christmas decoration capable of varying its color.

"How far away do you think we are?" Daniel asked.

"Close," Aussik answered. "Our waypoint is just ahead."

"Drop to 4-D. Let's ease into this," Zeeno commanded. Aussik made the adjustments, producing an instant feeling of dizziness while dramatically clarifying the scene ahead.

The horizontal white line expanded vertically, separating into multiple colors. Long undulating waves of blue, pink, white, and green stretched across their path in an ever-churning cloud. Multicolored streaks continued to shoot out toward the ship, but the view from 4-D now revealed the source of these sparks—a roiling cloud above the waves like a thunderstorm in fast motion. The overall effect felt like floating on a raft near the brink of Niagara Falls where billowing mists hinted of an apocalyptic waterfall ahead that threatened to pull them over the edge.

"We're there," Aussik said, pulling his red lever to neutral. "The dagger waypoint."

Doing his best to ignore the fireworks ahead, Daniel searched for nearby wreckage but found none. Their position in 4-D made picking out 3-D objects about as likely as recognizing someone's face on a flat paper photograph held edge-on. To be effective, they'd need to be smart about their search. But if anyone had the tools, this crew did.

19 CAPTAIN

"WELCOME TO THE EDGE of the universe," Zeeno announced.

The dramatic performance of undulating blue, white, and pink waves, turbulent mist, and multicolored sparks continued to fill the ship's forward viewport. The edge of the universe—if that's what this inexplicable boundary represented—seemed determined to live up to its moniker. Daniel could almost hear the thunderous waterfall ahead, could almost feel the vibrations as the substance of physical space crashed onto the surreal landscape of whatever indescribable reality lay beyond.

"Hell of a place to find a lost crew," Aussik said.

"They had a good view," Zeeno answered. "Time to do our job. Find them. Bring them home."

"Chitzas helping Chitzas!" Aussik yelled. Crewmembers below deck echoed his cheer, with Veronica adding, "And one Human too!" Daniel appreciated the inter-species camaraderie. Nala felt near.

While Aussik manipulated switches and dials over his head, Zeeno swiveled in his seat, facing Daniel and Sprig. "Here's the deal. Our scanners are good, and the data pack will give itself away with a transponder ping. Find the data pack and we find the crew too—if they managed to get into a 4-D bubble in time. But no guarantees, so don't get your hopes up."

Aussik studied one of the displays in front of him. "Nothing yet." He adjusted one dial and studied further. A magenta-colored disc surrounded their current position, but the display revealed no other bubbles regardless of zoom setting.

Zeeno tapped the quills on his chin. "We should have heard the ping by now. Double check the coordinates."

Aussik compared two screens. "We're at the waypoint, no question. And still aligned with their final vector, plus or minus."

Zeeno nodded thoughtfully. "Okay… no reason to panic. If the scanners can't find them, we'll do it the old fashioned way, with radar, infrared, and 3-D eyeballs. They're out there… unless they got zapped into electrons and protons." He mumbled the last part.

"How far is *out there*?" Daniel asked. Every position came with a margin of error. Aussik had already hinted as much.

"In your measures, a search area a thousand kilometers on a side will do," Zeeno answered.

Daniel did the math in his head. "So, a billion cubic kilometers to search. Small compared to light-years, but that's a sizeable chunk of space. Might take a while."

"Yes, it could. While we're here, how about you scientific types monitor for gamma. If you detect anything, we'll jump to 5-D. Hell, we'll climb to 6-D if we have to."

If Zeeno had access to six dimensions he'd kept it well hidden. Maybe it didn't matter. If Big Bang energy levels were nearby, the number of ninety-degree angles a captain and his ship were capable of constructing might only provide an illusion of safety.

They'd need to be smart about their search, and Daniel already felt something was missing. He recalled the statement made by the Litian-nolo Operations Commander that the Chitza distress message included data identifying two bubbles of extradimensional space. Yet now, they couldn't find them. Zeeno's dimensional scanner wasn't the problem. The display clearly showed a magenta disc surrounding their own ship.

They were fearless explorers, but Chitzas had their faults. Rushing to a conclusion was one. A good search plan would benefit from a more thoughtful approach, and Daniel could provide it.

"Imagine you're the captain of the previous mission, and you're hovering right here with the same view we have out to this bizarre, sparkling, misty cliff. Your mission is to explore, and your scanners aren't reporting anything bad. What do you do? Stay here and study it? Cross the boundary into the Chaos Field?"

"That's easy. You do a sniff test." Zeeno glanced to Aussik.

Aussik nodded his agreement. "Sniff test, no question."

Zeeno explained. "You drop down to 3-D and take a sample of whatever's out there. Run it through a spectroscopic analyzer to make sure the compression turbines won't get clogged by sucking up this blue-white foggy stuff. If it passes the sniff test, then you move on."

Daniel's mind kicked into high gear. The previous mission's data had indicated a Tau setting of zero. A full stop. He had to be sure. "Can you do a sniff test from 4-D space?"

Zeeno shook his head. "Not if you want accurate results."

"Then the sniff test might be what got them. While they were sampling down in 3-D, the radiation hit."

Zeeno nodded with his head down. "I see what you mean."

They'd come a long way only to identify the lost mission's fatal mistake. Of course, their captain hadn't known that ultra-gamma radiation might be just around the corner. Being the second mission to the edge of the universe had its advantages.

Daniel continued purely from logic. The pilots would need to confirm or poke holes in his thinking. "If they were sniff testing, then the 4-D bubble—two actually—identified in their final message data had nothing to do with them *being* in 4-D. Those bubbles were created *after* the sniff test."

Zeeno shrugged. "Their final message says it all. Abandon data. That's what creates a bubble, and you only do that if you're going down in flames."

"Then where is it? Blasted away by the radiation?"

Sprig spoke up. "Photons, no matter how energetic, follow straight-line paths. A direct collision between two massless particles is extremely rare, though in a high energy plasma a few could have ricocheted into four dimensional space."

"A few?" Daniel clarified. "Enough to give you a sunburn? Or enough to destroy metal, people, and the bubble itself?"

"Somewhere in between," Sprig answered.

"Which implies any abandon data bubble should still be there."

"Yes. It should."

Zeeno swiveled back to the control panel. "If you come up with any genius ideas, let us know, but Aussik and I need to get started on the visual scan." He turned to Aussik and ran down a checklist that involved binoculars and heat sensors. Daniel hardly heard it. His brain wouldn't allow it. They were still missing something important.

A strong shudder shook the ship, rattling seats and knocking Daniel off balance. He gripped the rail at the cockpit entryway's edge and held on tight. Groans deeper in the ship gave a sense of being caught in a giant's grip with enough power to twist carbon fiber ribs and struts.

Aussik lifted both paws off of his control panel. "Wasn't me!" The rattling and groaning soon faded, but nerves remained on high alert.

"Gravitational wave," Sprig said. The leaf braced against a knob on Zeeno's control panel but now stood tall. "Frequency, 30 hertz, amplitude, 0.73 percent."

Gravitational waves—literally ripples through space itself—were ordinarily generated from cataclysmic events involving stellar masses, such as two black holes merging into one. One of the most difficult phenomena in the universe to detect, clever scientists had figured out ways to measure these tiny wiggles of space even with a wave height no larger than a proton.

"How did that wave compare to typical?" Daniel asked Sprig.

Sprig answered with conviction. "At a distance of 100 light-years, two neutron stars in a binary orbit would generate a barely detectable gravitational wave with an amplitude variation of 0.000000001 percent. This wave was a hundred-billion times stronger."

Zeeno shrugged. "What does that mean?"

Daniel provided the answer, and with just as much conviction, "It means there's something big out there pushing space around. Whatever it is, it's close."

Sprig added, "We may be witnessing the physical effects of quantum decoherence on a vast scale. If a quantum field exists on the other side of this boundary, then energy crossing the boundary must decohere as it creates new matter. It may be the reason for the colorful flashes we see."

"I'm not good with waves," Aussik said. "Did that once at the ocean. Hey, get in, get out. That's what I always say."

The pilots returned to their visual plan with a renewed enthusiasm for *get in, get out*. Another disturbance—including a gamma blast—could erupt from this simmering volcano without notice.

Daniel appreciated the Chitza resolve, but he wasn't about to let their primary question slip away just because no one had yet come up with a reasonable answer: Why couldn't they find two 4-D bubbles they knew existed? Their scanner worked fine, and they'd double checked their position. The bubbles had to be here.

But where is here?

Once the problem had been restated, a new thought occurred. "Can your dimensional scanner find a 5-D bubble?"

Aussik paused in his switch flipping. "Sort of. They come up fuzzy."

One thought led to another. "How about 6-D?"

"Ha!" Zeeno turned around to Daniel. "Okay, I might have lied about jumping to 6-D. Even running both turbines flat out, we don't have enough power to do it, and neither did the last mission."

"But there's plenty of excess power outside when you're in a gamma blast." Daniel glanced back and forth between the two pilots.

Zeeno stared. "Damn, Human, you might be onto something."

Aussik stopped what he was doing and stared at Zeeno. "They boosted neutrino oscillation by opening the turbine inlets?"

The captain rocked his head. "Crazy... but under the circumstances..."

Aussik's paws flew across the buttons and dials on a dozen subpanels like a Chitza possessed. Daniel probed further. "What would a 6-D bubble look like?"

"Magenta," Zeeno answered without hesitation. "They're all the same color. It's the size that will throw you. A 5-D bubble viewed from 4-D space looks a lot smaller than it really is. So, a 6-D bubble... well."

Aussik leaned over his display. "Where are you, little 6-D bubble?" He brushed off some lint sticking to the screen. "Nothing nearby... wait..." He flipped a switch overhead then fine-tuned using a dial next to the display. He brushed the screen once more but a tiny dot, magenta in color, didn't go away. "Now *that* could be something. More of a microdot than a bubble. But I'd swear on my momma's furry kiss that little doodad is a couple dimensions above us."

Zeeno looked over Aussik's shoulder. "Color's right, but it's more of a fragment, and it's not even on our vector."

"But it's there." Aussik looked up. "Maybe the gamma blast tore it apart and sent it flying but it still could be part of a lifeboat maneuver."

Zeeno studied Aussik's display, scratching the fine quills on his chin. "Then where's the ping?" He pointed to an LED, unlit.

"Maybe they lost the data pack."

"Or maybe it didn't fit." Zeeno locked eyes with Aussik. "Get closer. Let's snuggle right up to this little blip and check under its skirt."

"I'm with ya, Boss." Aussik flipped open a cover to reveal a joystick and pushed right. The view outside drifted slightly. He'd shifted to manual flying. No navigation vector, no waypoints. Both pilots craned their heads looking for something tiny hidden among the colorful streaks of light.

"What's the lifeboat maneuver?" Daniel asked. The name alone sounded promising.

Zeeno answered without taking his eyes off the viewport. "A bad joke. A Chitza scout ship values mission data above all else. Generally, the data is too big to be transmitted along a 4-D filament, so if a mission is ever compromised the pilot ejects a data pack along with a transponder to mark its location. That's the abandon data procedure."

"A lifeboat for data, then. Your bad joke."

"But there's a kernel of truth to it. Eject a data pack into 4-D and you'll get a compact bubble no bigger than my fist. Lasts a long time. Centuries even. But if your compression turbines are still running at full speed, and you have enough time to set

External Targeting Mode—that thing Beets taught your friend, Tennah—then you can create a lifeboat for people too. Of course, whoever is doing the work goes down with the ship, but some can get out."

Aussik pointed out the viewport. "Got it!" Among the flashes of white, green, and blue, a tiny dot of magenta light stood out as the only colored bit whose light remained steady.

Zeeno spotted it too. "Get closer."

"We *are* close." Aussik lightly tapped his joystick until a colored marble hovered at the forward viewport like an eyeball staring back at them.

Zeeno shook his head. "Hell, you couldn't fit two whiskers in that."

"There's another one!" Aussik pointed to a second tiny spec.

"Wow!" Zeeno studied their latest discoveries. "Two bits, both tiny, and neither one pinging a damn thing back at us."

"But if they really are 6-D." Aussik pointed a thumb back at Daniel, the instigator of all this crazy talk. "Then they're bigger inside than they look. Plus, more dimensions could be tougher for a transponder ping to get through. Look at the perpendicular angle stats on this guy."

Zeeno checked the display. "Yeah, you're right. Both of you. This thing might be 6-D."

Aussik kept a firm stare on his captain. "Your brother did this. Zeeno 9 redirected the gamma blast into the turbine inlets."

Zeeno scratched his chin, staring at the magenta marble. He mumbled something in his own language, then slapped Aussik on the shoulder. "Fine work, my friend. You too, Daniel. All we need to do now is dock with it, knock on the door, and see if anyone is home... but how?"

Aussik shrugged. "Ya got me. I'm just a pilot."

"And a damn fine pilot. But we're going to need some muscle." Zeeno swiveled around and yelled. "Beets! Get up here."

The ship wobbled, rattled, and groaned as another gravity wave deformed the ship and caught everyone off guard. Zeeno fell out of the cockpit entryway. Daniel caught the Chitza before he went headfirst down the steps, and with one hand on the bulkhead rail managed to pull them both back to standing. The rumble slowed, then stopped, leaving the ship quiet once more.

"Bigger?" Zeeno asked. "Felt bigger."

"Sprig?" Daniel queried.

Sprig clung to a toggle switch sticking up from the control panel. "Frequency, 35 hertz, amplitude, 0.77 percent. Larger than the last one, but shorter in duration."

Daniel and Zeeno exchanged a look of concern, though the commander of the ship didn't seem ready to hoist anchor and hightail it out of here.

"We'll be fine," Zeeno said climbing back into the cockpit. Daniel was less cavalier about the recurring danger outside, but they'd come a long way and might be close to success, though what was inside these tiny bubbles was anyone's guess.

The ship's engineer poked her well-decorated head into the cockpit. Daniel squeezed to one side. She looked every bit as pissed as she had when they'd left Litia. "Fratz Aussik, you're killing my ship!"

"It's not me!" Aussik yelled back.

Zeeno pointed to the magenta marble hovering just above the viewport's glass. "That's 6-D space. Maybe. Probably! Dock us. Can you?"

Beets studied the object and grumbled. "I'd need an angle bridge."

Zeeno waited, saying nothing. The captain clearly had experience motivating the unmotivatable among his crew. Sometimes management came in the form of giving a team member space to work out the problem on their own.

Beets finally spoke. "I could salvage parts from the toilet."

"You could."

"Any survivors inside?"

"Might be, if we're lucky." Zeeno waited.

Beets thought for a moment. "That'll cost you more. I'll have to pull a downlink transformer from one of the turbines."

"Cool, but would it work?"

"Sure it'll work, but once the downlink transformer is out, I can't put it back in without a full calibration test bench—which I don't have—and running one turbine without a downlink transformer is going to make our full stops from here on out a living nightmare."

"Like... how bad?"

"Nightmare."

Beets stood firm. Zeeno took a deep breath. "Okay, fine. Do it."

"You got it, Boss. Give me a few." Beets brushed past Daniel and headed back down the ladder.

Daniel hadn't followed the problem or solution with any true understanding, but it probably didn't matter. The main point seemed to be that when it came to extra dimensions, something tiny could contain far more than its appearance would suggest. Beets had a plan to tap into that micro bubble to find out what it held.

"We'll need to go incremental," Zeeno told Aussik. "Cozy right up to it, and I do mean cozy. If anyone has the skills, you

180

do." He patted his copilot on the shoulder then hopped out of the cockpit.

"Am I in your way?" Daniel asked. He felt like the only crew member without a job at a critical point in their journey.

"Stay right where you are. We wouldn't be here without your ideas. Now we let Beets and Aussik do their thing. You and I are just the welcoming committee."

"You think survivors might really be inside that tiny space?"

"I don't think anything, but I'm prepared for everything."

Another gravity rumble arrived. Zeeno casually grabbed the rail at one side of the cockpit entryway, placed one foot on the step above, and with a stoic look on his face endured the twisting, shaking, and rattling like a gallant but diminutive George Washington crossing the Delaware.

20 SURVIVOR

BEETS HAULED A METAL shroud up the ladder between decks, then started loosening bolts on the top deck ceiling. Though curious about this latest operation, Daniel had long since learned to keep some distance between himself and the cantankerous Chitza. Zeeno did much the same, watching from the cockpit steps.

The shroud resembled a cylindrical wastepaper basket hammered from sheet metal and left open at both ends. Electronic components formed a ring around its outside. A rather large battery pack had been hastily screwed in below the electronics.

They had already suffered through two more gravity waves, with Sprig announcing the severity each time. Trending up. Zeeno remained stoically unconcerned, while Daniel tried to figure out how to motivate Beets to move a notch faster than lethargic. He'd offered twice to help, only to be met by a cold stare which only slowed things down.

Beets stuffed several bolts into a vest pocket, then swung a ceiling hatch inward. She shoved the shroud up through the hatchway. "Give me a tension check, Aussik."

"Clean and tight," Aussik yelled back from the cockpit. "Our doodad is spot-on overhead. Just give your connector a shove."

"Told ya," Zeeno said in an aside to Daniel. He'd predicted his team would figure out how to connect to the tiny chunk of higher dimensional space hanging above them. Daniel imagined the magenta marble as something much larger, spreading spherically in a direction not visible but reachable with the right technology.

In the language of Edwin Abbott's book, *Flatland*, A-Square was about to shove a specially angled tube into the ass-end of A-Sphere, who was floating just above the page.

"Pressure check," Beets called out, staring into the shroud positioned overhead.

"Stand by," Aussik said. "Pressure's good. Try sticking your head up there."

Beets motioned to Daniel to crouch under the shroud, then climbed up his leg like a four-year-old who turns their parent into a ladder. He didn't mind. She had finally accepted his offer to help. Sitting around had only made him anxious for what they'd find up there.

When Daniel stood, Beets easily reached up through the shroud. Her head disappeared into nothingness. Her body simply stopped at her shoulders.

"I will never get used to this stuff," Daniel said to himself.

The ship shook as a powerful gravity wave passed through. Daniel tightened his grip on Beets' furry legs while doing his best to keep her back spines from pricking his face. The wobble in space passed.

Beets' head reappeared when she crouched down, apparently none the worse for being temporarily decapitated. "I'll need a rope," she told Zeeno, then grumbled at Daniel. "Whatever you do, do *not* let go of me."

****

A thump sounded from below, another of the imagined waves that crashed onto the rocks in *some other place*. Not here. Not in this zero-g bubble of nothingness where floating debris included cans of much needed water just out of reach. This unholy place would be Nala's last experience of conscious life. She was beyond pissed about that.

She had zoned out several times in the last few hours, unsure if she'd been sleeping, oxygen deprived, or just bored with the lack of sensory input. The thumps *below*—wherever that was—had become more frequent, and stronger too, the only variation in this bleak pocket of nonexistence.

Tick. Clang. Scrrrape.

Nala's eyes snapped open. Her body instinctively twisted toward the new sounds. The grey fuzziness surrounding her looked the same, but she hadn't imagined the sounds. It could have been another collision of floating debris, but something about the slow scraping seemed *intentional*. Like someone unscrewing a jar lid.

She tried to speak, but her dry, swollen tongue felt stuck in place. "Hey!" she managed. For such an empty place, her shout disappeared without the slightest echo as if she were enclosed in cotton.

A sizeable piece of tangled plastic floated by. In the distance, she could make out several of those oh-so-needed cans of water. Or Chitza soda. Or rubbing alcohol. She hardly cared about their content, if only she could grab one and sooth her dry throat.

Nala caught movement at the periphery of her vision and twisted once more. Something brown, but it vanished as quickly as it had appeared.

No! There it was again!

A Chitza?

The head of a Chitza anyway. Before Nala could imagine macabre reasons for a head to be floating inside her bubble, it moved. Quills quivered. Eyes blinked. This bodyless head seemed alive and only twenty meters away.

"Hey!" she yelled again and waved her arms.

The Chitza head twisted toward her, but as another thump sounded, the head ducked down, disappearing into that undefinable region *below*.

The Chitza returned a minute later. Red-tipped quills. A female. And what was that glint? A metal ring hanging from one ear? Over a stubble of shaved fur?

"Beets!" Nala screamed. She flailed arms and legs in a weightless happy dance that started her body spinning but did little to change her position.

Two furry arms now rose from nowhere and threw a coil of twine toward Nala. About the thickness of a bootlace, the twine uncoiled from its momentum and drifted weightlessly toward her.

Nala pulled both knees to her chest to begin an in-place somersault, snagging the passing twine with extended feet and pulling it into her body. "Got it!"

She wrapped the twine around her waist, then added several loops around one arm to be sure it wouldn't slip away. If she'd been hanging in full gravity, she'd have to worry about the twine breaking from her weight, but in zero-g even dental floss would be strong enough to get her moving in the right direction.

Beets tugged. The twine became taut, and Nala moved ever so slightly. Beets tugged again, imparting a measurable velocity. A few more tugs brought Nala crashing into the open arms of the much smaller Chitza. Gravity suddenly appeared where there had been none, and the Human-Chitza combination plunged down into an invisible hole.

They crashed into a third body beneath Beets and all three slammed onto a hard floor in a heap of tangled arms and legs.

Beets scrambled away. Nala lifted her head. Daniel stared back, eyes wide, smiling. She screamed with joy, wrapping her arms around his neck. Daniel pulled her close, and they rolled across the floor like playful river otters. She brushed the hair away from his face to be sure it was really him, then squeezed him tight once more.

"I've never been so worried about you," he whispered in her ear. Daniel's familiar voice, Daniel's warmth, Daniel's smell, touch, and all-around wonderfulness. She was back. He had come for her just as she'd imagined.

Her voice came out scratchy, "How did you manage it? Are you like a Marvel superhero and Almighty God wrapped up in one? I mean, I was lost—*really* lost, like billions of light-years away... at the edge of the universe... in a hidden bubble no one else would find in a million years... *that* kind of lost."

Daniel kissed her. "There are a few things I'm really good at. But in this case, I had some help." They both lifted their heads from the floor, looking up at a circle of four Chitzas. Nala recognized them all.

"Don't stop on our account," Zeeno said with paws on hips. "This is riveting."

Beets nodded. "Irresistible—but in a disgusting kind of way."

Daniel rose on one elbow, speaking only to Nala, "We have an audience."

"Yeah, I noticed." Without taking her eyes off Daniel, she called out to the spectators, "Hey team, got any water? Human sized if you can manage it, I'm pretty thirsty." She kissed him hard on the lips. Beets recoiled further.

Nala raised onto one elbow and surveyed the upper deck of the Chitza scout ship. Everything looked in place. No damage anywhere. She swiveled to a seated position, happy to be back in gravity, if only an artificial form of it. Chitzas excelled at technology. Apparently, they were also pretty good at recovering from a blast of ultra-gamma radiation.

She pointed up into a shroud on the ceiling. "You know, Daniel, being stuck up there gave me plenty of time to figure out how this might end. My best case scenario was rescue by our quill-covered friends, but *you* are no less than a miracle. Daniel... in the flesh, this far from home. How did you get here? Some kind of Chitza teleportation technology?"

Daniel sat cross-legged next to her, eye level with the surrounding Chitzas. "I got here the same way you did. In fact, we followed your path."

The fourth Chitza handed Nala a large cup filled with water. Nala drank in one long swig. "Whew, I needed that. Thanks, Onner."

"It's Veronica, actually," the Chitza said. "Nice to finally meet you."

Nala put a hand to her mouth. "Oh. Jees... you're not Onner?"

"Well, I was. Onner 6, but I changed my name. You're probably thinking of my dodeca-twin sister, Onner 3."

The truth hit hard and fast. Nala felt stunned, stupid, and embarrassed all at once. And then she thought of lost companions. *Still* lost. Tears came to her eyes. "So, none of you are..."

Her mouth hung open as she swiveled around speaking to each Chitza in turn. "Zeeno? Aussik? Beets?" They each acknowledged the correct name. "I am so sorry. I know how Chitza families work, I just didn't put it together."

Zeeno spoke for the Chitzas. "It's confusing, I know. We're the rescue mission. We took Daniel with us."

Nala dropped her head into her hands. "Please tell me you found them."

"Not yet, but there's another bubble out there."

A strong jolt shook the ship with groans from metal spars and rattles from everything else. Nala matched its pattern to the thumps she'd been hearing all along. What had felt like ocean waves up there were something altogether different down here.

She stood, shaking with emotion. "We've got to find them. I heard their voices. Aussik, Onner, and Beets followed right behind me, then somehow the bubble split. It's been hours, but if I survived, they did too. Please, hurry!"

Zeeno signaled Aussik, who jumped into his seat in the cockpit. "Beets, get things buttoned up here. We'll make the same connection when we get to the other doodad."

"On it, Boss."

Nala moved out of the way as Daniel hoisted Beets to the ceiling where the Chitza's head disappeared beneath a shroud. Another jolt hit, jerking Daniel to one side and prompting a shriek from Beets.

"Whatever it is, they're getting worse," Nala said.

"Gravity waves." The vibrato voice came from a small leaf standing on its stem at the cockpit steps. *Definitely not my ship!* Nala thought.

She tugged on Zeeno's arm. "We need to get out of here. The gamma blast that got us came from a boundary—"

Zeeno held up a paw. "We know. We'll pick up the rest of the crew as soon as Beets is finished here."

"Working as fast as I can, under the circumstances," Beets called out from beneath the shroud. Sharp quills brushed against Daniel's face, but he held tight to the small Chitza. Beets tossed down one shoe, and then another. "These yours?"

Nala slipped her shoes back on, surprised that the Chitza had managed to snag them. "Oh yeah." She pulled the data pack still under her belt and handed it to Zeeno. "This was floating up there too. Will it help find the crew?"

Zeeno accepted the disc like a gift of gold. "I'll bet my boots they're inside the next bubble, but if not, we'll dig into the data. Damn fine job hanging on to it! Chitza Base will be thrilled to learn it's been recovered."

"All sealed up," Beets called out. The shroud was gone, with a hatch now bolted in place. "Pressure check."

"We're good," Aussik yelled from the cockpit.

Daniel lowered the Chitza back to the floor as the ship began to move. Through the cockpit entryway, Nala could easily see the sparkling boundary where her own crew had parked just before the radiation hit. Wavy bands of blue and white moved across the window as Aussik pivoted toward a magenta dot in the distance.

Daniel squatted next to Zeeno and spoke quietly. "Obviously, there's more work to do, but I'm grateful for recovering my wife." Nala joined them, wrapping her arms around Zeeno. He didn't seem to mind, in fact, he returned the hug.

"Just doing what we do," Zeeno said.

"Thank you, Zeeno," Nala said holding the captain by his furry arms. "But I'm worried about your brother. Once we left the ship, I never saw or heard him."

"One of those things... it's...whatever." Zeeno seemed flustered, either by the close contact with a Human woman or because Chitzas viewed risk as pure adventure and death as inevitable.

"Getting tricky up here, Boss," Aussik yelled. Zeeno excused himself, hurrying into the cockpit. Their work was far from finished.

With Beets and Veronica back at their stations on the lower deck, Nala and Daniel were left alone. Not quite alone. The curiously animated leaf hopped up Daniel's arm and perched on his shoulder.

"I am Sprig," the leaf said. It's voice had a pleasant vibration like the beating of a hummingbird's wings. Its edges varied in shades of red, giving a visual representation of each spoken word.

Nala reached out but there weren't any extended body parts to shake or touch, so she backed off. "Nice to meet you."

Sprig bounced slightly as it spoke. "You were trapped inside a six-dimensional bubble created from the energy of the gamma blast. The additional dimensions are also what protected you from the same radiation."

"Sprig is a physicist," Daniel noted. "Well, more of a cosmologist, assistant to a Litian-nolo professor of cosmology."

"Ahh," Nala said, not sure if the second title made any more sense than the first for such an unusual life form. "So, tell me, Sprig, I learned a lot about 5-D compression coming out here, but I had no idea Chitzas could do 6-D."

"Normally, they can't," Sprig said.

Without warning, the ship shook violently, instantly sending Daniel sprawling and knocking the delicate leaf from his shoulder. Nala went to her knees. Something smashed on the lower deck. Unlike the last gravity wave, this shaking didn't stop.

Aussik yelled over the rattles and pops. "Course is drifting! Our bubble diameter is dropping too!"

Zeeno called out. "Beets! We can manage the drift, but do not let us drop out of 4-D!"

"We need to get downstairs," Daniel said. "There's only one Human seat, but we'll figure it out." Strong rattles were interspersed with sudden lurches, making the ladder between decks difficult to negotiate.

"Compression is dropping," Beets yelled as they went by. "Don't ask me why. It just is."

"Reverse vector," Zeeno commanded. Twin turbines outside roared to life just as Nala reached their shared seat. She strapped in. Daniel sat against the wall, wedging himself against the seatback. Sprig clung to Daniel's shirt collar.

With shudders intensifying, docking with the second 6-D bubble seemed less likely by the second. They had their hands full trying to avoid becoming new casualties.

"Still drifting," Aussik said. "Something is dragging us."

Multi-colored flashes filled the view out the side window, increasing in brightness and frequency. The whine of turbines in reverse soared. Zeeno and Aussik seemed to be wrestling with the ship and losing.

The window suddenly erupted in brilliance. Daniel winced, covering his face with an arm. Nala slammed a window shade down. It crinkled and warped from the intensity on the other side.

"It's a gamma blast!" Veronica screamed. "Big one."

"Oh hell," Zeeno yelled. "Well, if we can't go backward, then forward!"

A lurch pushed Nala into her seat and Daniel against the bulkhead. She closed her eyes tight. Her heart raced.

Forward could mean only one thing: crossing the boundary. Zeeno had just commanded them into a place where stars and planets no longer existed, and space itself adhered to different rules. A place Jazameh had warned about. The Chaos Field.

21 CHAOS

BRILLIANT WHITE LIGHT flooded the ship as though its metal walls had been perforated by buckshot fired at close range by a hunter with malevolent intent. The ship twisted, deforming pretzel-like, or so it seemed, by forces incomprehensible and unseen. High-pitched screeches of metal binding against metal filled the air.

It felt like a jet diving through heavy turbulence then pulling straight up. Daniel slammed against the bulkhead and became squeezed behind the stanchion that supported Nala's seat. Metal groaned under the strain of their weight. Still strapped in, Nala gripped the seat's edges, embedding her fingernails into its padding.

"Seven G's," came the technical report from Sprig, who laid flat against Daniel's chest, pinned by the same acceleration that pressed Daniel against the wall.

For a brief moment the crushing force disappeared, replaced by weightlessness as though their roller coaster ride had tipped over the edge of a new cliff. But the crush returned, now from the top down, and worse than ever. The pressure squeezed the air from his lungs and drove his body into the floor. Daniel pushed back, urging his chin up from his chest to keep his windpipe from closing altogether.

"Uhhh!" Came an agonizing groan from Nala just above him. Her seat creaked with the strain. If the stanchion broke, she'd crush him.

Gravitational forces. Highly uneven, Daniel surmised, coming from whatever enormous mass was being created along the boundary. The force could have easily been seven hundred G's, not seven. But they were still alive, itself a remarkable outcome.

The crushing force eased. Jolts reduced to shudders, soothing the sounds of angry metal.

"Down to three G's now," Sprig offered. The leaf shuffled higher up Daniel's shirt, resuming its normal position on his shoulder.

The compression forces abated but left a confused sense of balance. Daniel suddenly felt upside down, or at least tilted off center, though he could find no rational explanation except that the slackening of force was now playing tricks on his inner ear.

"Gravity generator is still functional," Beets yelled. "Hang on to something. It'll pass."

She was right. The inner tumbling did pass. He reached up to Nala's seat and pulled himself level. "How are you doing?"

She looked pale. He'd at least had the advantage of a more prone position to keep the blood better distributed.

"Fun," she croaked through a grimace. "Let's go around one more time." Nala reached to the side window and slid the now-warped cover up a few inches. They both peered outside.

The blinding light had reduced to a glare that could be tolerated by a tight squint. Daniel searched for a blazing sun in their wake, but the remaining brilliance seemed to be coming from everywhere. A minute later, the glare had dropped enough to reveal a landscape unlike any other.

Uncountable white pinnacles stretched before them. Thousands. Millions. Curving peaks of every size and shape crowded across a never-ending landscape, undulating like static in an audio waveform graphic, though not limited to one dimension and not really confined even by two. Somehow, the up and down rhythms vibrated in and out, back and forth, and directions for which there were no words.

The pulsating landscape writhed as if alive, a sea of captured animals desperate to break free from restraints. Pinnacles leaped, then dropped away, competing against neighbors but lacking the energy to achieve anything more than a temporary advantage.

Nala pressed her face to the window. "Holy crap... the Chaos Field?"

She'd heard the name too, probably from Jazameh. But a name was one thing. Daniel wasn't ready to make sense of the visuals. Even Sprig remained quiet.

Though mostly white, the highest peaks flashed a mix of colors: mauves, chartreuses, and teals that popped into existence for a fleeting moment at the pinnacle's tip, then disappearing into a sea of icy white beneath.

Nothing of the writhing frost remained flat. The whole landscape tilted in undefinable ways, at times rampaging beneath the ship's window like moving mountains—as if they were flying above animated glaciers in the Himalayas. But a slight tilt of the head twisted everything sideways, pushing the pinnacles overhead as if their view outside derived from a moving camera position placed inside a complex computer simulation.

A taller pinnacle ejected a detached shiny globule of violet-colored liquid above its tip. The blob throbbed in varying ellipsoid shapes like a droplet of oil filmed in super slow motion. Languid movements above its parent lasted only a few seconds, then the globule fell back and was reabsorbed into the sea.

"All I got was a name," Nala said without moving her eyes from the window. "And plenty of encouragement from Jazameh to 'play it safe.' She forgot to mention the roller coaster part."

"I didn't get much more." Daniel wrapped an arm around her shoulder. He wasn't sure whether to blow this insanity off and spend their last few minutes of consciousness catching up on some long overdue kissing, or to explain what he'd learned about this place. She was, after all, not just his wife but a quantum physicist. For now—and only for now—he settled on physics. They weren't dead yet, and an informed physicist might help keep them that way.

"Tennah and Sprig both say it's a quantum field. Maybe *the* quantum field, but why we have a direct view of something quantum sized, I can't explain."

"We've shrunk?" Nala offered. Not seriously, but Daniel spotted the brainstorming technique that Nala often used when faced with the unrecognizable.

Sprig hopped off Daniel's shoulder to the window's bottom edge. "Expect distances to be meaningless here. If this is an eleven-dimensional string landscape, then time and space have adopted scales that have little comparison to our universe."

"There you go." Nala pointed an index finger toward Sprig. "We haven't shrunk, we're just… ahh, who cares. I'm surprised our bodies are still functioning. How do you cross into eleven-dimensional string space and remain intact? Even a proton would have a hard time keeping it together, yet here's an entire Chitza scout ship with six people onboard." She tapped Sprig's pointy top. "Plus one… sorry, what are you?"

"Enhanced biotechnical compositron," Sprig said.

"Of course." She gave Daniel the *I have no idea* look.

"Sprig is packed with sensors and does a good job matching measurements with theory. But how our bodily quarks are still glued together…" Daniel felt like he should have more to say but words were beginning to fail him.

"Tennah didn't explain?" Nala shrugged. "Yeah, I got the rundown about Sibyls and their revolutionary leader from my map provider, Jazameh, but she didn't mention anything about string landscapes. I doubt that quantum physics is a serious area of study for the Afeesh Tm."

"Tennah and Sprig say it's a quantum field—" Daniel stopped himself. "Wait... did I already say that?"

"You did."

His brain felt fuzzy. Nothing was coming out quite right. Time itself felt... *off*. They were unquestionably conscious and somehow protected from the chaos outside but that didn't mean they were completely insulated from the quantum weirdness playing out around them.

"We should be careful," Daniel said. "I'm not sure I'm a hundred percent cogent." It wasn't just his inability to turn thoughts into words, there was something else not right about this place.

"Me too, but I thought it was just dehydration," Nala said rubbing her temple.

"Let's check in with our pilots." Daniel headed for the ladder with Nala right behind. The turbulence they'd experienced had decreased to a background rumble, making movement about the cabin easier even if their inner ear continued to rebel against what their eyes claimed to be right side up.

Veronica and Beets looked up as they passed, then followed them up the ladder. The whole team gathered at the entrance to the cockpit.

Zeeno and Aussik weren't much better off, staring wide-eyed out the forward viewport to a pulsating sea of white pinnacles with multicolored tips. They glanced down at their control panels and back to the bizarre world outside without comprehension.

"Fantastic, our science team is here," Zeeno said as Daniel and Nala stuck their heads through the cockpit doorway. "It's not entirely unexpected, but I've got to say this Chaos Field is… hell, I don't know what it is but it's disaster on our instruments."

Several lights blinked. A few needles pointed to zero. Certainly not as disastrous as being melted by gamma radiation into globules of hot metal, but if Zeeno no longer trusted his instruments, Daniel had no reason to doubt his word.

"Are we still following Tennah's probability vector?" Daniel asked, agreeing with Zeeno that a destination and control were more important than making sense of the scenery outside.

"Far as I can tell," Zeeno said. "We still have waypoints, but where we're heading is anyone's guess."

Daniel could do better than guessing, but only slightly. "Tennah said waypoints inside the Chaos Field wouldn't be fixed coordinates. More like flips of a coin. Once we crossed that boundary, random probability is all we've got. Unfortunately, going backwards won't help either—there is no *backwards*. We can't rely on Euclidian geometry or even intuition."

"We're still inside a 4-D bubble," Nala said, pointing at one of Aussik's control panel displays. Daniel couldn't make any sense of the information presented, but Nala had probably learned more about how Chitza technology compressed space on her ride out.

Aussik answered. "We popped a few rivets back there, but yeah, the bubble held up and the turbines didn't clog, so that's good. Otherwise, we'd be nothing but a floating pile of screws and pins by now."

Nala shook her head. "Worse. If that 4-D bubble fails, we're looking at quantum deconstruction."

Zeeno's puzzled look kept Nala talking. "According to the Afeesh Tm, this is a quantum field. There's nothing tangible out there. This whole place is just a mathematical probability of finding a particle at a particular location—a wave function in the Schrödinger sense. Those pinnacles aren't flowing ice or anything

198

else made of atoms, quarks, or electrons. They're quantum oscillations. Superposition of the wave function. Bottom line, particles can't exist here."

"Or collections of particles?" Daniel asked, pointing to himself. The physics of chaos didn't sound promising for holding atoms together. Or bodies.

Nala twisted her mouth and shook her head no. "Step outside this bubble, you're fucked."

"Well, that could be a problem," Aussik said pointing to his display. "Our bubble may have held, but compression is still dropping. I can't seem to keep it fully inflated no matter what adjustments I make."

Daniel grimaced. "So, how long have we got?"

Aussik consulted his screen. "Hard to say. But the turbines are still working, so Beets and I might come up with something."

Zeeno swiveled his seat to face Daniel, Nala, and the crew. "Sorry, my friends. I got us into this mess."

The captain's eyes met Daniel's. It was a soft look that conveyed humble respect from Chitza to Human. Zeeno was almost certainly thinking the same thing as Daniel: the voice override to disengage the probability vector, discarded to maintain trust between them, might have prevented their current predicament.

But second guessing *what might have been* never got anyone anywhere. If Daniel had pressed his advantage, Zeeno might have eventually caved, leaving Daniel in charge. But once the gamma blast hit, only two choices remained: suffer, as the last mission had, or plunge headfirst into the Chaos Field.

Daniel nodded respectfully to their captain. "You made a command decision, Zeeno. Honestly, I had nothing better."

Zeeno scratched a quilled chin in thought. For once, their captain seemed to accept Daniel's assessment of their situation, both the good and the bad. There could only be one path forward. Tap the strengths of each crewmember, Human, Chitza, and compositron.

Sprig tapped Daniel's ear with the point of its leaf. "I have been observing."

At this point in their relationship, Daniel had gotten used to the leaf's style, roughly the same as a carbon monoxide monitor in your house that remained quiet for long periods of time only to shriek dire warnings when you least expected.

"Shoot," Daniel said, fully expecting more weirdness and-or imminent danger they'd neglected to account for.

Sprig didn't disappoint. "According to one theory of cosmology, a chaotic quantum landscape was the source of our universe, which implies that the most energetic peaks we see outside are capable of spawning more universes. The detached globule we recently passed may be one of those universes in its nascent stage. The gamma radiation we avoided at the boundary may be another, already spinning up its own Big Bang and partially invading an existing universe—our own."

Nala nodded her agreement. "If this is a nursery for baby universes, then time out there may be passing at a tiny fraction of what we'd normally experience. You know… a clock ticking in femtoseconds."

As a quantum physicist, she made a good counter to Sprig, able to confirm or deny the leaf's extraordinary cosmological theories and come up with her own extensions. Daniel, being more of a scientific generalist, might not have the same expertise these two could share, but he understood that an explorer skating along the edge of knowledge had a far higher chance of coming out alive if he could characterize the hazards surrounding him.

Daniel tossed out his own contribution. "Here's another twist for all you deep thinkers. What if this chaotic quantum landscape is primordial? Not just the source of new universes, but the foundation of reality? Universes come and go, but this place is eternal."

On more than one lonely evening with a glass of wine and nothing else to do, Daniel had tried to wrap his head around two of the most difficult concepts in philosophy: infinite and eternal, never ending and without beginning. The never-ending part was easier—just imagine a number line starting at zero and extending forever. Humans understood the task of counting and could picture a sequence of numbers disappearing into the distance. But the concept of eternal jarred the brain. How could something proven to exist have no beginning?

"There's a fair chance we've stumbled into the basis of reality," Daniel hypothesized. "This place could be the final answer in, *what came before that?* The bottom level of all levels. Time exists here, but locations are fuzzy probabilities. Whole new universes pop up right before our eyes while our own universe is nowhere to be found."

"Inspiring thoughts... but dangerous," Nala said, staring out the viewport at the hectic undulations. "Our only guide through this chaos is a map that can't tell us where we're going or how long we'll be here."

Aussik pointed to his screen. "The system *is* generating new waypoints, but I admit the current waypoint doesn't look any different than the last one."

Nala nodded. "Exactly what Jazameh told me when she loaded our probability vector. Don't expect the waypoints to be landmarks or to look like we're making progress. It's like solving a Rubik's cube puzzle—you won't know you're done until the last piece clicks into place."

"The Kyan Ta rumors were true, then," Daniel said. "You snatched Jazameh as your map."

Nala wheezed. "Now there's a spin. I didn't snatch anyone. I made a friend. That's how you defeat a shithead authoritarian—and trust me, I know a power-hungry dictator when I see one."

"Osperus."

"Right."

Daniel didn't mind the detour into more ordinary topics. It pushed away more depressing thoughts of being lost in the deepest recesses of reality. The rest of the crew seemed just as interested to learn how Nala had managed on the Afeesh Tm planet. Veronica even whispered "shithead" to Beets, a unique union of Human anatomy and swearing that made them both smile.

Daniel held Nala's hands. "I never doubted you for a second. In fact, I made a pretty good case to Tennah regarding your goodwill. I figured you'd secured a Sibyl to help, I just didn't know how you had managed it."

"Three days wandering the Afeesh Tm city trying to avoid Osperus and his goons. Yeah… I might have pissed him off with my comment about the injustice of men controlling women. Sibyls as slaves, and all that. Hey, these things happen. Once I met Jazameh, it all clicked. There are good people everywhere, even in the heart of a chauvinistic system."

"Jazameh and Tennah have work to do. When we get back home…" Daniel trailed off. First, they'd probably never get *back home*. And second, the concept of *home* had clearly grown far looser than Earth or Litia, or even the Milky Way galaxy. When lost in a primordial quantum field that bore no resemblance to any familiar reality, even a planet gigaparsecs from Earth felt a little like home.

Directly ahead, an enormous white pinnacle rose into their path, shimmered with blues and purples at its tip, then dropped beneath the ship as they slid past. Its movement felt ordinary in the sense of one object passing another, yet peculiar in an indescribable way. Even the amount of time it took to pass the next pinnacle felt dilated, like watching a slow-motion scene play out while high on a hallucinogenic drug.

There would be no turning back. Once they had crossed the boundary, they'd left their universe behind—possibly far behind if distance still had meaning. Randomness and probability now ruled their path forward, along with their chance of survival. The end could come at any moment either from a new Big Bang popping into existence and swallowing them up, or more simply from the continued decay of the extradimensional bubble that surrounded their ship and gave them refuge from the quantum landscape outside.

They had little choice but to continue on.

22   BREAKOUT

"OH, DEAR GOD IN HEAVEN this is delicious." Nala's whole body practically melted as she treated herself to another mouthful of ChitzaChow, a badly named but delectably aromatic blend of bacon, lasagna, and roasted green chiles stuffed into a buttered potato skin. At least, that's what the handheld food *tasted like*. Its savory aroma fared even better, selling the latest in Chitza cuisine even before the first bite.

"Glad you like it," Veronica said, casually leaning against her workstation desk. Nala sat in a newly crafted Human seat that Beets had fashioned from the remains of the shroud used in their rescue. "You looked kind of hungry. And don't worry about the size, we have lots more."

"Thank you," came the smothered response. Nala wiped her mouth with a miniature Chitza napkin. "With all the crazy, I almost forgot I'd only eaten one granola ball since being trapped, and who knows how long I was up there."

The trauma of her isolation had already begun to fade. It helped to be surrounded by resilient Chitzas. On top of building a new chair, clever Beets had also found a solution to their bubble shrinkage problem. With 4-D protection now shored up, the rest of the crew invented a new ChitzaCheer to honor their engineer: "*Beets aga teets, neg ama freets!*" which they said couldn't be translated into English because it would lose the rhyme, which was the best part about it.

It also helped when Zeeno explained that he'd managed to fire off a message back to base before they crashed through the boundary. Another rescue mission would surely be authorized now that they knew the precise location of the second 6-D microbubble. As for the crewmembers who were likely inside that bubble, Zeeno told them not to worry. "They'll just hibernate." Apparently, Chitzas could last for weeks without food or water though they woke up crabby—an unnoticeable difference in the case of Beets.

Best of all, having Daniel back in her arms helped to reset her outlook on this adventure gone wrong. With Daniel here, she could deal with the hard cold fact that they were getting further from home by the minute. Whatever lay ahead, they'd face it together. Besides, Daniel would find a way home. He did things like that.

Her handsome wizard of solutions relaxed in the original Human-sized chair, sometimes staring out the window, at other times closing his eyes for a catnap. He hadn't shown any sign of wizardry yet, but then, he'd probably had his own difficulties in his journey across the universe.

Give the man a break. He's not miraculous. They were in a difficult predicament, no question. Literally, beyond the edge of their universe inside a no-man's-land where quantum probabilities ruled. Or so, the Sibyls said. Over the past two hours, Zeeno had called out three more waypoints created by the vector that only Tennah and Jazameh understood. Outside, the white-pinnacled landscape continued to slide by. It gave a fair approximation of forward progress, but the far side of the Chaos Field could be anything from one waypoint away to a million. The Sibyls had only claimed they could navigate this landscape, not that the trip would be efficient.

Aussik appeared, dropping down the ladder from the upper deck and grabbing one of the savory snacks from Veronica's desk. He fixed his eyes on Beets as he ate. "The ship's on autopilot. Nothing's going on. Nothing to do but wait. I think it's time."

Beets stared back, emotionless. She sucked in a long breath. "You're right. It's time."

Beets stood, ran foreclaws through the quills on her chin, selected one of the longest, and plucked it out with a sharp snap. When her pinched eyes reopened, two tears of pain dropped out, but her clenched jaw and stoic expression never faltered.

She steeled herself and held up the plucked quill. "We'll need a target."

Aussik grinned wickedly. "It's got to be a Human."

Beets nodded slowly like a gladiator recognizing that the only path to victory would be through the dead body of her competitor. "Got to be."

Beets handed the quill to Aussik who ran a pen-sized wand along its length to sterilize it, measure it, or sharpen it—maybe all three. The slender quill gleamed in the cabin's overhead lights, needle sharp.

"Don't look at me," Daniel said, suddenly awake. "I'm not a needle kind of guy."

Nala laughed under her breath. "He's definitely not!" She rose from her chair. "I've got this. We played StickIt on the way out here. Kind of fun, in a weird way."

Nala squatted to Chitza level, staring Beets in the eye. "And you, my prickly friend, might be taking on more than you can handle." Nala slapped her chest with a hint of competitive ferocity, then reached out to Aussik who placed what looked like a circular beermat in her hand. The cardboard disc had a nondescript insignia printed on one side and a ring fastened to the other. Nala slipped her middle finger through the ring and raised the mini shield in a protective stance.

"I'll throw first," Nala said, reaching out for the quill.

"Not a chance," Beets growled as she slipped on her own shield, which protected significantly more of her smaller body.

Nala pointed. "Daniel. Got your olinwun?" She flipped her thumb.

Daniel reached into his pocket and retrieved a special coin he rarely traveled without. Known as an olinwun, he had carried the coinlike device back from 2053—inside his stomach no less. That future was now gone, but the coin remained as a keepsake.

"You call it," Daniel said to Beets. "Eagle or columns." On one side, a holographic eagle decorated the coin's face. On the other, a building fronted by stately columns. Beets called eagle. Daniel flipped. The coin bounced a few times on the floor, finally landing eagle face up. "Beets goes first."

Nala shrugged. "Fair." She backed away from Beets, lowered her stance and squinted at her opponent. "Okay, Chitza scum, do your worst!"

Beets stood tall, grinning as she twirled the sharp quill. Aussik took up a position on the sidelines as the official judge. Daniel moved forward to the Human-sized chair next to Veronica's workstation. He nervously fingered the olinwun, clearly never having witnessed this fight to the death—so, called. But then Chitzas embellished almost everything.

In the quickest motion yet displayed by the stout hedgehog, Beets leaped to twice her height drew her arm back and launched the quill at Nala like a javelin. Just as quickly, Nala flashed the diminutive shield up and to the right. With a distinctive *pwack*, the quill stuck in the dense cardboard.

Nala waggled her eyebrows, lowering the shield with the quill protruding from its center. "Nice shot."

"Nice feint," Beets said.

Aussik awarded three points to Nala. Yet, like a sadistic tennis match played with darts instead of soft fuzzy balls, this game had only begun.

Daniel apparently hadn't even noticed. He stared at his olinwun coin. He'd been flipping it as they played. His loss. He would miss her next practiced move, *le jeter en pointe*. Nala plucked the quill from her shield, turned, and walked a few paces back. She spun on one toe, ballerina-like, and threw.

Beets barely moved her shield, easily snagging the quill with her shield. "Ha!"

"Ha, indeed," Nala said, acting miffed but with a grin appearing at one side of her mouth.

"Even at three," Aussik announced.

"What?" Nala complained. "Did you see that twirl? Worth at least a half point." The judge remained unmoved by her plea, leaving the score tied.

While Nala prepared for her next defense, Daniel continued to flip his olinwun, now with Sprig observing the meaningless results from Daniel's shoulder. Given the obvious prowess of Nala's StickIt game, his disinterest felt a little insulting. He was even spinning the coin on Veronica's workstation, watching it until it fell.

Boys! Daniel could get distracted by the oddest things, but he also found insight in weird places. She'd ask him about the coin later—just in case the meaningless coin flips had somehow become meaningful.

Beets' next throw came without warning, launched underhand. Having been sidetracked, Nala wasn't fast enough, and the dart stuck into her thigh. She grimaced, looking to the ceiling. "Yow!" she groaned, pulling the quill from her pants leg. Painful, but she already knew the damage to skin and muscle would be slight.

Daniel looked up. "Are you okay?"

Nala waved him off. "It's fine. She's going easy on me. Chin quills don't have barbs. When the game advances to back quills, you really have to know your moves to stay out of the hospital."

Nala twirled the quill in her fingers, bent over like a baseball pitcher reading the catcher's sign, and snarled at Beets. "Be ready, Chitza bio-scrap, payback's a bitch." Half of the appeal of StickIt involved creative trash talk.

Beets crouched, maneuvering her shield like a pro. "Bring it on, hairless *dookah*. My barb already marks your rubbery skin."

Captain Zeeno interrupted their slanderous exchange with a yell from the upper deck. "Aussik, get up here!"

With their judge hustling up the ladder, both combatants rose from their crouches, staring at each other. Nala lowered her throwing arm. "He sounds upset. Time out?"

Beets nodded. She checked her workstation display. "Aha. Looks like we're in luck. Or in trouble."

"Strap in!" yelled Aussik from above.

This danger game was over. Nala dropped the quill and pushed Daniel out of her seat. He pocketed the olinwun coin and strapped into his own seat on the other side of their shared window. Outside, the view hadn't changed. A million pinnacles continued to undulate in a rhythmic dance across an unholy landscape. No random Big Bangs. No blasts of radiation. Yet something ahead had caught Zeeno's attention.

The ship rotated, bringing a black band into view. It sharply contrasted with the sea of white, forming a distinct horizon. Flashes of colors appeared along its length.

"Another boundary," Nala whispered.

"At least we have some experience." Daniel cinched his seatbelt tighter.

"Not sure about that. We entered from empty space, but what's on the other side now? A random multiverse could conjure up almost anything. Deadly radiation? Crushing density?"

Daniel seemed unconvinced. "Others have come this way before. The Sibyls were wary, but they didn't predict a dead end. However random, the path we're on is supposed to lead somewhere."

The black stripe grew taller as they approached. Zeeno shouted another warning to prepare, but for what? The ship tipped forward, feeling like a downhill slide. The black wall increased in height until it blotted out everything else. Torrents of colored sparks poured from its surface and a deep rumble shook the ship.

"Here we go again!" Veronica shouted.

The last gleams of white pinnacles vanished as darkness enveloped them. The ship's lighting system adjusted automatically, like driving into a tunnel. The rumble shook their seats and rattled cabinets affixed to bulkheads, then suddenly stopped altogether as they sailed into smooth space.

Outside, compression turbines hummed like finely tuned engines. Inside, the ship was strangely still. A full glass of wine balanced on the edge of Veronica's workstation wouldn't have spilled a drop.

"That's it?" Veronica asked Nala.

Apparently the high-G rocket ride they'd experienced on entry wasn't going to repeat on exit. Instead, darkness filled the window. Not a single point of light anywhere.

Zeeno called everyone up to the cockpit, and they scrambled up the ladder to learn their fate. The forward viewport didn't look any different. Black emptiness in every direction. Even Sprig couldn't find anything of interest to remark on.

"Any way to tell if this is a new universe?" Daniel asked. Evidence before conclusions. It was Daniel's way.

"We're still on the same navigation vector," Aussik said. "We never looped back or anything."

Nala pointed to Aussik's display. "Looks like we have a final waypoint, too." She had learned quite a bit about Chitza navigation on the trip out, including memorizing the Chitza numbering system and a good portion of their alphabet. "At Tau minus nine, we can be there in two hours."

Zeeno stared out to the blackness of space. "Any 4-D?"

"Nothing," Aussik said. The ship's scanner was always searching. It was the only effective strategy for finding life. Find a 4-D bubble—no matter how small—and you've found an advanced civilization. Aberrations of spatial dimensions were never natural.

"Hey, we've got a waypoint. Let's see where it takes us. Reconnaissance mode. Report anything unusual."

Beets and Veronica headed back to their workstations, leaving Nala, Daniel, and Sprig to watch the nothingness ahead. It was like surveying the Sahara for signs of anything other than sand. Rather boring.

A half hour went by with nothing to report except that they had covered another million light-years of nothingness. If they'd been in their own universe, they would have seen multiple galaxies by now.

Sprig was the first to report. "I detect matter. To the right. Cold. Inconsistent, but something is there."

"Shaped like a ring?" Daniel asked. It was a good guess. The Sibyls' map started from one 4-D ring. It might end at another.

Aussik had his eyes fixed on a display that typically revealed 4-D magenta bubbles—when they were out there. "I'm not seeing any perpendicular angle stats, so it's probably just rocks or ice. Definitely cold."

Zeeno held up one paw. "How about we get our bearings? Let's do a sniff test."

Before Nala or Daniel could raise an objection to the same maneuver that got the last mission into trouble, Aussik pulled his red handle to neutral. "You got it, Boss. Full stop coming up."

"Hang on to something," Beets called out. "Don't forget, I dismantled a downlink transformer to bring our survivor onboard."

"Oh, yeah," said their impulsive captain, a bit too late.

Both compression turbines spun into a reverse thrust whine. At first, it sounded like any other full stop, but then an earsplitting metal-on-metal squeal with a pitch high enough to break glass forced everyone to cover their ears. Finally, a loud clunk and a shudder throughout the ship made Nala wonder if the whole starboard compression turbine had just fallen off.

Aussik grinned sheepishly. "Full stop complete. Turbines spinning down normally... I think."

"Beets, Veronica, do a full systems check. We've been through a lot." Their captain waved to Daniel and Nala. "Bring your leaf guy and come with me. Let's get a good look outside."

Nala's curiosity spiked. Daniel's would be off the charts. Not enough to don a space suit, but that's probably not what Zeeno had in mind.

The captain halted beneath the ceiling port hole where they'd dragged Nala in from the 6-D bubble. "You're tall," he said to Daniel, waving to the closed hatch just above their heads. In fact, Daniel needed to crouch to avoid smacking into handles positioned around the hatch perimeter. "Twist the seal release... the one on the right."

Daniel grabbed a small metal handle and turned. A plate slid horizontally, revealing a transparent dome above with a view outside. Daniel stood tall, his head reaching well into the dome. Nala needed to stand on tiptoes but was rewarded by an extraordinary view now that they were back in 3-D space.

They had stopped alongside a glowing cloud where patches of green, blue, and red peaked from behind much larger bands of darker material that stretched into the distance, eventually disappearing into the blackness of space.

"Beautiful," Daniel said. "Looks like a dark nebula, but it's a lot bigger than what we see in the Milky Way. Reminds me of a supersized Horsehead Nebula. Can you get any data on it, Sprig?" Sprig hopped to the top of Nala's head, digging its stem into her hair.

"We are further away than it looks," Sprig reported. "This object is quite large and quite diffuse. One million light-years in length. Four hundred thousand in height. The size of Andromeda, the Milky Way, plus three more galaxies combined."

An enormous band of matter, but it bore no resemblance to a rotating spiral or any other galactic shape. "If it's not a galaxy, what is it?" Nala asked.

"It *is* a galaxy," Sprig answered. "But old and dying. I detect no active stars. The glow we see comes from embers of a million supernovae combined with billions of brown dwarf stars, slowly cooling. This dying galaxy contains a large amount of matter, but it has diffused so widely that the natural expansion of space now exceeds the pull of gravity. New stars and planets cannot form. We are looking at a graveyard."

"Heat death," Daniel said.

Nala knew the term. In fact, heat death was the projected end state of our own universe. Expansion would continue forever, with galaxies and stars separating as they aged. After trillions of years, entropy—the measure of disorder—would win, snuffing out the last bits of light to leave a cold, dead expanse of thinly spread matter. Depressing in a way, but she could think of several colleagues back home who would gladly accept a ticket to this remote place. Their research would provide new discoveries for a lifetime.

Daniel continued, "On the plus side, being stuck in a universe facing heat death is better than quantum deconstruction back in the Chaos Field. We're still alive. Who knows, there might still be a few planets hidden in all that dust, huddled close to their dying brown dwarf, eking out a dystopian existence in the final years of this universe."

"That's your plus side? Might want to work on your vision of our future."

"Just being realistic."

Zeeno scrambled up a set of rungs built into the bulkhead to reach the dome where Daniel and Nala looked out. "Let's get that sniff done to see if this dead universe is going to kill us too. Twist the next handle."

Daniel grabbed another of the handles around the dome. "This one?"

"That's it."

With a quick twist, a cylindrical tube rose a few inches just outside the dome. Zeeno asked him to press several buttons which initiated whirring sounds. Once complete, Zeeno shouted to Aussik back in the cockpit. "Got the sample."

Apparently, junior space explorer Daniel had just completed his first Chitza sniff test.

Zeeno dropped to the floor while Daniel proudly closed the hatch cover, looking almost like a regular member of the crew.

Back at the cockpit, Aussik studied diagrams spread across his screen.

Nala peered over his shoulder with equal interest. "That line is particle density?" she asked, pointing.

Aussik nodded and ran a claw down a series of bar graphs, each in a different color. "Broken out by type. Quark, electron, muon, tau ... well, you know the rest. The only boson we can detect directly are photons, but the others can be inferred by the atomic elements listed on the right panel." He pointed. "As you can see, we're picking up hydrogen plus a few strays."

"Fascinating," Nala said. "Helium and lithium too. Elements one, two, and three."

Aussik glanced up at Zeeno. "Sniff test looks good, Boss. No antimatter. Nothing dangerous. We only need gravity and some free protons to operate the compression turbines. I think we can safely say we've got both."

Zeeno patted his first officer on the shoulder. "Fantastic. As soon as Beets is finished, we'll continue to the waypoint." The captain took his seat and began preparations for their departure.

Daniel tugged Nala to the aft bulkhead. "You realize that unless we figure out how to get back home, Zeeno will just keep going as long as the supplies hold out. He'll always find something else to explore. I don't think he's bothered in the slightest that we're in a universe not our own. It's just another challenge."

Nala sighed. "Chitzas can be like that. I suppose we could try the reverse vector to get home, but you said Tennah didn't recommend that."

"She said it wasn't possible. Going into the Chaos Field bears no relationship to coming out."

"But her probability vector is taking us somewhere, right? Maybe we'll end up someplace just as cold and just as dead, but at least we'll know we made it to the end of the line."

"We'll eventually run out of food and water."

"So, we'll find your ice planet. Set up shop beneath the glow of its dying star." Nala smiled brightly, pulling Daniel in close and kissing him on the lips. "We'll build a cozy chalet at the foot of a glacier. Drink homemade glühwein every night and spend the rest of our lives chopping firewood and harvesting grass for the alien cows we raise."

"Wearing lederhosen and a Bavarian lace-up corset?"

Nala raised a finger. "Definitely sexy. You've got to admit that."

Daniel nodded. "Okay. Alpine chalet it is… after we find out where   this   vector   is   taking   us."

23 UNIVERSE 2

BEETS GAVE THE ALL-CLEAR, and Aussik fired up the turbines once more. At this point, shifting into higher dimensions had become routine; it was the stops that required advanced warning. Daniel didn't bother to return to his lower-deck seat and instead leaned against the doorframe leading into the cockpit. Sprig relaxed on his shoulder. Nala sat on the steps.

Dimensions shifted. Space compressed. The long band of dust backlit by a dim glow drifted by. The ship passed directly through one arm of it, but Daniel was unable to spot a single star. Sprig, however, noted several black holes with traces of accretion disks around them. If there were planets hidden in the gloom, they would likely be frozen solid. Nala's alpine chalet would remain a pleasant fantasy.

They could still do a U-turn, but re-entering the Chaos Field without a probability vector specifically designed for a return trip would be madness. This universe might be nearing heat death, but at least the matter sliding past their window was composed of hydrogen, carbon, oxygen, and other atoms that could be found on the periodic table. Their sniff test had proven it.

Even if they found an icy rock harboring the last remnants of life, being stuck in a dead-end universe meant isolation. They had no way to communicate back home. Friends and family would forever wonder what had happened to them. Their mission would be described as yet another failure, and if the Mission Two Chitzas were still hibernating inside a 4-D bubble, they would need to be rescued by someone else. Even the discovery of the Chaos Field and its scientific revelations about cosmology, eternity, and the birth of universes would be information that would never reach the home worlds of the Milky Way.

Daniel did his best not to dwell. Nala's naturally buoyant outlook—however imaginative—would keep their spirits up until they learned their fate at the end of this navigation path.

The pilots maintained a modest compression ratio as the ship cruised through the final stretch of space. They found no other bands of glowing dust. No galaxies either, spiral, elliptical, or any other shape.

When Aussik leaned back in his copilot's seat, Nala prodded him in the back. "Don't get too lax. Remember, we're in an unfamiliar universe."

"Aw hell, we're almost there."

"Well, not quite." She pointed to Chitza lettering on his display. "More than a million light-years to go." She had always shown a natural ability in languages, and Aussik seemed to notice too.

"*Eta qual tok, eh Nala?*"

"*Nab. Chi gink. Lak datica,*" she answered.

Nala's foreign words weren't surprising. Daniel had seen her do it before, and she'd spent more than a week with the previous Chitza crew.

Their exchange continued. After a particularly sharp comment from Nala, Aussik sat up straight. "*Den ka bah Afeesh. Seef teetsa gokk ... Bo?*"

Nala laughed. "*Bo,* my ass!"

She turned to Daniel and generously switched back to English. "He thinks we'll find another planet at the final waypoint, just like at Afeesh Tm. But I'm going with the Daniel Rice heat death theory. Aussik wants to make a bet."

Veronica popped her head up through the hole in the floor. "Loser eats a pink ChitzaPop." She waggled furry eyebrows.

Aussik grinned, showing canines. "You're on, girl."

Nala shrugged. "Risky, but I'll roll with it."

On any normal day, Daniel assimilated interpersonal complexities better than most. He even recalled the warning Veronica had given about consuming pink ChitzaPops while celibate. But the intersection of three highly spontaneous personalities might be more than an analytical guy could handle.

Piecing it together, if Nala won the bet, Aussik would hook up with Veronica. Or maybe Nala? No, probably Veronica, given the interspecies logistics and the fact that Nala was already married. Assuming Veronica, then perhaps a new couple would spring up from their bet. It would certainly be spontaneous, but not without hints of affection between them. Maybe Aussik and Veronica would build their own chalet in Nala's imagined alpine glen on the yet-to-be-discovered ice planet, and they'd all be neighbors.

But then, if Aussik won, and Nala ended up eating the aphrodisiac? There was always the lower deck broom closet.

Daniel laughed to himself. *Nothing like a little Chitza cheer to lighten the mood.* He more than appreciated his traveling companions.

Bet in place, they continued toward the final waypoint. Tennah's map had come with the expectation that travelers from far and wide would follow it, and, in spite of past disasters, Chitzas and Humans had finally succeeded. Their fate lay directly ahead. At their current compression ratio, they'd be there in less than an hour.

Sprig hopped from Daniel's shoulder onto the back of Aussik's seat, then leaped to the control panel. The leaf faced the viewport and twisted to the right. "Structure," was all it said.

"You see something?" Daniel eyes could manage only black.

Sprig trembled. "Unlike anything detected before. A web."

221

"Like from a spider?"

"In a way. Multiple strands. A weave of some kind, but each thread is exceedingly thin."

Nala popped up to peer out the viewport but after a few seconds of scanning, shook her head. Human eyes weren't the best of detectors when it came to dim objects in space.

Aussik reset his control panel display. "Hmm... nothing four dimensional out there. No... wait. Something is fading in and out. Weird. I haven't seen that before." The barest fog of color appeared on one side of the display. Not magenta, but a deeper purple, hardly distinguishable from the black background.

"Maybe it's fading in and out of 4-D space?" Nala offered. "You know... like it can't make up its mind about which dimension to live in." Her comment suggested life, but she was simply making sense of a phenomenon no one had yet encountered.

"Picking it up on the viewport now," Zeeno announced. They all looked up.

Silky threads emerged from the blackness. Crisscrossing. Barely visible, greyish purple on black. A web, of sorts, but less like the neat circular structure of a spider's web and more like the disorganized cobweb found in the corner of an attic.

Sprig hopped to the right edge of the viewport where it curved around the cockpit to provide a view out the ship's right side. "The web extends behind us too. They may reach all the way back to the boundary. I can't be sure, though, I wasn't paying attention." Even an intelligent leaf packed with advanced sensors had its limits.

More cobwebs appeared on the left side of the viewport. When the silky lines appeared directly ahead, Aussik backed off on the compression ratio, slowing their descent.

"It's not a galaxy, dead or alive. Not a nebula either," Daniel said.

"It feels organic," Nala said. "Can something organic be this big? It must be light years across."

"Millions of light years, if the first strands originated at the boundary," Sprig said.

"Stay the course, but let's ease into this waypoint," Zeeno said. Aussik reduced their forward velocity even further.

They approached the first tangle. Individual threads flew past, close enough to get a better view. Up close, each thread turned out to be a round tube with a glossy surface. Silvery grey in color with hints of purple that pulsed down the tube's length like a blood vessel pumping vital contents. One blocked their path, and Aussik used his manual joystick to dive beneath it. As they flew past, Sprig pivoted like a radar dish.

"Forty meters in diameter," Sprig reported.

"Whoa, that's no spider silk," said Daniel. "Big enough to drive a car through. Hell, a six-lane freeway." Distances and sizes in space were always hard to judge, particularly when the object had no recognizable markings. What had first appeared as a web of silk threads now felt more like a colossal network of flexible pipes, intertwined, haphazard in their direction or purpose, and pulsating like no structure made of PVC could.

Could they be tunnels? With no openings or windows, there was no way to determine what might be inside. Their random, ever-changing directions made it unlikely to be a transportation network.

"Kind of creepy, if you ask me," Nala said.

Daniel agreed. "A structure with an organic appearance and no discernable purpose located in the middle of nowhere. Why?"

Sprig scampered to the left side of the viewport. "Part of your answer is there." The leaf pointed its tip. While the cobweb maze continued in that direction, many of the threads ended abruptly, with broken tatters at their ends as though shorn off by an explosion. "I believe this web is a defensive barrier," Sprig said. "Or was such an obstacle in the past."

"Good guess," Nala said.

"More than a guess. I have remotely analyzed the residue left in this destroyed section. The explosive was derived from uranium. It leaves traces of an isotope which decays by half over 710 million years. This explosion occurred approximately 16 million years ago."

Aussik lifted his eye quills. "Long time. I don't know about Humans, but Chitzas were burrowing critters back then."

"Older than us too," Daniel said. "Whatever it is, it's ancient."

They continued past whole sections of the cobweb that had been shredded. Yet floating debris was absent, providing more evidence that the battle had taken place long ago. Aussik switched to manual control, tweaking his joystick as they ducked through the space between tubes.

Daniel took it all in, sorting through possibilities. With their final destination not far ahead, one conclusion stood out. "It seems the designers of our map—however smart they may have been— didn't get along with everyone they invited. They've slowed us to a crawl. That's got to be intentional. It's not a barrier, but it might be a speed bump."

They ventured deeper into the labyrinth at a no-wake speed. Gaps between threads narrowed. Slow cruise gave them plenty of time to run through a long list of familiar deterrents from history: castle walls, razor wire, 24x7 video cameras, electrified fencing, even crocodile-filled moats, which in Chitza history were filled with a swimming insect capable of burrowing through skin.

Almost unnoticed, glints of light began to flicker off the tubes ahead. The flashes increased as they progressed, bouncing around in the complex web. A minute later, they sailed out into clear space.

Black space returned, but it was now enclosed by an enormous wall of crisscrossing threads that spread out on either side of the ship. The wall gently curved overhead, giving a sense of interior space on a titanic scale. Hundreds of strobes positioned at regular intervals along the wall's surface flashed white pulses every few seconds. None were in sync. The flashes continued up the wall's face as it arched overhead to form a gigantic dome.

"Jesus, it's hollow," Nala said as she twisted to look up as best she could through the viewport.

The intensity of light from each flash provided a neat reference for the distances involved. Bright nearby but fading to pinpricks far overhead with only faint suggestions of flashes on the far side of the curving roof. In all, it was spherical in shape and enclosed an interior space thousands—maybe millions—of kilometers across to an unseen wall on the opposite side. You could fit a whole world in here. Maybe an entire solar system. Yet, it was lit not by any star, but by a fleet of light buoys defining the edge of a spherical sea.

"The light is harmless," Aussik confirmed from data on his display. "Wide across the spectrum, but not powerful enough to do any damage. Our ship could be made of paper, and we'd still be fine."

"Someone is watching us," Nala said.

"For an ancient place, it does seem rather active," Daniel added. "They slow us down, then ping us across multiple wavelengths to figure out who we are. Are we at the waypoint?"

Aussik said, "Close. The waypoint probably matches the exact center of this space, but it looks like it's empty. Nala won the bet." He heaved a sigh.

Daniel didn't disagree, but it would be an odd map to guide visitors across multiple universes, send them through a massive cobweb with probing lights, only to leave them in a hollowed-out pen with nothing to see.

His imagination ran wild. Were the surrounding lights more than radar sentries? Could the spherical web structure focus their energy at its center like a fusion reactor? Perhaps this voyage would continue into alternate dimensions, or drop to microscopic levels? Whatever it might be, something unseen was surely lurking at the center.

"Keep going. We might be surprised," Daniel said.

Even at their slow speed, they didn't have to wait long. Out of the darkness ahead, a dim object appeared. Very small, but shiny. They might have missed it altogether except for glints from the flashing lights.

Zeeno spoke. "A tiny ball?" Daniel nodded his agreement of their unlikely journey's end.

Aussik eased them closer. Silver-gray like the web tubes, it appeared to be perfectly spherical. A featureless surface gleamed like smooth pewter. A ball bearing floating in empty space.

Aussik glanced over his shoulder to Nala. "It's a planet. Bet won."

"An all-metal planet?"

"Doesn't matter what it's made of, I still win."

Nala shrugged, not seeming to care about their silly bet now that the center of this universe—and the map's destination—had revealed itself.

"Two hundred meters away. We'll park here," Zeeno announced.

Useful data since the ball provided no visual sense of its size. If it was a small asteroid, somebody had hammered it into a perfect sphere. Gravity alone wouldn't do it.

Aussik made the final adjustments, parking them in a hover, rather than an orbit.

"Should we ask it something?" Nala suggested. Her comment came out of left field, but it wasn't a bad idea. There had to be an intelligence around here somewhere, though it was equally possible the ball served only as a doorbell with unseen rooms beyond.

"They've been pinging us," Zeeno said. "Ping it back."

"Fair enough," said Aussik. He pushed a button and a blast of light shot out the front of their ship along with an audible ding inside the cockpit.

All eyes were glued to the oversized ball bearing, which now filled half the viewport. Glints reflected off its upper hemisphere, smooth and grey with nothing to mar the perfection of its curving surface. From its darker, lower hemisphere, a white fog appeared. The fog rolled from bottom to top like a planet-wide ocean wave. It soon enveloped the whole of the sphere giving it a fuzzy, whiter look with a glow around its edge.

"Wow, instant atmosphere," Nala said. "Now it really does look like a planet. Can we get more data?"

Sprig perked up. "I detect nitrogen and oxygen. The surface pressure is beginning to stabilize now… nine hundred millibars, at twenty-five degrees Celsius."

Daniel and Nala stared at each other in disbelief. Whoever was in charge had just produced a suitable landing site for both

Humans and Chitzas, evidence not only that their arrival had been monitored, but that their hosts knew all about them.

Before anyone had time to dwell upon its meaning, groans of metal sounded from around the ship. Daniel glanced left and right. Walls deformed. The cockpit where Zeeno and Aussik sat twisted. A hundred accompanying creaks dispelled any notion that these deformations were only a visual effect.

"Oh hell!" Zeeno yelled.

"On it!" Aussik yelled. He flipped switches as his whole control panel, normally flat, deformed into a standing wave.

From the left side bulkhead, a set of parallel blue bars slid through the metal wall of the ship like a giant litter box scoop passing through sand. Daniel expected the ship to be splintered into fragments any second, but the bars passed through bulkheads, through components bolted to the walls and ceiling, through electrical conduits—even through Beets, who stood next to Daniel. She seemed unharmed, watching in shock as two of the blue metal bars penetrated her body.

The same parallel bars pressed against Daniel's own body, pushing him into Nala. There was no time to wonder why a steel bar could in one second pass through solid objects, and in another push with the force of a hydraulic press. Together, wide-eyed and with hearts pounding, Daniel and Nala were swept through the opposite bulkhead, as if their bodies no longer had any substance and the ship had become entirely porous.

In Daniel's last view of the scout ship's interior, four confused Chitzas stared open-mouthed while their Human friends were scraped from the inside of one machine and transported to the surface of another.

24 SILVER

A CAGE OF PARALLEL blue bars opened simply by dissolving at one side, providing another hint of its unseen extra dimensions. The cage floor tilted slightly, depositing Daniel and Nala onto a smooth silvery surface. They watched in amazement as the remaining bars of the cage vanished one by one in a series of swirling wisps like smoke from a campfire.

Nala caught Daniel's eye with a wary unease, but she said nothing. They'd been extracted from the Chitza ship, dragged to the surface of a silver orb at the center of a mysterious alien structure. How? Why?

Daniel had always felt compelled to seek a basic level of comprehension for anything he didn't fully understand. Why do snow crystals form dendrite shapes? How does a bird as heavy as a goose manage to fly? An endless list created over a lifetime. Now he puzzled one more.

Why were they here? The navigation vector installed by Tennah had been their guide, but beyond "the wonders of distant places", neither she nor Osperus had provided insight into where the vector led.

Daniel pushed the toe of his shoe into the silvery surface. Smooth as glass, shiny like a clean sheet of aluminum foil, and soft like a polyurethane foam. When he lifted his foot, the indentation remained for a second before melting back flat.

A glowing white fog surrounded them, limiting visibility to a few hundred feet, though the curvature of this orb's surface could still be detected even in that short distance. He imagined a ball beneath their feet similar in size to the MSG Sphere in Las Vegas or the Biosphere in Montreal. Big enough to require twenty minutes to circumnavigate by foot. Not big enough to produce Earthlike gravity. Whatever held them to this surface was as artificial as its atmosphere.

In every direction, the shiny foil spread indefinitely, unmarred by surface features. Overhead, the foggy air glowed in diffuse light, hiding the Chitza ship that Daniel hoped was still intact two hundred meters away.

"I get the feeling we're being watched," Nala whispered. Daniel nodded.

A wiggle at Daniel's belt caught his attention. Sprig popped out from his pants line. "Is it over?" The leaf shivered.

"Just beginning, I'm afraid," Daniel answered. "But someone created an environment that precisely meets our needs, so at a minimum their intent is to keep us alive."

"Unless we're dinner," Nala said. "Fancy seafood restaurants let their lobsters roam in the nicest aquariums."

"There is that," Daniel acknowledged with a tip of his head. "Anyway, Sprig, I'm glad you're with us. We could use your abilities."

"I'll try to be of help." The leaf stood at the top edge of Daniel's belt, twisting on its stem like anyone would when surveying new surroundings.

Nala stroked Sprig's serrated edge, which seemed to calm its jitters. She squinted into the fog. "Can your scanners pierce this stuff?"

"Possibly. May I ride on you?"

Surprised, Nala offered her arm. "Be my guest." The leaf scampered up Nala's sleeve and took its usual lookout position on her shoulder. Nala made eyes at Daniel, suppressing a grin. "Seems you've been replaced."

"If we get some info out of it, I can handle the rejection." Daniel put an arm around her, careful not to knock off Sprig who made a three-sixty turn like an airport radar antenna.

"Nothing," Sprig said, slouching onto Nala's shoulder.

Nala turned her head, eyeball to leaf. "I almost hate to ask, but can you communicate with the ship?"

Sprig wilted further. "I cannot even detect the ship. This fog seems to be a layer of electromagnetic security. I would gladly inform Captain Zeeno that we are unharmed, but I have no way to do so."

"Okay then, I guess we explore the old fashioned way," Nala said. "Together, mind you. None of that 'we should split up' bullshit. This isn't a slasher film."

"Definitely together," Daniel agreed.

As soon as they started walking, Daniel detected movement at the edge of his peripheral vision. Nala saw it too. A hundred yards away, a silver post rose slowly from the surface. It stopped about hip height, then spread into a flat disc at its top. They exchanged an uneasy glance.

"Weird," Nala said.

"Weirdness is always worth investigating."

"Then off we go."

Each step felt slightly mushy, creating footprints that melted flat a second later. The post made no more movements, remaining fixed vertically like the beginning of a sturdy fence. They approached with caution.

The post resembled any four-by-four stuck in the ground. A round silver plate about two inches thick formed a cap. A five-fingered handprint in the plate's soft surface dissolved to flat, then indented once more as if an invisible hand had pressed down. The process repeated.

231

"Communication?" Daniel suggested. The handprint was about his size.

"It's a security doorbell. They want you to push it," Nala answered, not touching the plate herself.

"Which opens a secret panel revealing a staircase to the interior? Why the security? Why not just open the door?"

Nala waggled her eyebrows. "Aliens work in mysterious ways."

Daniel suppressed a grin. His wife had a knack for taking the edge off a dicey situation. "I'll consider their offer once I've learned a bit more. Sprig, got any ideas what this gooey silver stuff is made of?"

"Unknown," Sprig answered. "My optical spectrograph is functioning, but the surface material is not composed of elements in the periodic table. I wish I had more to tell you."

"No worries, discovering something unknown can often be just as valuable. Makes me wonder if this planet might be alive." It was only a guess, but Daniel had seen it before. At first, the moon-sized cyborg, Core, had appeared to be inanimate.

Nala walked in a circle around the post, noting how each footstep created a temporary trail behind her. "Coral is alive. Lichens too. Not terribly intelligent, but we need to remember this is not our universe. Here, anything is possible."

Daniel didn't disagree, though he wasn't yet willing to discard sensible boundaries. This place had air, gravity, light, and a reasonably solid surface. It supported sound waves, atmospheric pressure, and three-dimensionality. Even if this universe featured elements not found in our own, they shared enough in common to communicate with the aliens who had built this place—or with the silver orb itself if it turned out to be conscious.

The surface hadn't yet melted their shoes or given off disabling gases. "Okay, let's see what the handprint does."

Before Daniel could place his hand on the plate, its supporting post melted into a puddle and the plate disappeared back into the silvery surface.

"Too late," Nala said. "But…" She pointed behind him.

Daniel swiveled. Another vertical shaft rose up only ten meters away. It formed into a slightly taller post with an open ring affixed to its top. A second post rose a few meters away sporting a smaller ring. Then a third post with no ring at all.

Nala laughed. "It's a video game. You only get a few seconds to figure out the next challenge. We'd better hurry."

They ran, stopping in front of the post with the larger ring. At eye-level, Daniel peered through the ring. It aligned perfectly with the other two posts. "Huh," Daniel said. "It magnifies. The rings are lenses. The third post is holding a target. Looks like a bug."

Nala peered through the ring too, then they walked over to the third post. Indeed, a small, multilegged insect made from the same silvery substance perched atop a silver needle. "It's a telescope! Clever, but about what you'd find in a kids' science museum."

"It could still be communication."

"Hey aliens, we like your telescope!" Nala yelled into the fog. "That's communication too."

"For us, yes. For them? Who knows."

Sprig danced across Nala's shoulder. "There's more."

Further away, another silver shape loomed from the fog. Bigger, more complex, but from this distance Daniel could only make out an arch.

Nala linked to Daniel's arm. Together they walked toward the form—lured almost—by the next shiny object. A chill drifted

233

across the surreal landscape, real or imagined Daniel wasn't sure, but Nala pulled closer to him. Sprig rode in a crouch on her shoulder partially hidden in the locks of her hair.

"Hello!" Daniel called out as they approached the newest popup. Like the posts and telescope lenses, the arch and its surroundings were formed from shiny foil, but portions of this newest scene *moved*.

It was an ordinary creek, complete with silver rocks in its streambed and metallic mercury-like water that flowed around them, gurgling and splashing as it went. An arched bridge spanned the creek. On the far side of the footbridge, the figure of a large animal lay prone with heavy forepaws crossed one on top of the other like a resting lion surveying the savannah. All made from shiny foil.

"Wow," Nala whispered, soaking in the complex scene and its authentic sounds. Daniel stepped onto the footbridge, which creaked like wood from his weight. A silver wall rose at the apex of the bridge, blocking his path.

Daniel stepped back and the barrier dropped. He stepped once more onto the bridge and the barrier rose, very much like a video game puzzle, but this one was easily solved. The wall was only hip high.

He walked to the apex of the bridge next to the barrier. He listened to the flowing creek beneath his feet and studied the resting animal on the other side. The animal felt more like a statue, no different than the twin lions in front of the New York Public Library in Manhattan. The figure itself wasn't quite a lion. More alien. Feathers formed the animal's mane, and its heavy paws were adorned with claws the size of scythes.

As Daniel watched, the animal's head turned toward him. Its large eyes focused on him. Catlike. Fierce.

"Yikes!" Nala yelled from behind.

Daniel's heart leaped and he backed up a step. Sprig disappeared into Nala's hair.

Hanging hard onto Daniel's arm, Nala's voice quivered. "We're not in our own universe. It can't possibly be a lion."

"It's not even real," Daniel said with conviction. He remained steady, letting his heart calm. The animal's head turned forward again, resuming its survey of an imagined grassland spread before it.

"Nothing here is real," Daniel continued. "These are creations, projected from the substance we're walking on. The surface itself might be intelligent. It's presenting these three-dimensional shapes one at a time."

"Why?"

Daniel shrugged, then strode purposefully back to the barrier. "If it's a test, it's pretty easy." He hopped over the barrier, one leg at a time. The silver lion was now only a few steps beyond the end of the arched bridge. He walked to the animal, stood in front of its large head, then squatted to examine its paws. They flexed, extending long claws, but both paws remained in place beneath the complacent animal.

Daniel stood up. "See, it's a pussycat."

The lion roared, reached up with one giant paw and swatted toward Daniel. He leaped back, heart in his throat and stumbled backward across the squishy silver surface. Nala jumped the footbridge barrier and ran to his side.

The alien lion calmed, repositioned its legs beneath its body, and returned its gaze straight ahead.

"You okay?" Nala asked.

"Frightened, but the claws didn't touch me." They retreated to a safer distance well away from the creek.

Nala said, "That didn't feel like communication to me."

235

Daniel's heart finally settled. The body reacts instinctively even when the mind knows the danger is manufactured. "Yeah, me neither. If it was making a point, I haven't figured it out."

They walked on. The animal remained in place, and no other wild beasts popped up. Once they were far enough away, Nala laughed uncomfortably. "When I started playing with quantum space a few years back, I imagined a dozen ways I might die," Nala said in that lighthearted way she used when speaking of dark subjects. "Acceptable risks, really. I can handle a physics death, but I'd prefer not to be eaten."

"It was *not* a lion," Daniel reminded. "Someone is communicating with us."

"Badly."

"Okay, maybe the message isn't clear. Maybe we need to do some brainstorming to figure this puzzle out." He stopped suddenly. "Or maybe not."

Directly ahead, another silvery form rose up. It rotated. It flashed pinpricks of light in multiple colors. It spoke.

They hurried over, surprised to find a detailed model of a rotating galaxy. About ten feet across, the galactic disc angled forward with its axis attached to the surface while the rest slowly spun in a circle. Tiny pinpricks of light along the galaxy's arms glittered in orange, white, and blue. Red nebulae glowed, providing a marked color difference between this newest scene and the plain silver foil that had formed every other object they'd passed.

Most interesting, the rotating galaxy spoke to them with a female voice and American pronunciations. It could easily have been Nala speaking. "Four point three... one... three... identifier one eight seven one six." There was a pause, then the same sequence repeated once more.

"Are you writing this down?" Daniel asked Sprig. He'd do it himself if he had a piece of paper, but Sprig's memory probably equaled any computer.

"I have it," Sprig answered. "4.3, 1, 3, identifier 18716." Without context, the numbers felt meaningless. But it was the clearest indication yet of communication.

Nala squatted, peering beneath the galaxy and its stand, searching for the source of the voice. "Okay, so now they're speaking to us. The lions, tigers, and bears theory is hereby rejected, and Daniel's theory of alien communication is accepted with full apologies from the dumbshit gallery."

"You're not dumb."

Nala stood up, staring at the galaxy model. This time she spoke with sincerity. "No, actually... I'm not. Notice anything unusual about this model?"

Daniel studied the newest formation of flowing silver. The galaxy continued its smooth rotation with multiple arms twisting around a central hub. It accurately represented a galaxy. Nothing out of the ordinary. Finally, the discrepancy hit him like a smack in the face. "Ah, yes. Wrong universe."

"We've crossed millions of light years in this universe and saw one disorganized band of matter. Not a single spiral. This is definitely communication. They know where we came from."

Daniel nodded, thinking through the possible implications of a galactic model that represented his universe, not theirs.

Without warning, Nala jumped, grabbing Daniel around the waist. "Hang on, scientist, we've got company." She motioned with a jerk of her head.

Two humanoid figures loomed from the fog, coming directly toward them. They walked with a crisp gait, heads held high, and arms moving in synchronization with legs. Everything made from the same shiny foil.

"Showtime," she said, unlatching herself from Daniel and clearing her throat.

Daniel stood close at her side doing his best to think rationally while suppressing a range of more primitive emotions that never helped in a first contact situation.

One silver figure stood taller than the other. The shorter figure had coils of long hair framing the head. The glowing fog finally thinned enough to reveal familiar facial features.

"They're us," Daniel gasped.

Silver models of Daniel and Nala stopped only a few meters away. The smooth foil simplified some features but provided enough detail to make both faces recognizable. Daniel's angular jaw, his tall forehead, and thick eyebrows. Nala's elegant neck, prominent cheek bones, and large eyes. Shiny metal head to foot, but unmistakably *them*.

Apprehensive, Daniel stared at his doppelganger who remained motionless except for a slight rhythmic expansion in the chest. "Look at their feet," he whispered. Silver shoes blended into the surface as if they'd melted into place.

"It's like a mirror but creepy." Nala's silver model even sported a metallic rendering of Sprig on one shoulder. Sprig huddled deeper into Nala's hair. The silver version did the same.

The figures stepped closer. The silver model of Daniel reached out one hand. Fingernails and joints were finely crafted, even a hint of fingerprints at the tips. It extended an index finger.

Daniel hesitated, not sure whether to respond or recoil. Like the silver lion, would it lash out? His heart pounded, nerves on edge.

"He wants you to—"

"Yeah. I know."

Daniel lifted his own hand, momentarily hovered his index finger in the air, then touched the copy. No spark. No mind meld. Cool metal, nothing more.

Nala's silver model offered the same physical touch. Nala didn't hesitate, quickly tapping her own finger to the metallic version.

A new voice came quickly after. Not through the air and not a voice they could hear, yet the words easily resonated inside their heads.

"Welcome," the precise imitation of Daniel's voice said. "Your form is familiar."

25   REGISTRATION

DUPLICATES OF DANIEL AND NALA stood a few feet away, stuck to the surface of the silver planetoid where they originated. Their posture and facial expressions mimicked the Humans with fluid motions that could easily pass for the real thing.

The silver mouth of Daniel's model moved; its voice mimicked his. "We are Surveyors. Processing agents. Are your needs met?"

"We're breathing, if that's what you mean," Daniel answered.

"We strive for health throughout the registration process," the Surveyor said. Oddly put, but always good to hear benevolent intent explicitly stated.

"Registration?" Nala asked.

Nala's duplicate spoke with a voice almost matching hers, if slightly more machinelike. "You have arrived at the Registration Station established by Choreographers. Welcome."

Their near-perfect Human shapes began to droop, melting into formless stalagmites. The pointy piles of goo then stretched to twice their height. Features reappeared. A narrow head with vertically slit eyes perched above a flat torso. Skinny arms hung on either side. Skinny legs bowed outward as if made of rubber. While there were no elbow or knee joints—nor ears, a nose, or mouth—the overall shape could certainly be classified as humanoid.

"We now take the form of Choreographers," a new voice announced. It no longer sounded like Daniel or Nala but came with a slight echo and auditory distortions that gave it a bubbly quality. "Choreographers are similar to your own form. Do you see?"

"Yes, quite similar." Daniel said.

The name Choreographer suggested people who excelled at creative design. Not exactly how anyone might describe the maze of woven tubes they'd passed, or the rather plain silver orb. These were functional structures hardly confused with choreographing a creative dance. But Humans often built plain rectangular boxes for homes and businesses yet were capable of vastly more inventive results when prompted to be creative. Perhaps the allusion to dance suggested an alien race with talents not yet seen.

As for the Surveyors, they might be anything from Terminator-style liquid metal machines to a single exotic lifeform unclassifiable by Human standards. They had identified themselves as agents, likely serving the Choreographers if these names carried the same meaning Humans would apply.

For Daniel, one thought stood out. *We've found the mapmakers.*

If true, then these Surveyors—or their masters—understood the Chaos Field. Perhaps they had crossed it themselves long ago, stood on the Afeesh Tm planet, and grafted bio-integration computers onto the heads of seven Sibyls. The Arc of Progression—as Tennah had named the curving silver plate above her ear—looked remarkably similar to several of the smooth metal structures that had extruded from the moldable surface.

Logic led to a second thought. *If they know the Chaos Field, then we still have a chance to get home.*

"Did the Choreographers create this place?"

"Choreographers create wherever they go," Daniel's Surveyor replied. "Their origin lies not far from this registration station. You may visit the remains if desired."

"Remains? How long ago are we talking?" Nala asked.

"More than the lifetime of a planet."

"So… billions of years?"

The Surveyors gave no reply. No matter, the origin story could wait. For now, Daniel needed his key question answered. "We crossed the Chaos Field to get here. Do you know it?"

"It is the whole purpose of the registration station."

Daniel and Nala exchanged glances. Daniel would be happy to hand over his phone number, Social Security number, and mother's maiden name if registration came with tips on how to get home.

Sprig peered out from behind Nala's hair, listening and observing without comment, as was its style. The leaf would make a good spy.

"In their journeys across this universe, the Choreographers discovered the Chaos Field. It required fifty generations to learn its secrets. Every universe, including this one and your own began from chaos and will end when chaos consumes it."

The Humans listened. Sprig emerged further, clinging to Nala's shirt as the Surveyors' story continued.

"Once the Choreographers learned the principles that guide chaos, they built and secured this registration station, then left to travel the unknown spaces beyond the Chaos Field. Universe after universe; there are more than you might imagine. In each, they sought people similar to themselves. Your arrival is evidence of their success."

Nala circled one of the Surveyors, studying its silvery form from all sides. "I don't suppose your traveling friends create giant four-dimensional rings as they go? We found one. Big as a galaxy. You can't miss it."

"A guidance marker," one Surveyor answered. Its metallic body twisted as Nala rounded it, yet its feet remained glued to the orb's surface. "Choreographers place these circular markers where best suited to draw visitors. Each visitor to the guidance planet at the marker's center is given instructions and a map to travel

243

between universes. Some survive their journey. Some do not. Some look like you. Others do not, though the trend is in your direction."

"Weird how we keep encountering humanoids on this trip," Nala said, mostly to Daniel. Though he had thoughts forming on this topic, for now Daniel kept them to himself.

"How many universes?" he asked instead.

"Any count we provide would be meaningless. A registration station can last only as long as the universe it occupies. Eventually, our time here will end. Eternity—and the Chaos Field—will continue. No one can know how many universes existed in the past, or exist now, or will exist."

"But you count anyway? You'll register us, which adds one more to the list?"

"You are already registered. Your small companion too. We observed your arrival. Examined your probability vector. You come from a universe previously catalogued: Mass four by three, spin one, element three scarce, identifier 18716."

Daniel recognized the number sequence at the end. "It's the galaxy model you presented to us just now."

"Yes."

The spinning galaxy bore no resemblance to collections of matter in this universe, as Nala had noted. These Surveyors had reached into the scout ship's navigation records to discover not just their home universe, but the Milky Way.

Nala stood motionless, deep in thought. She repeated the Surveyor's descriptor as if trying to make sense of its words. "*Mass four by three.* Four. By. Three. Twelve. There are twelve fermions—quarks and leptons—the fundamental particles of mass. Four rows in the Standard Model, each with three flavors of the particle type."

The Surveyor standing across from her answered. "You are correct. Some universes have more. Others group differently."

The light had come on for Nala. "Then your *spin one* must represent the forces in our universe. Except for the Higgs, which is a scalar boson, every gauge boson for a fundamental force has a spin of one."

Daniel smiled at his wife. The last part of the Surveyors' moniker now made sense too. "Element three scarce."

"Lithium," Nala said. "Element number three."

Daniel nodded. "They've got us pegged. For some reason, our universe comes up short on lithium. It's been a head-scratcher for every student of the Big Bang."

"And now we know," Nala answered. "There's no reason for lithium being rarer than expected, it's just who we happen to be over in the land known as Mass Four by Three, Spin One, Element Three Scarce."

"And the five-digit identifier at the end?" Daniel asked the Surveyors.

"There are many universes like your own."

"More than eighteen thousand?" The identifier certainly suggested such a number. If there were tens of thousands of physical duplicates, how many more universes varied by one or more fundamental parameter? Millions? Billions?

"Our registration task is large and has continued for some time."

Nala cozied up next to Daniel. "These two are super good at understatement."

"They're also key players in a big mystery—the map itself. All those zettabytes inside every Sibyl's head must have come from here. What I want to know is why? Why bring people here? Just to count how many survive the Chaos Field?"

Daniel's Surveyor loomed overhead. "Your question cannot be answered. Neither of you is equipped to comprehend."

"The fuck?" Nala planted herself between Daniel and the much larger Surveyor. Daniel started to reach out but decided to let it go. Once riled, Nala would find a resolution—her way. She might be petite, to paraphrase Shakespeare, but she was fierce.

Nala poked the air with her finger. "Who says we're not equipped? I could tell you a thing or two about quantum fields. Sure, this Chaos version might be the mother of all quantum fields. Super... let's study it. We hear it's primordial, eternal, and probabilistic. But if it's a quantum field, I assure you we are perfectly capable of comprehending it."

The silver figure remained in place, but its facial features flattened like the softest of metals withering under an intense heat lamp. It finally answered. "The field itself, perhaps."

"Then what are we not equipped to comprehend? The map?"

"The map is nothing, a tool no different than a utensil."

Nala took another step closer. "The map creates a probability vector to guide through a randomly fluctuating quantum field. We're not stupid. Neither are our Chitza friends who built some pretty impressive tech to bring us here."

She pointed a thumb back to Daniel. "Answer his question. Why do you bring people here if all you're doing is counting?"

Daniel smiled with pride. He couldn't have made the case any better.

The Surveyor shrank to Nala's height and reshaped itself into a Human form again, mirroring Nala's features but not her aggressive stance. Nala's voice returned too. "For your benefit, we will simplify our descriptions."

Nala glanced over her shoulder at Daniel. Her shrug said it all. *I'll take what I can get.* Daniel agreed. They'd arrived at a place unlike anything else in the universe, or perhaps any universe. They'd take their best shot at understanding it, and then figure out if they had a chance of getting home.

Nala's Surveyor spoke calmly. "The map is easily shared with any technologically capable species. Yes, you and the quilled pilots of your ship are capable of following it. But its probability vector did not bring you here. Creation brought you here. Evolution brought you here. Time brought you here."

Nala backed down—just a little. She didn't look disturbed, more perplexed. Daniel felt the same. The Surveyor's list of things that brought them here made little sense.

"In the distant past," the Surveyor continued, "a time you call 13.8 billion years ago—the Chaos Field sparked your universe into existence... as it did... as it does... and as it will for uncountable more universes. One of many, your universe is a large collection of matter within expanding space. Profound in its own way, but miniscule in comparison to the totality of reality."

Any discussion of the multiverse could always be counted on for shock and awe. Clearly they were talking big numbers.

The Surveyor continued. "Over uncountable eons of time continuing even now, your evolutionary success confirms reality, reinforces it, and shapes it. You are a proud species. Rightfully so. You are a product of the evolution of reality. Your path to this station helps to reinforce future evolutions of new life, new universes, and of reality itself. Reality learns from you, adjusts based on your uniqueness, and evolves toward a greater good."

"Very deep," Nala said. "And still obscure."

Daniel agreed. The Surveyors seemed heavy on grandeur and thin on details. But he had picked out enough from the soliloquy to summarize it in question form. "You're saying you need us. Registration helps you, incrementally. We represent a small step toward your goal of a greater good. Is that it?"

"You are correct."

It felt a lot like big data, the routine activity of every social media company: collect volumes of personal information with no prospect to opt out, then use it for purposes defined solely by the data collectors but never quite explained to anyone else. The Surveyors showed no outward hostility or gave any hints of nefarious purposes. They'd been condescending, not belligerent, but did that mean their idea of a greater good matched anyone else's?

Back home, sweeping generalizations were a sure-fire way to obscure an underlying intent. Daniel threw out the obvious question. "You want to register more people like us?"

"Want? No. The trend toward people that look, function, and behave like you is a byproduct of the original placement of guidance markers, the ring you observed in your universe. It is a recognized bias introduced by the Choreographers long ago and not easily corrected without extensive travel. As Surveyors, we collect and process information. We do not travel. The Choreographers created the original structure. If they still exist, they may be adding to it even now. We cannot know for certain since remote activities are measurable only through new registrations."

Nala turned to Daniel. "These guys are duty bound. Condescending machines subservient to the Choreographers who are off galivanting around the multiverse. Or dead."

Daniel nodded, hoping these *condescending machines* wouldn't take offense to her blunt but accurate characterization. They controlled an extradimensional claw that could drag people out of a spacecraft. They might have a few other tricks up their silver sleeves too.

"Your registration is complete," one Surveyor reminded. "You are free to leave."

"Good to hear," Daniel said while mentally sorting through the unfathomable distances he and Nala had traversed in the last week. "Unfortunately, we got here via a probability vector that can't be reversed. We'd like to return to our own universe, but honestly, we don't know how."

The Surveyor answered, "To return, create a new probability vector configured for your navigation system. All map couriers can perform this simple task."

Dang.

They'd crossed billions of light-years in two different universes. They'd survived a landscape of chaos that words couldn't adequately describe. Yet now they were being told that the path home required a Sibyl. They needed Tennah.

"We had a map courier. We had to drop her off to handle a personal matter, so now we're on our own," Daniel said. Not quite on their own. The mapmakers themselves—or at least their agents—were standing right in front of them. These Surveyors might be condescending, they might only be traffic accountants, but it was worth an ask. "I'm hopeful that you could supply us with that return map."

The Surveyors gave no reply. A minute later, their figures melted back into the silver surface of the orb.

26 ENHANCEMENT

PRO TIP FOR TRAVELERS CROSSING the Chaos Field: if you intend to get home, bring your map courier with you. The outbound path bears no resemblance to the inbound.

Beginner's mistake, but then Tennah herself, who had on occasion joined crews traveling to the boundary, hadn't realized she would be needed for the return trip. Inadequate Sibyl training perhaps, or a hesitancy, given the obvious dangers of jumping headfirst into a primordial nursery for new Big Bangs.

Daniel held no hard feelings. He reserved his frustration for the Surveyors, who had offered no help or instructions. They'd simply melted into the orb, leaving Daniel and Nala standing alone on a fog-enshrouded silver surface. Even the artistic extrusions—the telescope, footbridge, alien lion, and rotating galaxy—had been reabsorbed into the surreal surface.

"You pissed them off," Nala suggested.

"They're pissing *me* off." Daniel paced, thinking mostly about the nothingness that surrounded them. "How do we get ourselves into these jams?"

Nala plunked herself down, sitting cross-legged on the slightly compressible surface. "Hey, at least it's an intellectual conflict."

"Which is better than…?"

"Better than battling slime-dripping alien baddies. You know… valiant hero bashes one monster after another in his struggle to reach the *Scimitar of Truth*, the only weapon capable of slaying the evil priest of magic, Sauron McGollum!"

She smiled. "Now I'm not saying you wouldn't be good at that evil priest slaying business… you would. I can picture you in your flowing robe, braided hair down your back, light saber—"

"You're mixing your epic fantasies."

Nala hopped up, draped herself around him, and smothered his cheek, neck, and ear with kisses. "Daniel my love, your bulging biceps might not measure up to Aqua-Super-Batman, but you're my hero. Always have been. I wouldn't be standing here if you hadn't trekked literally across the fricken universe to find me. And it's not the first time either."

Daniel immediately brightened. How could he not? He returned her kiss. "You're right, we'll get home somehow."

"Well, I didn't say *that*. But even if we're stuck in this universe, we'll make do. We've got Chitza friends with a capable ship that's stocked with food. We'll find a planet, then you and I can go all Adam and Eve."

Daniel hugged her tightly. "We'll plant an apple tree."

"Garden of Eden women are into apples."

"But first we need to get back to the ship." He stared straight up into foggy air. Somewhere above, the Chitzas orbited. The scout ship would be perfectly capable of landing if only they knew where to go. A silver extrusion in the form of a kilometer-high sign that read, "Land here!" would help.

No extrusion appeared from the fog. But something else did. Two new figures. Small, furry. Not silver at all.

Nala took two halting steps, then ran toward them. "Aussik! Veronica! You found us!" She hugged both Chitzas, taking care not to tangle with their quills.

"We got directions," Aussik said.

"From silver people even taller than you!" Veronica added.

"After they registered us," Aussik finished.

Daniel joined them, relieved to see at least half of the Chitza crew unharmed. "So, you landed the ship?"

Aussik shook his head. "Naw, after you two got scraped out I was checking for damage. Next thing I knew, the same blue bars swept through and dragged us out."

"Zeeno was fuming mad," Veronica added. "He's never happy about intruders. But twice! He's probably loading the— oh, we're probably not supposed to tell you about the JammerBlaster."

Daniel held up a hand. "At this point, I'm not sure I want to know. What I'd rather see is the ship parked, and Zeeno waiting for us to board. Unless he and Beets were clawed out too?"

Aussik and Veronica shook their heads and spoke in unison, "We would have heard them."

Aussik explained that the Surveyors pointed them in the right direction, but within minutes they zeroed in on Daniel and Nala just from their voices. Apparently, Chitzas had exceptional hearing.

"We saw a jutka monster," Veronica bragged. "Very rare. They live in the swamps on our planet, but this one was made from the same stuff we're walking on. This place is crazy, but I like it."

Nala eyed Daniel. "In our case, the figure was a silver lion. Not real of course. Daniel thinks the Surveyors were trying to communicate. But we did just fine talking with them, so now I think all those silver figures were there just to hold our attention."

While they shared their common experience, Daniel kept an eye peeled for any new extrusions. It seemed unlikely that the Surveyors had abandoned them. After all, they were registered visitors. Perhaps the blue bars would appear once more and return them to the ship. For that matter, Zeeno might get antsy, land, stick an ear out the hatch, and listen for voices. It wasn't a terribly large planet.

Motion in the distance caught his eye. It definitely wasn't Zeeno or the ship. A rolling wave deformed the surface. The wave grew in height as it neared, splitting into three parts. Higher in the

253

middle than on the sides. Just as it seemed the wave would sweep over them, it froze.

The two side waves coalesced into blobby pillars about Chitza height. Halfway up the central wave, a hole opened, allowing a clear view to the fog behind. A flat, hip-high platform emerged just below the hole, extending straight out toward them like a bed awaiting an occupant. Several projections extruded from around the perimeter of the hole like robotic arms. Some arms were articulated. Others just a cylindrical bar that projected into the center of the hole with an array of tools set on a rotating chassis: hooks, needles, and flat metal tabs. It reminded Daniel of a medical scanning machine, but one only an evil doctor could love.

One of the squat blobs slid across the surface and stopped in front of Daniel. A bubbling voice sounded. "Installation of a probability vector requires a receptacle. You?"

Nala glanced to Daniel then back to silvery figures. She jumped in front of Daniel. "Not him, use me."

"Wait, wait." Daniel pushed her aside and studied the machine behind its operator. The tools pointing into the hole included one that looked like power drill, complete with a set of drill bits at its business end. Another looked like an oversized tube of toothpaste, but it glowed with radiant heat as the air around it shimmered.

Next to the bed-like platform, an open-top container was filled with a collection of electronics components—LEDs, capacitors, possibly a few integrated circuits. But unlike electronic parts found on Earth, these featured short wires sticking out from their base that wiggled like a vibrating strand of spaghetti. They appeared to be alive.

This machine had been sent to perform an installation, and Daniel had a good idea what the finished product might look like. "Don't do it," he warned Nala.

"A probability vector requires a receptacle," the silver blob repeated.

Nala grabbed Daniel's arms and pushed him back. "They need a receptacle to hold the map data. A volunteer to become a Sibyl. That's me."

Daniel remained firm. "No way in hell I'm going to let this thing screw a metal plate into the side of your head."

Nala looked into his eyes. "Daniel... this *thing* is offering a new map. It's our way home."

He turned to the pillar blob. "Why do you need a receptacle? Can't you download a new probability vector data directly into our ship? It's parked right above us. It might even have landed. Just plug in."

The machine operator's voice remained steady without emotion. "A probability vector requires a *biological* receptacle." Its vocabulary might be limited but it seemed to understand Daniel's request. He didn't like its answer.

Nala kept pushing Daniel away from the machine. She wasn't half as strong, but she could put up a good fight when she wanted to. "Daniel, it's the only way. I learned about the Arc of Progression when I met Jazameh on the Afeesh Tm's planet. It's not just a computer or even a data store, it's an interface to a biological component. The combined intelligence is greater than the sum of each part. It's why they need Sibyls. Connecting directly to the ship won't work—a probability vector is more than a download, it takes a person."

Daniel succumbed to Nala's insistent force. "Okay... then I'll do it."

Nala shook her head. "Not a chance, big guy. Your head has already been scrambled by time entanglement. We're not going there again. Besides, there's a reason that the Afeesh Tm Sibyls are all female."

255

"Oh yeah? What?"

She threw up her arms in frustration. "Fuck if I know... but there is one. Jazameh said so. She said they stuck an Arc on a male once, and it didn't work. I don't know why. I don't even think Jazameh knew why. Maybe it's that male stubbornness all you guys have."

She smiled, sweetly. "Daniel, I'm the one who screwed up. I knew where the Chitzas were going, and I didn't tell you. I made you chase me across the universe. So, it's my turn to carry the load. I can do this."

Daniel wanted to wrap his arms around her. Pull her away from an unthinking machine bent on creating a *combined intelligence.* Keep her safe. Whole. Unaltered.

But he didn't. He released her.

She kissed him. "Think of it like new jewelry. It'll be pretty."

Daniel sighed. She clearly had more information than he did, and she'd learned it from the source—an Afeesh Tm woman who had first-hand experience with the device.

Nala turned to the machine. "I'm your receptacle."

Veronica tapped Nala's hip. "I'm female too."

Nala countered. "Doesn't work for Chitzas. You're too small."

Veronica scrunched up her eyes. "I'm pretty sure you just made that up."

Nala pointed to the machine. "See the operating table? Human sized. Besides, I'm just a passenger. You're our Safety Officer. We need you unaltered to get us home... safely."

Daniel had seen Nala's persuasive arguments before. Veronica never had a chance, though he admired the Chitza's courage. Veronica shrugged and backed away.

Nala hopped onto the bed like a patient in an examination room. "You want me to lie down?" she asked, then did it anyway. She pulled the hair on her head back, exposing Sprig who scurried out from its hiding place and leaped several feet through the air, landing on Daniel's shirt. The leaf ducked into his shirt pocket. Only its tip peeked out.

The operating table began to retract into the hole, centering Nala's head beneath silver protrusions. With an array of surgical instruments just inches away, Nala's eyes shifted nervously. Daniel stood by her side, holding her hand. The two silver blobs merged into either end of the standing wave, adding to Daniel's eerie feeling that the orb's whole surface was conscious in some way.

A silver arm with a rounded pad at its tip pushed against the side of her head. From the arm, two clips unfolded. One secured itself to the top of her head, the other below her chin.

Daniel steeled himself for the procedure ahead. Painless integration between a Human brain and an electronics circuit board seemed unlikely. Nala pinched her lips and closed her eyes. Her grip on Daniel's hand tightened.

The alien power drill rotated through a selection of bits and other pointy things. It stopped on an innocuous glass marble. A second later, a blue laser shot out, hitting Nala's head just above her ear. Locks of hair fell away, exposing smooth, brown skin as the centimeter-wide beam moved in a succinct stripe from left to right, then doubled back to cut another row. The smell of burning hair wafted across the operating bench, but her skin showed no signs of damage.

A nozzle tool sprayed a light mist, leaving a coating of white powder across her skin. Then the toothpaste tube clicked into position. Its red glow throbbed like a stove's heating element varying between medium and high.

"Be ready, this one might be hot," Daniel warned. Nala nodded rapidly, eyes still tightly closed.

The tube touched behind her ear and crept forward leaving a gooey silver stripe behind. The goo stuck like thick paint. Nala squinted in a grimace.

"You okay?" Daniel asked, afraid to hear the answer.

"Sort of," she said through gritted teeth.

While the arm drew its bead of molten metal, one of the articulated arms plucked an LED from the plastic container of parts. Its wiggling appendages looked like an insect caught in pinchers. In one swift motion, it pushed the LED into the goo, then repeated its actions snatching multiple components from the container one at a time. Each component had its own set of wriggling legs, and each was flicked into a specific place in the silver goo.

Nala winced with each new prickly part added to her scalp. "Yes it's hot, and yes it hurts… but I can manage," she said with conviction, which provided Daniel not one bit of reassurance.

They're putting live bioelectronics into your head, he wanted to tell her, but didn't, in part because he really had no idea if the wriggling feet were truly alive.

More liquid metal flowed. More wriggling electronics embedded themselves. The agonizing installation finally completed with a bright flash of light which firmed the molten metal into a hard plate. The toolsets returned to their initial positions, and the clips retracted from her head and chin.

The operating table pulled away from the hole and Daniel helped Nala to a seated position. She peeked out from slit eyes, touched the side of her head, and winced. "What does it look like?"

A crescent plate of shiny silver rose a few millimeters from her scalp like an oversized item of avant-garde jewelry. Its larger lobe curved behind her ear. A smaller lobe in front ended in a point at her hairline. Several of the electronics had sunk beneath the silver surface, but a few protruded above creating small bumps. One by one, each bump lit up in various colors, activated by an unknown power-up process.

"They did a good job," Daniel answered. "Clean lines." There were more visceral descriptions he could have given, but there was no need to disturb the patient any further. What's done is done.

Nala tightened both fists. Her voice whined with a nervousness unlike her. "Daniel, it's reaching in. I can feel it, tingling. Getting deeper. I think it's connecting to me."

Daniel ached for her, wishing she hadn't done it but admitting that her motive had merit. Ugly or beautiful, adornment or scar, Nala's new alien interface could be their best hope to find a way home. The installation had been painful to watch, but its integration was apparently only beginning. Daniel imagined generations of Afeesh Tm girls suffering through something similar when an existing plate transferred from one person to the next. Nala might not be the first to experience *integration*, but that didn't make the process any less intrusive.

Its job complete, the wave machine packed up its tools and rolled back into the fog. Veronica and Aussik joined Daniel in a tight circle around Nala. The small Chitzas looked up with sympathy and concern. Nala lowered her head in concentration, lightly touching the LEDs as more of them lit.

From the fog, the Surveyors reappeared. Daniel positioned himself between the alien forms and Nala for whatever protection he might provide. His patience with these agents had grown thin. Their actions lacked empathy, both for visitors to this orb and for innocent bystanders like the Afeesh Tm, who now lived at an intergalactic crossroads for no reason other than their similar form to the Surveyors' masters, the Choreographers.

And now they had coerced Nala into accepting a bio-integration. At the very least, it was a gross infringement of bodily autonomy, but Daniel imagined potential side effects, even changes to her mental state. His only comfort were thoughts of Tennah, who despite having the same device embedded into her skull, had learned not only to accept it, but to value it.

Nala kept her eyes closed, gently rubbing her temple. She seemed to sense the Surveyors. "Oh, you two are something else. Holy crap, this is a major head rush. But you knew it would be, didn't you? Bastards."

The silver figures stopped ten feet away, silently watching as Nala coped. Daniel kept one arm around her and the other ready to fend off any further contact. Aussik and Veronica stood to either side. The quills on their backs bristled.

Nala twisted in discomfort, eyes still shut tight, voice tired. "I can feel the data. A whole bunch of it. And code... I guess it's code. There's an organizational structure to it all, sorting itself out. Indexing stuff for fast retrieval. Jesus Fucking Christ, I'm turning into a computer."

For Nala, profanity came with her personality, but generally limited to those times she was most agitated. Daniel had seen her upset, but this felt different. She'd been wounded, and her distress seemed to be getting worse, not better.

"Hang in there," Daniel whispered, then to the Surveyors, "Some help here? Is there something she should be doing to make this easier?"

"Bio-integration of the Arc varies across species. Her progress is normal."

Nala tensed, pushing clenched fists under her chin. Her closed eyelids squeezed even harder. "Uhhh!" she moaned. Her legs buckled. Daniel did his best to support her weight.

"How much longer?" he shouted to the Surveyors.

"Not long. The integration must proceed to completion."

Veronica stroked a paw against Nala's hip. The Chitza's quiet whimper sounded like a dove cooing. Even shy Sprig popped from the pocket on Daniel's shirt and crawled up to a perch on his shoulder. The leaf shivered.

"Would it be easier if you sat down?" Daniel asked. Nala shook off the question, pushing upright but wrapping both arms around Daniel's neck and hanging her weight on him.

She took a deep breath, speaking through gritted teeth. "Almost there. I think the last few bits are falling into place."

A minute later she took a deep breath and put more weight on her own feet. "I have to admit, it's a tight way to organize that much data. I see it, I feel it, but I have no idea how it got that way."

"What is it?"

She shook her head gently, a good sign that the pain was finally subsiding. Her eyes remained closed. "Hard to explain. It's like looking across an ocean, but every wave, every swell, every little current or eddy is all there. Easily measured... and somehow... *monitored* for fluctuations all the way down to the microscopic level."

"Chaos?"

"I guess. But chaos that's understood. Even managed. It's like the Goddess of the Ocean magically passes a hand across its surface and causes one tiny ripple to grow into a tidal wave. More than that... it's like *I'm* that goddess." Nala shook her head, stronger this time. "I can see across this ocean. Every ripple is

261

right there for me to touch. But there's something wrong. The ocean is wrong. It's not true chaos. Not really."

She opened her eyes wide, finally rejoining the here and now. She stared at Daniel. "Holy shit, it's not even random."

Nala let go of him and turned an intense gaze at the two Surveyors. Her gaze seemed to question the new information inside her head with astonishment—and a touch of fury.

Nala faced the silver forms. "Are you fucking kidding me? There's a seed?"

Both Surveyors shrunk to Human size. Their features reconfigured to mimic a Human face. They spoke in unison. "With the seed in your possession, a chaotic distribution of probabilities can be transformed into a useful navigation vector. But as you now recognize, once the meaning of the seed is grasped, you also gain a glimpse into the true nature of reality."

Nala calmed. She looked tired. But she nodded as the Surveyors spoke, and a sense of comprehension spread across her face.

Daniel's education in mathematics included a fair understanding of the relationship between the words *random* and *seed*. But he had no idea what Nala or the Surveyors were talking about.

27 REALITY

PARALLEL BARS FORMED INTO a spheroidal cage and swept Daniel and Nala away from their Chitza companions and away from the orb's surface with no more than a cursory warning from the Surveyors about *targeted molecular filtering*. Presumably technology that was capable of selecting a specific collection of molecules—skin, bones, organs, plus the air surrounding the body—then pushing that collection into a 4-D bubble and depositing it elsewhere. In a 2-D sense, the maneuver was no different than applying a postage stamp to an envelope.

Daniel found himself standing next to Nala on the upper deck of the Chitza ship, exactly where they had been extracted only an hour before. Nala leaned against him. Her body trembled. "Weak knees," she said, but he knew it was more than that. She now sported a metallic plate on the side of her head. Colored LEDs glowed and flashed. As she'd said herself, she'd been turned into a computer.

Seconds later, another cage swept through. Veronica and Aussik magically reappeared looking rattled but otherwise unharmed.

Zeeno emerged from the cockpit and welcomed them back. "I wasn't worried," he said. "Best damn crew in any universe. I knew you'd figure it out." His congratulations ended as soon as Aussik tapped the side of his own head to inform Zeeno that Nala had become their new map.

Zeeno took one look at Nala and twisted the tiny quills above his eyes. "She doesn't look good." Together, Zeeno and Daniel helped a disoriented Nala down the ladder, where Beets sat at her workstation.

"Let's give her some rest before we do any downloads," Daniel said. He supported his wife at one elbow. She wobbled, clearly dizzy.

Nala wasn't having any of it. She pushed Beets out of the way and leaned both palms on the workstation desk. "I'll rest later. We need to get this done now, while it's still fresh in my mind. Plug me in."

Daniel had seen Tennah do it, but watching Beets attach a data transfer wire into his wife's head was far more unsettling. Tennah had years of experience downloading data and configuring probability vectors. Nala faced her first installation only minutes after major brain surgery.

She steadied herself with one hand against the ship's bulkhead, closed her eyes and waited. Beets monitored the workstation display as numbers scrolled across. The high-speed download seemed to drain Nala further, but when Daniel suggested they break it into phases, she brushed him away again. For reasons only she understood, the material in her head needed to come out.

Ten minutes later, the transfer finished, and Beets pulled the plug. Nala collapsed into the tiny Chitza chair. She ran a hand through the remains of her hair on the plate side, swallowed hard, then began studying the dual displays at the workstation. Her eyes darted. At times she pushed buttons, demonstrating an awareness of the Chitza technology without any training.

She worked for another fifteen minutes, sometimes pausing to go back and modify something she'd already completed. At one point, she hung her head and didn't move for a minute, either concentrating or nodding off.

"It's okay to rest. Lean against me," Daniel offered. She'd been through a lot and had to be nearing her physical limit.

Her head jerked upright. "Almost there." She took a deep breath and continued.

The metal plate on her head was surely the source of newfound skills, but her intensity came from a more personal place. Passion for her work had always been a part of Nala, but now it felt unnatural. Uncontrolled, as if it might drag her to a depth from which she might never recover. The obvious signs of fatigue made Daniel nervous that physical collapse could come at any moment.

He motioned to Veronica. "When this is done, is there someplace on the ship she can lie down?"

"I'll fix something up." Veronica whisked away. Given the tight confines of the Chitza ship, she wouldn't be able to do much, but Daniel appreciated the effort. The upper deck entryway and its cold metal floor might be as good as it got.

Nala kept at her configuration work for another ten minutes, at one point wiping tears from her eyes, but waving Daniel away when he tried to comfort her. She seemed unsure at times, but she faced an unfamiliar navigation system and techniques implanted into her brain by an alien device.

Finally, she pushed herself upright. "Best I can do." She wrapped both arms around Daniel's neck and melted into him.

"I got you," he said, lifting her limp body from the ground.

"This way." Veronica led to the back of the ship. Two large drawers had been pulled from a cabinet and stacked along the wall. They were still filled with supplies. The empty cabinet now formed a cubbyhole large enough for a Human to lie down. Veronica had lined the space with soft blankets.

"Perfect," Daniel told Veronica. He helped Nala lie down in the tight space, then crawled partially in himself, sitting with his back against the bulkhead and cradling Nala's head in his lap. Her eyes never opened, but a gentle motion in her chest assured she was finally getting the rest she needed.

Veronica squatted and caressed Nala's hair. "Sleep well. We'll do our best to give you a smooth ride."

"Thanks, Veronica. Go do your job. We'll be fine here."

"She's going to be okay, isn't she?"

Daniel nodded. "She's strong."

Veronica handed Daniel a can of Chitza soda from the supply drawer, then left. A few minutes later, the ship's turbines rumbled to life. Somehow, nestled into the comfortable cubby, the vibrations felt calming. If Nala had managed to set things right, this ship would soon be heading back across this mostly empty universe toward the Chaos Field. And, if they were lucky, toward home.

Daniel didn't need a window to sense their slow path back through the cobweb of tubes surrounding the Surveyors' silver planetoid. After an hour, the ship accelerated. A slight disorientation accompanied their jump into higher dimensions where compression would then carry them across light years of empty space with the occasional band of cold matter.

For now, their goal was simple: survive the Chaos Field once more and return to their home universe. The one called, Mass Four by Three, Spin One, Element Three Scarce, Identifier 18716. One universe among uncountable possibilities.

The ship's floor vibrated from spinning turbines. Chitzas quieted throughout the cabin, and Daniel finally relaxed for the first time since they'd departed from Afeesh Tm. Nala's eyes twitched in deep sleep. Lights glowed on the side of her head. He used his fingers to comb hair over the panel.

My beautiful wife, he thought.

Still as beautiful as the day he'd met her at Fermilab, Daniel had never been the kind of guy who ignored physical features. Nala was easily the most attractive woman he'd ever been with, and it wasn't hard to see even greater beauty inside, now that they'd been together for several years. Vivacious, spontaneous, and with a sharp wit, this woman would forever stir him.

Was she now tarnished? On the outside, slightly. But with time and patience, the plate could eventually be ignored, maybe even appreciated as a new part of her exotic glamour. What might be happening on the inside worried him more. If the bio-integration had damaged her joyful personality, he would hurt forever.

Daniel shifted to get comfortable, taking care not to awake Nala. He could use some sleep himself, but his mind wouldn't allow it. There were far too many events in the past twenty-four hours to sort through, analyze, organize, and ultimately fit into a mental image that made sense.

The most disturbing came from Nala minutes ago. "It's not random," she'd said when the new panel on her head had powered up. She had described its flood of data as an ocean with waves, eddies, and microscopic fluctuations that could be monitored and managed. Her description felt like the Chaos Field, which made sense given that the whole purpose of this device was to allow the wearer to create a probability vector capable of navigating across this bizarre quantum field.

But Nala and the Surveyors had also spoken of a *seed*. Moreover, he understood their talk to represent mathematics, not botany.

Scientists had long recognized the mathematical underpinnings of nature. The force of gravity, for example, varied precisely by the square of the distance between two masses. But probability was different. Probability required mathematics only as a counting system for random variation. Unlike gravity, probabilities weren't deterministic. There was no equation that provided the outcome of the flip of a coin based on past results. Even after ten heads in a row, the results of the next flip could not be predicted.

Mathematically, probabilities were best understood through a bell-shaped graph—the so-called normal or Gaussian distribution. Flip a coin a hundred times, and the most probable outcome would be fifty heads and fifty tails. But repeat this exercise, and you might see fifty-five heads. Occasionally, even sixty heads. Very rarely would the outcome of one hundred coin flips be eighty heads but it was not impossible. The resulting graph—a smooth curve highest in the middle and dropping away to extremes on either end—was the best representation of any random event.

Random event.

Many things unpredictable were not necessarily random. The height of a growing child depended on age, health, the height of their parents, and environmental factors. Lightning strikes were not randomly distributed, they were closely correlated to zones where thunderstorms occurred. Surprisingly, birthdays weren't randomly scattered through the year. Large datasets proved that birthdays fell more often in July through October than in other months. The act of conception enjoyed a favored time of year, nine months prior.

But quantum physics was absolutely, positively random. The chance that an electron would be found in a given position relative to its atomic nucleus was random. In the two-slit experiment, the chance that any single photon would pass through one slit and not the other was random. A neutron decaying into a proton, an electron, and an electron antineutrino to produce a radioactive click on a Geiger counter was not just an unpredictable event, it was a *random* event. At least, it was supposed to be.

Daniel struggled with Nala's comment as quantum probability data filled her head, "It's not random." Event probabilities for any quantum field *had* to be random. There could be no other choice. To declare something fundamentally quantum not to be random would be like saying that radioactive decay was only allowed on Tuesdays.

Could reality be hiding a mathematical secret? Could there be a quantum field that broke the rules? Though the words between them had been few, Nala and the Surveyors seemed to have the answer for the Chaos Field. "There's a seed," they'd said.

The concept of a random seed stood at the intersection between mathematics and computer science. Computer programmers routinely used random numbers to simulate the actions of game characters or shuffle a deck of electronic cards. *Give me a random number between one and fifty-two,* the solitaire card game programmers would ask before laying out the cards. In reality, they got something different. A computer was not capable of duplicating the randomness found in nature. Every step executed by every computer in the world was determined by the previous steps. A computer could do nothing by chance.

So, programmers wrote code to generate *pseudo*-random numbers that faithfully reproduced a normal distribution of probabilities. For example, to ensure that the likelihood of drawing the ace of spades from a shuffled card deck was precisely one out of fifty-two, no higher and no lower. To do this, they initiated their random number generator with a seed—a starting point. A seed was simply a unique number, often the current date and time down to the millisecond. Insert that seed into the code, and you got a set of numbers entirely determined by the seed but that *appeared* to be random.

A typical random number generator could produce a billion sequential numbers indistinguishable from random. But anyone who knew the seed could reproduce those numbers in exactly the same sequence. The seed became the key. Without it, events appeared to be random. With it, secrets were revealed.

Nala had apparently grasped something fundamental. She'd seen it immediately when the Arc powered up. Perhaps every Sibyl saw it too, but the Afeesh Tm weren't educated in mathematics. Nala was.

The Surveyors confirmed it. They had agreed with Nala that a probability vector designed to navigate the Chaos Field depended on a seed. The implications were staggering. If the Chaos field lay at the foundation of every universe, and its true nature appeared random but was not precisely random, then what did that say about any other random event in every universe generated from a Big Bang?

A deep secret is hidden at the heart of reality.

He could express his conclusion in thought, but he couldn't intellectually digest it. Not yet. He'd need Nala awake and engaged. Strangely, his discomfort didn't stop at her revelation of seeds and randomness. The name Choreographer—along with its meaning—jumped to the forefront of his mind.

28 RANDOM SEED

NALA SLEPT, DANIEL PONDERED, and the Chitzas piloted their ship across a universe not their own. Veronica rummaged through the supply drawers that she'd removed from the cabinet and pulled out two packets. She inserted them into a wall-mounted heater then handed one to Daniel. "You look like you could use some comfort food."

The scent of stir fried noodles wafted from the open packet. Veronica sat on the deck across from Daniel and slurped up her own noodle snack. Daniel tasted his, as delicious as any dish from a five-star Cantonese restaurant.

"Good times, huh?" Veronica asked. "On the road, new places, new adventures, and good company."

"Do Chitzas ever stop?" Daniel asked.

"Stop what?" Veronica gave a sly grin. "Getting into trouble?"

"Yeah, that."

"Chitzas never back down, especially when there's exploring to do. As I said, good times." Her voice quieted. "How is she doing?"

Daniel tucked one of the blankets around Nala. Her sleep had been restless, interrupted by occasional fits when she mumbled unintelligible warnings. Each time, she eventually calmed and snuggled closer to Daniel.

"I guess we'll find out when she wakes, but deep down she's one of you. An explorer."

"You are too," Veronica said.

"Debatable," Daniel said with a grin. "My type of exploration involves connecting the dots. Speaking of which, I have an experiment that needs your help." He pulled the olinwun coin from his pocket and tossed it to Veronica. She held up the holographic coin with a puzzled look.

"Flip it in the air ten times," he told her.

Veronica did as he asked, while Daniel recorded the results of each flip. Sprig stirred from its position on his shoulder. The coin performed as reasonably as could be expected of any coin.

"Even," Sprig said. "Five heads and five tails." Veronica returned the coin to Daniel, and he duplicated the same ten flips, this time getting four heads and six tails, a perfectly reasonable variance in a random world.

"Nothing wrong with this universe," Daniel said, then explained to Veronica. "When we were inside the Chaos Field I flipped this same coin forty or fifty times and it landed with the eagle side up every time."

"Ooh! I like it."

"You like it? The results suggest an aberration of reality."

"Exactly. That chaos place is freaky cool. When we get back to the boundary, we should do some other experiments. Like, what happens if you look in a mirror? Do you see somebody else? Or maybe you see yourself, but you're inside out?"

Daniel appreciated her active imagination. "Absolutely, let's do that."

Nala opened her eyes, blinked a few times, then smiled.

"Sleeping beauty awakes." Daniel caressed her cheek. "How are you feeling?"

"Better," Nala said. She looked around the narrow cubbyhole. "Nice setup. I've slept in Tokyo hotel rooms about this size."

"Veronica is quite resourceful."

Nala's smile returned. "Thanks, Veronica. I needed that."

Her personality remained intact, but that happy fact didn't eliminate Daniel's primal urge to dig fingernails under the panel's edge and rip it from the side of her head. Which—given a dozen electronic parts that had embedded their wiggly legs into her skull—would be a very bad idea.

She pushed herself to a sitting position and ran a hand above her ear as if she were checking to see if it had been a dream. "New haircut. A bit shorter than I normally go. Maybe when we get home, I'll buy some hoop earrings to go with it. Where are we, by the way?"

Veronica finished her meal and crumpled the packet into a ball. "You didn't miss anything. The fun stuff is still coming up. Aussik said he'd warn us when we got to the boundary. We're following your waypoints!"

Nala paled. "Daniel, it's not random. None of it," she said, as if repeating her pronouncement would clarify both how and why nature would disobey its own rules.

"I know," Daniel said. He showed her the olinwun and explained the results they'd just produced compared to what he had observed in the Chaos Field.

Nala pulled her legs close to her body and rocked. "It's a primordial quantum field. Jesus, if quantum chaos isn't random then nothing is."

Daniel understood her distress only too well. The foundation of her life's work had been shaken, a consequence not easily accomplished given that quantum physicists like Nala were used to results that didn't match common sense. She routinely explored theories conventional scientists wouldn't touch but even that work depended on a few bedrock principles. Random quantum fluctuations were as bedrock as it got.

"I should have paid more attention to my coin tosses," Daniel said. "But you knew something was wrong as soon as the Arc powered up."

Nala touched the alien panel like a wound she couldn't help but examine. "Wasn't hard to see. I can still see it. The stuff in my head is skewed. Imbalanced. You know, like if you poured a ton of gravel into a pickup truck and the truck bed ends up slightly tilted. You don't have to count the pebbles to know there's more on one side than the other. You spot it right away."

"And the random seed?"

"Yeah, weird. A bothersome kind of weird." The blank look on Veronica's face gave Nala a reason to include her in their somewhat technical conversation.

"In my work, I sometimes need to write computer code. We'll use a random number generator to create a sequence of numbers that have an unpredictable pattern but a uniform distribution. You know... spread evenly, with equal weight to each number like you're picking lottery balls from a rotating cage."

Veronica nodded, though it wasn't clear if Chitzas had lotteries.

"Casinos use random number generators too. If the results aren't random, gamblers will scream that the system is rigged and never play again. But a random number generator inside a computer isn't the same as a rotating cage of balls. It begins with a seed, a number that gets things started. If you know the seed, you know the upcoming sequence of numbers. To foil cheaters, gambling machines produce a thousand random numbers every second and the machine only grabs one when you press the Play button. It introduces enough chaos to give the impression of randomness."

She stopped, sighed, then stared at Daniel. Her eyes glanced sideways to the panel on her head. "But this thing... it's like stepping into the backroom at the casino and discovering how it all works. And like the casino, it turns out that reality isn't quite random either."

"The seed?"

"Seeds. Plural. Iterative too. Seeds generating seeds that feed into an algorithm so complex it makes a typical random number generator look like a dripping faucet next to a waterfall. When I write code, the seeds consume eight bytes in computer memory. Not eight thousand—eight. But even that tiny bit of memory can store a trillion possible starting points. Now... inside my lovely new jewelry..." She touched one of the LEDs, glowing red. "The seeds in here are each a zettabyte. That's one billion terabytes, and the code these seeds feed into is several more zettabytes. Altogether, it's a billion trillion times more complex than any random number generator Humans would ever write."

"Wow," Daniel said.

"Wow," Veronica repeated, though she still looked baffled.

"Wow exactly," Nala said.

Sprig leaped from Daniel's shoulder and landed on Nala's lap. "Your Arc device produces results indistinguishable from random," the leaf said. It had been following Nala's explanation well.

She leaned forward to Sprig. "If somebody wanted to play a trick on scientists, this is exactly how they'd do it. Pretend there's nothing to see. Make everything look perfectly natural on the surface and a hundred layers below. Rig it so anyone would have to dig ridiculously deep before they'd notice a single discrepancy from true random. So deep, only an obsessive fanatic would be that skeptical."

Daniel's thoughts spun chaotically as her point landed. He didn't like it one bit. "Randomness in nature is a lie, but it's a damned good one."

Nala pressed her lips together. "There's more."

"More in your head?"

"More to the story. The deception doesn't end at quantum scales. It's bigger."

"I was afraid you might say that." He'd been contemplating the ultimate impact of the Surveyors and their registration station for a while now. Guesswork, but an adventure across two different universes had provided a few clues. Unlike Daniel, Nala hadn't been observing the bits of evidence. She had been directly exposed to secrets hidden deep in reality. With Nala awake and fully rested, he could hear it from the source.

"Do Chitzas learn statistics?" Nala asked Veronica. "Standard deviations from a mean? Random distributions?"

"You mean math about coin flips?" Veronica answered. "Chitzas used to have coins but that was way back when my great grandmother was just a cub."

"Maybe your grannie knew that statistics can tell you how much a sample deviates from a larger distribution of random events? For example, if Daniel flips his coin a hundred times and gets fifty-five heads and only forty-five tails, is that normal? Statistics can tell you. It computes a standard deviation, in this case roughly one sigma, one standard deviation from the average. Now, if Daniel gets sixty-five heads that's a three-sigma event which only occurs once in 750 tries. If he flips seventy-five heads out of a hundred, then it jumps to a six-sigma event, which only occurs once out of 500 million tries."

"I get it," Veronica said. "A measure of 'how weird is this result?'"

"That's it, that's sigma. The data in my head tells me how the Chaos Field fluctuates, which gives me a good idea about how it spawns new universes from new Big Bangs. The Surveyors told us there are a lot of universes like ours, maybe hundreds of thousands, or more. Who knows? Not me. But I do know one thing. Spawning a new universe isn't random. Not quite. If it was perfectly random, a universe like ours would be a six-sigma event. It would only occur once every 500 million times. But that's not what's happening. Our universe is more like a one-sigma event. Common. Every fourth or fifth universe is the same as ours. Same Big Bang, same quantum fields that produce six quarks and six leptons, even the same lithium deficiency that we have."

"Which creates the same chance of life," Daniel interjected. "Maybe even the same forms of life."

"Seems possible," Nala agreed. "But the data in my head isn't about life, it's about quantum fluctuations—and not just inside the Chaos Field. *Every* quantum fluctuation. With each new Big Bang, a ridiculous number of quantum particles are created... quarks, electrons, photons, whatever. And each one is a fluctuating field, something physicists have understood for more than a century. But those quantum variations? We thought they were random—and they're close to random. But deep down, every particle that makes up everything in our universe depends on a seed that's so well hidden no scientist has ever found it."

"Yikes," Daniel said.

"Yikes," Veronica echoed, and this time she probably understood the insanity.

"Quite impossible," said Sprig. "Your conclusion implies not only a mathematic basis for quantum reality across multiple universes, but a deliberate action to manipulate it. It implies a god, and multiple cosmological studies by renowned Litian-nolos have proven there is no such intelligence."

"But did those Litian-nolos discover the seed?" Daniel asked.

"No."

"New information then," Daniel said. "Time to adjust our thinking."

277

Nala gave him a glance—an intimate connection between them. They'd stayed awake on more than one late night discussing religious concepts, and Daniel had always maintained a consistent stance on the lack of evidence for anything supernatural.

He wasn't suggesting a god, but a mathematical seed at the heart of nature—regardless of how complicated that seed might be—had deep implications. We'd need to stop thinking of our world as *natural* and begin to recognize that every tiny bit of existence could not only be calculated, it could be manipulated. It would take time to sort out the big picture. For now, he had a good idea where to begin.

"Choreographers," Daniel stated with conviction. "Who knows how they did it, but they've been tinkering with the quantum code."

Nala shrugged. "And there goes Daniel off the crazy cliff."

"Crazy? Yes. Wrong? No."

Nala shrugged. "I'm not arguing, I agree with you. But it's still crazy. Flesh and bones people manipulating the fundamentals of reality? If you promote that idea, you'll make the flat-Earth nut cases look as conventional as afternoon tea with King William."

"But a choreographer is a designer," Daniel added.

"Rock solid evidence. These guys were gods. Gods who danced."

"You mock."

"I do. But I still agree with you. I'm just preparing you for the peer review ridicule you're bound to get. I'm nice that way."

Daniel paused, listening.

The ship suddenly lurched, slamming his head into the cabinet's metal wall. Nala and Veronica crashed into him in a tangle of arms and quills. Sprig was thrown from his shoulder and disappeared somewhere into the rear of the ship.

"Boundary!" Aussik called from the deck above. "Sorry! Slight miscalculation!"

Daniel pushed Nala upright with one arm and untangled his shirt from Veronica's prickly body. "So much for a warning. Is everyone okay?"

Another shock slammed the ship. It wasn't Aussik. Randomness appeared to be alive and well in the Chaos Field.

29 RANDOM CHAOS

WITH HARD SWERVES SLAMMING him left and right, it took Daniel three tries to climb the ladder to the top deck. When he finally succeeded, he spread prone and pulled Nala up behind him. Zeeno had been yelling for her, presumably blaming their newest map provider for the mess they were in.

Handrails on either side of the cockpit entrance barely kept them upright through a barrage of jerks and smashes. Zeeno sat left, Aussik right, both firmly strapped into their seats. A chaos of jagged ice pillars filled the forward viewport.

Immense frosted cliffs soared past the ship to either side, with more craggy blocks of white appearing around every corner. It felt like a high-speed jet rocketing through the depths of a glacial crevasse that split off in every direction.

Aussik tweaked his joystick, but his actions were too little too late. Every few seconds, the ship slammed into one of the glistening cliffs in an explosion of ice shards. "They're coming too fast!" the pilot yelled.

"How did we get inside an ice maze?" Zeeno screamed at Nala. "There's something wrong with your waypoints!"

"It's not ice," Nala yelled back. The ship took another direct hit from a monumental column that rushed toward them, slamming Daniel and Nala against each other in the narrow opening to the cockpit. "The Chaos Field is pure energy, but fluctuations can feel solid when the force is strong enough."

Nala's alien head panel might be giving her data not available to anyone else, but a quantum physicist also had the talents to make sense of the scene ahead. The ice columns bore little resemblance to the landscape of pinnacles they'd passed through before, except that the primary color was still white. Perhaps on the trip in, they'd been *above* it all—if directions had any meaning in this place. Now down in the fray of fluctuating probabilities, the Chaos Field was living up to its name.

Daniel leaned into the cockpit for a better view. The slot canyon soared far above and below. Coarse edges along the icy cliffs vibrated chaotically, and gaps in the crevasse narrowed without warning making the job of threading the needle nearly impossible.

Aussik banked hard to avoid the next vertical cliff, but the right side of the ship glanced off a jagged ice spire. Screeching metal vibrated throughout the ship. How any vessel could survive such a collision, let alone dozens, was hard to understand.

Daniel pointed to Aussik's big red lever, the one he'd regularly used to back off on Tau and reduce their speed.

"We've tried," Zeeno yelled. "Can't slow down, can't even climb out of this. Nav system is locked. It's got to be bad waypoints." Zeeno's assessment rang true, Aussik's red handle was already in the neutral position.

"Sorry," Nala yelled. "I might have screwed something up. I'll need Beets' workstation to figure it out."

"Do it!" Zeeno yelled.

"I'll help her," Daniel said, giving Aussik a pat on the shoulder. The Chitza had proven his excellent piloting skills, but he had his paws full this time.

With teamwork, they managed to descend to the lower deck. Nala braced against Beets' workstation and against Beets herself, but the bigger jolts were too much to manage, throwing her to the deck several times. Daniel formed a second side to the Human-Chitza brace, giving Nala better stability, but progress toward a solution remained slow.

Daniel could only imagine what must be going on inside her head. With a new alien device inlayed over her brain, she had configured the original waypoints while in a state of exhaustion. Not optimal, especially for her first probability vector, and something had gone terribly wrong. But the current turmoil seemed even less conducive to quality work.

Nala gripped the edge of the workstation. "It's coming too fast. I could use some real-time data of what we're up against. A radar feed? If I could figure out how to get us above this frozen layer we might rise into a higher dimension of the string landscape."

With no pause button to work things out, they'd need to think quickly. Daniel did. "Use Sprig?"

"There's an idea."

"I'll need to find him first. Poor little guy went flying when the jolts hit."

Leaving Nala to fend for herself, Daniel made his way to the deck's aft end. The drawers Veronica had pulled out were overturned with their contents spilled everywhere. Sprig might be buried in the mess—a potentially fatal situation given the leaf's delicate structure.

"Sprig! Are you back here?" Daniel yelled.

With booming impacts reverberating throughout the ship, Sprig's tiny voice would be nothing but a whisper. Daniel concentrated, filtering out the creaks and groans until he heard a small peep from the aft bulkhead. He peered into a crack between two wall-mounted components. "Sprig?"

A tiny stem stuck out a millimeter. It wiggled. Daniel gently withdrew the leaf, bent in half.

"Ow! You look pretty beat up." He unfolded his friend, which left a deep crease across Sprig's midsection. Tiny claws at its stem opened and closed. "Is there something I can do for you?"

"Liquid," Sprig squeaked, barely audible.

Daniel found a can of Chitza soda from the scattered supplies and poured a stream over the leaf. Not water—not even sterile—but the pink soda would have to do.

Carbonated bubbles hung to the leaf's serrated edges. Its branching capillaries soaked up the liquid, swelling the crease and giving Sprig a pink glow.

"Better, thank you." Sprig's voice strengthened. "But an experience I do not wish to repeat."

"We're in a tough spot. I know you don't like pockets, but…" Daniel slipped the leaf into his shirt pocket, leaving enough sticking out to observe the surroundings—a wild assumption about Sprig's sensory system.

Back at the cockpit, Aussik still battled against ice crevasses left and right. Red lights flashed across a diagram of the ship on his display, with bold Chitza lettering impossible to ignore.

Daniel lifted the leaf from his pocket. "Sprig, we need to get a data feed into Nala's head. Distances, approach velocities, that kind of thing. Remember when Tennah sucked an entire language out of you? Something like that. Can you do it?"

Sprig hadn't suffered trauma from that experience, but Daniel had no idea how Tennah had managed the data transfer. Wi-Fi? Or something more closely tied to biology?

"One moment," Sprig said. Its surface quivered. A red tint circled its edges like an *in progress* animation. "I have detected a short-range transfer protocol on the deck below. Its signal is not coming from Beets, Veronica, or any of the ship's workstations."

"That narrows it down." Daniel snuffed out creeping thoughts of his wife as a cyborg. She simply had new talents—some they needed badly at this moment.

"I am now connected." Sprig turned to face the onslaught. Given the speed of icy obstructions coming at them, even a military airborne radar system would struggle to keep up. Sprig twisted left then right. "Closer to the viewport please."

Being too big to fit inside the small Chitza cockpit, Daniel reached out with his arm. Sprig scampered down to his hand, stretched tall, and froze in place. A slight tremble along its serrated edges was the only evidence of activity.

"This is great!" Nala yelled from below. "Approach velocities, distances, and angular momentum too. Fantastic!"

Apparently not satisfied with its performance, Sprig leaped from Daniel's hand onto the control panel and found a small knob just beneath the viewport to attach its stem claws. The screeches and jolts continued, but the leaf held firm and never wavered.

"Resolution is even better," yelled Nala. "Hang tight everyone. I'm working it."

A few minutes later, Nala called up one more time. "New waypoints initialized. Paws off the controls, Aussik. Just let the ship glide."

Aussik released his joystick. The ship smashed once more against a sheer cliff spraying chunks of quantum ice everywhere, then angled up, rising from the deep crevasse toward open sky above. Seconds later, they soared into a hazy glow above the chaotic landscape of undulating white pinnacles that stretched without end in every direction.

Nala clamored up the ladder and joined Daniel at the cockpit entrance. "We made it!"

Daniel hugged her. "Amazing work, but how?"

"Remember your coin flipping weirdness the last time we were here? I figured it out. With a little help." She rubbed the metal side of her head. "I'll tell you later."

Zeeno grinned. "Nice teamwork. You're good at this, little leaf guy."

Sprig hopped across the control panel and leaped back to Daniel's arm. The crease across its midsection hadn't healed but the wound didn't appear to be crippling.

"Damage assessment!" Zeeno yelled to his crew.

Aussik examined the ship diagram that continued to scream in bold red letters, then flipped several switches overhead. Veronica and Beets hurried around, inspecting anything that creaked or hissed—there were quite a few. One by one, the red flashes on Aussik's diagram switched to yellow. A few disappeared altogether.

Aussik folded his arms and leaned back. "Better, but still not great, Boss. We're low on power, cabin pressure is down, and I doubt our landing gear will ever work again. We'll be alright as long as we keep the turbines below fifty percent and stay out of 5-D. But we'll need repairs whenever we find a place for a full stop."

Zeeno turned to Nala. "You've got to get us out of here. Correctly this time."

"Sorry, Zeeno, my first vector didn't account for the probability of loop causality, one result influencing the next."

"Loop cause…?"

"Don't worry about it. Unless you're flipping a coin or shuffling cards, you won't see it. Daniel discovered the problem last time we were here. Turns out when you're inside a quantum field that's not quite random, you can get caught in an infinite loop. Waypoints looping back on themselves. My mistake."

Zeeno unbuckled and turned to Nala with a stern look in his eye. "You looked like hell when Daniel dragged you in here. I need you to straighten out that mangled head of yours. Power down. Do whatever Humans do to relax. Then get us out of here, preferably back to our own universe, but I'll take whatever I can get."

"Really, Zeeno, the waypoints I just loaded should get us home."

"You sure?"

"Pretty sure. There are still probabilities involved, but no more loop causality. This vector should take us through the boundary right where we came in."

Zeeno nodded thoughtfully. "I like that. We could finish the rescue."

Nala nodded with him. "Once we cross the boundary, space is real. No more probabilities. Those 4-D bubbles should still be there."

"Okay. Then we continue—but you get some rest. I need my crewmembers sharp."

"Wait... I'm a crewmember?" Nala stammered.

Nala had never taken commands well but in this case Daniel agreed with Zeeno. He gently pulled her away. "She'll relax. I'll supervise."

The rest of the crew went back to their duties while Nala and Daniel slumped to the deck just outside the cockpit.

"The new waypoints really *should* work," Nala told him. Daniel nodded without comment. Failure or success, she'd given it her best try under difficult circumstances. Daniel couldn't ask for anything more.

She leaned her head on his shoulder, possibly because she appreciated his support but more likely to prove to Zeeno that she knew how to relax. Sprig curled up between them, looking like it needed a break too.

Twenty minutes was all they got.

"Boundary ahead," Aussik announced.

They hopped up. A black ribbon stretched across the viewport, sparking and popping in multiple colors. Taller than their first time, the ribbon rapidly grew as they approached. Aussik fiddled with the controls. "We're accelerating, and I don't have the slightest idea why."

"Bring compression to zero. We'll coast through," Zeeno offered.

Aussik pulled his big red power handle to neutral. Turbines wound down to idle. A few metal-to-metal screeches made it clear that their primary propulsion system was in dire need of service.

"Still accelerating," Aussik said.

Seconds later, a dark wall enveloped them in a chaos of sparks all around. Without seats, Daniel and Nala held tight to the bars at the cockpit entrance but at least they'd have a good view. Like a roller coaster dropping from its highest perch, they flew through a barrage of sparks and soared into empty blackness beyond.

A sudden deceleration threw Daniel and Nala halfway into the cockpit. The ship stood on its nose like a hard braking airplane, then slammed back to level with shudders throughout the cabin.

The racket changed to quiet. Nothing and no one moved. Fingers relaxed their death grip on rails and seat arms. Outside, compression turbines at idle produced an uneven wobble that gently rocked the ship.

The ship slowly rotated in place, bringing a towering wall of multicolored sparks into view. It stretched above, below and into the distance left and right, eventually fading into the blackness of space.

"We're back in 3-D," Aussik said. "Kind of got thrown out of our bubble, I think. No filament deployed."

"Radiation?" Zeeno asked.

"None."

"Anything pulling on us?"

"We're steady as a rock. Nav is showing a solid coordinate position now. Haven't seen that for a while."

The boundary wall slipped to the side of the viewport as the ship continued to rotate in place. In the distance, Daniel could make out a faint galaxy, unmistakably spiral in shape. The previous universe had no such structures. If Nala's guidance had worked, they were home, though Earth would still be far beyond the cosmic horizon.

"Instability along the boundary could still occur," Sprig said, its claws gripped tight to Daniel's collar. "If capable, I recommend we leave this place."

Zeeno flipped a switch and turned a dial. "Not until we've found those bubbles." Two magenta dots appeared on his display. "Got 'em. We're back where we started."

Aussik grabbed his joystick, ended their slow rotation, then pushed forward. The ship rumbled back to life, moving toward the dots in the distance. One would be the bubble where they found Nala. If there were Chitzas inside the other, this mission would soon be complete.

Nala sensed it too, glancing nervously at Daniel.

The first marble passed by the viewport, but its bottom had been lopped off like a grape sliced in half. "Huh, that's different," Daniel said. "Did we do that?"

"Naw, it's cracked," Aussik said, looking at Zeeno. "Beets didn't crack it, did she?"

"How could she?" Zeeno answered. He spoke over his shoulder as they made their way to the second magenta dot, not far away. "A cracked bubble means it's been sliced open to 3-D space. We do it as a marker for anyone else who comes by. Tells them the bubble has already been examined and there's nothing inside. But cracking a bubble takes tech we don't normally carry on a scout ship."

"Which means someone else has been here," Aussik said. "Might have been a Chitza ship, but we're not the only ones with bubble crackers."

The second marble slipped into view. It too had been sliced into a hemisphere. Zeeno paused in thought. "I'm damn sure that thing was whole when we left. Somebody has definitely been here."

"Somebody who rescued the last crew?" Nala asked hopefully.

"Hard to say," Zeeno answered. "You heard their voices, so they must have been inside. But they sure didn't crack it themselves."

"Base sent a salvage ship," Aussik suggested.

Zeeno shrugged. "Sure, a salvage ship has crackers, but those old junks couldn't climb to 5-D even if you fed an ionized stream of Selenium plasma directly into the turbines. How would a salvage ship get here so fast?"

Aussik shrugged too.

Zeeno told Aussik to get underway. As the turbines wound up, the captain turned to Daniel and Nala. "At this point, we're crippled. Slow going at best. Chitza Base could help, but to send a message we need an existing 4-D filament. Lucky for us, I know where we can find one."

He returned his attention to Aussik. "Lay in a course for Afeesh Tm."

"Good thinking, Boss." Aussik had already pushed his red handle forward creating a new 4-D bubble. They'd limp back to the planet at the center of the ringed galaxy and make whatever repairs they could manage on their own. They could also tap into the communications filament they'd left behind and send a message for help. It might be weeks or even months before a slower salvage ship could reach them, but Chitza Base wouldn't leave their scout ship hanging.

With a few million light-years to go, turbines running at half power, and time to spare, the crew took turns resting. Chitzas could apparently fall asleep within seconds and only needed an hour before snapping awake, instantly alert and refreshed.

Nala used the time to wash up in the tiny bathroom while Daniel cleaned up the mess from spilled supplies, resealing several torn-open food packets that would still make an instant five-star dinner. Sprig swept up the crumbs with a sequence of surprisingly agile back flips.

The two Humans and their leaf ally gathered at the aft of the lower deck and talked quietly between themselves of randomness, Surveyors, and the heat-death universe they'd left behind. This rescue mission had morphed into a journey of discovery, and Daniel could never rest until he had sorted through the implications.

Aussik broke the quiet of the ship, calling down from the upper deck, "We have arrived. Maybe."

Back at the cockpit, they stared out to a grand galaxy. Spiral arms glowed with uncountable white dots. An enormous ring smoothly arced around the right side of the galaxy. But on the galaxy's left side, only broken segments of the ring remained. Gaps and holes riddled what should have been a smooth surface. In some places, whole sectors were missing.

"That's not how I remember it," Nala said.

"Same here," Daniel said. On their first pass through this galaxy, he had compared the rings to those of Saturn. Smooth, with glints of light off a polished surface. This ring looked incomplete. Pockmarked. Though landscapes look different depending on your direction of travel, this scene didn't match their first experience at all. "It can't be the same galaxy."

"Get closer," Zeeno commanded. "Forget the ring, we're looking for the communications filament we laid down. It'll be no wider than a plucked hair, but these things are damn sturdy. They hang around."

It took twenty minutes to reach the galactic center. Slow by Chitza standards, but quicker than any Human ship by a thousand years. A single yellow star finally appeared ahead. Its second planet bore a striking resemblance to Earth.

Unfortunately, no magenta line appeared on any display. Either the micro filament they had deployed had evaporated, or they were in the wrong place.

Zeeno scratched his chin, stupefied. "Can't catch a break. Oh well, no point in continuing with only half our normal power. We'll stop here and do our best to get this ship polished up."

It wasn't hard to understand Zeeno's decision. With the Milky Way still fifty gigaparsecs away, getting home at their current rate would take a lifetime. A full repair would be essential, in fact, their only hope.

"We cling to our technology," Daniel mumbled to himself. "Once it's gone, the immensity of space really sinks in."

Aussik announced they should prep for a full stop. Everyone hung on to something, and the pilot pulled his handle all the way back. The ship screeched, twisted sideways, bounced, and twisted again. Daniel pictured a bicycle slamming to a sudden stop and throwing its rider down a slope head over heels. Metal grated on metal, a hard sound to ignore. Serious effort would be required to get this ship back to working order.

"Bubble burst. Orbital insertion," Aussik said.

Zeeno called out. "Your ship, Beets! I want a repair plan by the end of the first orbit."

"On it, Boss."

The captain swiveled to Daniel. "Beets is good, but she's going to need help this time. Can you be our reconnaissance guy again? Go down there, check things out. See what kind of materials we can get our hands on. A sheet or two of titanium would be helpful."

Daniel raised his brow. "Unfortunately, the Afeesh Tm are better with wood and stone. Even a sheet of tin would be a tough scrounge, but I'll give it a shot."

A yell came from Veronica. "Uh... Daniel, before you go down there, there's something you should see." Zeeno motioned for Daniel to head to the lower deck. Veronica would also be the person to send him to the surface via their cigar-shaped drop tank.

Nala followed Daniel down the ladder. At her workstation, Veronica stared at an image of mountains, trees, and lakes from an overhead view.

"You found something?"

"Plenty. First, it's the right planet. That's the same city we targeted last time. But check it out. These people have been busy."

She pointed to a structure rising from the forest, a grey platform resting on four legs. As she moved the image left or right, a 3-D effect showed a tall concrete tower supporting a flat helicopter pad near its top. Several domes surrounded the pad.

The tower easily soared a hundred times higher than the trees. How anything that size could have been built in a day—or even a year—Daniel could not guess. Had he missed it on his first excursion to the surface? He looked up to Nala.

"Don't ask me, I was down there for several days but I never saw anything like it. Their tallest building was three stories."

Veronica tapped Daniel's arm. "It's twenty daks tall. That's like three or four kilometers in Human measures."

Daniel checked the image for a shadow. Regardless of the sun angle, a quick comparison to other shadows confirmed Veronica's number. This structure soared above everything else, a colossal achievement in engineering, especially for a primitive society like the Afeesh Tm. It implied the Afeesh Tm had brought in outside help. But unless this tower had somehow been ferried in overnight, its presence also implied something even more disturbing.

Daniel said, "I'll go down and find Osperus or Tennah. Doesn't matter which since my question will be the same."

"And your question is?" Nala asked.

"How long it has been since we left?"

Nala stared, her face blank. "Holy shit. I'm going with you."

30 TIME

AIR ROARED OUTSIDE the narrow capsule that confined two Humans and one animated leaf. Daniel clenched his teeth in a stupid grin while Nala screamed in a unique combination of terrified and thrilled that only an out-of-control roller coaster could provoke. Pinned inside the slender tube face to face, they'd both made the plunge to this planet's surface before. But like many death-defying thrills, a ride inside a Chitza drop tank turned out to be better the second time around.

Nala laughed and yelled simultaneously. "You just know those deceleration blades are going to deploy any second, but it still puts your heart in your throat."

They had no seatbelts or handrails, but there was little reason. Pressed against opposite walls, an industrial engineer couldn't slide a piece of paper between their bodies. Sensual, enjoyable, but frustrating too. When Daniel kissed her, she kissed back, then noted the third party within their tight confines.

Sprig repeatedly hopped between their shoulders. Nervous, excited, or embarrassed by their show of affection, it was hard to tell. Surprisingly, the delicate leaf hadn't yet complained about a voyage that featured non-stop mayhem. Nor had it fussed over the crease across its midsection, a reminder of the anatomical damage that any creature would suffer after being folded in half.

Clouds rushed by the windows, and a whir gave the first indication that the deceleration propeller had deployed. Presumably the drop tank's automation had accounted for the extra weight of two people, plus one leaf.

Now just minutes away from landing, Daniel felt confident they could handle whatever they might encounter. Sprig and Beets had modified the ship's short-range electromagnetic data network, boosting its signal so that Sprig could both send and receive data packets even from the planet's surface. Likewise, Zeeno had offered *JammerBlaster* air support if needed. The existence of this mysterious weapon—accidentally disclosed by Veronica and finally admitted to by Zeeno—would be their backup if things on the surface went south. This time they'd come prepared.

A shopping list of materials needed for ship repairs wasn't the only reason to make second contact with the Afeesh Tm. Daniel accepted Nala's assurances that they had not stumbled into a duplicate universe, but he was far less sure of *when* they had arrived. Roughly twenty-four hours had passed since they had dropped Tennah off at the derelict Chitza ship orbiting this planet, and no one builds giant structures overnight. He had no explanation except that they had traversed the mother of all quantum fields. Twice.

Never assume that anything quantum will conform to sensible.

With deceleration rotors thumping, buildings now appeared through the windows. The drop tank seemed headed for a landing in the center of the village. Their speed slowed further as they approached touchdown. Passersby hurried out of their way, and the drop tank settled onto a pavement of cobblestones.

Nala opened the hatch and squatted to peer outside. "Didn't hit anybody." She stepped out. Daniel followed.

The sun stood high in a blue sky. A fresh breeze with scattered white clouds mimicked any fine spring day on Earth. They'd landed in a town square filled with people, some hurrying past, others quickly forming a circle—curious, but keeping their distance. Unlike Daniel's first encounter with Afeesh Tm fur trappers, these people wore jackets over pants or simple dresses belted at the waist, clothing more suitable for a store clerk.

Daniel waved. "Sorry to bother you, I hope we didn't scare anyone." Sprig translated, though its meek voice didn't project well in the outdoor breeze. No one replied. No one left either.

"Can someone direct us to the government building? I believe where Osperus works?"

When Sprig translated, a murmur of hushed voices in private conversations spread across the small crowd. Daniel could only make out the occasional repetition of *Osperus*.

A young man came running across the square, broke through the circle of onlookers, and stopped in front of Daniel. A wide grin spread across his face. "It is you!" he said in English.

He wore a white collared shirt with a tight-fitting waist coat and pants that ballooned near the top. Narrow pant legs tucked into black boots. He looked rather dapper, maybe nineteen or twenty years old if the man lived on Earth.

"Have we met?" Daniel asked. There was something familiar about him.

"I help... to capture you!" the young man said. His words were stilted but easily understood. "We camp deep in the forest one night, then take you to our cliff house. You don't know me, but I know why. I was smaller." He held out a hand level at his chest.

Daniel paused to absorb the implications of his claim. He wasn't telling a story about how fast Afeesh Tm children grow.

"How long has it been?" Nala asked.

"Yes, well... more than eight years now." Then he added, "Our years are close to yours. Eight, yes. I am good to see you again!"

Daniel stared at Nala, comprehending the young man's story. He believed it to be true but had no theory for how one day could have turned into eight years.

Nala shook her head. "We've crossed between two different universes, maybe they're out of sync somehow?"

"What's your name?" Daniel didn't want to come across as a foreign inquisitor, but he felt a need to confirm such startling news.

"Esperion," the man said. Several people behind him nodded. His name might be the only part of the conversation they understood but the crowd seemed curious enough not to disperse.

"How did you learn to speak our language, Esperion?"

"From Leader Tennah. She taught many students. Leader Tennah says learning languages opens doors for us. Humans came to Afeesh Tm when I was small, but today only Chitzas. We learn their language too, but yours is better. More Humans will come now that you have returned, yes?" He smiled brightly exposing the single ridge of white teeth that reinforced the anime character look all Afeesh Tm shared.

"I'm not sure," Daniel told him. "Can I speak with Tennah? Does she still live at the cliff house?"

If eight years had really passed, they would need to be careful. Tennah's revolution may have been successful, but on Earth even new leaders with the best of intentions sometimes strayed from their revolutionary goals. On the plus side, the Afeesh Tm had used the time to educate their youth in new languages, and they'd built an impressive tower.

"Leader Tennah is in the Hall of Sibyls." Esperion pointed to a large stone building at one corner of the town square. It seemed Veronica had landed them at exactly the right place.

Nala picked up on the young man's other revelation. "Are Chitzas here now?"

Esperion replied, "Last year, many, but now only two, Ambassador Qalla and an engineer. Is it true that Humans travel with Chitzas?"

"It is true," Nala answered. "Is Ambassador Qalla also at the Hall of Sibyls?"

Esperion squinted. "No. At the People's Skyway, maybe." He pointed in another direction where town buildings gave way to the surrounding forest. In the distance, the base of a grey tower rose straight up disappearing into the layer of clouds. "Should I take you there?"

"Tennah first," Daniel said. "Thank you for your help, Esperion. And you might be surprised, but I do remember you like it was only yesterday." His night as a captive had been spent around a campfire that included several children. Esperion was almost certainly one of them.

The young man beamed with increased stature. He turned, parting the crowd with waves of his arms like a concert security guard leading the headliners to the stage.

Daniel and Nala followed across the town square, conferring privately among themselves. "Eight years? When we didn't return, the Chitzas must have sent another mission to find out what happened to us. They never give up. That's probably who cracked open the bubbles we found."

Nala rushed her thoughts. "Which means they rescued my crew but ended up with another disaster—us. Esperion mentioned that a few Humans came here, so news about us must have made it back to Earth. Missing and presumed…" She glanced up at Daniel. "Oh shit, my mom thinks I'm dead."

"Don't go there. We don't know for sure what happened."

"Esperion isn't lying, did you see his face?"

"No, he's not lying. But let's find Tennah and work it out from there."

They followed Esperion into a stone building that Daniel didn't recognize from his meeting with Osperus. Esperion guided them through hallways with inlaid marble floors and electric lights on the ceilings. They stopped at a guard station where Esperion spoke in the Afeesh Tm language. The guard gave Daniel and Nala a hard stare, then motioned for them to wait. He disappeared through a doorway and returned with several people in tow.

One was Tennah.

Her hair was cut shorter, exposing the Arc of Progression still embedded into the side of her head. Its silver surface matched the accent colors of an elegant gown that reached the floor. Lines around her eyes and mouth suggested aging—only a little—but the fact that she had aged at all confirmed Esperion's story. Daniel and Nala's voyage to another universe had taken far longer than a day.

Tennah's mouth opened, and words finally formed. "Could it be true?" She stepped forward and reached out to touch Daniel's face. "You have returned? My long lost friend, Daniel?"

"It's good to see you again, Tennah. You look well."

"You have not changed at all."

"I haven't. But then, I only left yesterday."

Her eyes grew wide.

Daniel nodded. "It's true. We crossed the Chaos Field to another universe. There and back in one day. My lip is still tender from ripping off a sticky wax your warriors spread across my mouth when you captured me… yesterday." He pointed to his upper lip though there was probably nothing much to see. "Strange, isn't it?"

"I… I don't know what to say. You left years ago. Seeking your wife, as I recall." Tennah reached for Nala's hand. "My dear, you are as lovely as I knew you would be. Jazameh remembers you fondly and speaks of you still. How can it be that we do not agree on the time that has passed?"

Nala returned the gentle gesture with a squeeze of Tennah's hand. "Daniel is right. From my perspective, Jazameh left with me three days ago. We don't know what happened. Something about the Chaos Field."

Tennah sighed, tears filling her large eyes. She stared up to the ceiling. "Spirit above, I have failed so many visitors. Before me are two more, thankfully alive, yet I have failed them too. They have lost years."

Tennah kissed Nala's hand. "I am deeply sorry. These quests to journey where no one should go are madness, they always were. When you left, I vowed to put an end to it. We expelled Osperus and his cronies. With help from our Chitza friends, we began a project to dismantle the ring that surrounds our galaxy and lures visitors here. Our new tower, the People's Skyway, has already dimmed this odious ring. Ultimately, we will erase it. But while our work continues, my vow stands. No one departs this planet for the Chaos Field. Not the Chitzas. No one. Daniel was the last to receive a map."

Never one to mince words, Nala pointed to the panel on Tennah's head. "But you still wear the Arc." Nala's own panel had remained concealed beneath her hair. Anyone would need to look carefully to notice it.

Tennah nodded. "Seven Sibyls. And yes, most of us are still bonded with the Arc of Progression. Once we banished Osperus, the Sibyls assumed leadership across our land. Today, each Sibyl stands with an equal voice. Each carries the wisdom passed to us by the Arc of Progression."

"But some Sibyls removed their Arc?" Nala asked. Daniel wanted to know too.

"Only one, Jazameh. The extraction left physical scars, but her character remains. Her computational abilities have diminished

301

but she has told me several times that she does not regret her decision."

"Good to hear." Nala turned the right side of her head toward Tennah and pulled back her hair.

Tennah's mouth fell open as she caught sight of the Arc. "Was it forced upon you?"

Nala shook her head. "A decision I made. We wouldn't be here without it. But I'm glad to hear it's reversable. A woman should always be in control of her own body."

Tennah stroked the side of Nala's head. "The Arc can be extracted, but do not take the operation lightly. Jazameh suffered for weeks. You should speak to her."

"I'd like to."

Tennah brightened as a thought occurred to her. "Then we will have a banquet in your honor. I will invite Jazameh and the other Sibyls. Most gave up hope for survivors, but now that you are here and we begin to understand that elapsed time in the Chaos Field is not what it seems, their hope will be renewed."

Daniel had no disagreement with Tennah's effort to dismantle the signpost that brought visitors here. Sibyls had been passing out maps for centuries, ensuring that knowledge about the boundary and the Chaos Field would carry forward among advanced species from many galaxies. But if the Afeesh Tm preferred to end their participation, they had every right to withdraw.

"We'd be honored to attend your banquet," Daniel told Tennah, "But before we set the table is there someone who can help us obtain materials for ship repair? We struggled to get this far."

"Yours were among the first Chitza ships to arrive. Today, Chitzas come and go regularly. We even have a mechanics shop that provides services. I am sure they can help." Tennah spoke to one of her assistants standing a few paces behind, then returned her attention to Daniel. The assistant left. "He will let the Chitza ambassador know you and your crewmembers have returned."

Nala spoke up. "Not everyone. My ship was destroyed at the boundary. It's why Daniel came after me. They found me but not my crew. Can your assistant check on them too?"

"No need to check. The early Chitza missions are well documented and remembered—a sad chapter in our pre-revolution history. The crewmembers of the first Chitza mission were murdered by Osperus. As you describe, the second mission was caught in a storm of deadly radiation. Their courageous captain managed to get everyone out but himself. Today, we honor this captain on a plaque near our memorial to fallen revolutionaries."

"But his crew was rescued?"

"They were. Rescuers found two lifeboat bubbles. They assumed—correctly it seems—that their third mission pulled you from one bubble and brought you onboard. But then, were lost themselves. Tragedy after tragedy. It became a turning point in public opinion. Even Chitzas, natural explorers that they are, began to question the wisdom of continuing into the Chaos Field."

"Having been there, I can't disagree," Daniel offered. "But now that we're back, your sad chapter of history is improving."

"So, it seems!" Tennah agreed. "We will joyfully amend our documents and the plaque!" Tennah's assistant returned and whispered something in her ear. "Tell your pilot to dock at platform two, halfway up the People's Skyway. The ambassador, along with a chief mechanic, will meet them there."

"Fantastic." Daniel turned to Sprig. "Contact Zeeno. He'll be happy to learn about the repair facilities, but he's going to be wary about docking. Tell him that the politics down here have improved in their favor. Be sure to mention the Chitza ambassador by name. Zeeno might recognize it. Oh, and... never mind. We can cover the details about the rescue of the previous crew when they get here."

"Done," Sprig said. "Zeeno's reply, *Are you damn sure?* My response, *Quite*. His response, *We're on it*."

Daniel smiled at Tennah. "My leafy friend is as efficient as the Chitzas. We Humans—as our Captain Zeeno has pointed out to me—tend to be wordy."

31 CELEBRATION

SEVERAL HUNDRED AFEESH TM crowded into what used to be Osperus' medieval office, now converted into a dining hall with a soaring ceiling above, narrow windows on one side, and elaborate embroideries hanging on the other. Daniel found comfort in a revolution that had deposed the old guard without destroying the beautiful buildings created by the regime.

Daniel and Nala ushered Zeeno, Aussik, Beets, and Veronica into the grand hall. They were met by Ambassador Qalla, who had once been a scout ship captain himself. The ambassador's assistant joined them too, and the six Chitzas quickly became the life of the party. They did more drinking than eating, but considering the noise level at their end of a long, communal table, they were making new friends among the Afeesh Tm.

Daniel and Nala anchored the other end of the table, joining Tennah, Jazameh, and five other Sibyls who had each traveled from far flung regions to meet the Humans. Each Sibyl provided heartfelt declarations of regret and affection, along with the ever-present greeting, "You look like us!"

Sprig plunked itself down on the table in between mugs of ale and plates of food, scooting away whenever someone mistook it for a mint leaf or a toothpick.

Their conversation ranged from boundary physics to Chitza persistence—apparently, exploring the Chaos Field was still a longer-term goal for Ambassador Qalla. Each Sibyl agreed that their map-making days were over, though several remained curious about the universes that lay beyond, especially the origin universe for the Choreographers.

Jazameh said it best. "We have each created probability vectors, yet none of us has followed our work to its ultimate endpoint." An Afeesh Tm woman of small stature, Jazameh's auburn hair was cut short. Small scars where the Arc once attached to her head were noticeable, though not jarring. Daniel tried not to stare.

Nala spoke with Jazameh like old friends who hadn't seen each other since college, even though it had only been a few days for Nala.

"This silver planetoid," Jazameh asked, "why did the Surveyors call it a registration station? Who or what were they registering?"

"Us," Nala answered. "Who we are, where we're from, how we got there. They pointed out our resemblance to the Choreographers."

Jazameh soaked up the new information. She seemed a more studious person than their revolutionary leader, Tennah. "It would explain why our ancestors were selected to become Sibyls and why the Choreographers built a ring around our galaxy. Visitors to our planet come in all shapes, but I find it intriguing that Humans, Afeesh Tm, and Choreographers share the same shape. Are we special in some way?"

"Probably not," Daniel said. "But artificial selection always produces a bias."

"Explain, please," Jazameh said.

Nala pulled Daniel's arm. "Daniel has a theory. Well, he always has a theory, but this one's a whopper."

He and Nala had already spoken about his ideas on the Surveyors and the Choreographers, and he'd put more thought into it since then. It was speculation—not scientific theory—but so far all the puzzle pieces made sense.

With all seven Sibyls waiting, Daniel had a ready audience. Time to reveal his *Theory of Reality*.

"I kept asking myself the same questions each of you bring up. Why entice people to pass through the Chaos Field? Dangle an intriguing map, stir up rumors of exotic places beyond, perhaps even emphasize the dangers involved. You'll get takers, if only for the challenge of exploring places no one has ever been. But what purpose does it serve? The Surveyors would only tell us that they registered visitors as part of an evolutionary process. They said that each new registration works toward a greater good. But what? And how? They wouldn't say, but once they installed the Arc onto Nala's head she figured out one piece of it right away. I suspect it's something you all know."

Nala took over. "The Chaos Field is not random." Multiple Sibyls nodded in agreement. The Arc spoke to each of them in the same way it spoke to Nala. The only difference was that these Afeesh Tm women didn't have Nala's education in math and quantum physics.

"There's a seed," Nala told them. "Its existence means quantum fields are deterministic, not truly random. Every Sibyl knows how to use this seed when computing a probability vector. But you probably don't realize that you're computing a solution to what astrophysicists call the *quantum wave function of the multiverse*. Sorry, it's complex stuff, but that's what consumes the zettabytes in your heads. The key takeaway is that you're making a straightforward computation, not flipping a coin. Daniel thinks it's even more than that."

Daniel took the handoff. "The Chaos Field creates new universes. It's a foundational quantum field. Think of it as reality at its most primitive level. Bedrock. There's nothing beneath it and it has probably existed forever. You could say that, while universes come and go, the Chaos Field is, always was, and always will be.

307

"But the Chaos Field evolves, at least that's what the Surveyors implied. It's not static. It keeps changing, and I think I know why. There's a structure surrounding the Surveyors' planetoid—a complex web of organic tubes. Designed for security, but it might also be a computer or maybe an interface into the Chaos Field. Sprig thought the web might extend all the way to the boundary. Somehow the Surveyors are able to change its seed. When you change the seed, you change the Chaos Field. It's a deliberate action on their part, coming from a plan established long ago by the Choreographers."

Daniel had their attention. "Each time a new civilization arrives at the registration station, the seed changes according to the registration data received, and the Chaos Field changes too. Just a little. New universes continue to bang into existence but with the new seed. It creates a slight bias—a gentle push—so that new universes tend to match *successful* universes. When Humans and Chitzas registered, the Surveyors counted our shared universe as one more success. Maybe they counted it twice since there were two species. The Chaos Field adjusted, producing even more universes like ours. That's what scientists call artificial selection, the same mechanism we Humans use to breed dogs or make our foods more resistant to microbes. But the Choreographers created an artificial selection process on the grandest possible scale—reality itself."

Daniel paused to let his description sink in. His audience members weren't scientists, but they were smart people, and their Arcs gave them access to data that could instantly confirm the points he and Nala were making.

Nala added one more. "The Surveyors told us they see a variety of visitors, just as you do on Afeesh Tm, but they said the trend is in our favor. Meaning, they're seeing more people who look, and act like us."

"It's part of the original design," Daniel added. "Once they figured out how the Chaos Field worked, Choreographers traveled from universe to universe seeking life. Where they couldn't find life, they moved on. But when they found life—when they found *intelligent and curious* life—they stopped. They asked those people, or forced them, to become a gateway to the Chaos Field. Their built-in bias focused on species who looked and acted like them.

"In our universe, they chose your planet and brought the Arc of Progression to your ancestors. In those days, the Chaos Field was probably spewing out all kinds of universes, haphazardly. Nala says a universe like ours should be a rare six-sigma event in a truly random scenario."

Nala jumped in. "But now our universe is a far more common one-sigma event, according to the data in our heads. Right?"

All seven Sybils nodded in agreement. Something inside their heads made sense of the explanation in ways Daniel could only imagine. The Sibyls themselves were evidence that his theory might be correct.

"In science, when you commonly find something that should be rare, it's usually evidence that you don't understand how things really work. Our type of universe bangs into existence more frequently than we expect. Why? Now we know. It's because of an evolutionary process established by the Choreographers long ago to create a so-called, *greater good*, as the Sentinels explained."

"Does this mean we were pawns to the Choreographers? Slaves?" one of the younger Sibyls asked.

Nala reached out to the fresh-faced woman and held her hand. "I hope you don't think of yourself that way. You were part of a tradition that provided visitors with a service—visitors like us."

Daniel added, "Curiosity sometimes gets the better of Humans, and Chitzas. We should have listened more closely to your advice on the dangers of the Chaos Field. Tennah tried to convince me not to go, and Jazameh did the same for Nala. The responsibility for lives lost is on the visitors to Afeesh Tm, not you."

Tennah had been quiet until now. "It helps that you have returned. We may never know the fate of everyone we sent. But if time is poorly defined inside the Chaos Field, perhaps other travelers will return a hundred years from now to tell our descendants that only a single day has elapsed."

Another Sibyl who had been quiet, also spoke up. "Leader Tennah... initially, I opposed you. I believed my map skills were essential, even graced by the Spirit above. You convinced me otherwise. And now that I hear Daniel and Nala speak of Surveyors, Choreographers, and the *greater good*, I shudder. Who is to say which good is greater? Osperus? These Choreographers? Certainly not me. You were wise to end our participation. I stand with you. Educated, informed, and sovereign over my mind." Tennah embraced the woman. The rest of the Sibyls placed a hand on the two.

A brighter future lay ahead for these people. No longer haunted by past deeds, they could take pride in themselves by rising above their former status as uninformed players to become custodians of precious knowledge. With the Arc, they intuitively understood how universes formed and how nature worked at its most fundamental level. The foundations for astronomy, physics, cosmology, and evolution had already been established. No need for their equivalent of Copernicus or Galileo to get a renaissance rolling.

Through the evening, they spoke of other topics: a focus on an equitable society and advancement of education. Chitzas came up several times. Early in their relationship, the Afeesh Tm had asked for Chitza help in dismantling the four-dimensional ring

310

surrounding their galaxy. Using bubble cracking technology, Chitzas then designed and guided the construction of the People's Skyway. Four kilometers tall, the new tower supported an array of compression turbines at its tip. All day, every day, the tower targeted small patches of 4-D space thousands of light-years away and deflated them back to ordinary space. Another fifty years would be required to make their galaxy invisible to 4-D scanners. Only then, Tennah told them, would the Afeesh Tm be free of their past.

Tennah left the conversation and moved to the other end of the table to speak with the Chitzas. When she returned, Nala asked what she'd said to them.

"An apology," Tennah said. "Something your crew probably needed to hear directly from a Sibyl. The first mission resulted in Chitza deaths. We can fault Osperus, but every Afeesh Tm citizen shares in our past. One thing I have learned over many years: never leave a regret unspoken."

"Wise words," Nala said.

Tennah took Nala's hand. "Now on to happier things. There is one more event of importance before our banquet is finished." She stood, pulling Nala up from the bench where she sat. "Come with me."

The other Sibyls rose too. Conversation down the length of the table quieted as the women followed Tennah up a staircase to a loft overlooking the dining hall. There they formed a circle with Nala in the center. The hall quieted to a whisper.

Tennah's words were difficult to hear from below, but they were meant for the select group. At one point, each Sibyl put a hand on Nala's head, touching the Arc embedded there. When the ceremony finished, the Sibyls returned single file and scattered across the room to rejoin the rest of the diners. Nala returned to Daniel.

"I've been inducted!" she said, eyes sparkling. "I'm officially a Sibyl, part of their sisterhood!"

She wiped tears from her eyes, and Daniel wrapped his arms around her. "What an honor. And a responsibility too."

More tears streamed down her cheeks. Nala smiled brightly as she wiped them away. "It's not like I'm going to create more probability vectors. I mean, I could, but why would I want to?"

Daniel pulled her close. "Why would you need to? The galactic ring will be gone in fifty years or so. After that, anyone who wanders past this galaxy won't even know the Afeesh Tm exist. Sibyls might retain their Arcs but they—and you—have no need to venture into the Chaos Field again."

"That was part of the ceremony," Nala explained. "The decision to remove the Arc is left to each Sibyl. That goes for me too. When I think about it, I can see how to extract it, but honestly I'm not sure I'm ready to try."

Daniel was getting used to the alien attachment on his wife's head. It hadn't affected her personality. It had enhanced some of her abilities, but the same could be said for a class in painting with acrylics. "Take your time. If you decide to rip it out, I'll be there with the alcohol wipes."

Crude, but Nala smiled anyway. She pecked him on the cheek. "My nurse on standby for open-head surgery."

Daniel smiled too. "I see a symmetry in your new group. Jazameh relinquishes her Arc, and they add you to the guild. The Afeesh Tm tradition of seven Sibyls continues. Maybe you should hang with them for a while."

"That's pretty much what Ambassador Qalla wanted too. Hang with Chitzas. Maybe take another shot at the Chaos Field. They never give up."

"Intrepid explorers right down to their core."

"I adore Chitzas. I love my new sisters too. And sure, maybe we'll hang out with the Afeesh Tm for a day or two while the ship is being repaired. But as soon as Beets declares we're ready to depart, I'm grabbing that seat. Really... I just want to get home. Milky Way. Earth. Santa Fe. That home."

Daniel nodded. "Yeah, me too."

32 ETERNITY

GALAXY AFTER GALAXY flew past the Chitza scout ship in a never-ending stream of matter pulled together into stars, planets, and life. Fully repaired, the ship once more compressed vast reaches of three-dimensional space with ease. Daniel stared out the side window on the lower deck, soaking up the colossal scope of existence.

Heading home. A home still gigaparsecs away, but the Chitzas knew the way.

Nala stood aside Veronica's workstation, chatting with the amiable Chitza about topics that Daniel had long since tuned out. He wasn't being anti-social, but even after outlining his Theory of Reality to the Sibyls, the implications of the Choreographers' plan hadn't been fully digested. Quiet times without distractions were often his best friends.

For hours, Daniel had spoken only with Sprig, who clung to his collar. Together, they had reviewed evidence pointing to a vast collection of universes continuously spawned from a primordial quantum field. The idea that quantum fluctuations weren't random disturbed him—and Sprig too—but nothing forced reality to conform to sensible boundaries.

The unexplained eight-year time shift would require further study. Was time ill-defined inside the Chaos Field as Tennah had suggested? They might never know the answer.

At the banquet, Beets had casually suggested that a thousand years could have elapsed back home. "I read about it once. Something about relativity and time dilation." Beets seemed completely unconcerned, but the idea that a thousand years might have passed—with everyone they knew now long dead—threw

Veronica into a tizzy. Ambassador Qalla had countered that he hadn't noticed any difference the last time he'd messaged Chitza Base. But their last-deployed communications filament had evaporated a few months ago, leaving them no way to confirm. Plus, the ambassador was pretty drunk.

Daniel had stepped in with science. Chitza ships crossed the universe by compressing space, which had nothing to do with time dilation, the speed of light, relativity, or even Einstein. Though galaxies flew past the window, the ship wasn't really moving. Instead, space compressed, like zooming in with a telephoto lens. Eight years elapsed in one place would be eight years anywhere.

Everyone seemed satisfied with Daniel's answer, but that didn't quell the uneasy feeling. Years *had* passed. Nala's mom, her only family, would be eight years older and probably worried sick about her daughter. Daniel's own sister would be in the same predicament.

Without a filament, they couldn't send a message, but they'd get home soon enough. There would be tearful reunions and some explaining to do, especially among family and friends.

An hour later and a hundred more galaxies, Aussik called out from the upper deck. "Andromeda!"

Nala and Daniel climbed the ladder to witness their return to familiar territory. The massive Andromeda galaxy filled the viewport then slid to one side revealing a barred spiral directly ahead. Home had never looked so good.

"*Assap Tijakk*," Aussik said. "Otherwise known as the Milky Way. Hey, Veronica, *Assap* juice time!"

"On it," came a squeak from below. Clanks and a whirring sound hinted of something special brewing from their five-star hostess.

"Drop to 4-D," Zeeno commanded over the noise.

Aussik adjusted their compression factor, and the galactic view expanded like a folded-paper scene in a pop-up book. Their forward progress slowed as they eased into one of the arms spinning off the central bar of the Milky Way. A white glow slowly resolved into millions of tiny dots. Individual stars began to fly past, providing the first feeling of reaching the galaxy's edge. A glowing red nebula whizzed past like a cloud pierced by an airplane on final approach.

Veronica popped up the ladder with a tray of shot glasses, each filled with a bubbling liquid. A purple fog flowed from the glasses, leaving a swirling cloud behind. Beets followed, waving the purple fog away.

"*Assap* juice?" Daniel asked as Veronica handed out shot glasses to everyone. The Chitza only winked her response. A sly half-smile, half-snarl revealed one gleaming canine.

Zeeno raised his glass, and everyone else followed. "*Eps gat ta lep toe, fir danna ekk pap, fir jex ekk pap, fir Assap Tijakk!*" the captain cheered.

"*Eps gat!*" the Chitzas cheered back, with Daniel and Nala scrambling to respond in the foreign words. Everyone downed the bubbling drink in one gulp. The purple liquid burned on the way down and gurgled in Daniel's stomach. His pupils dilated and his head spun with an instant buzz.

Nala stared back at him, her eyes wide. "Wow!" she croaked. "That's a hell of a welcome home drink." She leaned in close to Veronica and whispered, "I haven't learned enough of your language yet. What did the captain say in his toast? Something about a flying snake?"

Veronica shook her head purposefully. "Not touching that one! You'll have to look it up when you get home."

"I have the Chitza words recorded," Sprig announced.

"And?" Daniel asked.

317

"Like Veronica, I would rather not translate them, if you don't mind." Daniel and Nala shrugged in unison. Some things were probably best left for the imagination.

"I have Litia locked in," Aussik announced. It seemed they would be returning to their starting point, the moon Litia orbiting the gas giant Nolo. Perhaps Theesah-ma would be waiting for them, but with an eight-year lapse, she and other Litian-nolos may have forgotten all about the Humans who once visited their moon.

"Filament acquired," Aussik said. Daniel hesitated to interrupt the pilots during their approach, and while he didn't know what they might do with the communications thread, it sounded like a positive development.

Zeeno checked his display. "Well, what do you know? We just received arrival instructions. The same crap we always get coming into Litia with all the same mistranslations." He laughed, then pointed to alien lettering at the top of the message. "The date-time stamp proves an eight year gap. We've been gone for a while, my friends."

"Better than a thousand years," Nala said.

More stars passed. Aussik slowed their approach further. One star ahead remained fixed in the viewport's center.

Zeeno twisted around. "Better take your seats. The first full stop after major repairs can be a little... wacky?" He glanced to Aussik.

"Yeah, wacky is the right word," Aussik agreed.

The shudders, twists, and dizzying flips were every bit wacky. No one cared in the slightest. They were home, or close enough.

****

318

With impossibly long strides, Theesah-ma hurried down an arrivals corridor and skidded to a stop. The giant wrapped her long, jointed arms around Nala, lifted her off the ground, and shook her like a rag doll with Nala laughing all the way.

"Lovely Nala, I knew you would return! My hope never faltered," the six-meter tall Litian-nolo cooed. Her normal silky smooth voice was peppered with piccolo tweets as if a tiny songbird had suddenly taken shelter in her larynx.

Daniel was next in the giant's powerful hug. "Lovely Daniel, you are a lost treasure regained!" When she lifted him, Sprig leaped away, landing on Nala's sleeve. The leaf scrambled up to her shoulder safe from the unwanted squish.

Theesah-ma folded multiple knee joints to bring her flat face down to Human level. Widely spaced green eyes sparkled amid iridescent skin shimmering with violets and blues. "Eight years!"

She showed no signs of aging, but Litian-nolos often lived for several hundred Earth years. "It's only been a couple weeks for me," Nala said.

Daniel started to explain their transition from one universe to another, but Theesah-ma interrupted. "I understand. I know. Professor Alosoni-eff predicted it!"

She grabbed them once more, squeezing tight as Sprig leaped back and forth within the mass of bodies. Daniel would be happy to rejoice in the Litian-nolo's warm embrace all day, but curiosity won out. "The professor predicted our eight-year delay?"

Theesah-ma stepped back, reaching out to Sprig who hopped to the tip of her arm. She lifted the leaf to her face and spoke to it like Mary Poppins did with friendly robins. "Dear Sprig. So wonderful to see you once more. The professor missed you. But he was not idle in your absence."

She turned her attention back to Daniel and Nala. "After your disappearance, more Chitza missions voyaged to the cosmic

319

horizon. They returned to Litia with stories of past failures but also of a Chaos Field. When the professor learned of it, he set his mind to understanding its nature… and its effects on travelers who dared to enter it. He warned us that time could never be synchronous among independent universes. He compared the Chaos Field to a lake with three outlets. One leads to a gentle stream. Another to a tumbling cascade. A third to a waterfall. The flow of time, he told us, would depend upon the energy from which any new universe is born. The professor warned that traversing between universes guarantees an irreversible offset of time with each crossing of a boundary. He advised us to be patient. Travelers beyond the horizon may yet return, he suggested. We communicated this to both Chitzas and Humans. Lovely Daniel, lovely Nala… you were missed but never forgotten."

Sprig practically danced across Theesah-ma's hand. "I must reunite with the professor."

Theesah-ma quieted and held Sprig close. "Please understand that Professor Alosoni-eff is now in hospice care."

Daniel recalled meeting the elderly Litian-nolo, frail and wrinkled at the time. "I hope we're not too late."

"Not likely," Zeeno interjected from his position at the back of the group. The Chitza captain stepped forward and held out a paw to Sprig. "Come with us. We can help."

Daniel puzzled over Zeeno's offer, but when Theesah-ma lowered her arm to Chitza height, Sprig hopped onto Zeeno. The leaf had never touched a Chitza before.

Their captain announced in a clear voice. "Stand by, we'll be back in a snap. Then we're departing for Earth, and I want both of you onboard. Skip the portal, a scout ship is way better. Trust me, you want to make a grand entrance to your own planet. Adds flair. Besides…" he looked down, scuffing his boot on the floor, "Eh, we've never been to Earth. We hear there's good food there. Fun places too, and we're due for a shore leave."

"Las Vegas!" Aussik and Veronica shouted together. Even Beets nodded her head.

The image of inebriated Chitzas around a lively craps table was easy to picture. Daniel held out a hand to their captain. "I can't imagine a better way to return home than alongside the best deep-space crew in our universe or any other. And yeah, we've got good food. When we get there, try our ice cream."

Aussik perked up. "Iced? Sounds cold. I like it already."

Daniel wrapped his hand around Zeeno's much smaller paw. "Speaking for all Humans, we'd love to have you as our guests. Thanks for everything, Captain."

"Good. Stay put, we'll be right back."

All four Chitzas and Sprig left, leaving Daniel and Nala to wonder how anyone could visit an elder in hospice care and be *right back*. Theesah-ma didn't hesitate to provide the answers they needed. "Today will be the professor's last," she said with no hint of gloom.

"His last?" Nala asked.

Theesah-ma nodded. "On Litia, hospice is suspended animation. The consciousness remains alive even after the body dies. Machines can prolong the effect for years. Hospice ends when the patient decides. Chitzas understand this. As do I. The professor remains conscious only to see his assistant once more. He will rejoice at their reunion, I am certain. But once goodbyes are exchanged, I am equally sure the professor will deactivate consciousness support."

Daniel and Nala exchanged a glance. Nobody on Earth offered such a compassionate yet decisive end to life. But they should.

Nala said, "I'd hate to be the reason they're rushing Sprig's reunion. Maybe we should use the portal."

Theesah-ma's eyes twinkled. "Lovely Nala, this day is a joyous event. Even for the professor. Perhaps *especially* for the professor. Captain Zeeno is right. A Chitza scout ship has never landed on Earth before. Wouldn't that be something to see?"

Even with their impulsive nature, Chitzas had proven to be trustworthy partners and good friends. If Daniel had any sway, all four would receive presidential medals and be invited to parties in capital cities around the planet. Or a free hotel room in Vegas, if that's what they preferred.

"Pull up a chair, we'll wait," Daniel said.

Nala held Theesah-ma's hand. "Come with us to Earth. You can't fit in a Chitza ship but take the portal. You'll probably beat us."

"I will come," Theesah-ma said, "but only when you are settled. Your names have been in the news of Earth for many years. Even now, your arrival at Litia is announced far and wide. You will be welcomed home as heroes."

"For what?"

"I have read your history. Seventeenth-century explorers of the Americas. The first astronauts of the twentieth century. All welcomed home as heroic adventurers."

Daniel tipped his head in agreement. "We do tend to celebrate the wrong people for the wrong reasons. We cheer their footprints and leave their scientific discoveries unnoticed."

Nala shrugged. "Yup. The reporters will ask us what it was like beyond the cosmic horizon."

"And since it's just more space, you'll answer with a yawn."

"I will. Then I'll try to slip in a comment about quantum fields not being random before they cut to their morning show host who will ask about Chitza mating habits."

Daniel sighed. He guided them to a spaceport seating area and picked a chair small enough for a Human. Nala and Theesah-ma sat across. He would ponder all they had learned for the rest of his life, but they were only hours from encountering a horde of Human reporters. Theesah-ma was right, they'd be peppered with questions.

"So, what's our story? The story we want scientists to investigate and teachers to explain. The story that inspires artists to create profound works that will speak to people you and I could never reach. What do we want to say that those reporters will never ask?"

Most people would have laughed it off, but Nala had always been good about taking his deepest thoughts seriously. "Probably something about Surveyors and Choreographers? I don't know. You're better at connecting the dots."

Daniel had to think about his own question. The best questions were the ones that didn't have an obvious answer. "I guess it's a story about conflict and wisdom. Remember the web surrounding the Surveyors' orb? Some portions of it were destroyed. Maybe ages ago by someone angry about what the Surveyors were doing—pushing nature in a direction of their choosing, altering fundamental truths by manipulating reality at its most basic level. Does anyone have the wisdom to do that? And even if they're smart enough, do they have the right?

"Look at our own galaxy. It nurtures thousands of planets that support life. Look at our universe. Billions of galaxies, most pretty similar to the Milky Way. And now we have proof of a multiverse that continuously spawns new universes across a span of time we can't even imagine. How can any one species have the hubris to

323

think they should be in charge? It doesn't matter that the Choreographers were the first to discover the secrets. Or that they figured out how to manipulate the code. Shouldn't the basis of reality be sacred?"

Nala laughed uncomfortably. "It's like finding out your neighbor is a god. Has been all along. Enlightening, but disturbing and unfair."

"Yeah. Disturbing, mostly because there's nothing we can do about it. No matter how or why it started, who are we to stop a process that has been going on for millions of years?"

"You're overthinking it," Nala said.

"I do that," Daniel acknowledged with a shrug. "But I'm not wrong." Daniel pointed to the side of Nala's head. "There's another part of the story."

Nala pulled back her hair, then released. When it fell just right, the metal plate was mostly hidden. Hardly noticeable unless you knew just where to look. She spoke with conviction. "It's for you and a few close friends. That's all. It's nobody else's business— including that wireless interface that Sprig tapped into. I can control it. Nobody gets into my head unless I say so."

"Good," Daniel said with the same conviction. "If the reporters ask, I won't say a word."

The spaceport lounge was a comfortable enough place to wait. As promised, the Chitzas soon returned. Sprig rode on Zeeno's shoulder, giving the tiny leaf a somewhat larger persona when compared to a diminutive Chitza.

Zeeno stopped, put his paws on hips with his crew gathered in a tight grouping behind him. "Ready to go?"

"Sprig too?" Daniel pointed.

"Science Officer Sprig is now one of us."

Sprig stood tall. The dark veins on its surface pulsed. Even the crease across its middle had improved to the point of being a proud battle scar rather than a disabling wound.

"A damn fine addition to our crew. We could use a..." Zeeno gave a puzzled look to Sprig.

"Enhanced biotechnical compositron," Sprig said.

"Exactly. We can use that kind of capability. Our next mission has already been assigned. Cross the horizon again but in the opposite direction. Who knows what we'll find out there?"

"After shore leave on Earth," Aussik added.

"Yes, yes, after shore leave," Zeeno confirmed. "Two weeks! Never been authorized before. Seems we've earned some clout with the higher ups."

Nala asked, "You're not going home first?"

"Why would we do that?" Veronica squeaked with a sparkle in her eye. "Out there is advvvvventure!"

"Adventure *after* shore leave," Aussik reminded once more. He tugged on Veronica's elbow quills. It almost looked like an affectionate thing. Veronica kicked him in the shin but that could easily have been Chitza affection too. Reporters on Earth would no doubt be fascinated.

"Chitzas roaming Earth for two weeks," Daniel said to himself. "This I've got to see." He reached out to stroke Sprig's serrated edge. "Congratulations Science Officer. I have a feeling the next mission will be an amazing experience for you."

The surface of the timid leaf shined a little brighter now. Daniel would always keep a visual memory of his shy friend clasped to the Chitza's control panel while the scout ship ricocheted off icy crevasse walls deep within the Chaos Field. Bravery could be learned. Sprig had proven that.

****

White marble columns fronting the Jefferson Memorial contrasted with a cloudless blue sky. Cherry trees along the Tidal Basin exploded with pink flowers. A glorious spring day in Washington, D.C..

The whine of a low-flying jet interrupted the serenity. Tourists and locals strolling on the scenic walkway stopped, looking up to a solitary black wedge gliding across the sky only a hundred meters above the treetops. Twin turbines at its isosceles corners provided an audible impression of a commercial jet, but the craft's stubby triangular shape seemed to lack the aerodynamics to remain aloft by airflow alone.

The black wedge slowed further as it approached the Capitol Mall and banked right. People on the ground below began to run along the park's many pathways—not away but *toward* the craft. The fastest among them almost kept up.

Two military helicopters dropped from higher altitudes and leveled off directly behind the wedge. No missiles were fired, no guns fixed their sights on the spacecraft. Instead, the helicopters flew in formation with the ship, providing an escort. Word had gotten out. Though alien, this wedge was no invader. It had already made low passes over Paris, London, and New York. And now Washington. For the first time since Humans had joined the consortium of galactic civilizations, Chitzas had come to Earth.

The drone of spinning turbines lowered in pitch as the craft settled toward the lawn in front of the US Capitol Building. Capitol Police ran down the steps, their sidearms holstered, but sure hands ready. Government officials poured out of the Rayburn House Office Building to the south. Onlookers gathered in a growing circle around the ship.

326

Turbine exhaust overturned a nearby garbage can, blowing empty coffee cups and burger wrappers across the lawn. Struts lowered from beneath the craft, then pressed into the soft grass. The engines quieted. Turbines spun down.

The alien ship stood no larger than two flatbed trucks parked cab to cab at a thirty degree angle. Most Humans already knew Chitzas were small. Comparisons to knee-high hedgehogs had made the rounds, but when a ramp lowered and a single Chitza stepped out, those stereotypes fell away.

No hedgehog, this Chitza wore crossing leather straps with a collection of unidentifiable devices holstered at its waist. Mostly fur-covered, short spines stuck out from its chin, elbows, and ankles. Longer spines formed a ridge down its back. The Chitza looked left, then right. It grinned, revealing canine teeth.

The crowd now stood ten deep. A few called out, welcoming the alien. Most stood, stupefied. Even after visual preparation from countless news reports, a sight so foreign must first be absorbed and processed before it can be logically incorporated into, *this is okay.*

A teenage boy turned out to be the bravest among the growing throng. He ran up the ramp, extending a hand to the smaller Chitza. "Are you Captain Zeeno?"

The Chitza shook off the question, casually pointing behind. "Naw, the captain's inside. I'm Aussik." He tugged on the boy's hand. "Got any ice cream?"

The boy's eyes lit up at the unexpected alien request. He turned and ran to a pushcart vendor not far away.

More people gathered, edging right up to the ramp until Capitol Police arrived and reorganized the circle to give the ship space. At the top of the ramp, three more Chitzas stepped out, one with a small green leaf standing erect on its shoulder. Last to emerge were two Humans, their faces instantly recognizable to Americans and most everyone else living on planet Earth.

After eight years lost in the depths of space, Daniel Rice and Nala Pasquier had finally returned home.

33 MILKY WAY, EARTH, SANTA FE

DANIEL FLOATED EFFORTLESSLY with only the backside of his head resting on stone decking. Warm salt water provided a buoyancy that fresh water never could. As a bonus, when electrolyzed, the NaCl molecules temporarily broke down into sodium and chlorine, helpful to keep a swimming pool sanitized. Spool, to be pedantic, a combination spa and pool. Smaller, quicker to heat, with bubble jets when you wanted a massage.

The backyard spool was one of the reasons they'd bought the house in Santa Fe—eight years ago, according to the real estate agent who had managed the property for them in their absence.

The rumors were true, Daniel and Nala hadn't been forgotten. But their discovery hadn't been fully absorbed by the people of Earth. Word of the Chaos Field had transformed the study of cosmology, but not much else. No religious upheavals. God had endured the past eight years. Heaven hadn't crumbled. A few new cults had sprung up, but most people had taken the newest story of genesis in stride. Those who ignored science remained blissfully unaware that the ultimate secrets of reality had been exposed.

Nala sat across from Daniel on a ledge that jutted out where the jets turned the water turbulent. Theesah-ma floated in the deep end—only six feet of water, but enough to keep the giant suspended.

Spring was often chilly in Santa Fe but with Theesah-ma visiting, they'd found an excuse to fire up the heater and jump in the pool. Floating would provide Theesah-ma with relief from Earth's heavier gravity, or so the pretext went. Nala completed the therapy by fixing three killer margaritas with an endless refill supply on standby in the patio fridge.

"Such lovely green mountains." Theesah-ma said. Her silky voice spanned several octaves with lilts on words like *lovely* that sounded vaguely Irish.

The Sangre de Cristo range dominated their view to the east. With no fence or neighboring houses to interrupt, a broad vista of olive-colored sage and dark-green junipers eventually gave way to Ponderosa pines in the foothills. Snow blanketed the higher peaks producing a stark contrast with the deep blue of a cloudless New Mexico sky. The Litian-nolo had quickly zeroed in on the green colors of Earth. Her own planet featured purple plants. Retinal instead of chlorophyll.

Theesah-ma kept her iridescent head above the water to protect the breathing accessory she wore. It added a trace of hydrogen sulfide. It even came with a built-in straw, perfect for sipping margaritas.

Nala had her own hardware to consider. Though she'd already proven that the alien plate attached to the side of her head functioned perfectly well after a shower and shampoo, the swimming pool might be a different case. She hadn't dunked yet.

"Sorry," Theesah-ma said. "I have changed the subject once more, haven't I?"

Snowcapped mountains and a dome of clear blue sky would turn any conversation toward things more casual. Their topic so far had been deeper. Mystical even. Maybe it was the margaritas, but for the past hour they'd been speaking of the origins of the universe.

"The water affects me," Theesah-ma explained. "We carry a protein in our skin that rapidly duplicates when saturated. Medical researchers say the reaction can affect the mind."

"Should we get out?" Nala asked.

"No, I enjoy floating. Please ignore my interruptions. You were talking about scales of time and space."

"Unreasonable scales," Daniel said.

"A word that implies a limit of logical thought," Theesah-ma said.

"Mind boggling is the common phrase here on Earth. Billions of stars in a galaxy, a trillion galaxies in a universe, and an untold number of universes created by the Chaos Field over a ridiculous span of time."

"Forever," Nala added. "It makes no sense any other way."

"In my heart, I agree," Daniel said. "You can't keep asking 'what came before that?' At some point in the layer after layer of reality there can only be one of two answers. Either nothing came before... or, *before* has no meaning because the most fundamental layer is eternal. Personally, I'm not a fan of the *something from nothing* scenario, but I have to say, the concept of eternal is also pretty hard to digest."

"How can anything have no beginning?" Nala said, almost as a complaint. Theesah-ma watched their rapid back and forth.

"No beginning," Daniel confirmed. "No spark. No creation. Nothing preceding it because it's always been there. But that doesn't mean it hasn't changed. Maybe a gazillion years ago, the Chaos Field was more primitive, lacking the complexity we saw. Maybe back then, it could only spawn universes in a few variations. We can never really know, but the Chaos Field we see today could have evolved from something simpler."

"Evolution for physics. I like it."

"No reason to restrict evolution to biology. As long as you can represent something physical in data, and you have a mechanism like natural selection to change that data, then physical constructs could evolve too. How big is your seed again?"

He meant the random number generator seed inside her head. They were on the same wavelength, and she answered quickly.

"Altogether, about three hundred zettabytes. Seeds, plus code, and a few miscellaneous things I haven't yet figured out. Might be an instruction manual in there, but nobody reads that stuff." She flashed a wicked smile.

Daniel sat up straighter in the pool. "So, one zettabyte is ten to the twenty-first power bytes, right?" Nala nodded. "That's a trillion gigabytes. A big number. Compare it to DNA. A human genome consumes about one gigabyte in a computer. So, your seed data could store three hundred trillion genomes. Big enough to record the genome for every person alive today, plus all of our primate ancestors—hell every mammal all the way back to the first Mesozoic rodents. Alternatively, you could store the DNA for intelligent species on three hundred trillion planets."

Daniel paused. "I guess what I'm saying is that *we* could be somewhere inside that seed. Us, and a whole bunch of other species too."

Nala's eyes went wide. "They took our DNA."

"The Surveyors?"

"Yup. Think about it. Remember when that silver post popped up?"

"The one with the handprint on it."

"Yeah. You didn't want to touch it, so it went away. And what did they put up next?"

"Uh... the telescope to view the bug."

"Right. It begged to get close and look through that first ring. I know my eyelid touched it. My breath too. They sampled our DNA."

Daniel nodded. "You're right. They were testing us. Chitzas too. Leap over that bridge barrier to test our motor skills. See how we react when a lion takes a swipe at us... grab our DNA and encode it in a seed. Keep doing that over millions of years..."

Nala finished. "And you encode a preference for the kind of people who arrive at your registration station."

"Exactly. Sprig and I talked about the humanoid thing on our way home. The Surveyors told us that the humanoid shape is trending. If so, then why are we unique in the Milky Way? We've been to Jheean. We've met every known intelligence in our galaxy, and none of them look like us."

"What did Sprig say about it?"

"Not much, but he did seem annoyed. I had to tell him that I wasn't arguing *for* the humanoid shape, only that in their zeal to establish a network of Sibyls, the Choreographers set up a system biased toward humanoids—just not in our galaxy. Then I realized that we're conditioned to think of the Milky Way as being spectacularly vast, but it's really just a tiny corner of the universe. It supports twenty-four intelligent species, including us."

Daniel flashed both hands in a so-what gesture. "Twenty-four. That's nothing. It's like looking at twenty-four pixels of a digital photo and trying to decide who is in the picture. It's too small a sample. We'd need to explore Andromeda, Triangulum, Whirlpool, Pinwheel, and a bunch more galaxies. Find all of their space-faring species. Even then, it would be a small sample compared to the whole universe. If we keep searching, we might find the same bias."

"So, 1960s TV sci-fi was right. Aliens look like us but with pointy ears."

Daniel smiled. "Maybe TV writers were just wrong about the scale. Boldly going where no one has gone before requires getting outside our galaxy."

Their distinctly non-humanoid guest spoke up. "Is diversity in form and demeanor a good thing for biology?" A pointed question, delicately put.

"*Touché, mon ami*," Nala answered. "Diversity is most definitely a good thing for biology. Makes us stronger. More resistant to the dangers we face. So, why bias the Chaos Field toward anything? Just let it be random. I bet it *was* random before the Choreographers and their Surveyor dipshits started screwing around with it."

Nala pointed a finger at Daniel. "Brainstorm. What happens if somebody—maybe us—decides to firebomb their place?" She tapped the metal plate on the side of her head. "And trust me... I remember how to get there."

They often played the brainstorming game and usually to good effect. A mental exercise more than an action plan; she wasn't necessarily suggesting they climb aboard the next Chitza flight to the cosmic horizon.

Nala continued with enthusiasm. "So, we light the place up. Shred their web barrier with lasers, melt their silver orb with a few thermonuclear devices. We put a permanent end to the so-called fine tuning they're doing to the Chaos Field seed. Eventually things go back to random, and we're heroes. Fair?"

Daniel shrugged. "Fair. But one minor point... for anything eternal, there's no such thing as permanent. With unlimited time and constant fluctuations, you can't expect any configuration to stick around forever, which means that the Choreographers' manipulation will eventually end and something else will replace it. For that matter, who is to say the Choreographers were the first? Periods of manipulation could be cyclical. Ultimately, any mountain of solid granite wears away to sand. When time is unlimited, you have to expect an infinite number of permutations."

"Okay, I buy that. Is cyclical reality good or bad?"

"Good, I'd say. It's natural. Mountains become sand then erode to become sediment which later is uplifted into new mountains."

"Which requires underlying processes. Plate tectonics, rain, and rivers in the case of granite mountains."

"And random—or nearly random—fluctuations in the case of the Chaos Field."

Nala judged. "I'll accept that. So, firebombing might satisfy our urge to set things right, but in the grand, grand, grand scheme of things, it's just another blip."

Daniel sighed. For such a colossal topic, it rested on a foundation of simplicity. Once something changeable was deemed eternal, then all else derived from eons of time.

"Vastness on an unfathomable scale," Daniel finally said. "A foundation that evolves, resets, and evolves again, over, and over."

"We've existed before." Nala announced. It was another of her non sequiturs. Daniel gave her his best puzzled look.

"We're still brainstorming, right?" She smiled sweetly.

"Sure," he replied.

"Then we've existed before. Eternal ensures infinite. With time never ending, every combination of particles, energy, and events must repeat. Our universe, our world, us. We have to repeat in infinite variations."

Daniel nodded. "Got it. I agree. It implies we'll exist again too. Professor Alosoni-eff pulled the plug on his current life likely believing that his consciousness will someday open different eyes to a new life. From his perspective, no time at all will pass between incarnations."

"Deep stuff," Nala said.

Theesah-ma rose slightly out of the water. "You two amaze me. Every time. Your exchanges are a delight. Your passion combined with intellect. Such a joy to observe. Please ignore comments we sometimes hear. Those who say Humans do not... *measure up*."

"Measure up to whooom?" Nala mocked Theesah-ma's silky voice, but they'd become such good friends she could probably get away with it. "Toraks? We've got those grumpy centipedes beat easily. Chitzas? Hey, our buddies are fun, but their eyes would gloss over ten minutes into this conversation. How about Litian-nolos? Even there, I could make a good case for Humans."

Theesah-ma stared at Nala like she might be on the verge of mocking Americanized vowels. She didn't. "You could make a case. You wouldn't win, but you could try."

Daniel drifted across the pool to his wife's side and settled onto the underwater ledge where warm jets provided a lower back massage.

"Why don't Litian-nolos brainstorm like we do?" Nala asked Theesah-ma.

Daniel snuggled in close, resting his head against the pool deck. Nala's hair fell around his face. Up close, the smooth brown skin of her slender neck stretched forever. A blue light twinkled at one end of the Arc, only an inch from Daniel's eye. An indicator of her thoughts? Or a monitor, continuously sampling the trillions of quantum fields above, below, and inside her?

While Nala and Theesah-ma continued their conversation, Daniel pulled inward. Perhaps it was the warm water, or the gentle gurgle of the pool jets. Perhaps a lingering buzz from the margaritas or the comfort of returning home after having been so far away.

Daniel looked up, his view filtered through the strands of Nala's hair. A cumulonimbus cloud hung in the sky. Its white puffs performed a slow motion explosion of condensation, defying gravity to reach ever higher in the sky. Above the cloud, blue sky would eventually give way to the blackness of space.

Half a moon, easily visible in daylight, gave away the game. Stars were up there too—at this very moment—temporarily hidden by the blinding light of the nearest star among them. Once night fell, with the right optics, you could spot the dim yellow star where Theesah-ma's home planet of Litia orbited. If you knew where to look, you could find several other home worlds too. Twenty-four space-faring species inhabited the Milky Way galaxy, separated by vast stretches of space.

Andromeda would be up there too, another impossibly grand assembly of stars and planets just waiting to be explored. Further out, a hundred more galaxies in the local cluster, some named, some numbered, each unique. Every collection of stars, dust, and gas bore the marks of its own history spanning billions of years into the past. Some formed blobs, others slowly rotated in place. Islands of matter and energy within an immensity of emptiness.

The Afeesh Tm were out there, too far away to be seen no matter how big the telescope, but they existed. Even the boundary of the universe didn't mark the end. Reality continued far beyond, across infinite distances and an eternity of time.

He reeled his thoughts in, pulling distant locales and colossal spans of time back to one place and one time. Here and now. Daniel reset, then drifted once more, this time in the opposite direction.

One lock of Nala's silky brown hair cascaded across his eye. If he tried, he could focus on a single strand. The infinitesimal width of one hair could only be measured against other microscopic objects: a fiber of cotton, a spec of pollen. Yet, it would take a dozen red blood cells stitched together end to end to wrap around a single hair's circumference. Going further down into the microscopic world, that red blood cell would look like a baseball stadium next to the average virus, which in turn would appear mountainous next to a proton.

There would be little point in going further. Down at the quantum level, a proton would appear fuzzy, certainly not like a

337

ball. It's position would be indistinct, its movements hard to judge. The closer you got to picking out *where* it could be found, the more difficultly you'd have in measuring its motion. Uncertainty could be counted on; quantum particles refused to be pinned down. Scientists had a name for it, the Heisenberg Uncertainty Principle, a concept built upon a foundational idea at the heart of quantum physics.

Random.

Daniel reset once more, returning to the here and now. He lifted his head, stared at his beautiful wife, and slowly pulled her hair back to fully expose the metal arc embedded in her head.

Her conversation with Theesah-ma stopped. "It's still there, Daniel," Nala said without moving. "Not going anywhere. No plans to rip it out."

"Sorry, I wasn't thinking about that."

The alien device stored a random number seed of unfathomable complexity. Far more than a navigation tool, the seed applied to any quantum particle. Every proton, every neutrino, every photon. Inside her head, Nala held the key to unlocking the universe.

"What's up? You've been awfully quiet over there. Spill it."

Daniel let go of her hair and spoke barely above a whisper. "It's not random. Nothing is, and you hold the key. The Heisenberg Uncertainty Principle doesn't apply to you."

"Mmm." Nala tilted her head back and forth. "Yeah, I suppose I could compute an electron's path around an atom. That'd be cool. I'll have to try that sometime."

Daniel floated around to face her. "It's more than that. Think about it. With enough input and enough computing power, you could examine every particle. Every synapse firing in your brain and mine. Every atom moving around us. You could turn chaos

338

into determinism. You could know what is going to happen before it happens."

Nala scrunched up her nose. "I… really doubt it. But I see your point. It's a deterministic universe, not random. Assuming you have access to the key."

"Which you do."

"Yes, I do." She leaned forward and kissed Daniel on the lips. "Don't worry, I won't go all Quantum Goddess on you. No pulling your thoughts out of your mind. But I have to admit, knowing what's going to happen before it happens would be handy when we head back to the Surveyors and firebomb their registration station."

Daniel gave his wife a cold stare.

Nala lifted her eyebrows. "We *are* rebels."

Theesah-ma floated over. Her flexible head curled at its edges. "Quite dangerous too."

Nala nudged Daniel. "TM's getting the hang of sarcasm. It's going to be downhill from here."

Daniel smiled, wrapping his arms around her neck, and pulling her tight. "I wouldn't miss it for all of the worlds in all of the universes."

THE END

AFTERWORD

Excuse me while I ponder how many worlds there might be out there. Too many to count, but numbers are overrated. I'm confident—even more confident than I was when I started writing this story—that there are enough worlds out there to fill every niche in my imagination and yours too. Enough worlds that there will certainly be another world to experience when I'm done with this one. You too. The probabilities are in our favor. Eternity is on our side. With eternity, everything *must* occur, repeatedly.

Unless, of course, reality isn't random. In that case, all bets are off.

Thanks for reading. I hope you enjoyed the story and the colorful characters who played their parts in it. Once again, I had fun writing it. Shall we dive into science for a few more pages?

First up, the cosmic horizon (also called the cosmological horizon, or the visible universe) is a spherical boundary with Earth at the center. Its radius is a ridiculous 46 billion light-years. Every photon that we see with our eyes or through a telescope exists within that sphere. There are more photons emitted by stars *outside* that sphere, but we'll never see them. The distance between us and any star *over the horizon* is increasing faster than light can cross it. The universe is expanding, every chunk of space is swelling, every day, every year. No one knows why. There's something called dark energy, but that's just a name. No one knows what it really is.

"But wait!" you exclaim, "the universe is only 13.8 billion years old! Shouldn't the horizon be 13.8 billion light years?" Surprisingly, the answer is no.

Think of space as a grid of squares. Then imagine that each square grows by 1% over some period of time, say, a million years. That means the square next to us is 1% further away after a million years. But the next square over is 2% further away, then 3%, etc. A square that is 100 squares away becomes twice as far away as it used to be. A 1000 squares away, becomes 20 times further. It's multiplicative. The further out you go, the greater the multiplier. Eventually, you'll get to a square that is expanding away from us faster than light could travel the distance—even though nothing has really traveled that distance. The grid has simply grown larger.

Here's a good video from Physics Girl (Dianna Cowern) that superbly explains the cosmic horizon: https://fb.watch/l6hcf1Ak1v/ (As I write, Dianna is still bedridden, six months after getting sick from Covid. Best wishes to Dianna and her husband. We miss her enthusiasm for science and the wonders around us.)

One more thought on astronomical distances: we commonly use the poorest measure, light-years. It feels like a speed, not a distance, and it gets confused with the speed of light. It shouldn't. We should all switch to parsecs. Astronomers have. One parsec equals 3.26 light-years. Don't worry about where the parsec unit came from, it almost doesn't matter. A parsec is simply a convenient distance measure for stars and galaxies. For example, Alpha Centauri, Procyon, Sirius, Altair, and other nearby stars are between one and ten parsecs away. The center of the Milky Way is 34 kiloparsecs away. Andromeda galaxy, 780 kiloparsecs. The cosmic horizon is 14 gigaparsecs away. A gigaparsec is as big a unit as you'll ever need.

Okay... more fun stuff! Lithium! Where is our lithium? We sometimes read news items about running out of lithium for batteries. It's true, Earth is in short supply of element number three, but there's something even stranger: our whole universe seems to be short on lithium. Nonsense, you might say (and you might be right)! But cosmologists (astronomers who specialize in the Big Bang) have long wondered why measures of lithium don't match theory. This graph shows the measured abundance of each element in our universe:

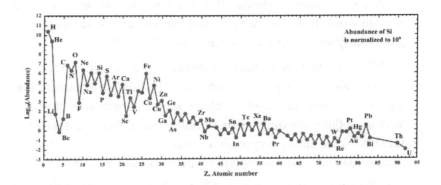

Hydrogen is first, at the upper left. Quite abundant. Then helium. But then a big dip down to lithium, beryllium, and boron. Then back up to carbon, where things settle into a smooth drop all the way to uranium. Cosmologists have a good explanation for why beryllium and boron weren't manufactured in larger quantities at the birth of our universe, but their explanation doesn't work for lithium. According to well-established Big Bang theory, there should be three to four times more lithium than we measure! Earth should be smothered with lithium. It should be more common than carbon. But it isn't.

Over the past several years, astronomers have come up with various explanations for why stars consume lithium in their furnaces and why it isn't released back into space through supernovae explosions. These explanations might be right; the jury is still out. Being a rebel, I decided to have some fun with it. And so, I described our universe as "lithium deficient" from birth. It's just who we are within the grand scale of the multiverse! Other universes were better behaved children.

343

Next topic: words. This is, after all, a book of 90,000 words. In Chapter 23, Aussik rattles off words in Chitza, ending with a question, "*Bo?*" Nala answers him with, "*Bo*, my ass!" It's Chitza, so it could mean anything. But I'll confess. *Bo* is actually a Korean word. It means "what?", and for Koreans, it seems to be a particularly strong form of surprise, like "What!?!?!"

When I lived in Manila in 2012, my wife and I regularly watched Korean soap operas on TV with English subtitles. Fun shows, but they inevitably include scenes where one character says something startling—like admitting his father is actually the CEO of some mega corporation—then three other characters go wide-eyed and chime in together with a resounding, "*Bo*?!?!" The English subtitle would appear below, "What?", and my wife and I would be rolling across the couch, laughing hysterically. Korean soap operas seem to include a "*Bo*?!?!" scene in every episode, every show.

So, now I know two Korean words: *kamsahamnida* (which means, thank you) and *bo*.

Sibyl is another word worth mentioning. I didn't make it up, it comes from ancient Greece. Sibyls were women who provided prophecies (presumably for a fee). I guess back in those days, everyone wanted their palms read, Greek style. One Sibyl who lived in Erythrae (about 70 kilometers northwest of Athens), wrote her predictions on a set of leaves. The leaves could then be arranged so that the first letter of each prediction formed a word or phrase, providing proof to the customer of the Sibyl's mystical talent!

Hmm. What do you get if you rearrange the first letter of each chapter in this book? Probably gibberish, but if it spells out "the Sibyl of Erythrae foresees chaos", I'll be a believer.

Let's move on to distance scales, one of the themes in this story. The scale of our universe is unquestionably vast. But words like *vast, grand,* or even *incalculable* and *limitless,* don't convey just how big this universe really is. Even zoom-out style video visualizations are tough to absorb because you lose track of your starting point. For this story, I decided that watching whole galaxies zip by a window hour after hour like fenceposts along a highway gave the best feel for the incredible scale of space that surrounds us. I hope it gave you that sense too.

Science fiction usually sticks to adventures inside the Milky Way galaxy. But not always. Have you read *Tau Zero* by Poul Anderson? It's written almost like a documentary, but it's the only story I've ever read that provides a plausible method to traverse the whole universe. How? Build a ship that can approach the speed of light, and, for you, time will slow down. As you accelerate, time dilation opens up the whole universe, even if everyone you ever knew back home—and Earth itself—are long dead.

In *Quantum Space* (Book 1 of this series), I started using the Greek letter *tau* as a measure of spatial compression. The same letter was used in *Tau Zero,* where it's a measure of the ratio between clock ticks aboard a very fast ship and clock ticks outside. The ratio approaches zero, as the ship approaches light speed.

Back to the science in this story. I have three more topics to expand upon: probability in the quantum world, something from nothing, and the cosmology of the multiverse. Heavy stuff! But I'll try to keep it light.

You've probably heard that fundamental particles like quarks and electrons are *quantum,* which means they exist as discrete packets. And while a world made from tiny building blocks is easy to grasp, nature doesn't let us off that easy. Every quantum particle is also a wave. I won't go into why this is true because I've mentioned the quantum particle/wave duality in other books.

Afterword

You can find good descriptions on the internet, like this one: https://www.youtube.com/watch?v=Hk3fgjHNQ2Q

Let's take it a step further. A quantum particle is not only a wave, but its position in three-dimensional space is described by a *probability field*. A good example of a field is the tip of a magnet. Hold another magnet nearby and you can feel the fields they create, even though you can't see them. When I was a child, magnets felt like pure magic.

A quantum field is just as real as a magnetic field, and just as marvelous. It's the mathematical probability of finding a quantum particle at a particular location. For example, a 50% chance that the particle will show up at nearby point A, and a 0.01% chance it will be found way over at distant point B. Because it's also a wave, we don't know exactly where the particle will be until we measure it. But we *do* know the probabilities where it *might* be. Erwin Schrödinger won the Nobel Prize for his equation that computes location and momentum probabilities for any quantum particle. Here it is:

$$\frac{-\hbar^2}{2m}\frac{\partial^2 \psi}{\partial x^2} + V(x)\psi == i\hbar\frac{\partial \psi}{\partial t}$$

Physicists use this equation all the time. You couldn't design a nuclear power plant or a Geiger counter without it.

So, does that mean that reality itself is random? If the fundamental particles that make up everything can't be pinned down except by a roll of the dice, does that mean nothing in life is deterministic?

You decide. But in 1964, John Bell devised a robust quantum experiment to distinguish between random and deterministic. Early experiments in the 1980s were inconclusive, but Bell's Test was finally resolved in 2015 by Alain Aspect and others. Their conclusion: quantum particles are inherently unpredictable.

Reality at its core is truly random. There are critics, though, who to this day say nature might harbor an undiscovered property that explains why something that *appears* to be random is actually quite different.

I took that idea and ran with it. Sci-fi allows us to play upon the mysteries in science, which can be a whole lot of fun.

Next up: something from nothing. This is the idea that our universe and the Big Bang that created it, is not dependent on an underlying engine. Nothing initiated the Big Bang; it simply sprang from nowhere. Strange as it sounds, this nearly magical genesis is entirely possible. Theoretical physicist Lawrence Krauss wrote a whole book about it (*A Universe From Nothing*). I read it three times trying to understand it, and Krauss is a good writer. The concept itself was the issue (for me). What is nothing? It's not just empty space. To make sense, nothing must be truly nothing. No space, no time, but also no rules. It's what Aristotle called First Cause.

Krauss describes matter and spacetime emerging from nothing as necessary conditions of a quantum fluctuation. Nothingness, Krauss says, is unstable. It cannot remain nothing. But suggesting that nothing suddenly blossoms into a volume of space containing matter requires underlying rules—quantum fluctuations, for example. Time itself is a rule. Without time, you can't have an event, which a fluctuation most definitely is.

Aristotle concluded—correctly, I think—that there can be no First Cause. Some portion of reality is, and must be, eternal. Aristotle labeled the eternal part, God, which I think is a handwaving copout (manufacturing a fantasy to explain the genesis of reality doesn't sit well with me). But I do agree that at least some sliver of reality *must be eternal*. Time itself would then be eternal, and an engine of creation (however primitive) would allow a Big Bang to create a universe, or many universes. We either accept an eternal engine, or we have to go with the something-from-nothing scenario, which (for me) is even harder to reconcile.

Finally, I wanted to talk about the latest thinking among cosmologists. Cosmologists are theoretical physicists and astronomers who specialize in questions like, how did we get here? You'd be hard pressed to find a cosmologist who didn't agree on two things: the Big Bang started our universe, and in the earliest microsecond of existence, a strange phenomenon we call inflation exploded the universe's size from a quantum dot to an energetic soup the size of a solar system.

Cosmologists then describe (in fair detail) how matter coalesced from energy, when the first atoms formed, when the universe first became transparent to light, and on to the first stars and galaxies. There's loads of evidence for the Big Bang and inflation theories, primarily because big telescopes not only look into deep space, they're looking backwards in time. We can see the first light. It's out there if you look far enough. It tells us what the universe was like 13.8 billion years ago.

Today, cosmology is a rapidly changing field. Cosmologists continue to study the first few microseconds of the Big Bang, but they also work on theories for how the bang got its start. There are lots of competing theories that adjust as new information comes in from our most advanced telescopes.

I like to compare developments in cosmology to the science of DNA. In the 19th century, no one knew about DNA, but Charles Darwin showed that species evolved, and Gregor Mendel exposed the mechanism: a *gene* passed from parent to child. It took another hundred years to discover the shape of DNA (Francis Crick, James Watson, and Rosalind Franklin, in 1953), and its AGCT base pairs (Fred Sanger, in the 1970s). Jump ahead another forty years, and

Jennifer Doudna and Emmanuelle Charpentier invented genetic scissors called CRISPR capable of snipping out a DNA section and replacing it with something else. Incredible progress of an extremely complicated science, but it took 150 years before geneticists could claim a full understanding of DNA.

Cosmology feels similar. The expansion of our universe was discovered in 1924 by Edwin Hubble which led to the Big Bang theory. By the 1950s, Big Bang had been accepted by most astronomers (beating out the earlier static universe model). A multiverse theory (multiple Big Bangs) was first described by Hugh Everett in 1956, including what Everett called the "universal wave function", the mother of all quantum wave functions, derived from Schrödinger's equation.

In 1979, Roger Penrose pointed out that the universe we see is both homogeneous (smooth in regard to matter) and isotropic (looks the same in every direction). He calculated an extremely low probability of this happening if initial conditions were random, thus giving rise to the anthropic principle which says that our universe must be fine-tuned for life. If it were not, we wouldn't be here to observe it.

In 1981, inflation entered the picture (proposed by Alan Guth) and by the 2010s, many cosmologists had resurrected Everett's multiverse idea, even if they weren't in complete agreement.

Now in 2023, cosmology feels like it's at the Crick/Watson/Franklin phase—that is, about midway through a 150-year process that resembles the discovery path for DNA. We now have several incredible telescopes capable of peering back to the origins of our universe, and the cosmic microwave background mapped by the WMAP and Planck missions have provided a wealth of evidence for the Big Bang, inflation, and hints of a multiverse.

The most recent cosmology theories now explore reality on a much larger stage, in part to avoid Penrose's conclusion that we are somehow special. Cosmologists today ask, "Can we define models and find evidence that we live in one ordinary universe out of many?" The answer so far: yes we can.

In 2006, Laura Mersini-Houghton, Richard Holman, and Tomo Takahashi established a mathematical framework that describes a quantum *landscape* capable of generating Big Bangs. They made a reasonable assumption that, at its birth, our universe was a quantum-sized particle. Then, they used Everett's universal wave function to compute the probabilities of its existence in various states. Mathematically, it turns out, our universe may be pretty ordinary. Not exotic, not special, not specially crafted to support life. One of many, and commonly produced.

Which brings me to Laura Mersini-Houghton's astonishing book published in 2022, *Before the Big Bang: The Origin of Our Universe from the Multiverse*. I couldn't put it down, not even the second time I read it. Mersini-Houghton is a PhD theoretical physicist and a professor at the University of North Carolina in Chapel Hill. She collaborated directly with big names in physics, like Roger Penrose, Michio Kaku, and Stephen Hawking, and now she provides us with a rational explanation of nothing less than *the basis of reality*. She describes a foundational quantum landscape that gave birth to our Big Bang and describes the quantum mechanism whereby a vast collection of universes routinely spring into existence over an eternity of time.

This is not sci-fi. It's real cosmology, in fact, the latest in scientific thinking. Better still, there are tantalizing hints from recent data collected by the Planck survey of the cosmic microwave background radiation that Mersini-Houghton's view of reality is correct.

Her theory begins with a quantum landscape of peaks and valleys representing every possible way Hugh Everett's wave function of the universe could produce a physical universe. Each peak or valley is a discrete point of vacuum energy—*potential energy* in physics terms, the same energy contained in a glass of orange juice sitting on the edge of a counter. Push it just a little, and you'll have an explosion of orange juice across your kitchen floor (your own personal Big Bang).

This theoretical landscape has a ridiculous number of peaks and valleys (1 followed by 600 zeros), each with a different potential energy waiting to be triggered. Picture undulating dots extending off into the distance.

What triggers a single dot to blossom into a new universe? Probability. The flip of a coin. The same random chance that tells us whether a photon passes through one slit or another (in the famous two-slit experiment) or whether an orbiting electron will be found at point A or B.

But not every point in this bizarre landscape has an equal chance to be the site of a new universe. Some places (peaks) are highly unlikely to convert their potential energy into space and matter. Others (stable valleys) have a far greater chance. But with 10^{600} options, this landscape has plenty of *high valleys*—stable pockets with a large potential energy. Those are the ones that produce a universe like ours, which neatly explains Roger Penrose's concern that a high energy universe like ours is extremely unlikely to occur. Mersini-Houghton's landscape shows that it can and will occur many times over.

Afterword

The landscape of a universal wave function is first described in Chapter 18 by Sprig, then mentioned again by Nala in Chapters 21 and 31. I gave it a name: the Chaos Field. And while my fictional story can take us there, the real world equivalent would likely be far more abstract and only physical at a quantum level.

Yet, Laura Mersini-Houghton's theory may be more than a mathematical explanation of how universes could be produced from random quantum fluctuations of a universal wave function landscape. If her theory is correct, it pulls back the curtain on a new form of reality that we may never see with our eyes but is just as real as any star or planet.

The big question: how can we find out if this quantum landscape is real? As it turns out, Mersini-Houghton and her collaborators have figured out several ways to experimentally test for it.

If the landscape converts potential energy into a quantum particle (called an inflaton, which then kicks off inflation to create a new universe) then, like any quantum particle, it could be entangled (a quantum property commonly found in photons). Mersini-Houghton theorizes that we might find evidence of that primordial entanglement in the earliest snapshot of our baby universe: the cosmic microwave background, or CMB. In fact, she made seven predictions of "anomalies" that could only exist if our universe is part of a multiverse, and she believes they have already found six of them. As she says in her book, "In less than a decade, six of our seven predictions had significant if not definitive proof to support them. Our seventh prediction, which involves the motion of galaxies relative to the expansion of the universe (known as 'dark flow'), remains an open question." So, while there's still some debate, there's a fair chance that at least part of the landscape theory is correct.

If you'd like to hear it from Laura Mersini-Houghton herself, watch this video *How to Find a Multiverse*: https://www.youtube.com/watch?v=OAL1-vzMvmA&t=18s

How was that? Deep stuff? Good. That was my goal. My brain is still spinning from everything I've learned while writing this story. Cutting edge science never ceases to amaze me!

I'd love to stay in touch (Amazon doesn't give authors information about readers). Please go to http://douglasphillipsbooks.com and add your name to my email list. I'll keep you informed about upcoming books, and I promise I won't fill your inbox with junk. Also, at my website are pictures related to the stories and color versions of each book illustration.

I hoped you enjoyed this fifth book in the Quantum Series. If you did, please consider writing a short review. It doesn't matter if there are already a thousand reviews, yours will be unique, and future readers pay more attention to the most recent reviews anyway. For information on how to leave a review, go to http://douglasphillipsbooks.com/contact.

Thanks for reading!

Douglas Phillips

ACKNOWLEDGMENTS

If you're a writer, I highly recommend joining an authors circle. It's a place (physical or online) where you gather with peers and exchange chapters (or whole books) for critique. The process is a bit intimidating at first, but the right group can provide needed feedback without deflating every hope and dream you've constructed for yourself since childhood. CritiqueCircle.com is one of those groups. This time I owe thanks to Darren Cook, Kathryn Hoff, and Landon Knauss for your valuable feedback. I really enjoyed reading your own stories, and I hope we'll do it again in the near future.

Thanks to Terry Grindstaff for correcting my misplaced commas and other mistakes. Proofreading takes a lot of concentration. I really admire your grit and your enthusiasm for the task!

The colorful cover for this book came from Dane Low, who is quite the artist and a great collaborator for crafting an eye-catching design that tells its own story in a single glance. Thanks Dane!

A big thank you to a great team of Beta readers: Calvin Clark, Nancy Bisson, Bill Gill, Jay Moskowitz, Jeff Cantwell, Juliana Greco, Jim Shurts, Keith Lavender, Rick Spencer, John Stephens, William Lea, and Marlene Phillips. I forced these fine people to read the book in two parts (divided at the end of Chapter 20, right at a major cliffhanger). The split Beta made things easier for me but harder for them, yet they provided excellent insight that only comes when a variety of viewpoints are considered. I had fun during Beta, I hope everyone else did too.

And finally, thanks to you for reading! I'm thrilled to have an audience for my style of science fiction. If you enjoyed this book, please take a few minutes to leave a review on Amazon or Goodreads. Independent authors—those of us not associated with the high-price New York publishing firms—flourish or flounder based on reviews from readers like you.

FROM THE AUTHOR

Quantum Series

Quantum Incident —Prologue

Quantum Space —Book 1

Quantum Void —Book 2

Quantum Time —Book 3

Quantum Entangled —Book 4

Quantum Chaos —Book 5

And more...

Phenomena

Lost at L3

For these and other works by Douglas Phillips, please visit http://douglasphillipsbooks.com. While you're there, sign up to the mailing list to stay informed on new books in the works and upcoming events.